Look what people are saying about Kathy Lyons…

"A sexy new approach to the military hunk stories."
—*RT Book Reviews* on *Night After Night…*

"If you enjoy reading books with Alpha males, then *Night After Night…* is definitely a book for you! This book comes with some seriously kinky and steamy sex scenes and a very modern happy ending!"
—*Night Owl Reviews*

"Detailed, empathetic characters mix with a fascinating plot and sizzling sex to make one extraordinary tale."
—*Affaire de Coeur* on *Night After Night…*

"This book is hard to resist."
—*Affaire de Coeur* on *In Good Hands*

"Lyons' latest is a fun, flirty and unexpectedly kinky book."
—*RT Book Reviews* on *Taking Care of Business*

LIVING
THE FANTASY

BY
KATHY LYONS

First published in Great Britain 2013
by Mills & Boon, an imprint of Harlequin (UK) Limited,
Eton House, 18-24 Paradise Road, Richmond, Surrey TW9 1SR

© Katherine Grill 2012

ISBN: 978 0 263 90629 5
ebook ISBN: 978 1 472 01191 6

14-0613

Harlequin (UK) policy is to use papers that are natural, renewable and recyclable products and made from wood grown in sustainable forests. The logging and manufacturing processes conform to the legal environmental regulations of the country of origin.

Printed and bound in Spain
by Blackprint CPI, Barcelona

A *USA TODAY* bestselling author, **Kathy Lyons** has made her mark with sizzling romances. She adores unique settings, wild characters and erotic, exotic love. And if she throws in a dragon or a tigress here and there, it's only in the name of fun! An author of more than thirty novels, she adores the fabu-lousness that is Mills & Boon Blaze. She calls them her sexy treat and hopes you find them equally delicious. Kathy loves hearing from readers. Visit her at www.kathylyons.com or find her on Facebook and Twitter under her other pen name, Jade Lee.

Brenda, you made this book awesome.
THANK YOU!

_1_

OMG I'm going to kill this client!

ALI FLORES LAUGHED as she looked at the text message from her best friend, Elisa. Apparently some guy had hired Elisa's modeling agency to find an actress for him but he couldn't verbalize what he was looking for. Go figure. A guy who didn't know what he wanted in a woman. What were the odds?

Ali was smiling as she texted back.

I'm still coming for lunch. Have to get out of here!

She'd just hit Send when her boss popped his head into her cubicle.

"Hey, Ali, did you proofread that brochure?"

"Right here," she said as she handed over the document. "But I really think the photos could be better—"

"Great. I'm having a terrible time getting those promotional pens out of China. Can you call their customs department for me and get it worked out?"

"Because I speak such good Chinese?" *Not.*

"Because you're the best. Thanks!" And off he went with a wave. She wanted to scream. How the heck was she supposed to navigate Chinese customs? But she didn't say a word. Instead, she grabbed her phone and typed out another quick text to Elisa.

My boss knows exactly what he wants: me, chained to my desk. Until I DIE!

She had to get a new job. Truthfully, she had to get a new life, but what? And how? She dropped her chin on her hand and stared at her computer screen. And as she glared at the blinking cursor, she imagined a knight in shining armor stepping up to her desk to rescue her. He'd take her away to his castle, he'd shower her with jewels, and…and he'd probably ask her to mother his seven screaming brats from a previous marriage.

Not!

Ali groaned and started pulling up all the correspondence with the Chinese factory. But as she worked, her mind kept churning on her own life problems.

Ali believed in happily ever after. Perhaps that was the problem. She didn't just believe in it, she ached for it. She obsessed about it. She wanted it with a hunger that filled her fantasy life to overflowing.

But she needed some way to shape her dreams. It wasn't like knights in shining armor were wandering around Houston looking for her. And she wasn't really a damsel in distress. Truth was, she didn't know who or what she was.

She'd been a quiet child growing up, buried in books because that's what she liked. She and her single mom had been happy up until she was ten. Then suddenly her mom up and married a guy with two sons, both younger than Ali. And if that weren't enough, Mom got pregnant just a few months later.

Ali went from the girl who liked to read to the girl who changed diapers, did laundry and screamed at the boys to stay out of her room. In the end, she escaped to college only to quit when the money ran out.

She'd got this job as a secretary to the head of PR in a hospital. Talk about being unimportant. The hospital saved lives. Her boss kept the hospital looking good so it could save lives. And what did she do? She made sure their booth at a health fair was well stocked with promotional pens. Sure, she wasn't screaming at toddlers anymore, but she was working just as hard screaming at customs or tracking UPS shipments or doing whatever menial task her boss threw at her.

Other people had passions, they had goals and a purpose. She had fantasies about handsome pirates not because she liked pirates but because she didn't know what she did like. And she wasn't going to find out sitting here filling out customs forms.

It was time to make a change. So she whipped out her phone and texted Elisa.

Lunch NOW. We're going to find me a new life.

KEN JOHNSON WAS SEARCHING for a queen. And for some ridiculous reason, he couldn't find one. Maybe because Queen Guinevere didn't exist in Houston. Still, he was determined to try. He was now at his seventeenth modeling agency praying that the woman he sought walked through the door. But so far, he'd been sorely disappointed.

Ken was CEO of Quirky Games, Inc., and he was about to launch a new adventure game that he hoped would take the geek world by storm. But in order to do that, he had to throw a huge publicity campaign that included gaming conventions, comic conventions and even a theme-park opening. And after years of experience in the geek gaming world, he knew that every event hinged on one thing: the actors who played the characters.

Any model could strap on a corset and a sword. Put a babe

in a brass bra and kids would look, but they wouldn't necessarily buy. These days, players needed more than a hot chick before they invested the hours to get fluent in a game. They needed a goal, a challenge and, most of all…a queen.

His queen needed to be divinely beautiful but so approachable that boys would immediately want to talk to her, be with her, play the game for hours just to spend more time around her. She needed to be reserved enough to seem mysterious, and yet so warm that you believed she could strap on an apron and serve chocolate-chip cookies. Sex goddess and Betty Crocker, all rolled into one.

That was the queen he wanted, and damn it, she was nowhere to be found.

"I need a break," he said, shoving up from his chair. He was in the primary conference room of the last modeling agency on his list: OMG Action! But just as all the others, every woman who'd strutted, shimmied or swaggered in front of him had left him cold. Not just cold, but vaguely nauseated. They were certainly beautiful, but the personalities beneath the flawless skin and high cheekbones were arrogant or just plain over-the-top.

The agency owner, Marilyn Madison, pushed out of her chair and teetered on her ultra-high heels. "Mr. Johnson!" she cried, panic in her voice.

Then her assistant—a very sweet young woman named Elisa—offered him yet another folder of pictures. "If you could just tell me what look you're going for, perhaps in this pile—"

"I don't care about a look," he said for what felt like the billionth time. "I need the woman to *feel* right, and these girls just don't." And with that he stomped out the door. He didn't stop until he'd pushed through the doors of the elegant glass foyer, but as the office was on the thirty-seventh floor, he ended up standing in the hallway near the elevator bank.

He toyed with the idea of just leaving the building. He

could be at his favorite comic-book store in twenty minutes. Except, of course, he was an adult today. He had a company and—more important—twenty employees who needed him to make Winning Guinevere into a multimillion-dollar success. Their jobs and his life savings depended on it.

Eight years ago, he'd been fresh out of college with a computer-science degree and a hunger to make it rich. He had a cool game written, and he and his best friend, Paul, had marketed the heck out of it and sold a zillion copies. Quirky Games, Inc. was born. But that was eight years ago. Since then, they'd launched one game after another to only middling success. Winning Guinevere was their last hope, and Ken was pouring everything he had into it. Which meant he had to find the right Guinevere. Without her, he might as well declare bankruptcy now.

He took a deep breath and tried to think. Maybe there was a compromise somewhere. He ran through different scenarios in his mind, but every one just made him sigh. Everything hinged on the woman. He couldn't compromise there. It would compromise everything.

He was on the verge of muttering curse words in Klingon when the elevator doors dinged. He didn't look out of curiosity—his eyes were just focused in that direction. But since his eyes were aimed at the elevator door, he could hardly fail to notice when *she* walked out. Normal height, nice curves and thick dark hair pulled back into a neat ponytail. He caught a flash of flawless skin, high cheekbones and enticing legs that had enough muscle to be strong and enough softness to be sexy. She wore a dress of muted blue and a sweater that covered her curves but didn't hide them.

And none of that made him leap off the wall until he heard her chuckle. Low, throaty and so damn sexy, he felt his jaw drop in shock. It seemed to fill the air and vibrate in his soul. Sexy and *warm*. Chocolate-chip-cookie warm.

Oh my God, had he just found his queen?

He pulled himself together—a lot harder to do than it should have been—and scrambled for a way to introduce himself. Meanwhile, she turned out of the elevator alcove and headed down the hall toward him. Her eyes were trained on her cell phone. That was apparently what had made her laugh because a second later, she did it again.

Wow. He felt this one in his spine, and every part of him leaped to follow her. The words were out of his mouth before he could think twice.

"Excuse me, miss…" he began, but then his voice trailed away. What could he say to this woman?

She looked up, her eyes going wide as she realized she'd been so focused on her phone that she hadn't seen him there. "Oh!" she gasped. "I'm sorry. I should look where I'm going, huh?" She immediately folded up her phone.

"No, no. My fault. I…uh…" He tried his best smile, his mind scrambling. The problem was that as smart as he was—and frankly, he was considered very smart—he'd never been very good at communicating with girls. He wanted to be suave and ended up just looking like a tongue-tied geek. Which was exactly what he was. "I was just admiring your phone."

She blinked and looked down at the cell in her hand. Ken noted with dismay that it wasn't a cool phone. It wasn't even a smartphone, which made it a virtual dinosaur.

"This phone?" she asked.

"Um, no. Actually I was just looking for a way to talk to you."

She smiled. "Bad luck then, choosing to talk about my phone. I'm just grateful it can handle text messages."

He stared at her, lost in her face. Flawless skin was right: like the smoothest latte ever, only with a dusting of gold. She seemed to be of Polynesian descent, which made her look exotic. But what really caught him were her meltingly chocolate-brown eyes. And, best of all, each of her cheeks sported a dimple.

She was perfect. Absolutely perfect.

Meanwhile, she put away her big clunker of a phone while he grabbed for something more to say. "So you must not be one of those ultra-plugged-in people. Internet, social media, a zillion apps just to get coffee?"

She shook her head, but didn't laugh. In truth, she seemed almost shy the way she ducked her head. But her eyes sparkled when she spoke. "Not me. Whenever I check my email, I get junk or more things to do from my boss."

He gave a mock shudder. "Hate that." Even though he was technically the boss, every time he opened his email he ended up with ten more things on his to-do list. Meanwhile, he tried to cover his ultra-slick phone with his elbow. She noticed of course, and gestured to where it was hanging like a lead weight on his belt.

"You seem kinda plugged in, though."

"Um, yeah. You never know when the urge to get a triple mocha latte will hit."

She lifted her chin, her eyes dropping to a sexy half mast as she murmured a long, appreciative, "Yummmm."

His blood went straight south. Not only did she sound sexy, but suddenly her expression sparked all sorts of dark things in his imagination. Meanwhile, she had straightened and was looking down the hall. Hell, he was about to lose her, so he scrambled for another way to keep her with him for just a moment longer.

"Um, really, I was just looking for a way to talk to you." Lord, was there ever a more lame way to approach a girl? Especially since he now realized he'd already said that.

"Talk to me?" she echoed. Then she flushed slightly and smiled back at him. "I mean, hello. Nice to meet you."

He held out his hand, but out of habit, he wiped it first on his pants. He'd spent so much of his adolescence with sweaty, gross hands that it was just an automatic gesture. Then he cursed himself for being an idiot. He was in a suit, for God's sake. And now she was wondering what had been on his hands when it had been nothing!

Mentally he sighed and tried even harder to be charming. He grabbed her hand and shook it too hard. "My name is Ken. Ken Johnson."

"I'm Ali," she said, as she glanced beyond his left shoulder. "And, um, I have a meeting…"

"Oh, right!" He stepped aside, his thoughts whirling. Could she possibly be going into the agency? Was God smiling on him? Could she maybe be a model?

She stepped past him, and he tried not to look like a creepy stalker. But that was harder than it seemed given that he was loitering in the hallway for no reason at all. Then it didn't matter because, *yes,* she pushed through the doorway of the agency.

She was a model and she was *hired!*

He stumbled after her, nearly tripping over himself in his excitement. He made it through the doors right on her heels. She turned at his noisy entrance, her eyes going wide and her lips parting on a sweet gasp of surprise. In the background, Elisa came forward, talking to the newcomer.

"There you are! I'm so sorry—"

"Don't apologize, Miss…" What was her name? All he could remember was Elisa. "Look, Elisa, this girl right here, I want her." Belatedly he realized he couldn't afford to pay exorbitant rates, and he ought to be negotiating. "I mean, assuming she's a reasonable price."

Both women gaped at him. It took him a moment to realize that Elisa had been talking to the newcomer, not him. Meanwhile, Elisa recovered first, her skin flushing a dark red. "Oh, no, Mr. Johnson. I'm sorry. She's not for sale."

He ground his teeth together. Damn it, she was already booked. He turned to the model, trying not to appear desperate. But he was desperate! "How long until you're available? Are there breaks? A weekend or two? I'm sure we could work things out."

He reached out to touch her arm, but Elisa quickly stepped between them. "Mr. Johnson, you don't understand."

He refused to let anyone come between him and his queen. He pushed Elisa aside as gently as he could. Fortunately she wasn't all that stable on her stiletto heels or he might not have managed it. Meanwhile, his eyes were on the woman he wanted.

"What's your normal rate?"

Instead of answering, his queen swallowed, and her eyes darted anxiously between him and Elisa. Uh-oh. Not a good sign.

"Look," he said, "I know this is unusual, but I'm not crazy."

"You just want to buy me," she said, her voice soft. God, she had the most beautiful voice. Just listening to it made everything in him go still.

"Hire you," he scrambled to say. "Hire you. To be my queen."

She blinked at him.

"Mr. Johnson!" snapped Elisa. "She's not our model!"

She wasn't... Oh! "So you're with a different agency?" he asked.

"Um, no," his goddess answered. "St. Catherine's Hospital."

He frowned and looked at her, his body actually lurching as he tried to understand her words. "Hospital? You're a…a…" He looked at her, mentally trying to fit her into the medical profession. Doctor? Nurse? None of that seemed to fit. "Um…"

"I work in the PR department doing events. Health fairs and the like."

"Health fairs?" His queen was…a PR girl? But that was perfect! She was in PR. She knew how to handle—

"Sorry. I'm just here for lunch." She gave him a self-conscious shrug and turned to Elisa. "Are you free yet?"

"Uh…" began Elisa, but then from directly behind them, the head of OMG Action! spoke, her voice cutting through the foyer in strident tones.

"No, she's not!" said Marilyn Madison. "Both of them are coming with me!"

Then the strangest thing happened. All three of them—himself, Elisa and his queen—all groaned at once.

2

ALI FLORES COULDN'T LOOK AT the cute guy who'd tried to flirt with her in the hallway. She'd figured out his problem. He'd assumed she was a model just because she was headed into the agency, and wasn't that just too funny! The idea of her as a model cracked her up. She wasn't tall, blonde or rail-thin. And she certainly didn't have the style sense to do anything like modeling.

Still, she had to admit she was flattered, even if he really needed to get his eyes checked. She had been looking forward to giggling with Elisa about it over lunch when Mad Marilyn saw them. That was their code name for Marilyn Madison, owner of the agency and somewhat of a bitch.

Last week, Elisa had taken Ali out to lunch for her twenty-eighth birthday. It wasn't until they were on their way back to the office that Elisa realized she'd accidentally paid using the corporate credit card. Sure, Elisa had refunded the money into the petty-cash drawer along with the receipt and the explanation, but Ali just knew the madwoman was going to ream them both out at the first opportunity. And now the time had come to pay the piper.

Too bad it had to happen in front of that cute guy she couldn't quite look at.

Ali mouthed the word *busted* to her friend, then turned

around to face Marilyn. Since she wasn't employed here, Ali fully intended to take all the blame. She wasn't exactly sure how she was going to manage that except that she was really good at constructing elaborate cover stories. She'd just have to make sure it was really good.

With that thought in mind, she pasted on an ultra-innocent smile and turned around. First off: start with flattery.

"Why, Miss Madison, look at you! You've lost weight!"

As expected, the woman stopped glaring long enough to shoot Ali an I-know-what-you're-doing smile. "Thank you for noticing," the woman said. "I've always thought you to be unusually perceptive."

Ali blinked. She had? Since when? As far as she was aware, the woman didn't even know her name. Then she had to mentally slap herself. Obviously, the woman was simply shooting back the same insincere flattery that Ali had given her.

"Now come along, you two," the woman said, punctuating her order with a glare at Elisa.

Ali shuddered. This was not good.

Then the woman turned a dazzling smile on the sweet Blind Ken, as Ali had now named him in her mind.

"Mr. Johnson, please, if you would give us just a moment, I'm sure I can work things out just as you'd like."

"But I'd like—"

"Yes," Mad Marilyn interrupted. "I know exactly what you want, and I'm going to make sure you get it. But first, I've ordered some sandwiches and coffee. They'll be up in just a moment. Why don't you wait with your VP in the conference room. I'll be just a moment."

Blind Ken had a VP? Wow, he must be the difficult client Elisa had been texting her about. The guy who wasn't happy with any of their usual models, but couldn't say why.

She looked up at him, and immediately regretted her decision. He was staring intently at her. He obviously wanted to say something but wasn't sure what. She could relate. She spent half her life thinking she ought to say something, but not knowing what would work.

The moment stretched on, and the pressure to say something—anything—built inside her. She took a breath at the very same moment he did, but then Mad Marilyn beat them both to the punch.

"In here please, Miss Flores," she said in a freezing tone.

Nothing to do now but shut her mouth and follow the madwoman into her office. At least Elisa would be in there, too, but one look at her friend's face and she could tell they were both equally clueless about what was going on.

She'd barely stepped into the large room when Marilyn started talking and rooting through files at the same moment.

"Shut the door, Elisa. Have a seat, Miss Flores. We really need to change your name. Never model under your real name. How do you feel about Flowers?"

Ali frowned, replaying the sentences in her mind. Nope. They still didn't make any sense. But Mad Marilyn looked up to pin her with a glare.

"Well? Do you like Flowers?"

"Um, yes?" Who didn't like flowers?

"Excellent." Marilyn pulled out a thick contract, set it down on the desk and started writing. "So your name will be Ali Flowers. You'll have the standard agency agreement, but before I can release you to Mr. Johnson, you'll need some training. Emergency training, if you catch my drift. But lucky for you, I can simply deduct the cost of that from the contract with GQ."

Elisa stepped closer after having closed the door. "I think you mean QG. Quirky Games."

Marilyn looked up and frowned. "What? Oh, right. These games. Ridiculous name. Quirky. Whatever. Now, Ms. Flowers, will you please sign here, here, here, and initial here." She pushed a pen forward into Ali's hand.

Ali barely managed to grab hold of the pen, but beyond that, she didn't move a muscle. She felt like an idiot—and a slow one to boot—but she had no clue what was going on and no interest in signing anything until she did.

So she carefully set the pen down. "I'm afraid I don't understand. Why would I sign an agency agreement with you?"

"So you can be GQ's Guinevere!"

"QG," she corrected. It was the only thing she understood. That they were definitely *not* talking about *Gentlemen's Quarterly.*

Mad Marilyn waved that away with an impatient snort. "Look, I understand you want more money. Don't we all? But I simply can't get you ready in time *and* forgo the usual agency cut. Believe me I'll be earning every cent!"

Ali shook her head. "But I don't want to be a model." The idea was laughable! "And why would you—"

"Marilyn, please," cried Elisa. Apparently, she understood what was going on. "Ali just came here for lunch."

"Well, what has that to do with anything? Look," she said, turning her laser eyes on Ali. "That man out there has a lot of money. He's been looking all over the city for some woman to play his Queen Guinevere in a summer promotional sweep. And now he wants you." She grabbed the pen and pushed it into Ali's hand. "So sign. Then you and I can make a lot of money."

Ali gaped at her. "Guinevere? Me?"

Marilyn rolled her eyes. "Yes, you!"

"But why?"

"Because he's a crazy man! You're not tall enough, you're not trained in any way and you could stand to lose a few pounds."

"Hey!" That was Elisa, not Ali. Sadly, Ali knew everything the woman said was absolutely correct.

"But I don't understand why," said Ali, her gaze going to

Elisa. Sadly, Mad Marilyn wasn't allowing anyone to talk but herself.

"It doesn't matter why, Miss Flowers. It matters that you say yes!" This time she forcibly wrapped Ali's fingers around the pen.

"But I don't know anything about modeling—"

"I'll teach you everything you need to know."

"—and I already have a job!" That last protest was pure reflex. After all, hadn't she just decided she needed to re-make her life? But modeling had never entered her mind as a possibility.

Meanwhile, Marilyn huffed as she sat back in her chair. "Shall I be blunt?" she asked.

As if she was ever anything else! "I'm not a model," Ali said.

"No, my dear, you're a secretary in a hospital PR department."

Ali blinked. How did Marilyn know that? "I manage events, coordinate publicity and logistics. It's an important job!" She said the words, but inside, she knew it really was a lame job. Sure, what she did was valuable, but all it took was an organized mind. She had that in spades. She was valued (at least she hoped she was) but from anyone else's perspective, she was just another cog in a very big machine.

"And now you have a chance to be something better. Something special! A Marilyn Madison Model!"

Ali didn't know how to answer. The idea of her as a model was just too far to go, and yet she was starting to think about it. Could she really be pretty enough to be a model? She wasn't ugly, but she'd never thought of herself as beautiful.

"Think of it!" Mad Marilyn pressed. "Your picture in the paper, screaming fans, cameras, a life under the lights! It's what every girl wants, and it's being handed to you on a sil-ver platter!"

Uh-oh. Wrong thing to say. As Marilyn started speaking,

the reality of what a model had to do started hitting. She'd be put on display. All those cameras! What if she said the wrong thing? What if she did the wrong thing? She would be promoting Blind Ken's product—whatever it was—but if she screwed up then that would reflect badly on him.

"No," she whispered. "No, I can't do that."

Marilyn released her breath on a huff of disgust. Then she shook her head. "Listen to me, Miss Flores. I know this is fast, I know this is a big change. But sometimes opportunity happens like that. It's there and then it's gone like that." She snapped her fingers with a loud crack. "So take it now while it's being offered. Otherwise it's gone." Again, she snapped her fingers and the sound seemed to echo in Ali's head. "Think hard. And think fast."

Then she pushed out of her chair and shot a glare at Elisa. "You're her friend! Explain the situation. Explain how great an *opportunity* this is." She straightened her very tight fitted jacket. "I'll go negotiate your fee." Then she was gone.

Ali waited a long time after Marilyn was gone before looking at Elisa. They were best friends, had been since college when they'd been assigned each other as roommates. They couldn't be more opposite. Where Ali was studious and shy, an introvert with a love of reading, Elisa was vivacious, spontaneous and had a burning desire to be a runway model. After she'd failed a dozen auditions, Elisa decided to use her brain and body a little differently. She interned at Marilyn's agency and was so good at it that Marilyn hired her as soon as the internship was over.

Elisa couldn't be a top model, but she could help other girls attain the dream. And now, apparently, her job was to see that Ali became exactly what Elisa had dreamed of. But Ali just couldn't do it. She couldn't be a model. She didn't know anything about it!

"Don't shake your head, sweetie," Elisa said as she pulled

up a chair. "Let me guess. You're thinking that you can't be a model, not because you aren't pretty enough—"

"I'm *not!*"

"The client says you are."

Ali didn't have an answer to that, so she buttoned her lip.

"You're thinking that you can't stand having people look at you. That you'd be the center of attention and that you'd mess it up somehow."

Ali sighed. "It's not fair of Marilyn to make you talk me into this."

Elisa shrugged. "Don't think about me right now. Let's talk about you."

"I can't be a model!"

"You keep saying that, but what really is stopping you?"

"I have a job."

"And didn't you just text me that you wanted a new one?" Elisa pulled out her phone and paged through to the right text message. "Oh, I'm sorry," she said. "What you actually said was: 'We're going to find me a new life.'"

Ali sighed. Sure she'd said that, and she'd even meant it. "But I can't just change my entire life over lunch."

Elisa shrugged. "Like Marilyn said, sometimes things happen that fast."

"Don't you dare snap your fingers!" Ali groused. Of course Elisa didn't have to. Ali still had the sound of Marilyn's *snap* echoing in her brain. But even as her heart was starting to think of the possibility, her brain was busy coming up with reasons she couldn't possibly do this.

"I'd be a lousy model." She'd spent her life on logistics and organization. It had been a necessary survival skill while managing her three younger siblings. "My skills are great *backstage.*"

Again, Elisa just shrugged. "Maybe it's time to learn some new skills."

Sure it was. But modeling? "I haven't a clue what to do."

"Well, that's easy enough. We'll teach you. And besides, you're not going on a runway. You're just dressing up and talking to people. You do that every day."

"I talk to people at health fairs. About finding the right doctor and managing their blood pressure."

"And now you'll talk to kids about a game. Really, Ali, you're incredibly smart. You'll get the hang of it in no time."

Ali tried to picture it. She imagined herself as one of those product girls she saw at health fairs, the ones attached to some drug company. They looked good, but dressed on the edge of too slutty, in her opinion. They were there to draw people to the booth so that they could try a sample of an over-the-counter medication. Or a new arch support. Or something. They were product girls, and…and well, what they did wasn't that hard.

"That can't pay enough compared to what I'm making now."

"Are you sure? That's what Marilyn's out there negotiating right now. And from what I saw, Mr. Johnson wants you bad. That means big-dollar bad."

Ali shook her head, but inside she was thinking. After all, Marilyn was right; every little girl wanted to be thought of as gorgeous, so beautiful people would flock to see her. But as a child she'd been much too shy and awkward to want anyone looking at her. There wasn't any big trauma in her background. She was just more comfortable watching the action than being part of it. She was the girl who made sure things ran smoothly, whether that meant making sure her brothers had their uniforms for the big soccer game or watching the UPS website to be sure the hospital booth arrived at the event stadium. It had taken her a year to be able to function smoothly in a booth, speaking clearly in a crowd without stammering or blushing.

"I can't lose my job," she said. "What happens when the promo sweep is over?"

Elisa leaned back. "What about a leave of absence? I saw the events he has planned. It's three months, tops. Good work for a model."

"I'm not a model." She said the words out of habit, but she was already softening.

"Don't think of it as being a model. Think of it as an acting job."

"Not helping."

"People won't be looking at you, Ali. They'll be looking at Mr. Johnson's queen."

Ali didn't even know how Elisa could say those words with a straight face. "How does a queen act? What if I do it wrong? It'll reflect badly on his game and this agency."

Elisa snorted. "You think too much about other people. Let Marilyn worry about the agency. Let Mr. Johnson worry about his product. You're just being hired to stand around looking pretty. You can do that! Especially if you get paid really well for it."

Ali squirmed. She could tell that Elisa wanted her to say yes. But the idea was so ludicrous. And yet even as she said those words to herself, she wondered if she were lying. Obviously, it wasn't ludicrous. Not if Marilyn could really get her good pay. And yes, Elisa was right. Blind Ken seemed to think she'd be perfect for the job. He was delusional, but that wouldn't stop him from paying her.

"What if I get fired without pay?"

"You won't screw up, and Marilyn's big on up-front pay."

Ali gaped. "Can she do that?"

Elisa shrugged. "Not usually, but like I said: he wants you."

Elisa stopped speaking, waiting while a zillion thoughts spun around in Ali's brain. Elisa knew her well. She knew that she had to think things through. That she hated being bullied. And that...

"One last thing," Elisa said. "Today's text wasn't just out of the blue. You've been ready for a change for a while now.

Just last week you said you were getting frustrated. That you felt you were in a rut. You weren't going to get promoted, you'd topped out your pay at the peon level—" Ali opened her mouth, but Elisa stopped her with a pointed finger. A gesture she'd obviously learned from Marilyn. "Those are *your* words, Ali! 'The peon level.'"

Oh, right. She had said that.

"So maybe this is the shake-up you need, a summer of opportunity. If nothing else, think of it as a paid vacation. You'll only be on a stage a few hours a day. After that, you can sit around in your hotel room and read. Or maybe you'll go to the bar and get a drink. Hang out with your fellow actors. Come on, Ali, are you sure you don't want to try it? Just for a few months?"

Ali shifted uncomfortably in her seat, her mind continuing to race. Everything Elisa said was right. Absolutely everything. But could she do it? There were so many things that would have to work out right. The pay, for one. The leave of absence from her current job, for another.

"Tell you what," Elisa said, proving that she knew Ali was weakening. "Why don't you go out and chat with Mr. Johnson? Find out exactly what he wants. You'll see how easy it will be."

At the mention of Mr. Johnson, Ali felt her face heat. He was cute. She'd enjoyed the short exchange that they'd had in the hallway. He'd seemed real and, well, just her speed. That meant funny and dorky in a nice way. Not the silk-shirt-and-thousand-dollar-suit guys that Elisa usually dated.

She thought about working with him day after day. He wasn't tall, which was great. At five foot six, she hated feeling like a shrimp next to big guys. He had dark curly hair and nice brown eyes, though she'd noticed they were a bit red. As if he was already hours into a too-long day and it was barely one o'clock. But mostly she remembered how he'd made her feel: relaxed. As if he was just as nervous as she was, and so together they'd muddle along fine.

It was an odd thought to have after just a few minutes' conversation, but the feeling persisted. Maybe it was his smile—warm and genuine, but still holding a hint of anxiety. As though he really wanted to make a good impression. Which made her smile because, honestly, what über-rich guy wanted to please her?

In short, the answer was yes. She could imagine working every day with him. In truth, she thought it could be really awesome. She'd just have to stop thinking of him as Blind Ken. He was Mr. Johnson from now on. Her boss…maybe.

"Okay," she finally said.

"Okay, you'll do it?"

"Okay, I'll go talk a little more with Blind Ken."

Elisa snorted. "You cannot call him that. And he's not blind! How many times have I told you that you're way more beautiful than you think?"

Ali shrugged as she straightened up from her chair. Then she rubbed her hands nervously along her skirt and wished she'd refreshed her makeup. "Do I have time—"

The door burst open and Marilyn stomped in looking for all the world as if she was ready to wrestle a bear. "Are you done? Did you sign? Can we go meet the client now?"

Guess there was no time for a makeup refresh. "Yes, I'll meet Mr. Johnson now."

Marilyn froze, her gaze darting to the unsigned contract.

"And then," pressed Ali, "we can decide about an agency agreement."

But first, she had to impress the hell out of Blind—er, Notblind Ken. The CEO of some quirky company. And when exactly had she stepped from normal world into wonderland?

3

KEN DIDN'T KNOW WHETHER to be depressed or dive head-long into a Desperate Act. It was obvious that he had erred badly. Having finally found his queen, he'd assumed she was a model (Mistake number one), stalked her like a psycho creep (Mistake number two), declared he "wanted her" and tried to buy her for a weekend or more (Mistake number three), and then when he'd finally realized his error, he lost the opportunity to explain himself (Mistake number four). Marilyn had whisked the woman away only to return fifteen minutes later to negotiate the woman's fee as if she were bartering the crown jewels.

And in all of that, he got the distinct feeling that his Guinevere—a Ms. Ali Flowers—had no interest in being a model. So now he was faced with two choices. He could either give up entirely—not really an option. Or he could try again with Ali. But how? What to say to explain that he wasn't creepy or insane? And how to convince a hospital PR rep to quit her job to come work for him for a summer? Because he could pay her well, but probably not *that* well.

He was still chewing on that thought when Marilyn finally realized he wasn't going to negotiate any fee until he talked to Ali again. She clicked her teeth shut and pushed up from the table. "I'll be right back," she snapped, then tugged on her short jacket and stomped out.

Which left him sitting in the conference room with Paul, his vice president of marketing, while staring morosely at the table. Fortunately, Paul knew just how to talk to him.

"So, you're sure this is the woman?"

Ken nodded without even taking his chin out of his hand.

"No one else will do?"

Ken shook his head.

"And she's not even a model."

Ken shrugged.

"So basically, we're screwed."

"Unless I can charm her into quitting her job for us."

"Uh-huh. Screwed." Then Paul paused. Ken knew what was coming. Paul was tall, dark and baby-faced cute. Not exactly handsome, but a man who looked and dressed the part of a marketing executive. And if one of them was going to charm Ali, then it would probably be Paul. "Do you want—" Paul began.

"No. Absolutely not. You stay quiet." Both of them were startled by the vehemence in his words.

"Ooo-kay."

"Let me sink or swim on my own here."

Another long pause. "You know you're not being entirely rational, right?"

Ken had no response to that. Of course he wasn't being rational. But apparently, he didn't care. Especially as Marilyn's office opened up and out she came with one sharp-taloned hand gripping his Guinevere's arm.

Ken shot to his feet, yet another mistake (number five) as his chair nearly flopped to the floor behind him. Fortunately, Paul had fast hands and grabbed it. *Get a grip!* Ken ordered himself. But it was hard to hear his own thoughts over the pounding of his heart.

The conference-room door opened and the ladies entered,

Guinevere first. Ken searched her face, hoping for a clue, but he saw nothing that reassured him. Her face was composed, her eyes were alert, but there was a general air of wariness about her. And no wonder. She probably thought he was a total sleaze.

Time to start being charming. He pulled on a smile.

"Hello, Miss Flowers. I'd like to—"

"Flores."

"—apologize. I must have sounded like a… What?"

"Flores. My name is Ali Flores."

"Oh." He could have sworn Marilyn said Flowers. Great, now he was really screwing up. "Um, I apologize. For getting your name wrong and for acting like a lunatic earlier."

She smiled, a soft curving of her lips that did not show teeth. It was a reserved smile, and he found he liked her all the more for it. It softened her face without bowling him over with a polished exterior. It made her feel more real, and he found himself relaxing at the sight of it. She was a normal person. Hopefully, she understood that he was a normal guy—one who made mistakes.

Then Marilyn had to spoil the mood by hauling out a chair and strong-arming Ali into the seat. "Excellent! Now that that's out of the way, let's sit down and talk details."

Ken bristled. He had a Neanderthal reaction to seeing anyone manhandling his queen, even if the man-handler was a woman. But before he could say anything, Paul leaped into the breech. Great, his employee got to be the hero before Ken could do more than glare.

"You know, Marilyn," Paul said, "I believe I need to go over the contract with you in detail. We're not signing anything until I get a few questions answered."

"But what about—"

Paul took Marilyn's arm and physically pulled her off Ali. "I'm in charge of the contract part. My boss is in charge of the campaign and the company as a whole. So you and I are going to talk turkey somewhere else. Now." Then he all but shoved Marilyn out of the room. He was half a step out of the door when he somehow managed to grab hold of Elisa. "You, too," he said. Then he glanced back at Ken and shot him a wink. "Sink or swim, buddy." Then he was gone.

Ken released a slow breath, beyond grateful to finally have Ali in the room alone. But right on the heels of that relief was the knowledge that it was all up to him now.

He tried another smile. "Okay, so now they're gone."

She nodded, but didn't speak.

"So we're clear, I wasn't trying to hire you as a prostitute or anything earlier. I thought you were a model. I was trying to book you—"

"I know," she interrupted. "I figured that out."

"Oh, good. Because I was afraid…" He swallowed. Stay on track. "So I'd like to hire you as a model. But you work at a hospital. Then Marilyn said…well, she said your name was Flowers."

Ali grimaced. "She wants me to change my name."

"Don't you dare!" Then he flushed, belatedly realizing that he had no right to tell her to do anything with her name one way or the other. "I mean, Flores is a great name. And Flowers is a stupid one."

Her lips curved a little more and her eyes seemed to sparkle. "Don't you like flowers?"

Was she teasing him? He didn't know and so he didn't know how to respond. "Um, well, sure, they're pretty and all. And you are, too, so, you know, Flowers would be okay if you really want it. But I don't think you should change who you are. Unless you want to change your name. I mean—"

She laughed, that soft chuckle that pressed every damn happy button he had. Then she pressed her hand to her mouth and her eyes widened. "Oh, sorry," she gasped.

"For what?"

"I, um, I shouldn't have laughed like that."

"No, you should have. I'm falling all over myself today. I'm sorry. I'm trying to impress you and doing such a damn bad job of it."

Again her laughter bubbled up, though he could tell that she was still trying to hold it back. "That's so funny," she murmured.

"Yeah, I get that a lot," he drawled. Usually when he tried to impress a girl. Once again he was choosing *sink* over *swim*.

"No, no!" she exclaimed. "It's funny that you're trying to impress *me*."

He frowned. "Why wouldn't I try to impress you? You're beautiful and charming. And I want to hire you to be my Guinevere."

She sobered and her expression showed true confusion. "But why? Why would you want me?"

And wasn't that just the question of the hour? Paul had asked that, Marilyn, too. He gave the same answer that he'd given them. "Because you fit the part. You're real." He gestured to the stack of model photos on the table. "They're not."

She tilted her head, and he nearly lost himself in the curve of her neck as it met with a nice jaw, swooping up into a perfect shell ear.

"I bet if you'd met them, they'd be real, too."

He snorted. "I have met them. Every single one of them paraded before me all morning. I only have to talk to them for half a minute to realize that they're…well, they're just like Marilyn."

Her eyes widened. "Which part? Mad Marilyn where she decides my name should be Flowers? Or Scary Marilyn where she tells me I've got a dead-end job and that there's nothing special about me unless I take classes from her and lose weight?"

"Don't you dare!" Then again, he remembered that he didn't have the right to tell her what to do and not do. "I mean," he hastily amended, "don't take classes from her.

She'll turn you into one of them." He touched the nearest model photo and pushed it to the opposite side of the table.

"But I should lose weight?"

"What? No! You're fine! And I can't wait to see you in a corset." Oh my God, had he just said that? "I mean…I think you'd look great in a…but not in a skanky way, you know. It's the costume… And you're beautiful in just what you're wearing."

She laughed. "I got it! Guinevere wears a corset."

Thank God. She could understand his babbling. That was a plus as he seemed to be babbling a lot right now. And he really needed to stop. So he took a deep breath and decided to go for broke.

Sink or swim.

"Okay, here's the truth."

She looked up at him, her eyes dark, her skin flawless, and her lips—wow, those lips. He kept getting lost in looking at her mouth. And so, while he was still dazzled, his words began to flow.

"Back in high school there were two girls. Well, there were a lot of girls, but there were these two in particular. Stephanie was flawless. Tall, blonde, volleyball star and a mouth that was always dewy-moist like in those lipstick commercials."

She blinked, and then she absently licked her own lips. His groin tightened at the sight. Her lipstick had mostly worn off, but that just made her more natural in his mind. No cosmetic mask, so to speak. Just her, clean and pure.

"Did you win her?" she asked.

"Geek me? No. But I did hang out around her at a couple parties, listening at the fringe, trying to fit in."

Her lips curved. "I know it well."

"And then one day I went from her crowd to the food table. I was munching on some chips when I started talking to Heidi. She was on the volleyball team, too, but wasn't the star. She had a scar right here." He pointed to a place right above his lip. "We started talking movies, then chemistry class, then philosophy." He snorted. "Well, philosophy the way two sophomores in high school would."

"How long did you two date?"

"That's just the point. We didn't. Not for another year and a half. But suddenly, I realized the difference between beauty and substance. Stephanie's beauty ended up just leaving a bad taste in my mouth because it wasn't real. But Heidi had substance. I could talk with her. We ended up being friends and that was so much better than being attracted by Stephanie's flawless beauty." He gestured to the pile of photos. "These girls are just another pinup, but you're someone I can talk to. I could do it in the hall, and I can do it here. You have no idea how powerful that is. It means the world to me and will to the kids who are going to buy my product."

She stared at him and he just looked back. Did she understand? "But actually, I'm kind of shy."

He smiled. "I know. It's like the difference between a whisper and a shout. I'll tune out a shout. Everyone shouts. But a whisper? Now I'm intrigued. Now I'm leaning in to hear more."

She blinked, and he wondered if he'd caught her. She'd certainly captured him. It wasn't just her unconscious beauty, which certainly grabbed him. It was the way she bit her lip when she was thinking. The way she listened when he spoke. And the way she thought about what he said without just throwing back what she thought he wanted to hear.

"Let me explain what I'm planning." He pulled a series of screen captures out of his folder and pushed them to her. "We're launching this game." He pointed at the cover image of Winning Guinevere.

"Wow. She's gorgeous." She traced the woman's face with a long, tapered finger.

Looking at the design, he made a quick decision. "I'm changing the cover design. Blondes are overdone."

She glanced at him but didn't comment. So he took a deep breath and plunged into his pitch.

"Winning Guinevere is a take on the King Arthur legend turned video game. Players can be anyone in the legend they want—knights, fair maidens, Merlin, King Arthur or Lancelot. They can even be Mordred if they're so inclined."

"The betraying bad guy?"

Ken nodded. "He's there to muck up the works, so to speak. But the core of the story is between Arthur and Lancelot. Who will Guinevere choose?" He lifted the page to show her another picture. "That's you. Guinevere."

She peered down at it. "I don't look anything like her."

"But you *feel* like her. And besides, I'm changing her look to reflect you."

Her eyes widened. "You're not serious."

"I am serious. I can't express how important it is to have the right Guinevere. She will make the campaign that should launch the product that—" He cut off his words. He probably shouldn't tell her that this one product could make or break his whole company.

"And you think I'm Guinevere."

"I know it."

She looked back at the picture in front of her. Then taking a deep breath, she turned the page, looking deeper at the product specifications. "The point of the game is to win…me?"

"You. Your love. Your gifts."

"Seriously?"

"That takes on very specific meanings depending on the player's score. Plus, if they work very hard and do very well, then they get a discount on the purchase of Winning II."

"And kids will do that? Spend hours on the game just to get a game bonus that isn't even real?"

"And a sales pitch for the next game. Yes, they will."

She looked skeptical.

"Trust me. They will because the game is that good. But

I have to get them playing the game in the first place. I have to get them started, and I have to show them you."

"Me."

"Yes, you. Beautiful, sexy as hell, but approachable. Someone who would bestow royal gifts. Someone who understands them and is worth the time and money."

"But I don't understand them. I don't—"

He waved that aside. "You *do* know them, you just don't realize it yet." He huffed out his breath on a sigh. "Look, I know this doesn't make any kind of logical sense, but I know what I'm talking about." At least he prayed he did. "You're Guinevere, and I'd like to hire you to spend the summer with me."

"With you?"

He flushed, his mind going to all the wrong things. "I mean, on tour with the whole crew. It's an entire summer of buses and hotels. You'll get time off, I swear, but it'll be in a different city each week."

He pulled out the schedule to show it to her. Not surprisingly, her eyes widened in surprise. "That's a lot of dates."

"Like I said, at least one every week. We do a different step in the story in every city. We start with Arthur and Guinevere getting married at the first stop, but with Lancelot in the wings. Then the next week there's affection from Lancelot. Next Merlin plays a hand. After that, there's Mordred causing problems. It builds throughout the summer until there's a showdown between Arthur and Lancelot."

"Who wins?"

"You're Guinevere. You get to decide." Then he flashed her a grin. "Well, actually we'll see how the fan choices go. We'll be blogging and getting fan commentary throughout the summer. In the end, the fans choose for you."

She smiled up at him. "That sounds like a lot of fun."

"It is. Exhausting but fun." He pushed another page forward and prayed that she didn't flinch. "This is the pay schedule. We cover all expenses and travel. I'm sorry, but my company is being cut to the bone to do this launch. I'm afraid I can't offer more than this." It was a lie. For her, he'd pay a lot more. He'd find the money somewhere, somehow. For her.

She nodded slowly, chewing on her lower lip as she looked at everything.

"And, um, I'm sorry, but I think the agency will take a cut of that. Marilyn will insist on that. Even if you don't have a contract with her right now, I did meet you here."

"Yeah," she said softly. "I can't see Marilyn giving up her piece of this."

He sighed. After agency fees, the dollars weren't great. Not bad for a summer actor. Good pay, actually. But he had no idea what she made at the hospital. He probably shouldn't have reminded her about the agency fees. Let her think she was getting the whole amount so she had more incentive to say yes. But he didn't want to lie to her, even by omission. Still, he was very aware that he might just have blown it.

"You understand that this is all take-home pay," he said. "We're covering all expenses."

She nodded.

He waited. There was nothing more to say, but God he wanted to. He wanted to beg her to say yes. And as he sat there watching her, seeing the curve of her face, the fullness of her breasts and the feminine arch to her back, he started wanting other things, too.

She flipped through the pages and started reading the contract, her lips pursed as she concentrated. He looked at her lips and starting thinking of other things. What she might also do with those lips. Of what he could do to her to erase the furrows on her forehead. Of what they might do together that had nothing to do with contracts and everything to do with a whole lot of naked wonderfulness in bed.

That's where his mind went and it was wrong, wrong,

wrong! He was her employer—or he wanted to be. So he forced his thoughts down a more professional track.

It took him a while.

"So," he finally asked. "Is this enough to make you quit your job at the hospital?"

She shook her head slowly. "No."

His heart sank.

"But for a summer leave of absence? Yes."

4

THE NEXT FEW WEEKS PASSED in a blur for Ali. The first worry was that she couldn't get a leave of absence from her job. That turned out to be the easiest task on her list. Depressingly so. It's not that her boss tossed her out the door. The man just sighed, asked her if she was sure—she was—and then approved it. It was a measure of how underappreciated she was there.

At least her coworkers were sad. Especially as she passed off one project after another into their hands. Ali consoled herself with the thought that in her absence, her boss would realize just how much she did around there. She couldn't bear thinking about the opposite possibility: that no one would even notice she was gone. That was just too depressing for words.

Then there was passing off her plants, getting Elisa to check in on the apartment, and lastly to convince her family she wasn't insane. She failed in that last task. Her mother rolled her eyes and asked who could possibly want Ali as a model. Not the most supportive attitude, but Ali was committed now. And even if she wasn't, there was something that kept her headed toward her bizarre summer:

She'd started fantasizing. About her multi-cabillionaire boss. She'd always had a rich fantasy life. After all, she'd started out as a latchkey kid to a single mom. Plenty of alone time, plenty of time to lose herself in her imagination. That habit had continued well into adulthood where her imagination took on a decidedly mature aspect. And it was no different when she started dreaming about Ken.

It started out simply enough. As long as she was going to be working for the man, she decided to look him up on Google. There weren't a lot of news items on him, but there was a ton about his games. The man apparently was more interested in getting press for his product than for himself. Her kind of guy.

There was nothing in the news stories about him being megarich, but that didn't seem to matter to her libido. In her fantasies, he was über-rich, über-awesome and über into her. It all built off his smile. He smiled just like she did—a little nervous, a little happy, a little puppy dog. It was cute as hell. And the fact that he talked with her—his attention fully focused on her—well, that was an aphrodisiac all by itself.

Most people were kind enough to start by looking at her during the conversation, but all too soon, they were looking away. She didn't know if she was just too boring to hold anyone's attention or if people just didn't have that long of an attention span. She'd learned to keep everything she said to short sound bites. She delivered her information, and then let whoever wander away. But that hadn't happened with Ken. His attention had been like a laser light. At first it had been a little uncomfortable. But now, in retrospect, she really got off on it.

She wondered what it would be like to have him look at her like that during a date. Or better yet in bed. Yeah, her libido didn't work by half measures. She wanted her guy to have that kind of intensity with her as he did *everything* to her.

She'd spent many a happy night picturing his eyes. But then she belatedly realized the man was going to be her *boss*. Oops. But even knowing that, she couldn't stop herself. Didn't matter what she did to distract herself, Johnny Depp morphed into Ken, Orlando Bloom…same thing. Two kisses into her fantasy, and he became Ken. Even Brendan Fraser, who had his own laser gaze, soon became Ken.

She would just have to remember that Ken could be her fantasy man at night, but during the day, he was strictly professional. Which worked great until they had their first face-to-face a couple of weeks prior to the promo tour.

It was a simple evening get-together at the offices of QG. Everyone involved in the tour was there—Ken, looking slightly harassed; his marketing VP, Paul; and five others. Ali arrived late, of course. She was still wrapping things up at work and had been caught in a meeting. So when she walked in the door she was feeling flushed and very *not* together. She *hated* being late.

That was bad enough, but then she got a look at her co-workers. They were all *gorgeous*. Every single one of them. Even Ken who—objectively speaking—was the most average-looking of them all. Even he was oozing sexiness thanks to her nighttime fantasies, especially as his face lit up the moment she walked in the door.

"Ali! Great! I was getting worried something had happened to you."

She swallowed, reminding herself that this was not fantasy playtime. He was her boss, and she should not be wondering what he looked like undressed. "Sorry. Got caught up in a meeting."

"Bad one, huh?" he asked. Lord, there were six other people in the room, but he just talked right to her. Which, naturally, made her libido do a little happy dance, making the rest of her all soft and liquidy.

"N-not bad," she stammered. "Just awkward. I'm unloading all my work off onto other people, and they don't like it."

"I get that," laughed a honey-warm voice behind her.

Ali spun around and came face to chin with a blond god

of a man. Holy moly, she'd known he was gorgeous the moment she walked into the room, but up close he was downright intimidating.

"Hi," the god said in a steadily deepening voice. "I'm Blake, aka Lancelot, on a quest for gold that, thanks to your influence, becomes a noble mission for good." Then he waggled his eyebrows. "I think you get to knight me!"

"Um…hi," she said.

"Yeah," said Ken, tugging her toward a seat. "Everybody, this is Ali Flores, our Guinevere. Blake, you want to grab those folders and pass them out? Thanks. Then we'll go around the table and introduce ourselves. We're going to be living in close quarters this summer, so I hope we can all be friends."

Everyone took a seat. Because Blake was handing out folders, he was the last to find a chair and ended up being the farthest away. That, actually, was a good thing for Ali. He was too beautiful to be real, and she felt a little uncomfortable next to a man who was so much better-looking than she was. Sadly, everyone there was better-looking, or so it felt to her.

Blake was the only male actor. The others were girls of the bouncy, perky type. Blonde, brunette and redhead, they were clearly chosen because they were both beautiful and friendly. Except as the introductions went around, she realized that the blonde was Tina, Paul's assistant and troupe costumer. The brunette was Ashley, aka Morgan le Fey. And the redhead was Samantha, who would be a tavern wench. Ali just nodded, pretending she knew what that meant.

She'd already met Paul, the marketing VP who would double as Mordred, betrayer of King Arthur. And naturally, Ken would play the king.

Obviously, the others were well used to this type of thing. They introduced themselves easily, talked about their acting experiences and the parts they would play, then gushed a little about how excited they were to be here. But when it came time for her to speak, Ali got flustered and tongue-tied. Unlike them, she had absolutely no experience whatsoever.

"Ali?"

"Um, right." She felt her face heat to crimson. "I'm Ali Flores. I'm Guinevere. And…uh…I'm happy to be here." It was a lie. At the moment, she wanted to be *anywhere* but here.

Then there was a long, awkward pause. Rationally, she figured it wasn't really a long or awkward pause, but her imagination expanded it into something hideous. Good God, how was she ever going to learn how to do this in two weeks?

Fear started building inside her, but she kept it locked down tight. She'd already taken a leave of absence from her job, so she was totally committed. She'd just have to learn fast. So she paid extra attention all through the discussion of itinerary, accommodations, the game and costumes. Costumes were the most awkward because, apparently, the models/actors already had a lot of the things they'd need. The girls all had corsets, daggers and leather pants. Ashley had a neck chain that she'd been given as a joke. Blake even had his own sword and fur boots!

What did Ali have? Um…a blouse? Comfortable shoes?

"No problem," Ken said with a warm smile. "That's why Tina's here. She'll get together with you this weekend and get you all fitted."

"Unless we can meet during the week?" asked Tina hopefully.

Ali shook her head. "My last day is next Wednesday."

"That's okay," said Tina in a very perky voice. Was Ali going to have to learn perky? "How about we meet at Spiked Leather on Saturday morning? The owner knows me. He'll give us a good deal."

Ali could only smile and nod. Spiked leather? She didn't remember Guinevere wearing anything that resembled spikes.

"That's settled," said Ken. Then he smiled at her. Lord, if it weren't for that smile, she might have bolted right then.

"We'll need everyone to come next Thursday for the photo shoot. The address is in your folder."

Photo shoot?

"And finally, we're giving each one of you a copy of the game. Read the instructions. Memorize the product specs. And most of all, play it. A lot. Starting Thursday, you're all on my dime. I expect you to spend all that extra time playing the game. When you're not here, you should be trying to win Guinevere. Bring your friends over. Play with them, too. I expect every one of you to have gotten at least to Adept level by the time we leave."

There were laughter and giggles all around. Apparently, for everyone else, finding playtime with the game wasn't a problem. They all had gaming machines and friends who would fall over themselves to play. Samantha even giggled that she was so going to be queen with her brothers this weekend. They were dying to get their hands on this game.

The best Ali could do was paste on a smile. It had been a major accomplishment to hook up her DVR and connect up cable. She didn't know an Xbox from a doorstop. Her brothers would know. They played enough video games, but they were more likely to play the game themselves and keep her out of it. No way did they have the patience to teach her. Besides, they both had jobs now and were busy with their own lives. Hell, what was she going to do? Then Ken touched her arm.

"Ali, do you think you could hang back for a bit? I'd like to talk with you if you've got the time."

"Uh, sure." She might have said more, but at that moment Paul came rushing up, camera in hand.

"I know you haven't had time to have head shots taken, so I figured I'd just get this started here. If you could smile for me?"

Ali tried, but the sick feeling in her gut was getting worse. She obviously wasn't doing it right because Paul dropped the camera and gave her an equally wan smile.

"Hmm, okay. Try this. Just lift your chin. Disdain. That's good. Aloof? Yes." He aimed the camera back to her face, and she belatedly realized it was shooting video, not taking still photos. Over to the side, the others were leaving, but Ali was still able to imagine their disdainful looks as she tried to show one emotion or another as Paul hopped around.

Then Ken stopped the man with a slight touch. "Do we really need to do those now?"

"Well, not normally," Paul said with a slight grumble. "But *somebody* wants game Guinevere to look like Ms. Flores. The sooner we get some digitized images, the better."

Ken shoved his hands in his pockets and looked awkward. "Oh. Right." Then he glanced at Ali. "Sorry. This will only take a moment."

"But—" she began. Too late. Paul had the camera rolling again.

"It's best if I get all sorts of natural poses," Paul said from behind the lens. "Hey, Ali, how do you feel about zombies?"

She blinked. "Um…bad?"

Paul chuckled. "Depends on the zombie, but okay. How about mass genocide? Republicans? Democrats? I'm looking for a strong emotion here."

Ken stepped in. "Let's go with the basics. Chocolate cheesecake."

Ali gave him a grateful smile. *That* she could be passionate about. "I once offered to have sex with the next person who brought me a slice of black silk pie." Then she immediately blushed. Had she said that aloud? "I was…um…I was in my apartment alone with my boyfriend at the time."

Thankfully, Ken clearly thought it was funny. Paul flashed her a grin along with an eyebrow waggle. "And was it everything you hoped for?"

Ali shrugged. Might as well go with honesty. "Cheesecake, yes. Boyfriend, no."

"Okay, last questions," inserted Ken. "Ever seen someone kick a puppy? Trample flowers in the park?"

She frowned. "When I was a kid, we had a pet cat who was a huntress. I did everything I could to stop her, but she still caught things. Mice, bunnies, birds. It was awful the way she'd play with them. It was worse when she ate them."

"Okay, that's gross," Ken agreed. "But it is their natural instinct."

"I know. But it doesn't mean I wanted to watch her do it. Or that I wanted her to gift me with her kills."

Suddenly, Paul dropped the camera. "Perfect! That's enough for the techies to get started with. Thanks, Ali!" Then with a wave, he moved over to the brunette who was just grabbing her coat.

Ali barely had time to remember he'd been filming her when bam, he was gone. It was rather disconcerting.

"He's a high-energy kind of guy," Ken said from where he stood beside her. "Especially right before a launch. He gets really jazzed on all the details and excitement."

She watched as Paul simultaneously helped Ashley with her coat, passed Tina the camera while issuing instructions and still had time to flirt with Samantha.

"How many lattes a day does he drink?"

"Put it this way. I told him to just buy Starbucks. It'd be cheaper."

Ali giggled, pressing her hand to her mouth as she did it.

"Don't cover up," Ken said as he gently pulled her hand down. "I like seeing you smile. Seeing you laugh is even better."

Here it was. She'd been dreading it from the very beginning. It was one of those moments straight out of her fantasies where he had some reason to touch her and then they ended up just staring at each other. In her dreams, it took about two seconds for her to end up in his arms. Another ten before she was in his bed. But in real life, all she could do was look into his eyes and scream at her libido to shut up. No go. She just stood there looking while her nipples tightened and her belly trembled.

Hell.

Meanwhile, Ken seemed equally caught. He just looked at her, his eyes widening. She wondered if it was panic or terror. Part of her labeled it clear lust, but that came from her libido, which made up stuff all the time. She ignored it. And then suddenly, Paul was there, clapping his hands and completely breaking the moment. Ali jerked at the noise. So did Ken.

"Okay, Ken, I've got a zillion details to work out, but I've changed my mind about hanging around here eating dinner with you. I'm doing it at home with brandy and a cigar."

"He doesn't really drink brandy or smoke cigars," Ken said in a low voice.

"I certainly do! But you're right. Tonight is more likely to be hard lemonade. Can't stand being in this building one more second and besides, there's a Bulls game on tonight."

Ali smiled. "That's what my dad's doing tonight. He's a big fan."

"Good man. Anyway, I'm outta here." Tina rushed in with a big food sack and handed it to Paul, who promptly dug inside it. "Which means you get two subs." He tossed the first wrapped foot-long sub at Ken, then the other.

"Hey!" cried Ken as he fumbled to catch the flying food. He got the first, but didn't have a hand for the second. It caromed off his fingers and toward Ali. Thankfully, she had good reflexes. She managed to snatch it out of the air before disaster struck.

Fortunately, Paul had stopped throwing things. He just dropped the rest of the bag on the table. "I won't toss the drinks at you. I know I'd be the one to clean up the mess."

"Damn straight you would," answered Ken, but Paul wasn't listening. He'd already grabbed Tina's arm and was asking her something about latex body paint. Two seconds later,

Ken and Ali were the only people there. Not a problem, according to her libido. But Ali was working hard to be professional, so she firmly squelched the ideas running rampant through her brain.

"Um, you wanted to talk to me?"

"Oh. Um. Yeah. I noticed you got kind of a panicked look when playing the game came up."

She swallowed. "Uh, yeah."

"Not a big gamer?"

She shook her head.

"Ever played WOW? Warcrest? Legend of Zelda?"

She bit her lip and looked down.

"Okay," he said slowly. "You understand, don't you, that I need you to know this game inside and out? How to play, what to do—everything about it that you can learn in the next week."

She nodded, feeling miserable. How the hell was she going to do that? But even as she was about ready to give up the job, her mind started playing out possibilities. Maybe she didn't have a friend who was up on all the major games, but she knew where a game store was. She could talk to the guys there. Maybe they could teach her how to play. And while she was still thinking of ways around her problem, Ken pushed a sub sandwich into her hand. She looked at it then back up at him.

"Eat up," he said. "Because right after this, you and I are going to party in the lounge."

She stared at him, her lust doing a happy dance that was wholly inappropriate. Finally she managed, "Wh-what?"

"Adventure, mayhem, sex!" he quipped as he leaned across the table and snagged the food bag.

She swallowed, not knowing how to answer.

"Don't worry. I'm really not that good at it. Not compared to the other guys. But at least I can make it fun."

"What?"

He turned to her, his eyebrows raised. "We're going to play the game. We've got it all set up in the lounge. I'll walk you through the basics, then we can play it together." He frowned. "What did you think I was talking about?"

"Um…nothing. The game. Of course." Not like her libido was stuck on the word *sex* or anything.

"Trust me. I go easy on virgins."

She had absolutely no response to that.

5

KEN LEANED BACK in the couch, his gaze on Ali. She had her lower lip caught between her teeth as she frowned at the screen. He didn't even consider giving her a hint. First, because he had before and she'd told him quite clearly that she wanted to figure it out on her own. Second, because he had total faith that she could conquer this particular puzzle.

Because he'd learned in about ten minutes that she was smart.

She'd obviously not grown up with video games. Her eye-hand coordination wasn't lightning-quick and she didn't have the fluidity with the game controller that gamers did. So during fight sequences, she was at a severe disadvantage. But this game was as much about smarts as it was about fighting. In fact, he'd made sure the designers put in at least one smart solution to get past every obstacle. Brute force might help, but it wasn't the only way.

"What if I try…this!" She rapidly moved her avatar around and experimented.

He didn't answer. He already knew it wouldn't work, but it was a good thing to try.

"Well, shoot," she said and once again she started biting her lower lip. Even, white teeth. Red wet lip. God, he was hard for her. Hell, he'd been hard for her from the beginning.

Sadly, he was her boss, so he held back. Besides, she was thinking and that was too sexy a sight for him to interrupt.

She grabbed her soda off the table and took another swig as she stared at the scene on the television. Then she thumbed through a few other screens, looking for a clue.

"Wait a minute…" she said.

There! She'd found it.

"Can you—"

"On it," he said, quickly maneuvering his avatar to help hers.

"I'm going to—"

"I'll brace you like this—"

"Now together—"

Bam! The Impenetrable Wall tumbled to the ground.

"Woo hoo!" she crowed, dropping the controller on her lap as she fell backward into the couch. "Damn, this game is hard!"

"You seem to be flying through it."

She looked up at him in surprise. "Really?"

He nodded. "Really."

Then she looked down at the game box. "Well, the game is designed for teens. I suppose I ought to be flying through it, huh?"

He shook his head as he leaned back into the couch right beside her. They were close enough to touch. In fact, he shifted his leg enough that their knees and some of her calf touched.

"That's mostly a violence-and-sex rating. A lot of these puzzles will stump a teenager."

She laughed. "Well, that's reassuring to my ego. I'm smarter than the average sixteen-year-old."

And sexy, too, with her eyes dancing and her lips wet and so close. He wanted to kiss her. She was thinking it, too. Or at least he thought she was. Her gaze had dropped to his mouth and her body had stilled. The air froze in his chest. Could he? Could she?

Guess not because she abruptly looked away. "Gee, um, what time is it?"

Stifling his disappointment, he glanced at the clock on the gaming machine. "One twenty-seven."

"In the morning?" she gasped as she leaped off the couch. "Holy crap! I've got to go to work tomorrow. Er…today!"

He straightened slowly, shoving his hands into his pockets rather than reach for her. "Can you call in sick?"

"On my last few days there? Just because I stayed up too late gaming?" She blinked a moment then released a short laugh. "I never thought I'd hear myself say that."

He smiled. Impossible *not* to smile when she laughed like that. "Well, consider it research for your new job."

"I still gotta say goodbye to the old one first." Then before he could comment, she held up her hand. "And I'm not calling in sick." Then she sighed. "But I may take the afternoon off if I can't keep my eyes open."

He nodded. "Sounds like a fair compromise."

"I'll remember that, boss, if this happens again over the summer."

He was watching her slip on her shoes, noticing the flash of bright red on her toenails, when her words hit him. "Hey, that's not what I meant!"

She laughed. "Too late. You already said it!"

He released a fake grumble then started turning off the electronics. "Wait for me. I'll walk you to your car."

"You don't need to——"

He stopped her with a shake of his head. "It's a safe area, but there's no sense in taking chances. Besides, I need to get home, too."

She stopped arguing, and he quickly closed up the office. A couple of minutes later he had his satchel/briefcase strapped across his chest and together they headed for the elevators.

Fortunately, he'd had enough time to think of another conversation topic. Or perhaps an old one.

"So you don't have a brother or a male cousin or a boyfriend to show you video games?" If he were honest, it was the boyfriend part he was most interested in.

She laughed. "Actually, yes to all of those things."

His heart plummeted. Fortunately, she didn't seem to notice and kept talking.

"Three brothers, all much younger. A ton of male cousins and even a couple of boyfriends along the way. But none of them had the patience to teach me how to play. Not like you just did." Then she flushed. "Was it terribly boring for you? To wait while I figured things out?"

"What? No! I had a great time."

"Liar."

He held up his hand in a three-fingered pledge. "Scouts' honor. I had a great time. I like watching people figure things out." That was a lie. He liked watching *her* figure things out.

The elevator arrived and they stepped in. He let her push the button for the parking garage since he didn't know what level her car was on. Meanwhile, she kept up the flow of their conversation.

"You're a great teacher. And I gotta say that it's a well-designed game."

"Really? What parts did you especially like?"

She paused, eyeing him a little warily. "You really want to know?"

"Of course I want to know! You're a brand-new gamer! If I could figure out how to interest people like you, then my financial woes would be over."

She paused a moment, and her eyes narrowed. "You have financial woes?"

He sighed. "Don't worry. The launch is safe. Let's just say if the game doesn't sell well, then I *will* have financial woes. As in piles and piles of them."

She nodded, and he could tell she was thinking about that. But in the end she shrugged. "Okay, here you go off the top of my head. I really liked the story behind the game…"

She rattled off a couple of the early sequences, surprising him with her answers. At first he thought she was giving him just generic "girl answers" as Paul would say. In general, girls preferred quicker puzzles, less brute force. But then she warmed to her theme, getting more detailed in her comments and critiques of the story structure. By the time they made it to her car, he wanted to pull out a pad of paper for notes.

"Wow," he said, as she finally ended her comments. "That's just off the top of your head?"

She shrugged. "I read a lot. I like fiction."

"I'd like to hear more. Some of your ideas won't work with what we've already got, but a couple of those were brilliant."

She shook her head. "Now you're just stroking me. None of that was brilliant."

"You'd be surprised what a gamer finds brilliant. And believe me, that last idea about the character arc for Guinevere? That was brilliant."

She flashed him a coy smile. "Well, thank you. I'm glad I could help."

They'd made it to her car. It was a little yellow Saturn, and she unlocked it with her fob. The chirp of the car sounded loud in the garage. Exhausted as he was, he still hated to see the evening end. Apparently, she felt something similar because she turned to face him without opening her car door.

"This was a lot of fun. You've got a great game and…well, I just had a ton of fun. Like I haven't had in years."

"Rough couple of years?" he asked.

She shrugged. "No. Not really. Just settled into a rut. I work, I read, I occasionally have lunch with Elisa. I always thought my life would be more exciting. Instead, it's just kinda routine."

"You're shaking things up now. You're going on tour with us."

She smiled. She shouldn't have looked so good under the harsh parking-garage lights, but she did. She looked beautiful. He swallowed, feeling the need to touch her build inside him. "I, um, I really had a great time, too. And I really hope we can play more."

Her eyebrows rose and too late, he realized what he'd said had a double meaning. "More of the game?" she asked.

"Yeah, more of that," he said. And then he just did it. He kissed her. He'd wanted to since he'd met her, and she was right here.

She gasped in surprise, her body stilling in shock. God, this was wrong of him, but he couldn't stop. He stroked his tongue across her lips, tasting the cherry flavor of her lip gloss. Would she open for him? Or was he about to be shoved onto his ass?

She softened. It happened between one heartbeat and another. She was stiff and tight, and then everything in her seemed to give way. He would remember the feel of it until the day he died. The way she just relaxed into his kiss, tilting her head to give him better access and relaxing her body. She might have melted into him, or maybe he just pressed forward, trapping her body against her car. Either way, she opened herself to his kiss and he was quick to take advantage.

He thrust his tongue into her mouth. He stroked her teeth and the roof of her mouth. She teased back, curling her tongue around his and sucking once. That one action sent him around the moon. He framed her face with his hands and kissed her deeper. He ground his pelvis against her and groaned at the way she pressed back. She set him on fire.

Usually, he tried to think about being skillful with a girl. Usually, he tried to figure out what the right move would be. Not with her. He just kissed her. And he wanted to do so much more. So he let his hands move, feeling the silky softness of her cheeks then her neck. She was a wonder of curves, of hard bone in her shoulders and the soft mounds of her breasts.

She broke off the kiss, dropping her head back as they both struggled for breath. But he could not stop touching her. He shaped her breasts, feeling the bumps from the lace of her bra, but finding the tight points of her nipples infinitely more fascinating. Especially when she gasped as he stroked his thumbs back and forth across them.

Her knees softened and her pelvis rocked against his again. He had to touch her skin, so he slid his hands down and quickly pulled up her blouse. Then he slipped his fingers underneath to stroke the quivering silk of her belly. Meanwhile, he was kissing her throat, tasting the curve of her jaw, heating the trembling pulse of her neck with his breath. But he couldn't tell whose heart was beating faster—hers or his own.

He wanted her, so he slid his hands behind her back, fumbling for the catch on her bra. He wasn't skilled with this, and he was rapidly losing his ability to think at all much less perform a feat of manual dexterity. He just wanted to touch her.

"Ken—"

He did it. He popped her bra and quickly slid his hands around for his reward.

"Oh, Ken…" she murmured.

She had great breasts. They filled his hands, her nipples rolled against his palms, and when he held them she began to quiver in his arms. Her eyes were fluttering and her breath came in quick pants. And below she was rolling against him in a way that made him insane with want.

He felt her hands on his pants, but she couldn't find the button. It didn't matter because she hadn't the reach. Not with his hands moving down her skirt. It was perfect for what he wanted. Not too tight. Just loose enough to push up to her hips and let him slide a thumb inside her panties.

She cried out as he touched her and he nearly came. She was hot and wet and so responsive. And as he stroked her, she wrapped one of her legs around him. Just the feel of her surrounding him had him stroking her harder. Faster.

Then she cried out as her body clenched around his hand.

It was amazing.

But her movements dislodged his hand. And then he had to hold her up as she continued to climax. He didn't mind. He adored the sight of her flushed skin, the sound of her cry and the feel of her going wild in his arms. No fantasy he'd ever had topped this.

The moment passed. Her tremors eased. The leg she had wrapped around his hips slid slowly to the ground. And she looked up into his eyes. One second she was dazed, her lips curving in wonder. The next second, the joy was replaced by horror. Her gaze darted around, and he suddenly realized he'd just brought her to orgasm in a parking garage.

If he had the strength—and presence of mind—he might have tossed her over his shoulder and carried her to his bedroom. Or the lounge couch. But he wasn't a caveman. He was, in fact, her boss. And what he'd just done went way beyond unethical.

"Oh, no…" she whispered.

"Uh-oh," he said at almost the exact same moment.

Her gaze turned panicked.

"I was out of line," he said, as he took a hasty step back. Oh, hell, he didn't want to do that. His entire lower body screamed a protest at his brain, but he'd already done it.

Meanwhile, she was hastily straightening her skirt, but her bra was undone, which made her breasts jiggle distractingly. He shouldn't look, but damn it, he couldn't stop himself.

"I never…" she began. "I mean, I wouldn't… I don't—"

"I know," he said, forcing his gaze up to her face. "I've never either. Not…" He gestured weakly to the empty parking garage. Geez, he hadn't even had the decency to hit on her in the lounge. He'd pressed her up against her car. What the hell was wrong with him? He rubbed a hand over his face and tried to find something to say—something to do—to salvage the situation. Sadly, all he could think of was ways to press her back up against her car while she wrapped both legs around him and he—

Stop it! he ordered himself.

She was reaching behind her back. Obviously more dexterous than he was, she got her bra fastened in record time. And then she was just looking at him, mortification coloring her skin a dark red. Damn it, he still found that stunningly gorgeous.

"I'm so sorry," she whispered.

He wasn't exactly sure why, but those three words crushed him. He understood what she was saying. She hadn't meant for that to happen. She knew he was her boss and that what they'd just done was wrong on so many levels. But some part of him thought it had been right. Really right and really good. That same part was hoping she'd want to do it again soon. Maybe even in a bed or at least inside a building. In fact, he wanted it with a passion bordering on insanity.

But she'd said she was sorry. And from the look on her face, this was never, ever going to happen again. Which really hurt part of him even while his rational mind told him she was right. This couldn't happen again.

"Look," he said, as he took another step backward. "It's no big deal," he lied. "We're two consenting adults. Your employment contract doesn't begin until next week anyway, so I'm not exactly your boss yet."

"Right. Right," she answered, though he had no idea if either of them knew what they were saying.

"So," he continued despite his brain's warning to shut up. "So we'll both just pretend this never happened. It doesn't have to affect anything else, right? It was fun. It…um…it happened. No big deal."

She swallowed. "No big deal," she echoed.

"So, um, you're at your car," he said, gesturing to the obvious. He was still backing away, but this time he was trying to distance himself from his own stupid words. "Mine is up a level, so I'm…uh…" He pointed at the elevator.

"Right," she said, flashing him a weak smile. "Good idea. I need to get home anyway." She fumbled at the car door but managed to wrench it open.

"Home. Good idea," he said as he accidentally backed into a concrete post. "Ow."

"Watch yourself," she said with a too-high laugh. Then she practically jumped into her car and slammed the door. By the time he'd straightened off the post, she'd started her engine and was shifting into Reverse.

But she didn't move her car. Instead, she paused and looked at him. It was as if her whole soul was in that look. He could see everything there—the panic, the embarrassment, but there was a flash of joy, too. At least he prayed there was. He really, really hoped that she'd enjoyed what they'd done. Because he certainly had.

Then the moment was over. She ducked her head and nearly squealed her tires in her haste to back out of her space. Three seconds later, she was gone.

6

"HE KISSED YOU? Oh my God!"

Ali flushed. She was talking to Elisa, unable to keep from confessing what she'd done. "Um," Ali hedged. "He did a lot more than kiss me."

Elisa's eyes went round. "All the way?" she gasped.

Ali shrugged. "For me. Not for him."

"He didn't…?" She paused and then her mouth gaped open. But all too soon, her eyes started sparkling with laughter. "Um, really? How very… um…self-sacrificing of him."

"Elisa! This isn't funny!"

"I'm not laughing," she said, even though she was giggling between every word. "Well, not much. Actually," she said as she shifted to prim, "I think it's noble of him. Making sure you had a good time and all. You did have a good time, didn't you?"

"Well, yeah! A really, really good time."

Her friend squealed. "Or should I cry, 'Score!'"

Ali threw a nacho chip at Elisa then dropped her chin into her palm. They were in her kitchen trying to eat the food still in her apartment. That meant stale nachos with questionable bean dip. Frozen veggie burgers that were equally inedible when microwaved. Steamed vegetables that they'd already eaten because they'd wanted to begin with something healthy.

And now it was time for the final serving: chocolate-fudge ice cream.

"Stop laughing and tell me what to do!" Ali ordered as she went for the ice cream and two spoons. Forget bowls, they were going to dig straight into the carton.

"Do?" Elisa shot back. "Do it again if you can! And maybe let him enjoy himself, too!"

"He's my boss! He's your client!"

Elisa sobered. "Well, okay, so that is a hitch. But actors often bunny-rabbit around."

Ali handed her a spoon and popped the top off the carton. "Bunny-rabbit?"

"Yeah, sleeping—"

"I know what you meant. And besides he's not an actor. *I'm* not an actor."

"You are for the summer."

Ali sobered, recognizing her *real* problem when it was spoken aloud. The truth was that sure, it was unethical to sleep with one's boss. But people did it. And, as he'd said, they were both consenting adults. The real problem was that this was just for the summer. "So let's say we, that he and I—"

"Mambo the night away?"

Ali groaned. "Yeah, let's say we do that. What happens when it ends? What if we're still on tour? What if it ends when summer is over?"

Elisa gaped at her. "You've only had one spectacular moment in a parking garage. And now you're already on relationship-ending disasters?"

Ali sighed. She couldn't help it. She thought about things like that. It was the bad side of having a rich imagination. If she and Ken pursued a relationship, then what happened next? Her imagination took the what-if from hot sex to relationship to disaster. Three easy steps in a variety of different ways. "Any way I look at it, it's a bad idea. Besides," she said as she stabbed her spoon into the ice cream, "I don't bunny-rabbit."

Elisa sat back in her chair and looked at her with a suddenly serious expression. "No, you don't. So why did you?"

Ali stared at the scoop of ice cream and wondered if she should confess everything. She was still thinking when Elisa decided to start asking questions.

"Let's start with the basics. What's he like?"

Ali smiled. "He's cute. I think he could be hot with the right clothes and stuff, but mostly he's funny and comfortable. You know, the kind who wears a suit because he has to, but it doesn't quite fit perfectly. The first thing he does is strip out of his jacket and tug at his tie. And he's always running his hand through his hair so it's constantly messy in an adorable kind of way."

"We'll put that down as cute. Geek cute, but cute nonetheless. He runs a company, right? So he's rich."

Ali shook her head, remembering his comment about financial woes. "It's a small business, which means he's got the potential to be really rich. Or really broke."

"Hmmm." Elisa grabbed a pen and notepaper from the counter. "We'll put that as neutral."

"We're not doing a pro/con list about sleeping with my boss."

Elisa looked up with a grin. "Of course not. That would be tacky. We're doing a pro/con list about your boss, period. Whether you sleep with him or not is your choice."

Ali groaned, but Elisa was undeterred.

"Next question, is it about the sex or do you just like hanging out with him?"

"It is not about the sex!" Ali cried. But inside, she wondered. Because, of course, she had been fantasizing about him from the day she'd met him. She'd gone into that meeting strong in her determination to act professionally. But then they'd started playing the game, and she had such a great time. Plus it had been really late, so her defenses were down. And

then he'd looked at her, all intense and hungry, and...and...
"And he's a great kisser."

"Ah-ha!"

Ali started. Oh, hell, had she said that out loud? Apparently so because Elisa was busy writing that down in the pro column.

"Let's get a little more specific," Elisa said.

"You just want gory details."

"Damn straight. So give. If it's not about the sex—great kisses and all—then why do you like hanging out with him?"

Ali chewed on her lower lip as she thought. "He's smart, but he doesn't talk down to me like my brothers do."

"Your brothers are teenage dorks. Leave them out of this."

Ali nodded. "Okay, Ken listens to what I say and he knows just what I'm thinking. Or at least it seems like he does."

"So were you thinking about kissing him? Were you thinking about doing *more* with him?"

Ali didn't answer, but her flaming cheeks were more than enough to set her friend off into another squeal of delight. To which Ali responded by grabbing the ice-cream carton and putting it away.

"Hey! I wasn't done!"

"Yes, you are. Especially if you can't do anything but squeal. This is a real problem. He's my *boss!* There's no way a summer fling can turn out well."

Elisa lifted up the pro/con list and waved it in the air. "But you like him. As in really, really like him." She pushed up from her seat and went to give Ali a hug. "Look, I know you're Miss Ethical and all, but you're about to get paid to dress up in a costume and smile pretty. It's a summer funfest. Enjoy it."

Ali shook her head. "We're going to be living in really close quarters for the next three months. I can't even read his emails right now because I'm so embarrassed. How am I going to spend the next three months with him?"

Elisa sighed. "What did he say? After the...um..."

"Fireworks stopped?"

Elisa giggled, then promptly covered her mouth. "Uh, yeah. What did he say?"

"That we were consenting adults and that we should just pretend it never happened."

"Ouch." She wrinkled her nose. "Do you think it was bad for him? As in he didn't like it?"

Ali shrugged. "I don't know. I mean, he seemed to be enjoying it. Not as much as I was, but…" She groaned and dropped her head into her hands. "I can't believe we did that in a parking garage!"

"Oh, give it up. It's not such a big deal. He's not forcing you, is he?"

Ali's head shot up. "God, no!"

"And you're not going to sue him or anything."

"I loved what he did with me." Again her cheeks heated to crimson. "Why would I sue?"

"Then if it happens again, enjoy it. Don't look for problems where there aren't any."

Ali shook her head. "It's too much. It's too awkward. I'm going to be with him for three months. What if he hates me after one?"

Elisa shrugged. "Then you'll know that there are a lot more cons than pros on this list. You'll come home, see if you can pick up your old job earlier than expected and go on knowing that you tried something different."

"I can't."

"Ali! Weren't you the one complaining that you were in a rut? You're going to be a queen all summer, and being paid to do it! Kick loose and enjoy the ride!"

"But—"

"No buts! You want my advice? Here it is—act professionally around him. Just like he said, pretend nothing happened. But if he goes for more again—and you want more—then let it happen. See if the pros keep piling up. Who knows, this could be the best summer of your life!"

Ali bit her lip, knowing that Elisa was right. But she also worried about…well, about so many things. "It could all go horribly wrong, you know."

"Or wonderfully right. Ali, take a risk," she added as she grabbed the dishes and headed to the sink.

"Okay," she finally said, not sure whether she was agreeing to act professionally or to let something else happen next time she and Ken were alone together. Lord, how was she going to spend a summer acting professionally around Ken? It was hard enough when she'd only been fantasizing about him. Now she knew from experience just how awesome he was.

As she mulled over her dilemma, the phone rang. It was a number she didn't recognize, and her heart sped up to triple time in the hope/fear that it was Ken. But she couldn't keep hiding—not from his emails or his phone calls. So, taking a deep breath, she pressed the button to answer.

"H-hello?"

"Hi, Ali! Glad I caught you!" It was Tina, and Ali released her breath on a whoosh while she tried to calm her heart.

"Hey, Tina. What can I do for you?"

"Well, I managed to get you an appointment at my friend's salon. We've got some great ideas about your hair and I wondered if you could come now?"

"Now?" she gasped. "As in right now?"

"I know it's last-minute, but Marissa knows just what we want."

Ali shrugged. She'd signed a contract, after all. "Um, sure. You're not going to shave me bald, are you?"

Tina released a trill of laughter. "Of course not! You'll like it, I swear. And if you want, she'll give you a good deal on a facial, too. You know, to spruce up the pores before we start burying them under all that stage makeup."

"A facial?"

"I do one before every launch," she said. "It's my make-me-beautiful ritual."

"I've never had a facial before."

"Well, then this will be a special treat. I'll go ahead and schedule it for right after the dye job."

Dye job?

"See you soon! 'Bye!"

ALI GOT HER HAIR DYED. Not all of it. Just a shock of red down beneath her right ear. It took her about eighteen hours to adjust to it, but by the end of the next day, she loved it. Her mother, of course, thought it was appalling and cheap, but she did say that Ali's face glowed. She had to admit that the facial had been well worth the cost. Her skin felt cleansed and polished. And if it didn't, she had nearly two hundred dollars' worth of new face products to make sure that her skin felt especially pampered throughout the summer. Fortunately, QG paid for most of that.

Tina, of course, thought it had been an excellent purchase and wasted no time in discussing the makeup products that Ali also used. Fortunately for her pocketbook, Tina had all the stage makeup Ali would need. Not so fortunate, her date at Spiked Leather came up way too fast for Ali. She'd barely gotten used to her new hair when she walked into the leather shop.

Spiked black leather wasn't even the half of it. She also saw whips, chains and studs, all tooled into leather attire. She walked slowly into the shop, feeling as though her eyes were triple-wide and trying to envision herself in any of these things. Utility belt—she could do that. Leather pants, probably, assuming she didn't look like a cow in them. Cuffs and dog collars? Only if she had to. Leather pasties and all other variety of nipple or breast attachments—no. Same went for the female version of the codpiece. No way was she wearing a leather bikini or…well, she didn't even know what some of those things were.

"There you are!" Tina cried from the very back of the store as she waved Ali deeper in. "I've already gathered what I'd like you to try on. Don't panic. We're not doing any S&M stuff. Just corsets and the like. Fortunately, you're a real-world size. That makes buying off the rack so much easier."

"Real-world size?"

"Yeah. Sometimes trying to find stuff for models is like trying to make a toothpick look sexy. It looks really hot on camera, but it's all specially designed. And since we're not going to spend much time on camera, it's more about personality anyway."

Was she trying to say Ali was fat? No, no, of course she wasn't. But Ali couldn't help but be self-conscious about those extra pounds around her belly and creeping onto her thighs.

"Okay, I guess," she said. "What do you want me to do?"

"We'll start with the basics," she said as she led Ali into a dressing room. "Put on the white shift—that's the silk dress there—and we'll put the corset on top."

Ali held up the simple white gown. "Silk?" she asked.

"Last launch we did, I put the girls in polyester outfits that looked really pretty." Tina shook her head.

"Bad idea?"

"About a third of our events are outside. In the middle of summer. Trust me when I say, you want only natural fibers next to your skin. Unless you enjoy heat rash."

"Silk it is," she said as she ducked into the dressing room. Tina was right. The silk felt heavenly against her skin, but the dress just seemed to hang there. There was very little shape to it. And as much as she enjoyed the basic sheath dress, she'd always thought she was too curvy to wear it.

"Um…" she began.

"Come on out, and we'll start trying on the corsets."

Ali stepped out, but was immediately stopped by Tina.

"No, no. You can't wear a bra with a corset. That would just be silly!"

Of course it would, Ali thought as she rushed to pull off her bra. But then she was swinging free, so to speak, which in her mind meant swinging low beneath the sack dress.

"Um…"

"Trust me, Ali. Come on out."

Okay. She could do this. After all, it was just Tina out there. She hadn't seen any of the store staff when she'd walked in. Or at least none at the back.

Sadly, the moment she stepped out of the dressing room, she realized her mistake. There were other staff here. Two, to be exact. Two tattooed, pierced and Gothed-out guys in black. One was lanky, the other huge. As in motorcycle-gang huge.

Ali paled, but there was no time to run. Tina grabbed her and said, "That's perfect with your skin."

Ali looked down. The pale white did indeed look pretty right now in the middle of spring. "But I tan really, really easily. A month from now, every exposed skin cell is going to be brown."

"How brown?"

"My last name is Flores. You tell me how brown is too much and when I hit it, I'll start putting on sunscreen."

Tina pursed her lips. "Good to know, but you know what? I like a little ethnicity in my queens. The gaming world has way too many golden-haired Galadriels."

"The elf princess from *Lord of the Rings?*"

Tina nodded and flashed a smile. *Oh good,* thought Ali. *I got one right.* But that was the last moment of feel-good she had in a while. Especially as the guys came forward, each with a leather corset in his hands.

Tina grinned. "Aren't they pretty?"

The corsets or the guys? It was hard to tell because though Ali didn't personally go in for tattoos, Tina might be all over that kind of kink. Especially since the big guy was all muscles and ink.

"Ever put on a corset before?" Tina asked.

Ali shook her head.

"Well, welcome to your crash course. Actually, it's pretty easy. You just raise your arms." Ali did. "And then we tie you in."

Turns out Tina wasn't lying. It was really easy to wear a corset, assuming she didn't need to breathe. Because not only were the tattooed guys kinda hunky, but they were also pretty damn strong. Even the lanky one had the pull strength to completely defeat her ribs. Ali was strapped in, her ribs compressed and her breasts lifted from below. Then Tina had her turn this way and that as she snapped some photos. Two minutes later, the laces were untied and Ali could breathe. But then another leather contraption appeared.

Who knew there was such variety in corsets? Forget decorations, of which there were a zillion. Under the breast, over the breast, long line, short line. Then there was her personal nightmare: the W lift where the boning went under her breasts was like the hardest underwire ever. But that felt better than the big U that smooched her together so that her breasts seemed to meet right under her chin.

But on the upside, she did have quite a pretty waist when she was in one of those things. On the downside, someone else would have to put on her shoes because she couldn't bend over to do it. And then, suddenly, it was over. Or at least that part was.

"That's the last of the corsets. Let's look at the boots."

Finally, Ali let herself smile. Boots were something she liked.

Except, of course, she hadn't thought about *queen* boots. Apparently, Guinevere wore spike heels sharp enough to kill someone and high enough for her to kick an elephant.

Ali had never thought of herself as particularly clumsy.

She wasn't an athlete, but she could shoot a basketball and hold her own against her much younger brothers. She'd run a marathon, too. But apparently, that was nothing compared to walking around in five-inch spikes.

"Um, didn't Guinevere wear short gold sandals or something? I feel like I'm on my tiptoes on stilts."

Tina grimaced. "Yeah, those aren't going to work for you. Not with the platforms. How about—"

"Holy cow. My queen, you've ascended to the heights!" said a deep voice from behind her.

Ali spun around. Too late she realized she was spinning in shoes that turned her into the Empire State Building. "Oh shit."

Ken dashed across the small shoe space, half catching her, half overshooting and barreling into her.

"Oh crap!" Ken said as they teetered together.

Thank goodness for big tattoo guy. All he had to do was hold out his arms as the two of them fell against him. Sadly, Ali had landed on top-ish. Ken was squashed between her and the big guy. She scrambled to get off of him, but it wasn't easy in those boots. In the end, Tina had to give her a hand, laughing the whole time.

"Definitely not these boots," she said. Then she turned to Ken. "And now that you're here, we can get down to the real decisions. Meanwhile, Ali, why don't you get out of those boots and into those pants?"

Ali bit her lip, doing her best not to speak. But the words came out anyway. "Uh, hi, Ken," she began. "I didn't realize you were coming."

Ken flashed her a quick smile that looked a little awkward. Good, because Ali was feeling *really awkward*.

"Uh, hi. Yeah. I've got final say on the costuming."

Meanwhile Tina was booting up her iPad. Apparently, all those photos that she'd been snapping had already been loaded onto her pad. Ali peeked over the woman's shoulder to see a spread of herself in all those corsets and boots. And now...pants?

"Uh—"

"Just put on the pants," said Tina. "And don't bother with your bra. The corsets will come next."

Great. She was going to be swinging free right in front of Ken. And even worse, given how tight these leather pants were, he'd have a really good idea of exactly where every piece of candy she'd ever eaten was stored on her thighs and rear.

7

KEN LOST HIS ABILITY to speak. He'd known today's costuming meeting was going to be difficult. Usually he enjoyed picking out outfits with his female models. They loved the shopping, and he was able to direct them to the subtleties of what he wanted them to project. And it was a great way for him to get to know his models. If they gravitated toward the spikes and oohed over the sales guys' tattoos, then he knew that they would work best as steampunk models. If they fidgeted in black leather pants and tugged the corsets higher, then tavern wench was more their speed. Those costumes were equally fun, but the fabric tended to cover things more securely.

But what did he say to Ali? How did he even *look* at the woman without thinking how amazing she had been during her climax? He knew her taste and her scent. And he'd spent the past three days alternately planning ways to get her naked or creating elaborate schemes to keep them apart. He was her boss and he had a strict hands-off policy with all his actors. It just complicated things too damn much. Plus, his entire company was riding on the successful launch of this game. Why would he jeopardize that by having a relationship with one of his employees? Forget the problems it could cause to the launch, it was just too distracting for him right now. His company was at stake!

And yet, the night they'd spent playing Winning Guinevere together was the best night he'd had in years. Years. He didn't want to give that up—to give her up—just because his company was at a very crucial point.

It was maddening, and now he was looking at her in black leather pants that hugged every inch of her curvaceous body. And all he could think—beyond the obvious *I have to bed her now*—was how was he going to hide his total infatuation with this woman?

"Well," said Tina as she tapped the pen against her lips. "Those pants rock, but I'm not sure they're quite what we're looking for in Guinevere."

Ali swallowed nervously, her gaze hopping between the mirror and everyone else's faces. She couldn't quite meet his eyes, which was fine since he was having trouble looking up from the sweet line of her bottom and her muscular legs. And if he dragged his gaze upward, it was to see her breasts as they moved so distractingly. His thoughts—what there were of them—were distinctly X-rated.

Beside him, one of the sales guys laughed in appreciation. "Depends on what kind of Gwen you're going for. Lady of Pain, Queen of Spank Me. Or how about—"

"Not doing S&M," interrupted Ken before he got even *more* images in his head. "Let's go back to the shift and corset look. Show me those pictures again."

Tina nodded, but Ken couldn't stop himself from watching Ali as long as possible in those pants. He saw her nod and head for the dressing room, but not before she stroked her hand along her thigh. She liked those pants, he realized, but she was too professional to say so.

Normally he had trouble stopping the models from expressing their opinions. But that was one of the reasons he'd chosen Ali for this role. She was so reserved. Which told him he'd have to ask her for her thoughts.

"Ali," he said, freezing her in her tracks. *Don't look at her breasts. And not at her ass either!*

"Yes?"

"I'd like your opinion. You've played the game." Oops, shouldn't have brought that up. Her skin immediately flushed red. His probably did, too. "What do you think would be best? Keep in mind that we're appealing to teens, primarily."

She bit her lip, obviously thinking. Her gaze scanned the rack of clothing she'd already worn, then she finally answered. "You want classy sexy."

"But warm. Approachable."

"A hot older sister who is bringing you cookies and asking you very nicely, very sweetly, if you might please go on a quest for her."

He nodded. She understood things perfectly.

"Then give me a long shift—"

"We need to see your legs." Oops. Had he said that out loud? The truth was *he* wanted to see her legs.

"Right. Draping in back, short in front."

Tina started typing. "I can do that."

"Then a corset to give me a waist."

One of the sales guys perked up. "Red leather to match the shock in your hair."

She blinked, but nodded. Apparently she'd forgotten the totally hot change to her hair. "Perfect touch," he inserted as he glanced at Tina. "Great idea."

Tina flashed him a grin.

"So we've got the sexy," he said. "What about queen?"

Ali shook her head. "That comes with jewelry or trim."

Tina frowned. "I can get you a crown that drops across your forehead."

Ken started thinking. "King Arthur gives her the crown at the first publicity stop. Next stop has Lancelot giving you…"

"A necklace," inserted Tina.

"Right. Small fight between Lancelot and Arthur at stop

three, Merlin stuff stop four." He shook his head. "She's going to be buried in jewelry if we're not careful." Ali was too sweet to be covered up in all that stuff.

Tina frowned and looked up. "What about a weapon? A dagger or something. I mean, she's a warrior queen, too. Especially as the tension heats up between Arthur and Lancelot."

Ken smiled. "I like that." He looked over at Ali and knew she could be fierce. Someone just had to bring it out in her.

Meanwhile, Ali wasn't so sure. "But you want warm, too. Chocolate-chip-cookie warm."

"That's you," Ken said. "That's totally you."

She shook her head, obviously doubting him. "That's in the footwear. Fun, flirty…" She sighed as she looked at a pair of thigh-highs. "It's stuff I already have."

God, what he wouldn't give to see her in those boots. "Well, we do have those three steampunk days. That's the week when Lancelot and Arthur go to war. Guinevere needs to be a lot more kick-ass then. Plus, it'll be an adult crowd."

Tina looked up, her eyes narrowing. "You're thinking about those boots over there, aren't you?"

Ken tried to put on a neutral expression while, over to the side, Ali flushed an adorable pink. No way could he resist seeing her in them now.

Fortunately, the sales guy knew his job. He'd already disappeared to get a pair from the back. Five minutes later, they had the look. An over-the-breasts corset, shift and those beautiful thigh-highs.

"Wait!" said Tina. "Ali, take off the shift."

Ali blinked. "But—"

"Just corset and boots. Here, put on these." She tossed her a pair of black tights that were designed for just this purpose.

"Uh—"

"Trust her. Do it." That came from the sales guy and Ken flashed him a look of sheer annoyance. It came from pure jealousy. He didn't want any other man giving Ali suggestions like that. Or seeing her in an outfit like that. But he didn't disagree. He was rock-hard wanting to see it himself.

Ali nodded slowly, then disappeared back into the dressing room. It didn't take her long.

"I need someone to tie this tighter," she called from the dressing room.

"I got it!" Both sales guys were on their feet, but thankfully Tina got there first.

"*I've* got it, boys." Then she ducked into the dressing room. Two aeons later, Ken heard her satisfied grunt. "Yeah, this will definitely work for the evening ComiCon events."

Ken's mouth went dry. Fortunately he didn't need to speak. Tina would bring her out in a sec—

Holy moly. That definitely took Ali from PG to R. And in his brain, they'd gone straight to XXX.

Beside him, one of the sales guys whistled.

"What do you think?" asked Tina.

Ken had to swallow twice before he could speak. In the end, he could only manage two words: "Buy it."

ALI HAD A FEW DAYS to get used to the idea that she would be walking around in a leather corset for part of the summer. It almost kept her from obsessing about the way Ken had looked at her when she was wearing that outfit. The sales guys had been horny. That much she could tell. They'd looked at her with a slick kind of smile and she had immediately looked away. That kind of attention she did *not* like.

But she hadn't been able to resist peeking at Ken. He seemed like he wanted to jump her right then and there. That was frightening enough for her, but he seemed equally freaked out by the thought. His gaze had dropped to the floor, but then a second later, he was looking back at her. She saw him swallow—twice—and didn't that just do wonders for her self-esteem?

That costume—and the way Ken had looked at her—made

her feel sexy. Like a woman who was proud of her body and wasn't afraid to own herself and her clothes. She'd never felt that way before, and she relished the idea of it. Suddenly she was Sexy Ali. And whenever the joy of that started to fade, all she had to do was bring up the memory of Ken staring at her with hunger in his eyes and she was right back to feeling amazing.

That gave her the confidence to sail through the photo shoot where she did *not* wear the catsuit. Phew! It kept her excitement alive as she closed up her apartment and loaded her bags on the bus. It even had her smiling all the way up until she checked into her hotel room the night before their first event.

They were doing a small event. Just a gamer group in Dallas. There was going to be a party at a comic-book shop, and not even a big one, according to Tina. Samantha as a tavern wench would begin working up the crowd, playing off Paul, who would be snide and cynical as Mordred. Lancelot would wander through, but he was just there to help build anticipation for Guinevere and Arthur's wedding. Beyond the obvious "I wed thee, King Arthur," Ali's only job was to notice Lancelot. As she wandered through the crowd, she was supposed to be obviously interested in the handsome knight.

Ali had memorized her lines on the bus, so that was pretty easy, assuming she didn't stutter her way through her part. After that, she was supposed to mingle, talking up the game or just plain talking. That was it. Basic booth work with the occasional look at Lancelot. And so she kept reminding herself as she paced her hotel room. Booth work. She'd done it dozens of times. Of course, this time she'd be in a corset and half boots, but still. Easy peasy.

She was halfway to a panic attack when a soft knock sounded on her door. She nearly wiped out tripping over her own shoes in her haste to get to the door. Anything for a distraction.

And what a distraction! Ken was there, his hair looking even more rumpled than usual. His jeans and faded T-shirt looked comfortable on him. And for the first time she noticed that there was some muscle definition on his arms. Well, truthfully, she'd noticed it before when he was helping to load the bus, but this time she was up close and personal with them.

"Oh!" she gasped. "Was there a meeting or something that I forgot?"

He blinked then shook his head. "Oh, no! No. I…um…I wanted to talk to you."

"I'm not fired, am I?" It was a joke. Or at least half of one. Truthfully, she was nervous enough to welcome a firing.

He ran his hand through his hair and flushed. "God, no. Um, it'll just take…um…" He hesitated, looking into her room before flushing and looking down at the floor. Then he abruptly shoved his hands in his pockets. "So, would you like to take a walk?"

She exhaled. A walk sounded like a great idea. "I—"

"See, I'm going nuts like I always do before the first event. Paul is sick of me and threw me out of the room. We're sharing, you know. The others are down at the bar, but well, that just…" He huffed. "All those people make it worse. I'm sorry, you probably wanted some alone time. We've been stuck together on that bus for hours. I'm probably the last person you want to see."

She smiled at his rather morose expression. Clearly this man was on edge, even more than she was. "You always go nuts before an event?"

"No, no. Just the *first* event. After that, I'm too tired to get anxious."

She nodded. "So how many launches has your company done?"

"Like this with actors and a tour bus? Twice before. There were other little launches before that, but nothing on this scale. And nothing that makes me want to climb the walls like a chimpanzee on crack."

She laughed. He looked nothing like a chimpanzee, cracked or otherwise. "All right, monkey boy. I'm going to grab my shoes and I will be happy to walk wherever you want. Because I, too, am going a little nuts."

"Don't worry. You'll be great." It was an automatic response for him. She'd heard him say it to all the actors at one point or another in the past week. But she could also tell that he meant it.

Where he'd managed to find such confidence in her, she had no clue. But it was there, and it made her feel better. So she flashed him another smile then pulled on her shoes. Two minutes later, they were heading for the elevator.

"So where to, fearless leader?" she quipped.

He released a short laugh. "Didn't we just establish that I'm definitely not *fearless* tonight?"

She nodded as they got on the elevator and he punched the button for the lobby. "Okay, let me try again. What exactly are you worried about?"

He huffed. "There are a zillion things to worry about. The product launched nationally two days ago. If it flops, I could lose everything."

She swallowed. She'd forgotten that this was a make-or-break kind of deal for him. "I don't know how you do it, then. I'd be a nervous wreck."

"Mostly I bury myself in details. If you're focused on the little things, then it's hard to worry about the big things. Or at least harder. And we've already had some problems."

Her gaze snapped to his. "What? I mean, we have?"

He shrugged, but she could see the tension in the movement. "Not a big deal. Paul forgot some stuff, that's all."

"Important stuff?"

He sighed. "Yeah, important stuff, but I called my parents. They have a key to the office. Mom's overnighting some stuff to the hotel." He released a self-conscious laugh. "It's bad enough to call your mom for a rescue when you're twelve. At thirty, it's mortifying."

She laughed as the elevator finally arrived. "I doubt you do it often."

"Even so. Plus I hate the expense."

"I understand that. One time, we had this health fair at this hotel…" She regaled him with the story of her biggest show disaster. You couldn't do events without some sort of hiccup. By the time she was done, he was smiling and they were out of the hotel.

Fortunately, it was a balmy night in Texas. They were in a safe area right across from the comic-book shop where the event would be. They headed off toward the walkway that would lead to the nearby mall, walking in a comfortable silence. But at the corner, she turned to study his face. The lighting was harsh beneath a streetlight, so it picked out the furrows in his forehead, the slight hunch to his shoulders. Wow, he really was wound tight.

"So what set this off now? Why right before the first event?"

"Because there's nothing to do now. It's all done or in Tina and Paul's hands. But at the same time, it's also when the most things are unknown. I don't know how this group is going to mesh over the summer. I don't know if someone's going to be toxic or someone else is going to break a leg."

She laughed. "I think that's something actors say for good luck. 'Break a leg.' It's not going to happen."

"It did last year. The girl before Tina insisted on wearing ridiculous shoes even during teardown."

Ali laughed. "She didn't."

"She did on the second week. Tripped and snapped her ankle. We dropped her off at a hospital in New Jersey and had to leave her there the next morning."

"Okay, so you're good, then," she said. "You'd have to be

cursed or something for a broken leg to happen on two tours in a row."

He stopped dead in the center of the walk and groaned. "Do you know nothing about tempting the fates? You don't say things like that!"

She laughed because she knew it was a joke. "And here I thought you were a numbers guy, without a superstitious bone in your body."

"I *am* a numbers guy. But when there aren't numbers available, I'd fall back on praying to a voodoo priestess if I thought it would help."

She narrowed her eyes and looked around. "Sorry. I don't see any voodoo priestesses around. Maybe she has a kiosk in the mall."

He chuckled, the sound coming out lighter than before. "Good idea. We'll check there. But just in case she's closed, keep an eye out for a wishing well."

"Deal."

They walked in silence again, and Ali enjoyed the nice evening weather, the companionable walk to the mall, even the idea that there might be something fun to see inside the mall. And then about five feet away from the door, Ken completely destroyed her sense of peace.

"I also wanted to talk about that thing I said we didn't ever need to talk about."

8

KEN FELT READY TO jump out of his skin, but was trying to be mature. In truth, the last thing he wanted to do was discuss what they'd done in the parking garage. Not that he hadn't thought about it. It was practically *all* he thought about. All the tour worries were just distractions from his Ali obsession.

The problem was that he could see the same awareness in Ali's eyes every time they looked at each other. Ever since that night, her body did a kind of freeze whenever they ran into each other. It didn't last long, but it was there. Her shoulders tightened up. And once he thought she might have ducked around a corner to avoid talking to him. Sure, it could all be in his imagination, but he didn't think so.

Not that he blamed her, of course, but they couldn't continue the whole summer with her doing that. So he'd decided to confront her about it. Except right now she was being especially sweet, which made him think he'd imagined the whole thing.

"Oh," she said, obviously cringing. "Okay."

"I get the feeling that there's been some awkwardness between us. Not that I blame you or anything, but am I right?"

She licked her lips in nervousness, and his blood went straight south. Fortunately, she started talking so he hoped he was able to cover.

"I…well, yes, I suppose, but…" Her voice trailed away, and she looked distinctly uncomfortable.

"I'm so sorry, Ali. I didn't want— I shouldn't have…" He swallowed and forced himself to concentrate. "It was completely my fault. It won't ever happen again. I hope you won't leave the tour because of this. We really need you."

Her eyes widened, and then she squared her shoulders. A martial light entered her gaze and she abruptly grabbed his hand and pulled him away from the central mall entrance. Since this was an indoor/outdoor mall, she was able to lead them down a charming path that was currently empty of people.

"That's just it," she said when she finally slowed down. "I liked what we did. I like you. But you're my boss and this is weird, and I'm so sorry." Her last dozen words came out in a rush.

He knew he should say something, but his mind had completely stalled out on the fact that she liked him. Because he liked her. A lot.

"So…" she said and gestured to a restaurant/bar that was still open. "If we're going to keep talking about this, can we go into the bar?"

"You need some liquid courage?"

She flashed him her adorable smile that she half tried to hide. "No, I just like playing with the pink parasol."

"An umbrella-drink fan. I can work with that."

She rolled her eyes. "*Every* guy can work with that."

He paused a moment, wondering if there was an extra meaning in there. Was she thinking he was hitting on her? He wasn't. Not that he didn't want to. But…

He forcibly pulled his thoughts to a stop. She wasn't suggesting anything. She was just talking with him. Friend to friend…sort of.

"Uh, then we should go in," he tried.

She nodded. And then it was the awkward, you-first-no-you-first movement into the bar. How he longed to go back to the ease of just three minutes ago. But he'd started this— he could hardly complain when he'd been the one to make it awkward. Eventually, they worked it out and soon they were sitting at a table.

"Order whatever you like," he said. "My treat."

She smiled but then shook her head. "I think you're paying for enough," she said. "This one's on me." Then she leaned in. "You see, I've found this sweet deal for the summer. Costumes, makeup, parties all summer long. And I'm getting *paid* for it!"

"Wow," he drawled at her obvious joke. "What kind of sap does that?"

She smiled. "Only the best kind." Then the waitress appeared and she ordered a Malibu pineapple drink. He asked for a beer and nachos.

"Unless you want something else," he said, belatedly realizing that he should have asked if she wanted an appetizer.

"Nachos are great! Besides, aren't we leaving Texas tomorrow? Last stop before the food gets bland."

"A spicy girl, huh?"

"Within reason. I never saw the sense behind setting my mouth on fire just to prove my testosterone quotient."

"Brothers?" he asked.

"Boyfriend." She rolled her eyes. "I was definitely *not* impressed."

"Well, never fear with me. I promise to run screaming from any jalapeños."

"So you don't like spicy?"

"I love spicy if it's the right type." He flashed her a wink. It was not his best move. In fact, it wasn't his move at all, and in high school, he'd created a zillion of them. But with her, he found himself doing things on the fly without second-guessing himself so much. That was a good thing. Truthfully, it was a *great* thing. It wasn't that he was incredibly awkward around girls. But spending his past ten years buried in work had made his flirting skills extremely rusty.

Fortunately, she just laughed. Not so fortunately, the conversation stalled. The arrival of the drinks helped cover for a minute or so, but all too soon, he was sipping his beer and trying desperately to think of something cool to say. Thankfully, she stepped into the breech.

"My cousins really love Winning Guinevere."

"You played with them?"

"I took it over to their house a couple of days before I left. They told me I wasn't half bad for a girl."

"Ouch! Damned by faint praise."

She shook her head. "Not really. Their sister, my other cousin, is a tomboy and can kick her brothers' butts when it suits her. So I took it as a compliment whether they meant it that way or not."

He nodded. "Sounds like a wise choice."

"They said it's much better than your other game."

He grimaced. "Which one?"

"Leaper."

"Oh, yeah. That one bombed."

She started playing with her paper umbrella, spinning it in her fingers, opening it and closing it. He found himself fascinated by her fingers. Her hands were girl's hands, long, tapered fingers ending in sweetly contoured nails with fresh nail polish. She'd opted for a soft tone, a coral or something like that. Probably because it matched a costume. Tina was obsessive about details like that. He found he just liked it. Pretty, not bold, but with a shimmer that made him think of hidden depths.

"Did you throw a launch for that one?" she asked.

"Huh?"

"A launch like this for Leaper. Your game that—"

"Bombed. Right. No, that was early days. Before I figured

out that what I enjoyed in a game was not necessarily what the market wanted."

"So you liked Leaper?"

He nodded. "Loved it. Still play it sometimes."

"I'd like to try it."

He looked up and abruptly grinned. "Now you're just being nice." She opened her mouth to deny it, but he held up his hand. "Nope, you can't take it back now. You've promised to play it with me. After this launch is over. At the end of the summer, you and me, a Leaper party."

She smiled, and he watched those dimples appear again. "Agreed. I'll bring the nachos."

He groaned. "Hell, that means I'll have to find a blender to make...er, that."

She reached out and grabbed his beer to take a slug. "Nah. Beers are great." Then she pushed over her drink. "Here, you take the Malibu. I just wanted the umbrella."

He hated fruity drinks. Too much sweet, but he let her make the switch and drank every drop. And by the time it was gone, they were talking much more easily. They hit the normal topics—game design, bad marketing and bad girlfriend mistakes for him. Her topics were stupid health-fair customers, favorite college classes and bad boyfriend mistakes.

By the time they'd stuffed themselves on nachos and he'd finished another Malibu—she'd ordered it over his protests— they were laughing freely. He was coming to like fruity drinks, plus they could mock fence with the little umbrellas. Then the bar was closing—how late was it exactly?—and the two of them rushed giggling back to the hotel.

Honestly, it felt like a date with him walking her back to her room. Probably the best date of his life given that they were still laughing. That made it the most natural thing in the world to kiss her at the door, right? To press his mouth to hers, to lean against her body as he felt all its glorious hills and valleys. And she was kissing him back even as she opened her hotel-room door.

He hadn't meant to follow her inside. He really hadn't. But they kind of fell inside. He caught himself right before he toppled her to the floor. He wasn't that huge a guy, but she was definitely smaller than him. He didn't want to flatten her.

But she just kept going down to the floor, even when he tried to hold her up.

"You're too nice," she said as she dropped to her knees.

"You're too drunk," he shot back, even though he was laughing as he said it. "Come on, let's get you to bed."

"Hmmm," she said, shaking her head. "I'm not drunk after two beers."

"You had four."

"Did not!"

He frowned, trying to think. How much, exactly, had she had?

"That's what I keep thinking," she said. "You're too nice."

"I'm really not."

"You were in the garage," she said as she undid his belt buckle. He tried to jump backward, but he was trapped against the dresser.

"Ali!"

"And now it's time for you to get your turn."

He tried to stop her. He really did. But she was determined and within seconds, any blood in his brain rushed straight south. She was caressing him right through his pants. He was rock-hard, and at her first touch he nearly jumped onto the dresser. But there was no strength in his legs and what she did felt so good.

His jeans were unbuckled and pulled down in moments. He could have fought her. Hell, he *should* have fought her, but it had been a long time since he'd felt a woman there. His life had been his business for years now and…

Sweet heaven, he couldn't breathe. She'd already pushed

down his clothes and now had him gripped in a hand with just the right tension.

"Ali," he groaned. "You don't—"

She took him in her mouth, all wet and hot and sure. That's what got him. She seemed so shy at times, but for something like this, she knew just what she wanted. And it was him! He'd braced his hands behind him to hold himself up. But now he reached a hand forward to touch her hair, to stroke her cheek.

"Ali," he tried again. "Don't. We shouldn't—"

She sucked him. Hard. And what she was doing with her tongue... He couldn't think. He was thrusting into her mouth, and he didn't intend to. This was so wrong.

"Oh, Ali," he breathed, feeling the charge build right behind his balls. His butt had gone tight, his legs were growing stronger, and his blood was beating to the pulse of her suction. But he couldn't do this. It wasn't right.

Reaching down, he grabbed her shoulders. He tried to be gentle, but everything in him was growing urgent. And if he didn't do this now, it would be too late.

"Ali!" he cried, as he forcibly pulled himself backward. He slid out—hell—but it was the right thing to do. "I can't let you do this." He said the words, but he didn't move himself out of her hand.

She didn't answer. She just looked up at him with a coy smile. God, she was beautiful. Not in a supermodel way, but in a mischievous, I-am-having-so-much-fun way. Which was a thousand times better. Her eyes sparkled and those dimples flashed. And then she did two things that undid him completely. First, she was smiling as she caught her lower lip—all flushed and red—in her teeth. And second, her thumb rubbed right below the ridge of his head.

Lightning washed his vision white and he surged forward toward her. He didn't want to release, but there was no stopping the rush and it was amazing. His whole body went into it. And his consciousness, too, because he was sure he blacked out for a moment.

But when he came back to himself it was to hear her giggling. He opened his eyes, horrible guilt washing through him. Then he saw her, and it just got worse. He'd released... over her.

"Oh, no," he breathed. "Oh, God. I'm sorry. I—"

"It's just a T-shirt!" she laughed as she pushed up from her knees. He scrambled to help her, but she was quick and graceful. A ton more coordinated than he was at the moment.

"Ali—"

She grinned at him, then ducked her head right before she disappeared into the bathroom. He was left standing there— or leaning there because his legs wouldn't support him—with his jeans at his ankles and his face burning. Worse, his brain kept spinning back and forth between what-have-I-just-done and can-we-do-that-again?

It took him a moment, but he forced himself to pull up his pants. He barely had the hand coordination to button himself when she came out, all smiling while her eyes danced with merriment.

He took a breath. "Ali, I…" He what? He had no freaking idea what he wanted to say.

And then, to his horror, she yawned. It was a tiny yawn, and one that she obviously fought. But one glance at the clock told him it was beyond late. Nearly 3:00 a.m.! Of course she was yawning. But talk about ego-crushing.

"Ali," he said, the words forming without conscious will. "That was amazing and I really enjoyed it. Though I'm sorry about your shirt."

She glanced down then shrugged, pulling it off with a quick tug. He didn't think he could get hard again so fast, but damn if his body didn't respond lightning-fast to her. Creamy skin, a red, lacy bra—red!—and then she dropped backward onto her bed with a whoosh, her arms completely spread open.

"God, I feel relaxed," she said.

She felt relaxed? The only solid part of his body right now was his growing boner.

"Ali, I want to climb into bed with you right now. I want it more than anything else," he said.

She rolled onto her side and flashed him a come-hither smile.

"I'm trying to be responsible here," he groaned. "You're drunk. *I'm* drunk. This is so not a good idea."

He watched as awareness entered her expression. It slipped in slowly. First her brows narrowed a bit, then her eyes widened. She blinked a few times before she seemed to realize she didn't have a shirt on. Her hand came up to cover her chest, and boy, did he mourn the loss of that sight.

He stepped forward, taking her hand in his. "Don't cover up. You're beautiful. And I'm a horrible boss who ought to be brought up on charges."

She shook her head. "No, no! This was all my idea!"

"Can I kiss you good-night, Ali? I really, really want to."

She shifted up onto her knees on the bed. Again, she was so graceful and her face was so beautiful. He just stood there and watched. Then he touched her face. It wasn't that he thought about what he was doing. He just started touching her. He caressed her cheek, he framed her jaw with his palm, and then he bent down to claim her lips.

Sweet. She was so sweet. And the lust was pounding through his body like a freight train. He took her lips and possessed her mouth. Then he nearly threw her to the bed and did what any caveman would.

But he couldn't. He was her boss and he'd started this evening trying to make up for what he'd done with her in the parking garage.

It was the hardest thing he'd had to do ever, but he ended the kiss. He pulled back, he touched her face, he stole a look at her gorgeous breasts even though he shouldn't. And then he forced himself to back away.

"Thank you, Ali Flores."

"For what?" she quipped. "I was just returning the favor."

He had no answer, but apparently one came to his lips anyway. "Thank you for being you." Then he backed out of her room.

ALI HEARD THE DOOR TO HER ROOM click shut and dropped backward onto the bed with a whump. She wasn't nearly as drunk as she'd pretended. That was her dirty secret. Tomorrow she'd have the excuse ready—oh my, I was totally smashed when we did that—but tonight, she couldn't lie to herself. She'd wanted him to make love to her. And she'd wanted to drive him wild with a blow job.

She'd obviously succeeded with the second. The first had been stopped by his honor. Hell, who'd have thought that she'd be annoyed by any guy's sense of honor!

On some level, she knew he was right. She wasn't thinking exactly clearly right now. But they'd had so much fun this evening. She hadn't laughed that hard in years. They'd even played a mock sword fight with their umbrellas! He was a great guy and she wanted to have hot sex with him.

That was the bold, honest truth. And now she had to respect his sense of honor—sigh—and climb alone into her cold hotel bed. If she was a good, wholesome, honest person, she wouldn't tempt him again all summer.

She giggled as she pressed her face into her pillow. Guess she wasn't a good, wholesome or honest person. Who knew?

9

ALI WASN'T NERVOUS before going on stage. No, she was more of the get-sick-and-pass-out variety of panicked. She hyperventilated. She had sweaty palms. And nothing anyone said to her made it any better.

She'd been thinking of this summer as basic booth work. It was, except for the "show" part. The wedding between Arthur and Guinevere was on a *stage,* and her one middle-school experience with being on stage had been a disaster. That had been over ten years ago, but she still remembered walking to the center and forgetting every line.

"Wow, do you look good in that outfit or what?"

Ali turned to see Ken smiling at her. He was looking regal in his King Arthur getup. Tunic, belt, boots and a robe that swept the floor as he walked. Once again she noticed muscle definition, this time in his legs. Nice! And quite the distraction from her current difficulties.

"Nice costume," she managed to say.

"No one's going to be looking at me."

Ali looked down. Silk sheath, corset about to burst and classy-looking half boots. She did look sexy. She even *felt* sexy, which was awesome. Normally that would be a great thing, except that it was somewhat hard to breathe *and* be sexy. It had taken two of the girls to tie her into this thing, and she seriously doubted that any blood flow was going up to her brain.

Normally she would take a deep breath to calm her nerves, but that wasn't going to happen. The best she could do was stand tall and breathe into her upper lungs. Which naturally lifted her chest a little higher. Which the guys seemed to appreciate. She just hadn't realized how constricting it was to look sexy.

"Um, thanks," she said. Normally a heartfelt compliment like that would have bolstered her confidence. It did make her smile, but one look out at the audience had her breaking into panic.

The "small comic-book shop" was actually pretty big because they didn't do anything small in Texas. What no one had told her was that they had shifted the event to the main mall stage. At the moment, there were a few hundred people in the audience, and a few thousand more shopping.

"Tell me again why I thought this was a good idea," she said.

"Because it's fun."

She shot him an incredulous look, and he just laughed.

"Trust me, Ali. You're going to be great. Just be yourself." Then he peeked through the curtains at the crowd. "And don't forget to look longingly at Blake."

She grimaced. Blake was Lancelot, and yes, he sure did look pretty. But she didn't want to look at him. She wanted to stay with Ken. Preferably in another state and far away from any crowd.

"Ali—" Ken began, but at that exact moment, the music started. Standing in the wings, they got to watch as Samantha, the tavern wench, came on stage and started talking about the royal wedding. Paul bantered back as Mordred with snide comments appropriate to the villain of the piece.

The crowd got into it, especially as Blake started wandering through as Lancelot. He, too, got to make some witty remarks. Most of it was unscripted, and all of it was fun. Which made Ali abruptly realize how sunk she was. Extemporaneous banter? She sucked at that!

"I can't do this," she said, her heart sinking.

"Not a problem," Ken answered as he gently dropped a hand on her shoulder. "I don't want you to do what they're doing."

She glanced at him. "Yes, you do. You want me to work the crowd, to get them excited about the game, to—"

"I want you to be you. Stand on stage and smile. Say your lines and when it's time, step down into the crowd and just talk to them."

"But—"

"Ali, you can do this."

It was almost time for them to go on stage. She could hear the steady march of the mini-play behind her. But Ken didn't let her look out there anymore. Instead, he turned her to face him.

"One more thing, Ali," he said.

"What?"

"To the day I die, I will always regret walking out of your room last night." Then he kissed her. Deep and full on her mouth.

It was obviously a ploy and it shouldn't have worked. But it did. After all, she'd been aching for his kiss forever. And just because it came now, right before she was going on stage, did nothing to take away from the power of being pressed up against his body again. Of feeling his tongue sweep in and possess her in a very elemental way. She opened for him, she melted into him, she did everything but strip him naked and take him to her bed. And then, damn him, he slowly pulled away.

"Until my dying day," he murmured. Then he grabbed her arm and shoved her onto the stage. She barely had time to recover her balance. No time at all to regain any sense of equilibrium. But that was okay because her first line was about how difficult it was to marry a stranger. According to legend, she and Arthur had never met before their wedding day.

Ashley sauntered up as Morgan le Fey. She was the female baddie, and she played the part to perfection. Guinevere was supposed to be young and naive at this point, so it was right in character when it took Ali two tries to get her words out. But she was able to do it, and soon she was settling into her role as she crossed to center stage. Except it wasn't so easy to walk in three-inch heels and there was an irregularity in the stage. Ali's heel caught and she nearly went down to the floor in an inglorious heap. Fortunately, she saw a young man start to jump up from his seat as if to catch her.

"Do you think you could help me?" Ali asked, her voice rather breathy. She didn't know if it came from just being kissed or from the fact that she was still wobbly, but apparently the boy heard. He was out of his seat and on stage in a flash.

The kid was about fifteen years old, gangly and with unfortunate acne. But he had a nice smile that she responded to. He took her hand and helped her walk down the stage.

"You're so kind," she said.

"Don't worry," he said. "I've got you."

She smiled her thanks. "Yes," she said, "you do. Thank you. You are very strong." She said it because it was true. He had a solid grip on her arm, and she was less afraid of falling.

Apparently, it was the perfect thing to say. He flushed a hot red and suddenly became her most devoted follower. He escorted her to her place on the stage. She spoke her lines and interacted with the other actors. And all the while, the boy stood right by her side, apparently very proud of his new position. A discreet glance at the crowd told her that a few of them were looking enviously at the young man, especially as she knighted him, giving him the name Sir Gary.

And at that moment, Blake must have realized he was

being upstaged. As Lancelot, he should be the one at her side. So he made a dashing leap onto the stage, introduced himself and then offered her his arm. Poor Gary was ready to retreat, but Ali would have none of that. She kept both "knights" by her side.

And then Ken came on stage. Or rather, it was King Arthur in full royal regalia. His voice boomed across the mall as he welcomed everyone to his wedding. He was every inch a king, and Ali couldn't help but stare. He was magnificent!

So when he held out his hand to her, she completely forgot Lancelot and Gary. She stepped straight up to Ken just like the queen she was supposed to be. Then together they turned and were "married" by Merlin, who was played by the owner of the comic-book shop.

Her lines were simple. All she had to say was "I do." But at that moment, holding on to Ken's hand and looking into his eyes, she had a flash of a real wedding. Of saying yes to marriage with this man who had made her laugh so hard last night. Who had given her a memory of ecstasy in a parking garage. It was ridiculous, and so very inappropriate, but she couldn't stop herself from thinking about it. From feeling it.

And then she said, "I do" as if she really did.

She saw his eyes widen in surprise, then darken with some sort of emotion. She didn't dare try to interpret it, but his hands were shaking as he lifted her crown. Guinevere didn't get a ring. Instead, she knelt before Ken and let him crown her.

She was supposed to look to Lancelot then. They were setting up a love triangle, after all. But she didn't want to. She wanted to straighten up and kiss her king as if they were gloriously in love. But she was *acting,* she reminded herself, so she forced herself to look sideways at Blake. Funny how she'd once thought him incredibly handsome. Right then, she wondered how the man was going to compete with the very regal Ken.

Then the show was over. Ken clapped his hands and invited all his guests to partake of refreshments and play the game that was set up on monitors all around the central mall area. Paul, too, stepped up and called, "Let the games begin!"

Within moments, a full third of the audience was organized around monitors, beginning the game play. The rest gathered around card tables to start with the tabletop play. Or at least pre-video play. It wasn't necessary to the game, but it could add an extra dimension. Plus, it kept people busy while others were using the electronics.

Seeming reluctant to leave, Sir Gary stayed by her side, handing out game pages, helping to explain the rules. He even spent a few moments entertaining an unruly toddler while an older sibling got time to play.

Lord, she didn't know how she'd managed to pick the one boy out of the audience who was a gem, but she had. She made sure to keep his duties light, and within about forty-five minutes, Tina showed up to escort both her and Gary back to the stage where the really large view screen was up.

"My, aren't you a lucky one," Tina cooed in her best tavern-wench voice. "Assisting our queen."

"It wasn't anything," Gary hedged.

"It was a very great deal," Ali responded. "And for your help, you shall now have a very great reward." She prayed she wasn't lying.

"Nay, Sir Gary Stevens," cut in Paul/Mordred in his booming voice. "Do you think it is an easy thing to win a queen's favor?"

"Er…" Gary began. "I, uh…"

"You must prove yourself worthy. You must show us on the field of battle! Are you prepared?"

Gary looked anxiously behind him at the audience. "Um, I haven't gotten to play at all. I don't know—"

"Then it shall be a true test of skill and cunning."

"Don't worry," Ali put in, squeezing his arm. "I believe in you."

Gary flushed and nodded, taking the game controller in his hand.

Paul grinned. "Then we shall begin."

And so, just as the audience had started to get bored, Paul and Gary caught their attention yet again as "Sir Gary" began his quest on the big screen.

It was fun to watch, especially with Paul and Tina making all sorts of wry comments. And when those two grew tired, Samantha stepped in and kept the audience in stitches by camping it up with Lancelot. Meanwhile, Ali slipped off the stage and continued to work the tables, helping where she could. Chatting when she couldn't.

Basic booth work. The idea was to keep the people happy and hanging around long enough that they finally ended up buying the product. Which, by the way, was selling at a very steady clip.

It turned out it was easy. She wasn't talking about blood-pressure medicines or cholesterol pills like at her old job. No, this time she got to talk games and books with a crowd of kids. Truthfully, she didn't understand half of what they said, but she knew enough to smile and laugh when it was called for.

It took about twenty minutes, but she realized that most of the kids didn't care that she didn't understand what they said. What mattered was that she listened. And she did, or at least she tried to. With what felt like hundreds of kids, it was hard to tell if she got anywhere with any of them. She did know that the time flew by. Six hours. Six hours! And it felt like ten minutes. Except for the fact that she was exhausted by the end and still the kids seemed to linger beside her, wanting to talk.

She worked with them patiently. Behind her, Tina, Paul and Ken were tearing down the equipment. The actors were laughing, pitching in with the work while congratulating each other on an event well done. But Ali was still with the remaining kids. And Gary. Faithful Gary who was flushed and happy from a successful campaign on the big screen.

She was beginning to feel the strain, wondering if she could keep it up much longer, when Ken appeared by her side.

"I'm so sorry," he said to the remaining seven holdouts. "I'm afraid my lady Guinevere needs to return to her duties. No rest for my queen."

The kids laughed at that, but not mockingly. They seemed to truly be happy to let her stay in character even when breaking off.

"But," continued Ken, "I'd like to hand you these coupons. They're a really good deal. Give them to your friends. Mail them to your cousins—"

"Give them to your girlfriends' brothers," Ali added, "so they won't interrupt your dates."

All the kids giggled at that. They were all too young to have a girlfriend, but that didn't mean they weren't blissfully imagining it.

"And," continued Ken, "if you have a gaming club or just a big group of friends, my email address is on there. Email me and we'll hook you up."

Thanks and appreciative murmurs went around as they all took the coupons.

"Don't thank me," answered Ken. "Thank Queen Guinevere."

They did. Every single one of them smiled at her and in all seriousness, thanked her with grave voices. She accepted their appreciation as regally as possible.

Then, just like that, the event was over. Ken took her hand and led her away. Behind her, the others were wheeling out the carts, and it almost looked like an entourage was following her out the door.

Amazing. Incredible. Ali couldn't believe it was done or

that it had been so…well, not exactly easy, but fun. It had been fun!

So why, in all of this, were her only thoughts about Ken, his kiss and the words *I do?*

10

Ali was asleep, curled up like a kitten in her bus seat. Ken had taken the seat across the aisle from her, hoping to find a moment to talk with her. But whereas everyone else on the bus was still high on the success of the event, Ali was an introvert. She could be spectacular in a crowd—and she had been—but at the end of the event, she was exhausted. Which meant that, unlike the extroverts who were chattering away toward the back, Ali was out, and Ken—who hovered between exhausted and exhilarated—sat a seat away and just watched her.

He'd never been so amazed by a person before. She'd made him laugh last night until his sides ached. She'd been terrified just before going on stage, but she'd come through just like the queen she was. She'd charmed everyone, himself included, and he was halfway in love with her. It didn't hurt that she revved his engine like no one else, too.

He couldn't stop thinking about the moment they'd said their pretend "I do." He knew it was pretend. He knew they were acting, but it had felt so real. She had been so beautiful and he had wanted to marry her. He'd wanted her to be his queen with a hunger that both stunned and terrified him.

He might have done something stupid then. He might have hauled her up and kissed her. But at that moment, she'd turned slightly and looked at Blake/Lancelot. That had been the bucket of cold water he'd needed. She was *acting,* for God's sake. And only a fool would take it as anything but pretend. But for those few short moments, he had felt like a real king with Ali as his queen.

He leaned back in his seat, letting his own eyelids grow heavy. This was either going to be the worst or the best summer of his life.

HE WAS KEEPING AN EYE ON HER. Ali was dead on her feet—or on her butt since she was sitting in the bus seat—but there was a simmering excitement in her blood that kept her from falling completely unconscious. Part of it was the certain knowledge that Ken was sitting right across the bus aisle from her just watching her as she pretended to sleep.

It should have felt weird. Instead, it felt exciting. Arousing. She could easily fantasize that she was curled up on a couch in her apartment while someone hot and exciting was standing guard outside. It wasn't like he was a Peeping Tom. In her mind, he was just like Ken—sweet and funny—only like a P.I. sent to protect her.

Because of his job, he'd be forced to look on as she slowly stretched on her couch then piece by piece, peeled off her clothes because it was so hot inside her apartment. And while Ken would be fighting the urge to burst through the door and take her right there on her living-room rug, she would be doing an unconscious striptease for him. Or maybe not so unconscious because maybe she knew he was there and wanted him to burst in.

She felt her nipples tighten and her core go hot and liquid. And that was really frustrating because she was on a bus with a half dozen other people. She wanted it to be just her and Ken.

Lord, when would she learn that she should *not* fantasize

about her boss? But she couldn't stop herself, and so, as the miles slipped by, she let her mind drift into some very pleasant places.

THEIR NEXT STOP WAS an amusement park where they would be for the next ten days. Their job was to do a show on the main stage once a day, and then draw people to their booth throughout the rest of the park hours. Which meant that, for the most part, Ali got up at eight, grabbed some breakfast, then put on her costume. They worked in shifts until the park closed at eleven at night with time off throughout the day to eat junk food and sneak in a roller-coaster ride or three. She then collapsed into bed at midnight or later, only to do it all again the next day.

It was grueling. The weather was hot, and though the booth had air-conditioning for the electronics, she was supposed to be outside in the crowd drawing people into the booth. So she stood in the sun in a leather corset and was very grateful to be wearing a silk shift underneath.

At least she didn't have the sunburn problem that her fairer coworkers had. Samantha, the redhead, was using industrial-strength sunscreen by the bucketful. Even Ashley, as the brunette Morgan le Fey, claimed she'd just come from a fight with a dragon who'd nearly burned her to a crisp.

She barely saw Ken, more's the pity. He was there, of course, but always working. The main stage show was supposed to reveal the rising attraction between herself and Lancelot. There were all sorts of feats of manly combat and suggestive flirtations. Truthfully, the only fun part for her was when Ken hit the stage as King Arthur. She knew she was supposed to be attracted to Lancelot, but she only had eyes for her king, especially the few times he strapped on a sword and started mock fighting. There was something about a guy with a sword that just turned her on.

But as soon as the stage event was finished, they were

right back at the booth selling the game. In short, the team used this time to settle into a rhythm. The main show became a well-oiled machine. The group all became friends, some closer than others. And Ali felt that her relationship with Ken was becoming entrenched in friendly camaraderie. Very nice, but it just made her nighttime fantasies all the more heated.

And then came the *hot* day. Not just hot, but a blistering 104 degrees. Everyone was cranky except for Paul. The VP of marketing loved it because where else would the public go when it was that hot but inside an air-conditioned booth? They were crammed to the gills every minute and sales were through the roof.

Meanwhile, Ken declared that no one could be outside for more than twenty minutes at a time. And Ali thought if she spent two more minutes listening to the stuttering of another prepubescent boy or smiled at one more tired mother with a cranky kid, her brains would boil. Literally boil right out of her ears.

She was about three seconds from losing it when Ken grabbed her arm and pulled her to a tiny alcove to the side of the booth.

"Oh my God, I'm going to explode." That was him speaking, and he'd taken the words right out of her mouth.

"My shift doesn't end for another ten minutes," she whispered. It wasn't quite 5:00 p.m., but she was counting the seconds until she could leave.

"You started a half hour early because Blake started throwing donuts at Samantha and I tossed them both out. So I declare your shift done. Mine, too."

She chuckled as he aimed her straight for a park exit. "I didn't realize the boss had a shift."

"Of course I do. It's the work-until-you're-going-to-kill-someone shift. And I just hit my limit."

"About damn time," she murmured as she climbed into the van. It was one of those ubiquitous white metal things and it usually hauled around the electronics. But everything was in the booth now, so what was behind them was an eerily empty stack of shelving units and snakes of cables piled into the corner.

Ken was a step behind her, hopping into the driver's seat.

"So where we going, boss?" she asked as she aimed the air vents straight at her overheated face.

"Name your favorite place to detox."

"A library."

He paused a moment. "Seriously?"

She shrugged. "You don't actually have to study in a library, you know. People always assume you are, but you can do just about anything so long as you're quiet."

His expression shifted into a slow smile. "Anything?"

She grinned, her mind going right where it always did when she had a moment with Ken—straight into the X-rated territory. "Just about."

"But I don't know any libraries around here."

"Good because what I really want is a swimming pool."

"God, yes. You read my mind." He immediately put the van in gear.

She sighed as the air-conditioning began to take hold. "Yeah, that would be lovely, except that there will be a zillion kids at the pool."

He nodded. "Yeah, maybe at our hotel. But you forget, I've done this summer trip twice before."

She rolled her head to look at him. "Yeah?"

He grinned. "Yeah. I'm also someone who understands about hotel chains and frequent user points."

Her eyebrows lifted. "Any hotel pool is going to be buried in kids right now."

"Trust me?"

"I do." She said it without hesitation, but his expression shifted.

"Ali..." That was it. Just her name, but she heard a wealth

of meaning underneath it. And it told her without words that he had been tortured by some of the same thoughts and feelings that she had. That he wanted something he shouldn't—not as her boss—and that this was a chance for them to express it to each other. Appropriate or not, he wanted to explore.

And so did she.

So she touched his arm. And then she got bolder and stroked her fingers down his forearm to touch his fingers where they were on the steering wheel.

"I trust you, Ken." *And I want you.* She didn't say the last part out loud, but maybe her eyes did. Maybe something in her words tipped him off because she saw his eyes darken and his nostrils flare. Then he took the freeway with a little extra gusto.

Twenty minutes later and they were walking into a cool lobby with very smartly dressed people standing behind dark mahogany counters. They didn't even blink at the way she was dressed. They simply smiled and asked if there was anything they could do to help.

"Is the presidential suite available?" Ken asked.

"One moment, sir," said the young man behind the counter as he typed on his keyboard. "Yes, it is."

Ken passed over his ID. "I believe I have enough points to have it for one night."

Again, nothing but a smooth smile as the man typed. Five minutes later and they were on their way up to the twenty-seventh floor with special gold keycards in their sweaty grips.

"You know what he was thinking," Ali said as they stood side by side in the elevator. The man probably thought she was a hooker, purchased for the afternoon. If it weren't so mortifying, she might have laughed at the situation.

"I don't care what he thinks," Ken all but growled. "So long as room service and the air-conditioning work, he can think anything he wants."

"Easy for you to say. You're not the one traipsing about in a corset and half boots." And if this wasn't the most bizarre hooker gear, she didn't know what would be.

He grimaced, obviously feeling remorse for his words. "You don't look anything like a hooker, Ali."

She arched her brows at him. "Doesn't matter—"

"And your face is too sweet to be mistaken for one."

She frowned, unsure whether to be insulted or complimented. No, she didn't want to look like a prostitute. But she didn't want to be thought of as so sweet that no one had lustful thoughts when they looked at her. She wasn't a nun.

"And besides," he added, "I'm in costume, too."

Barely. As boss, he got the most minimal of costumes. His kingly gear was in his cape and crown. Once he ditched that, he walked around in leather pants and an old cotton shirt. In some places, he might have passed as trendy. Thankfully, there wasn't time for her to answer as the elevator dinged. There wasn't even a hallway. The doors just opened onto a suite that was larger than her apartment. Cool air enveloped her so fast and so quickly that she sneezed. But that did not detract from what she was looking at.

A kitchenette, a living room, a bedroom and a balcony with… "It's got its own pool. Holy crap! There's a pool out there on the balcony."

"It's just a little one."

True. It was just a little kidney-shaped thing. But it was completely private because it was blocked on all sides by greenery.

"This isn't the presidential suite," she murmured. "This is the movie-star suite complete with ways to block telephoto lenses from the paparazzi!" She spun back to Ken. "Just how many frequent user points did you spend?"

He shrugged. "All of them." He joined her at the sliding door to the balcony. "I stayed here for a conference once."

"Here as in the hotel, or here as in up *here* with the kitchen and the pool and probably your own towel girl."

He laughed. "No towel girl, I swear. But yeah, they messed up my reservation and I ended up here."

"Lucky you!"

He shook his head. "That's just it. I kept thinking, what a waste! I worked the whole time and was never even here. All I did was sleep and grab an espresso on the way out the door."

"An espresso?"

He gestured to the kitchen counter where there was indeed a machine for espresso shots. "It only took me three tries to figure it out."

She laughed—a real carefree, relaxed laugh—for the first time in days. She was cool, standing in the lap of luxury, and alone with Ken. What more could a girl want? Except... "Oh, hell. I don't have a bathing suit."

"Sure you do." He stepped over to a closet and swung the doors open. There, folded neatly on one of the shelves, was a small variety of bathing suits from men's swim trunks to bikinis, with various one-piece suits thrown in. "Loaners. They're cleaned after every use."

"Oh my God. I've stepped into a Hollywood movie and didn't even notice."

He grinned. "Only the best for my queen." And then he sobered. "Look, I don't know about you, but I've been dreaming of that pool since the minute the thermometer hit sweltering. So I'm going to shower and change and submerge."

"Rock-paper-scissors-lizard-Spock for first use of the shower."

His eyebrows rose. "Wow, where did you learn that?"

"Paul taught me. We were fighting over the last pineapple slice." She held up her fist in the traditional rock-paper-scissors stance, all the while grinning because she'd surprised him with her geek know-how.

Meanwhile, he frowned in mock outrage. "Hey, those were my points that paid for this room!"

"And yet chivalry demands that you let the lady go first."

"Oh, my damnable honor!"

She raised her fist a little higher. "This is the only way to assuage both your honor and give you a fighting chance at being the first in the pool."

He grimaced but held up his fist. "Okay, but I warn you. I don't always pick Spock."

"Good to know," she said in mock seriousness. She didn't really care who showered first. There was plenty of time for both of them, but this made it fun. And she liked that she could banter with him like that.

They pumped fists and she won. He had indeed picked Spock. She'd correctly guessed that his earlier comment was a way to throw her off, so she'd gone with lizard, which poisons Spock. Which meant after a gleeful chortle, she danced happily into the bathroom. "I'll be quick!"

"That's what they all say!"

She laughed and switched on the light, only to gasp in stunned delight. The bathroom was roughly the same size as the bus. Or at least it felt that way. Whirlpool bath, extra-large shower, double-sink counter, not to mention a separate makeup area. She opened a closet looking for linens only to discover that there was a separate room for the commode.

Now she really did feel like a queen. Or at least a princess. Mindful of her promise to be quick, she started to undress. Or rather, she planned to, until she realized she was in a corset that tied in the back.

Oh, hell.

"Um, Ken?" She popped open the door and peeked out. "Ken?"

He looked up from where he sat at the conveniently provided hotel computer. "Yeah?"

"I need some help here." She stepped out and gestured behind her back. "Without help, I'm stuck in this thing."

"Oh, right. No problem."

He straightened up from the desk, and she stared at him as the pieces started falling into place in her head. So far this trip, she'd seen him working constantly at the booth helping to make sales or hunched over his computer. Except for their very memorable night before the mall event, he hadn't done anything else but those two things.

And now she was two minutes in the bathroom, and he was already on the computer. "Either you're a workaholic, or you're worried about something," she said.

"Workaholic," he said without missing a beat.

She shook her head. "I don't think so."

He gestured for her to turn around. "No, really. Definitely a workaholic."

She didn't move an inch. "No, my boss at the hospital is a workaholic. He's always at work and when he's not there, he's talking work. At lunch, at parties, on weekends when he's supposed to be with his kids, it's all jabber jabber jabber. Hospital this, publicity that, event extravaganza whatever."

He frowned. "How would you know that? You spend time at parties and weekends with your boss?"

"Sure. I remember one hospital-sponsored community event. I was there working. He was there with his kids."

"And?"

"And, he had his smartphone going all the time. Barely even looked up when his kid went to bat in the softball game."

Ken pursed his lips. "Well, I don't have kids but—"

"You don't exist with a phone plastered to your ear and an iPad on your lap."

He grimaced. "Yeah, I do."

"Lately, maybe. Because you're worried about something. And I'll bet if you had a chance to see your kid play softball, you wouldn't even have a phone with you."

"I always carry my phone."

"Really?" She looked at his belt where it was usually strapped. Not there.

He patted his belt, then cursed. "I must have left it in the van."

"Ding ding! I win!" she crowed.

"Because I forgot my phone?"

She nodded. "Because workaholics would never forget their phones and would be panicked if they did—"

"I am panicked!"

"You're irritated at yourself. But you're going to get over it and leave it in the van because I have mine." She pointed to the corner where she'd dropped her purse.

"I doubt we'd get the same kind of calls."

"No, but anyone who desperately needs to contact you will think to call me when they can't find you." She frowned, wondering if he could follow those confused words. "And now before you completely distract me, you're going to tell me what's the problem."

"There is no problem."

"Then you wouldn't have desperately needed this escape. You don't mind the crowds like I do."

He frowned. "The crowds bother you?"

"We're not talking about me!" she huffed. "And it's not so bad. But they do get exhausting."

He nodded. "I hear that."

"And I want to hear what the problem is," she said sternly. One month ago, she wouldn't have pushed so hard. After all, he was right: this was his company, not hers. But something about playing a queen on stage had gotten into her. She felt more assertive than ever before. It was as if she'd been forced to confront her shyness. After two weeks of playing Guinevere, standing up on stage no longer frightened her. And standing up to Ken seemed like child's play. So she dropped her hands on her hips and took a stab in the dark. "The release of the game was last week. I thought we were doing well."

"Our events are doing fine. Great, actually. But nationwide figures are…well, it's too early to count." He lifted his shoulder in a defensive gesture that she recognized from her own mirror. He was putting on a brave face, but inside he was worried as hell.

"How bad are the early indications?"

He shook his head. "Not that bad. And besides, it's not your problem. All you have to do is be my queen."

She snorted. "Well, this queen is also your friend. And as your friend, I want you to talk to me. What's the problem?"

He waited a long moment. She thought at first that he wasn't going to confess. But in the end, the weight of it all got him talking. His shoulders slumped, his hands slid down the sides of his pants as if he was looking for pockets and, most telltale of all, his gaze dropped to the floor.

"It's not so bad. There are sales. But, you know, they're about on par with Leaper."

"Leaper? The product that *flopped?*"

He winced and she immediately regretted her harsh word. "Like I said, it's early still. It's not like I get real-time sales reports."

"But there's a downloadable version, right? Not as complicated or as good as the big-deal one. But it's like a teaser to lure you into the more expensive version."

He nodded and didn't speak. So she prodded him.

"And those are the sales numbers you have been watching. Because you can see those in real time."

Again he nodded but kept his lips buttoned.

"Oh, hell, they're bad, aren't they?"

He sighed. "I think I need some beer. What about you? Or would you prefer another Malibu pineapple thing?"

She watched as he pulled out the room-service menu, seeing it for the avoidance tactic it was. Worse, it was avoiding via booze. Translation: sales were really bad.

Ah, hell!

_11_

KEN STUDIED THE ROOM-SERVICE MENU as if he was prepping for a final exam. He didn't want to talk about the dismal sales reports or what they might mean to his company. Talking about a disaster didn't help avoid it. Or wouldn't in this case. All he wanted to do was drink, eat and have sex. Not necessarily in that order.

"So," Ali said as she stepped right up to him. She was still in her corset, still looking like the queen he'd envisioned since…well, since he was a child. Not the actual look or costume. As always, the looks were secondary to what he felt around her: warmth, compassion, humor and a whole lot of sexy.

"I'll order dinner," he said. "What would you like?"

She touched his arm, and when he steadfastly refused to look at her, she touched his face. No way he could refuse her now. So he turned and looked right into her very beautiful eyes.

"First, Ken, answer one question. Is there anything we can do now to help sales? Beyond what we're already doing?"

He shook his head. If there was, he'd already be doing it.

"You and Paul have been over this a zillion times, haven't you?"

"I have. Paul's been…" He shook his head. "Paul's been distracted lately."

She frowned. "By what?"

"I wish I knew." And what a time for his VP of marketing to suddenly flake out on him. It wasn't anything overt, but the man just seemed half there at times. Paul went through the motions, but his mind was obviously somewhere else. Meanwhile, Ali had been doing some thinking on her own.

"First things first," she said as she turned off the computer.

"Hey!"

"You don't need to be looking at that. You need to be ordering dinner and thinking of ways to relax." She started flipping through the room-service menu. "What are you having?"

"Lasagna." It was his go-to meal when traveling anywhere.

She nodded. "Good choice. I'll have the spinach salad—"

He rolled his eyes. "You don't have to diet—"

"And the black silk pie." She flashed him a grin. "Why eat a meal when you can make one out of dessert?"

"Healthy and sinful. I like it."

"I think you should get the cheesecake. I mean, if you like cheesecake."

"What about the hot lava cake?"

She pursed her lips. "I can work with that, although that is two chocolate desserts."

"Hmmm, good point. Does that mean we're going to share desserts?"

She grinned. "I will if you will."

"Oh, I will. I more than will." He blinked. Had that made any sense at all? It was a small thing, but he loved the intimacy of sharing food with a woman. It was something he only did with a girlfriend. And though Ali wasn't at that status yet, he wanted her to be. And so he wanted to share desserts with a freakish kind of want.

She chuckled. "So I guess you'll have to decide what you're going to order."

He grinned and picked up the phone. He ordered beer—she didn't want the fruity thing—salad and lasagna, then all three desserts.

"Ooo!" she cooed. "I like how you think!"

He hung up the phone. "And I'd like to get you out of that corset now."

She blinked at him. "Wow, going for the gusto there."

He flushed. He hadn't exactly meant it as a come-on. Mild flirtation, certainly, but—

She burst out laughing. "Relax, Ken. I know you were teasing." She turned around. "And yes, please loosen this. I would really like to breathe again."

He went straight for her ties in back. After two other launches like this one, he was an expert at tying—and untying—corsets. But as he started tugging the knot apart, he couldn't resist looking at the smooth curve of her neck or the beautiful latte color of her skin. If she were his girlfriend, he would be kissing her neck right now. As he loosened the corset and pushed it down, he would nuzzle the shift open, as well. Eventually, both corset and shift would drop to the ground and he would wrap his arms around her. He'd slip his hands across her shoulders, down her arms, until he could slide in and cup her breasts. He would do it slowly, sweetly, and she would melt backward into his arms.

She took a deep breath, and from this angle, he could see the lift and lower of her breasts.

"God, it's good to breathe."

He nodded, even though she couldn't see it. He liked seeing her body move as the restriction on her torso eased. All women did it. They took a deep breath then kind of wiggled inside their corset. They stretched on each side and always sighed in delight as their body was freed. He watched Ali go through those exact motions, appreciating every second of the display.

"I gotta say, my back never felt so good," Ali commented.

"Usually after days on my feet, my whole body aches. With a corset, it's just my feet that burn by day's end."

"I promise to rub your feet after dinner."

"You *are* my hero!"

"But only if you promise to watch a movie with me while I do it."

She tilted her head. "What movie?"

He grabbed the guide and flipped through it. "*Terminator 3? Blade Runner,* director's cut?"

She choked back a laugh. She had a hand on her belly, holding the corset in place as she turned around to look at the guide. "Sci-fi action fan?"

"We could try *Space Balls.* That's sci-fi spoof."

"Yeah, it was too much to hope for a foot rub *and* a romantic comedy."

He mock rolled his eyes. "Way too much."

"Fine. How about…?"

They set about negotiating movie choices. She liked romantic comedy and mystery with a paranormal twist. He went for the science fiction that wasn't kid stuff and anime. In the end they agreed on the TV pilot of *Terra Nova.* Neither of them had seen it, but it had enough elements for them both to be happy.

"But first," she said firmly, "I need a shower."

"Yeah," he pretend-groused. "You said you'd be done like ten minutes ago."

She stuck out her tongue at him, a gesture that immediately sent his blood straight south, and then disappeared into the bathroom with a laugh. He sighed and dropped back down into the desk chair. He was just reaching for the computer when she called from the bathroom.

"And if you touch that computer while I'm in here, then I'm going to make you watch a Jennifer Aniston movie!"

He pulled his hand back with a snap. "That's so not

fair! What am I going to do while you're luxuriating in the shower?"

"Suffer!" she called right before the shower started.

He was suffering, he thought as he adjusted his pants. But it was a good kind of pain.

ALI SHOWERED QUICKLY, and boy, was it great to clean the dust and grime away. Then she put on one of the very lush hotel robes and stepped out. Ken was waiting right where she'd left him—next to the computer with a strange expression on his face. Kind of happy, kind of in pain.

"Were you on the computer?"

"Nope."

"What were you doing?"

"Thinking."

"Work thinking?"

"Nope."

She looked at him, at the slight smirk on his face and the way his arms covered his groin. Could he mean fantasizing thinking? The idea was kind of titillating. After all, she'd been doing her own kind of thinking in the shower. And way earlier, if she was honest. Back when he'd untied her corset, she'd felt the brush of his breath across her skin and it had set every nerve ending on fire. She'd wanted to sink backward into his arms and let him slowly peel the clothing from her body. And that fantasy had nothing on what she'd imagined in the shower.

"So, um, are you going to share?"

He shook his head. "I'm a man of mystery."

"You're a man who can have the shower if he wants."

"I do." He said it, but he didn't move.

"Um…waiting for something?"

"Yeah. I thought I'd just sit here and watch you put on a swimsuit first."

"Ha!" Then she threw an extra towel at him. "Go on. You stink."

"You'd look great in that yellow bikini there."

She looked at the garment. She'd never worn a bikini in her life. As a teen she'd been much too self-conscious to wear so little. Her brothers had teased her enough when she wore her one-piece. Then there was no time for swimming between college and her job.

"Come on," Ken said. "I'm nearsighted. I won't see a thing." He flashed her a grin that had her tingling from head to toe. "Well, not unless I get up real close."

Lord, she was thinking about it. She was thinking hard about it. But if and when she undressed for Ken, she wanted it to be sexy. Trying to put on an unfamiliar bikini was more likely to be awkward. So she just lifted her chin and said primly, "I think I'll stay in this robe, thank you." Then she walked to the window and stared out at the view.

In her imagination, he came up behind her. He undid her robe and took her slowly, from behind, right against the window. She waited, taut with anxiety and lust, but all she heard was his chuckle as he headed for the bathroom and quietly shut the door.

How could she be both disappointed and relieved?

Sighing, she went back over to the swimsuits. Did she dare? Guess so, because her hands went to the yellow bikini. A month ago she would never have worn something that skimpy. But just a week of walking around in a corset had changed her. She was bolder than before and had a confidence in her body that was completely new. That, or she was just rising to the challenge in his words.

You'd look great in that yellow bikini.

He made her want to see if she really would. And if his eyes would light up in delight when he saw her in it. Or maybe darken with lust.

She knew she was playing with fire, but she couldn't resist. Before she could change her mind, she dropped the robe and put on the bikini. Then in a fit of nervousness, she all but ran outside and jumped in the pool.

He came out ten minutes later. He, too, wore a robe and, after a glance at her in the pool, grabbed a pair of swim trunks and headed back into the bathroom. A moment later he emerged, looking a lot more fit than she expected. Nothing was left of the geek she'd first met except for the general size and build. Seeing him in loose red swim trunks—and nothing else—she could tell that his pretend swordplay had paid off. He wasn't athlete-trim, but he did have muscle definition and a nicely proportioned body.

"Very nice," she said as she grabbed hold of the edge of the pool.

"You wore the yellow bikini," he said.

"I did," she answered, though he couldn't have had any more than a glimpse of it given that she was hugging the near side of the pool.

"So let me see."

"Why? You already said I'd look great in it."

"Okay, so let me appreciate." He dropped down to the side of the pool. "You know I already think you're gorgeous. Didn't I mistake you for a supermodel when we first met?"

"A supermodel?" she laughed. "I don't think so. Not at Marilyn's agency." OMG Action! had a decent reputation, but it was a long cry from representing supermodels.

"Wow, do you split hairs or what? Come on. I'm sitting out here in all my flabby glory."

"There isn't a lot of flab."

"Right back atcha, Ali."

He was right. She was too old to be this self-conscious. Besides, she was the new Ali. The sexy, confident *queen* Ali. So she took a breath and pushed back from the side of the pool. She floated backward, letting him see all of her through the distortion of the water. Then she finally put her feet under her and stood up. The pool wasn't that deep where she was. It only came to her hips, so he got a good look. Thankfully, so did she...at his face.

She saw the curve of his lips as he smiled, and the dark appreciation in his eyes. His nostrils flared, and his fingers clenched the side of the pool. He liked what he saw. And from the sudden intensity in his eyes, she guessed that he liked it a lot.

"You're good for my ego," she said softly.

"You're hell on my self-control."

She swallowed. Right there, out in the open, was the invitation. She could tell him outright that she didn't want him to stay in control. She wanted him touching her everywhere and every way. Right now. She almost got the words out, but then there was a buzz from the intercom.

"Room service," said a voice through the intercom.

Saved by the buzz. But as he got up to allow the elevator access, she let her body slide back into the cooling water. It was time, she realized. Tonight, she was going to sleep with him.

KEN WAITED AT THE ELEVATOR for the food. He let the man push the cart in, but that was it. He didn't want anyone else nearby for even a second longer than necessary. Less than a minute later, he was back outside with her.

"Want to eat out by the pool or inside in luxury?"

"I think it's luxury either way, but I vote inside. I've gotten enough sun these last few days."

"You got it." He ducked back inside, keeping an eye on her luscious body as she toweled off. Hard not to get distracted with that beautiful sight right through the screen door. Somehow he managed to get the cart unloaded, putting plates onto the table in record time.

"You must have been a waiter at some point in your life," she said as she came into the room.

He frowned. "What? No."

"Come on. You dressed that table like a pro."

He looked down at the tablecloth, settings and flowers, then chuckled. "I wasn't a waiter, but my stepmother was. Every dinner at home, she made me bus the table."

"She taught you well," she said as she sat down.

"Good to know. That way I'll have a fallback if my business goes belly-up." He meant it as a joke. It *was* a joke, but he could tell by the way she bit her lip that he'd thrown a damper on the conversation. "Hey, don't worry—"

"If you say *my* salary's secure, I swear I will hit you. I'm not worried about *my* pay."

He swallowed, unaccountably touched. "Actually, I was going to say, don't worry. There's still plenty of time to turn sales around. We started the promo a little late."

"You did?"

He nodded. "Normally we'd have started pushing at least a month earlier, but the pieces weren't in place."

She frowned, and he recognized her figuring-things-out face. Sure enough, she put the pieces together quickly enough. "You mean you hadn't found the actors yet."

He hadn't found *her* yet, but why belabor the point? "We were delayed because I was picky, yes. But I count the time well spent."

"I sure hope so," she muttered.

"I *know* so. You've been bringing in customers by the boatload."

She still had that face on. "It doesn't matter how many I bring in, though. The few hundred or so I'm converting won't make a difference on a national scale."

"Don't underestimate the value of a few hundred and good word of mouth. In the internet age, a good event gets talked about way more than you think."

She nodded. "That's good. And I guess that a groundswell

could happen at any time. In the long run, a month or two sooner or later doesn't make any difference."

He smiled. Lord, he got hard as a rock when she said stuff like that. She was *smart,* and besides that, she understood business at an intuitive level. He'd met MBAs who couldn't follow his train of thought as well as she did.

But rather than lose himself in admiring her—something he was all too prone to do—he quickly sat down and started uncovering dishes. Lord, the lasagna smelled heavenly.

"Wow, that looks good!" she said. She was looking at his plate, not her salad.

"Want to share?" he asked, pushing his plate toward her.

"Nope. I'm saving room for dessert."

"Your loss," he said as he dug in.

In the end, she did end up taking a few bites, but mostly because he insisted. Then they both tucked into the desserts.

He made the decision quickly enough. It happened sometime between her moaning at her first taste of the silk pie and when she fed him a dripping spoonful of lava cake and ice cream. In many ways, the decision had been inevitable since he'd first seen her in the hall weeks ago.

He was going to sleep with her. A lot of times in a lot of ways. That wasn't the decision. What he decided right then was that he wanted to marry her.

And that thought scared him to the opposite side of the couch.

12

ALI LOVED THE SHOW. She loved hanging out with Ken. And she really loved the way he looked at her when all she wore was a bikini and a robe.

She shouldn't have done it. He was being all noble and sitting on the opposite side of the couch from her. But it wasn't that large a couch. And while they started out sitting all prim and proper, she relaxed as she got into the show. He did, too, resting his arm on the back of the couch. That gave her room to slide sideways—not on purpose—then she tucked her legs up beneath her. For warmth.

He leaned back a little farther, stretching his legs out. And then she was startled by a scary moment. That meant she jumped—sideways, of course—straight into his arms. Within another ten minutes, she was leaning against him, her head resting back against his shoulder, and all but purring in her contentment.

Then the show ended. She sighed in regret, knowing that she would have to leave the circle of his arms. That she would have to get dressed in that corset and dusty shift and go back to her hotel room. Just because she wanted to spend the night didn't make it a good idea. They'd hit a nice balance. She didn't want to upset that. So the last thing she should do was look up at him with lust in her eyes and invite him to kiss her. The very last thing she should do.

She did it anyway. She heard him release a sigh that she couldn't interpret. Relief, surrender, desire? Any and all of those applied to herself. It didn't matter. In a moment, his mouth was on hers and she was giving herself up to him.

His arm dropped to her back and he pulled her tighter against him. She felt his tongue thrust into her mouth, and she dueled with him. Normally her mind started thinking things as she kissed. It was a normal thing for her—a brain that would not shut up. But with him, all that mental noise stuttered to a stop. Her attention was on the thrust of his tongue, the pull of his arm and the way he supported her as he gently rolled her back so he could kiss her more deeply.

She let him do it. She'd wanted this for so long and now, finally, he was pushing her onto her back. Her robe gaped, just as she'd hoped it would. He broke the kiss to press more along her cheek, the line of her jaw and down to her neck. She shivered at the feel of his hot breath, the wetness of his tongue and the erotic caress of his mouth. Every inch he touched felt electrified. And that current was transmitted to every quivering cell in her body.

Her robe was open. She still had the bikini on underneath, but that still left lots of tingling skin for his hands to stroke. And when his mouth made it to her collarbone, he pulled back, his eyes dark while his hands tightened where they touched her waist.

"I was right," he murmured. "You do look fantastic in that bikini."

"Thanks," she said, not having any other word to use because most of her mind was on the smooth expanse of his chest. She was stroking the robe off his body, too, and he shrugged it off without breaking eye contact.

"It's beautiful," he said. "May I take it off you?"

"Yes, please."

And just like that, his fingers left her waist to untie the strings that held the tiny scraps of yellow on.

The air hit her breasts and her nipples tightened painfully. Or perhaps it was the way he looked at her that made them so hard. He was reverent as his palms came to her breasts.

Oh, he had nice hands—large and dexterous. She really liked what he did with her breasts. The way he held them was nice enough, but he did something with his fingers on her nipples. She didn't have the focus to know what, but it was like he was playing with them. Tweaking them, pulling them, moving them around. It was bizarre, and it made her giggle. It also made her so wet she wanted to slide right off the couch and onto him. All the way on.

"You're not supposed to be laughing," he said, his eyes dancing.

"You're supposed to be naked," she said.

"I—" He swallowed. He was thinking. She saw all the signs of it. The way his eyes narrowed, his brow furrowed a bit and, worst of all, the way his hands stilled. She couldn't have that.

She reached out and smoothed the lines in his forehead. "Don't think, Ken. You think too much."

"One of us should."

"No. Really we shouldn't." Then she surged forward and kissed him again. As deep and thorough as she could manage. She heard him groan, and his hands slid to her waist, gripping her hips.

Yes! She pulled him closer, but she didn't have the angle. Her legs weren't spread and he was on his knees next to the couch.

On his knees? When had that happened?

She felt his thumbs hook beneath the hip straps, slowly tugging them down. Perfect. Pushing forward, she took her weight on her legs and slowly stood up. With his hands right there, the bottom half of the bikini slid right down to her knees. And as an added bonus, she stripped out of her robe at the same time.

They'd had to break the kiss as she moved, but his mouth was right there at her belly, kissing her skin while her muscles quivered beneath his touch. When he started to kiss her lower, she leaned down, tugging at his arms.

"There's a bed right over there."

He looked over, then back up at her. She swore she could see his heart in his eyes. The lust and the need. But there was something infinitely sad in them, too. She was about to ask when he answered her unasked question.

"I don't have any condoms."

Oh, hell. She'd bought some, too, just in case. But they were back in her hotel room. She hadn't thought they'd end up at a different hotel.

Wait... "It's a high-end hotel. They've got to have them somewhere in here." She frowned as she looked around. Bedside table? Bathroom? "The gift shop certainly."

"Do you want me to call room service? I'm sure they'd bring some up."

She bit her lip, thinking furiously. Then her eyes happened to fall on where her corset was lying beside the bed. Nearby was a neat stack of his clothing, both costumes complete with long leather ties. Hell, his outfit even included a modern belt.

She bit her lip, thinking. Would he go for it? They hadn't even had normal sex yet, much less her brand of fantasy play. But the idea had taken root. In truth, she'd thought of it the very first day in the leather shop. It had grown more detailed in the nights since.

"There's something I haven't told you," she said.

His eyes widened with wariness. "That sounds ominous."

She half laughed, half shrugged. "Here's the thing. I was the only child of a single mom for the first ten years of my life. I was alone a lot, read a lot, and I developed this great imagination."

He nodded, but it was clear he didn't understand. She would have to make herself more clear.

"This great fantasy life."

She knew the exact moment he understood. His body jerked slightly, but not away. It seemed as though he'd just stopped himself from leaping on her, and that made her libido all the more bold. Then he had to clear his throat before he could speak.

"Fantasy life as in…sexual fantasies?"

She nodded. "There's lots of things we can do that wouldn't involve a condom. I mean, if you want to."

He nodded slowly, but his eyes had taken on a dark kind of intensity. "I want," he said, his voice thick enough to be a growl.

"Good," she said. "Because so do I." Then she stepped back from him, using the motion to completely step out of her bikini bottoms so that she now stood naked before him. She wasn't normally this bold, but this was her summer of fantasy play. Apparently, the Ali who wore yellow bikinis and leather corsets was a lot more confident about her body than normal Ali.

She took a deep breath. "Look, this is about distracting you, right? Keeping you from going nuts worrying about your company, right?"

He straightened slowly until he stood right in front of her. He was still wearing his bathing trunks, though the robe was gone, and his erection made an impressive tent to the fabric.

"I haven't thought about my company in a few hours, Ali. I swear."

"Good. Let's keep it that way." Then she jerked her head at the bed, amazed by her own boldness. "Go lie down on the bed. And lose the shorts while you're at it."

"Um—"

"And don't you say a damn thing about work or anything

else. We're total strangers tonight. No relationship except whatever it takes to keep your mind off…other stuff."

He paused, his hand going to her cheek in a slow stroke that had her toes curling into the carpet. "Except we do have a relationship. We're—"

"Friends. With benefits." She wasn't prepared to admit to anything else just yet. Because if she did, her mind would skip straight to the real problem: What would happen to their relationship after the end of the summer? So she held it at bay, focusing instead on a stranger fantasy.

"Ali—"

"I know you think this is unethical, but honestly, I don't care. I want to live something I've dreamed about forever."

His eyebrows shot up. "You've dreamed about…about…"

"A guy, spread-eagled on his back on the bed. You can be a stranger, my boss, a vampire or a leprechaun for all I care."

"I pick stranger," he said with a laugh. "Definitely the best option."

She laughed as he started moving for the bed, his expression both intrigued and a little frightened. He paused with one leg on the bed as he turned to look at her.

"You've been dreaming about that?"

"You have no idea," she drawled.

"Apparently not."

"I have hidden depths."

He grinned. "I like hidden depths."

"Really?" she said as she grabbed his belt and her corset ties. "Are you sure? Because I'm about to tie you down."

He barely hitched as he sat down. "I should have expected that."

"You're a smart guy. I bet you kinda already did."

He assumed the position, and yes, his erection was very impressive. Meanwhile, he gave her a challenging look. "Maybe. Do I get to tie you down later?"

She paused, then shook her head. "I don't think so. Because

I don't make promises to strangers." Then she went about the business of tying him to the bed.

It wasn't as easy as it seemed. The bed was ridiculously huge and she didn't know much about knots. But he lay obediently still as she used what she had to rope him down spread-eagled. He could break out easily. A twist of his wrists or a good hard jerk of either leg would release him, but that wasn't the point. It was all about the illusion of having the man strapped down and at her mercy.

Ali stepped back to admire his body. Lying on his back like that, she could see every hill and valley cut by his muscles. He wasn't bulky. She'd known that. But there was a leanness to him that became clear in this position. Especially with the hard jut of his penis.

Wow, he was rather nice-looking. And what was even nicer was the way his penis twitched when she came close, moisture already seeping from the tip. Without even looking at the dark hunger in his eyes, she knew he was half a breath away from throwing her down on the ground and taking her, condom or not.

She grinned. "You need to picture me in a black leather corset, stiletto boots and…um…a whip in my hand."

He flinched. "Really? Can't I just go with what's really here. I like that better anyway."

She blinked, pleased by his statement. So maybe she didn't need to play up the bondage part of it. Maybe she just needed to get to what she wanted to do.

"Here's the thing, Ken doll—"

"Oh, God, don't call me that."

Without even thinking, she reached out and flicked his penis with her fingers.

"Ow!"

"I'll call you whatever I want, Ken doll."

"Okay. Okay. Don't damage the…um…attributes."

She arched her brow. "I've heard guys name it all sorts of different things. I never thought I'd hear *attributes*."

"I have a very literate soul," he said primly.

She smiled. "Okay, literate Ken. Here's what I've always wanted to do. I'm going to climb on top of you—"

"I like that—"

"In reverse."

"Oh. Uh—"

"And if you please me, I'll suck on your…attribute. If you don't please me—"

"I get it. I swear I'll work very hard to be pleasing."

"Good idea." Then she just stood there. Good Lord, was she really about to do this? Sure she'd imagined it a thousand times, but she'd also imagined herself as a kick-ass demon huntress, too. Or as a supersecret spy or even a mild-mannered librarian. She had a rather rich, erotic, literature-inspired fantasy life. But that didn't mean she was any of those things in real life.

"Hey, stranger," Ken said, effectively cutting into her thoughts. "You have to swear to never repeat a word of this to anyone else ever. It would be rather, um—"

"Embarrassing?"

He nodded. "In fact, as far as I'm concerned, this night is *not* happening. I've already forgotten it."

She nodded, realizing that he'd just said the one thing to give her the courage to act on her fantasy. Anonymous sex play it was. And she was thrilled with the idea.

She stepped forward, but he twitched on the bed, holding out his hand to stop her as best as he could.

"Swear!"

"I swear, Ken. Not a word to anyone. You?"

"Never, ever. God, I'd never hear the end of it."

She grinned, then she climbed up on the bed.

13

ALI COULDN'T BELIEVE she was doing this. Sure, the kissing and teasing was easy. She kissed Ken's lips, took her time down his torso, then even played with his enormous erection for a bit. But then she went for what she really wanted.

She straddled his face while keeping her hand and mouth by his penis. He was tied down, so he couldn't move much. Which left her in complete control.

It was amazing. When she wanted to be pleasured, she simply lowered herself to him. His tongue was very clever and completely fearless. No delicate taste for him. He stroked her, sucked her, even thrust his tongue into her, making her go wild above him.

And when it got too much for her, she just lifted up. Her thighs were quivering, her back arching, but nothing stopped her from letting him do such marvelous things to her. Nothing, that is, except when she wanted to make it last. And she wanted to make it fun for him, too.

So she would lift away from him and play with his penis just as he had played with her. Lips, teeth, tongue, she used them all. And had the satisfaction of hearing him groan whenever she engulfed him. His hips were bucking beneath her. And she was so hot that she could barely support herself. Which meant it was time.

She lowered herself back down and felt her eyes roll back in her head as he began stroking her again. Her bottom was tightening, her breath was coming in short gasps, but she didn't forget him. She started to suck on him, doing whatever she could manage for him.

She heard him groan something, but the blood was roaring in her ears. She couldn't hear him. But she felt his last rough stroke of his tongue and she went flying.

Yes!

He was mere seconds behind her, and it was so good. For both of them, she thought, but it was hard to tell beneath her general tide of *yippee!*

She collapsed to the side, flushed and hot and happy. She lay there, luxuriating in the sweetness of it all. Had she just lived out a fantasy for real? Who knew she could be that daring?

Then she cracked open her eyes and saw that he was equally dazed, his gaze unfocused, his body sated. And there was that happy little grin on his face.

"Good?" she asked when she could find the energy to speak.

"Oh, yeah," he groaned. Then with a twist of his wrists, he escaped from his bonds. So much for her knot-tying ability. But he didn't go far. Just enough to stroke his fingers along the outside of her thigh.

"Mmm," she said in response.

She thought she heard his contented sigh, but it might have been her own. Either way, she drifted into sleep for a bit. The next time she opened her eyes was when she felt him shift. Her eyes opened, and she saw he was trying to get a blanket. But it was hard to grab given she was half lying on top of him and they were both on top of the covers.

Forcing herself to move, she straightened to a better position. But then her gaze caught on the pool. And right here was another fantasy. Skinny-dipping. She'd never swum naked outside before. And now was her chance.

"Wanna catch a mermaid?" she asked.

He blinked. "What?"

"That'd be me," she said with a giggle as she scrambled off the bed and headed for the pool. She'd only covered three steps before she heard him leap off the bed. She glanced behind her.

Yes, he had *leaped* off the bed and was dashing right for her. With a squeal of laughter, she scrambled for the sliding door out to the pool. She had it open and was jumping into the water barely an inch away from his grasping hand.

The water wasn't any escape, though. He landed in the pool beside her, and then he had her.

"Caught," he said as he pulled her flush up against his body.

Ooh! Wet, slick, hard manly planes. She liked his naked body in water. Apparently he liked hers, too, because he slowly backed her up against the side of the pool then proceeded to press all his lovely body flush against her.

"You are amazing," he said as he lowered his mouth to hers. But he didn't close the deal. Not yet. Instead, he rubbed his nose against hers and slid his hands down to her hips and thighs, gently tugging them open. She'd already spread her legs to keep herself upright, but with the water below her and him bracing her against the wall, she didn't need them. Without her consciously deciding to do it, she opened herself up to him, sliding her knees up along his flanks.

He didn't waste any time pressing against her. Not into her, just his long, hard length against her folds.

"Oh, God, Ken, you're good."

She felt his mouth curve into a grin. "I've waited my whole life to hear a woman say that to me."

She stroked her thumbs along his cheeks and kissed him

hard and deep. But she froze when she felt his organ shift. She pulled back abruptly, but there was nowhere for her to go.

"Ken!" she cried.

He froze. "I'm clean, Ali. Completely healthy."

She nodded. "So am I, Ken. But...but I can't risk a baby. I won't."

He nodded, though he didn't move his lower body. Not into her, nor away. Instead, he dropped his forehead against hers.

"I want you so bad," he said. "In every way possible."

She smiled, her insides warming to molten. "I've waited my whole life to hear a man say that to me."

He lifted his head and looked her in the eyes. They were so close, she felt as though she could see straight into his soul.

"Do I call down to the front desk? They can bring us up a whole carton of condoms if we want."

She giggled, which had her bobbing precariously close to danger. "A whole carton is rather ambitious, don't you think?"

"Not with you. I feel like I could go forever with you."

She grinned. "You stud muffin, you!" Then she sobered at his intense look. He wasn't interested in teasing right now. She could feel his taut muscles and knew he was holding himself back for her sake. But he didn't want to.

Part of her didn't want him to. Part of her wanted him deep and hard inside her right now. But another part was pushing to the surface, forming words and thoughts that she struggled to express.

"I really like you, Ken," she said softly. "I really like you a lot."

"Good, because the feeling's mutual."

"But—"

He groaned and closed his eyes. "But I'm your boss."

"That doesn't make a damn bit of difference to me," she said, a little startled by her own admission. She didn't believe in office romance. Or rather, she believed that it was a bad idea on all levels. But this had never felt like a real job to her. It was more like that fun thing I did on my summer vacation. So why not bed the hottie in charge? "Really, Ken, it doesn't matter in the least bit to me that you're my boss."

His eyes lightened with hope. "So, does that mean…?"

"It means the problem is deeper than that. And believe me, I know it doesn't make sense given what we just did inside."

He got a wolfish grin on his face. "I liked what we did inside. I liked it a lot."

She felt her face heat. Yeah, that was one dream come true that more than lived up to her expectations. "The thing is, tonight was about distracting you from…everything else."

"Ali—"

"No, listen. Tonight was a moment out of time in a summer out of time."

He nodded but he clearly didn't understand what she was getting at. She didn't blame him. She was groping in the dark for what she meant, too.

"The thing is, doing the rest—the normal rest—"

"Making love."

She bit her lip, an unwelcome rush of anxiety shivering down her spine. "Yeah, doing that isn't about being out of time. It's about—"

"Being serious. With another person."

"For real. Not for fantasy play, but—"

"Real life. Real relationship."

"And then what happens at the end of the summer?"

He didn't speak, but she could tell he understood. And from the way he was easing back from her, she knew neither of them was ready to face those choices. Not yet.

"Ken, I know that doesn't make a lot of sense."

He sighed. "It makes perfect sense. I'm just having a hell of a time convincing my dick."

She laughed, as she knew he'd intended. "That's okay 'cause I gotta say—"

"Don't say it!" he cried, his expression half desperate, half terrified. "If you say you want me, too, nothing is going to keep me off you."

"Oh," she said, biting her lip. That was exactly what she'd been about to say. "How about this? I'm going to get dressed and call a cab."

Now he really did look panicked. "What? Why?"

"Because I've got the first shift tomorrow morning. Because you're the boss."

"You said you didn't care about that."

"I don't. But others will."

He sighed. He knew it was true. She could see it on his face. "Ali, I want to keep seeing you."

"We've got the rest of the summer, Ken. Seeing me is not going to be difficult."

"You know what I mean."

She did. She knew exactly what he meant, and she wanted it, too. But she didn't know how to keep the various parts of her life separate. How did she date her boss, stay professional and still explore this newfound daring of hers? And how did she guard herself so that she wasn't a complete mess at the end of the summer?

"Dinner," she said. "A simple dinner date. Just you and me. We're going to be in Chicago next, right?"

He nodded.

"I've got a cousin there I'm going to pretend to visit. You're going to do business stuff. We'll meet up at a restaurant somewhere and have a normal date."

"I can do that."

"Good. So can I."

"Okay," he said. "A normal dinner date. But I'll pick you up in a cab behind the hotel."

She smiled. "Works for me."

"Just one more thing," he said as he slid right back up to her, bracing his hands on either side of her so that she was trapped between them.

"What?"

"I want to make you come one more time."

"Ken!" she cried, but it was too late. His mouth was on her breasts and he was tonguing her nipple. She arched her back. Her body was already simmering.

Then his hand was between her legs, his fingers thrusting deep inside her. She grabbed on to his shoulders. It was her only support except for where her back was against the tile.

He started rubbing her clit with his thumb. She cried out, her entire body tightening. He was wonderfully relentless. Stroke after stroke built the fire in her blood.

She came, but he was the one who cried out.

"Yeah!"

It was another hour of pool play before she found the strength to leave. Fortunately, that was enough time for her to return the favor to him.

The last thing he said to her before she left was "this is the best damn day of my life. But dinner in Chicago—that's going to be way better."

"Bold words," she taunted from the doorway. "Sure you can live up to them?"

He grinned. "Watch me."

14

"Hey, Ali! Got a second?"

Ali had just waved goodbye to a pair of enthusiastic new customers. And while she knew she was supposed to be cheerful and available to everyone—including fellow members of the cast—what she really wanted to do was go inside the booth and sit down for...oh, a year or so. But instead, she turned around with a smile that was feeling decidedly strained. Only an hour more to go on her shift.

"Sure, Blake. What's up?"

He flashed her one of his megawatt smiles, and, as always, Ali noticed that he was a pretty, pretty man. Blond good looks, a beautifully bulked-out torso and warm honey eyes that were more golden in the sunlight than brown.

"You're off in like an hour, right?"

She nodded. "Hallelujah. My feet are about to give up the ghost."

"Yeah, I get that." Then in a display that was decidedly *not* warrior-like, he dropped the tip of his weapon into the dirt. "And this thing is *heavy*."

"Well, at least you're getting a good tan." His costume required nothing up top and relatively little down below. Some days were leather pants, but in this heat, he'd opted for the leather shorts and boots. If it wasn't for the way he wielded his sword—usually with much more respect than where it was now—he looked more like a calendar pinup guy than Sir Lancelot.

He looked down at his sculpted and now golden-tan abs. "It's a living," he quipped.

"Yeah," she echoed back in the all-too-common actor refrain. "Somebody's got to do it. Thank God it's us!"

He grinned at her, but the expression was short-lived. And, as his dazzling smile faded, he took her arm and led her a couple of steps away from the booth. She thought he was heading for the relative shade of a nearby tree, but Samantha was there chatting with Paul and Tina. Blake did a sudden side step and they were heading for a booth that sold mead.

"Want one?" Blake asked.

Ali shook her head. It wasn't that she disliked mead. The honey-based drink was rather lovely. But the day was sweltering, she was tired and adding alcohol on top would just be dangerous. She'd end up…well, living out her fantasies on top of her boss or something. Not that that hadn't been amazing, but she was with Blake now, not Ken.

"I'll take a lemonade," she said.

Blake nodded and ordered a lemonade for her and a mead for him. He paid, too, which was rather nice. And then when he turned around to hand her the drink, he flashed her his nervous smile. It was every bit as beautiful as his megawatt smile, but it had an underlying note of vulnerability in it. And it made him look all the more boyish in a gorgeous sort of way.

"So, ah," he said, "I was wondering what you're doing tonight. We both get off shift in an hour."

"Nothing much," she said, which was a lie. She intended to relive every moment of what she and Ken had done together from beginning to end. With a special emphasis on the pool play because…well, why not? "What's up?"

"Well, I thought you'd maybe like to go out."

"Sure. Tina said something about—"

"Not with everyone else," he said, cutting in. "Just me. And you."

She blinked, taking a moment to process his words. "Like on a date?"

He winced and put a hand to his heart. "Ouch! You wound me, fair Guinevere."

"No!" she cried, though she wasn't sure what she was reacting to. Had he really just asked her out for a date? "I just didn't think you'd…that I'd…" She swallowed and tried to gather her thoughts. "I just didn't think you were into my type of girl." In the short time they'd been on tour together, Ali had seen Blake go after every gorgeous woman around, and she didn't mean in the tour group. She meant the customers. And in all fairness, he'd flirted with the not-gorgeous ones, too. Old, young, pretty, plain—he'd charmed them all with his smiles, his gentle teases and his infinite amount of charisma. But it was the stunning women with the svelte bodies and the come-hither smiles that he seemed to put extra effort into. To the point that he followed them around like a puppy on a chain.

"I'm afraid to ask—what do you think my type is?" he asked.

"The really pretty ones," she answered without hesitation.

He blinked. "Have you looked in a mirror lately?"

"Now you're just stroking me."

"Wow, Ali. No self-esteem issues there."

Ali bit her lip, both embarrassed and flattered. Then, for some bizarre reason she could not fathom, her gaze slipped sideways to the booth where, inside, Ken was working.

Blake must have seen her look and misinterpreted it because he was quick to reassure her. "It's okay with them."

Ali looked back. "With whom?"

"The bosses. Ken and Paul and Tina. And actually…" He flashed a self-conscious smile. "It was Paul's idea."

"Paul thinks you and I should go out?"

He shrugged. "Publicity campaign, remember? Guinevere and Lancelot dating in real life? If we snap a picture or two, then we can leak it to the blogs."

"So you're asking me out on a date to help the campaign?" She didn't know whether to be insulted or just amused.

"You've got to learn to play the paparazzi. Use them."

She pointedly looked around at the decided *lack* of cameras. "I don't think the rag mags are interested in us."

"So we help them. Come on. Let's just do it." He flashed her his come-hither smile. "I figured I'll get us a cab about an hour after we're done here. We'll go out for a nice dinner. Talk. You know, have a normal, everyday date."

"With the paparazzi."

"No. With a camera."

What could she say? If it helped the campaign, then she had to agree. Especially given Ken's worries the night before. Looking to the side, she caught sight of Paul watching them from his place under the tree. When he realized she was looking at him, he gave her the thumbs-up and an encouraging nod.

She returned the gesture. Anything to help sales. "I guess we're on."

"Great!" Blake said as he hefted his sword. "Dress nice. We'll go someplace that serves steak!"

BLAKE SHOWED UP at her door about twenty minutes late. Not a big deal. She used the time to fuss with her makeup for the ten-zillionth time. She was so used to the stage makeup now that her everyday stuff seemed too light, too subtle, too... not her anymore. But when she put it on heavier, she just looked like a preteen after her first attempt with her mother's cosmetics.

He smiled when he saw her, gave her outfit a once-over and then asked, "Is that what you're wearing?"

She looked down at her bright yellow sundress and brown sandals. She thought she looked nice. "Um, yeah. Why?"

"Oh, nothing. It looks great on you. You look great. I was just thinking that we clash." He gestured vaguely to his black denim jeans and silver silk shirt.

Ali frowned. She didn't think they clashed exactly, but he was right. They certainly didn't match. She was dressed summer dinner and a movie. He was dressed Hollywood night-club chic.

"Did you want me to change? It'll only take me a second."

He bit his lip, obviously thinking. Then he shook his head. "No, I'm being ridiculous. This is supposed to be a real date. And besides, the cab is waiting."

Of course it was. Because he'd been twenty minutes late. But she grabbed her purse, regretting that she didn't have a slim golden date purse. She did at home, but she hadn't brought it with her because, really, she hadn't expected to change months of datelessness while on tour. Guess she'd been wrong!

She watched his face, noting that it remained carefully neutral when she grabbed her brown leather purse with the painted butterflies on it. She'd found it at an art fair years ago and loved it. But it was, sadly, a little worse for wear.

"I'm sorry," she said. "I don't have a different purse."

"What? Oh, that's okay. I barely noticed." A lie if there ever was one. But he was smiling at her and his words were sweet even if she did know he was lying. Then he offered her his arm and they walked down the hallway like Ginger Rogers and Fred Astaire.

They got in the cab and he had to fumble with his iPhone as he tried to pull up the nearest steak house. In the end, she asked the cabbie to recommend someplace. He took them to a lovely restaurant with a fireplace and open grills. It felt rather Texan in its decor, and Ali suppressed a tiny squirm of disappointment. After all, she'd lived her entire life in Texas. It would have been nice to go to a restaurant that served something different.

They were escorted to their table and Blake looked around. "Rustic. Fun, but rustic."

"We can poke fun at the decor," she offered. "Decide if it's *real* Texan or just fake."

"Good idea. The antlers on the chandelier—fake."

"Thank God. I'd hate to think of—" she quickly counted the number of antlers shoved together to decorate the lighting fixtures "—thirty or more bucks being shot just to hide a lightbulb or two."

"The Stetson's real. Just real lame."

She wasn't sure about lame. It was just odd hanging there on the wall for decor. The people she knew who wore cowboy hats actually wore them. But they didn't hang them high on the wall as if they were supposed to be art.

The waiter came, and they placed their drink orders. Then Blake started a running talk on his last gigs. Ali listened, made polite comments, but soon her mind was wandering. She liked Blake and all, and he was certainly hot to look at, but it just wasn't the same as going out with Ken. Mostly because Blake talked about himself. A lot.

"Oh, God," Blake exclaimed, "I've bored you to tears. I'm not surprised. I've been gabbing away, and not finding out more about you. Which was the whole point, by the way. Finding out about you."

Ali blinked. "What? Why?" Okay, so that wasn't the most come-hither response she'd ever made. "I thought this was a publicity event."

"Well, it's that, too," he said. "Speaking of which…" He pulled out his cell phone and aimed it to take a picture. "Lean in close."

She did, and he snapped a picture only to look at it, frown, then make her do it all over again. About a dozen times.

"Blake…" she began as he stared at the last picture.

"It just looks too posed. And the resolution isn't good."

"Because it *is* posed and you're using a cell phone."

He nodded. "It's supposed to look like we were caught sneaking out. Let's get the waiter to take the shot."

And so it was done. Fortunately the restaurant wasn't that busy. The waiter was extremely patient as Blake made him take a zillion different shots. He paged through them as their food came.

"This one will work," he said as he showed it to her. But before she could get a good look, he had flipped to the next. "This one's awful. But you look good."

"I think you always look good."

He laughed. "Nice thought, but good isn't going to get me to Hollywood."

"That's where you want to be?"

"Isn't it obvious? I'm hoping this summer tour will get me some exposure. Better than summer theater, in any event."

"Blake—"

"Actually, it's Brian, but don't tell anyone."

"What?"

He laughed. "My real name is Brian. Boring old Brian. Not even with a *y*. So when I decided to go into acting, I took up a stage name to spruce it up."

"But Brian is a lovely name."

"Maybe. But it's the guy I'm trying to get away from, not who I want to be."

She set down her fork to concentrate better. "I don't understand."

He grinned. "Of course not. Because you're genuine. You like who you are, you're comfortable with it, and you don't look to everyone else for validation."

She blinked. That was unexpectedly deep, and she wasn't at all sure it fitted her. "Of course I want to change who I am. I want to be prettier, bolder, stronger in every way." That was, after all, a big part of why she'd decided to go on this Summer of Strutting in a Corset. It was so she could be more of everything she wanted to be.

He nodded. "But you're just doing the superlatives. I'm doing the *out*."

"Huh?"

He popped a bite of steak into his mouth, then gestured to her with his fork. "You're adding on to who you are. The base is set. You want to be *bolder, stronger*. I want to change completely. Erase Brian and replace him with Blake."

She frowned. "You mean the Blake that has to make sure my clothes match his, the one who is obsessed with pictures of himself and was twenty minutes late to pick me up for our date?"

He winced. "Yeah, sorry about that. I had to redo my hair like three times."

She blinked. His blond locks were gorgeous. "What was wrong with your hair?"

"The mousse was too thick, then too thin, then just all wrong. I was trying some new stuff, but…" He grimaced. "But you don't want to know about that."

"I want to know why you think Blake would be the least bit more interesting than Brian."

He sighed. "See, that's just it. Brian is obsessed with what to do to further his career. Summerfest or promo tour? Blog pictures with a girl or hot single guy at the bar? Brian is all work and no fun."

"And Blake?"

"Well, Blake is casual cool. He's quiet, noble and a real hero. He has to work out and eat well to keep his body working right, but it's not his primary focus. And Blake's career just happens because he's awesome like that."

"That sounds like a fictional character, not a real person."

Blake/Brian shrugged. "It's who I need to be to get ahead."

She processed what he'd said and tried not to compare him to Ken. Sadly, she did, and poor Blake couldn't compete with Ken's quiet confidence. "So, let me take a stab at the particulars. You were gorgeous in high school, and I know you played sports."

He nodded. "But I wasn't very good at them. I mean, I'm coordinated and all, but bashing people around in football just seemed like two walls of testosterone going at it. I really wanted to be a drama geek."

Ali toyed with her mashed potatoes, her thoughts on high school. "I didn't have the chance to play sports. The very idea was laughable in my mind. I'm just too clutzy. So I was the lighting tech."

"And the technical director, I'll bet. The one who makes sure everyone is where they need to be, and that everything is working just the way it ought."

She nodded. "I tried."

"Yeah, actors are lost without someone like you. Directors, too. You're the quiet organizers, and you're never valued enough." He snorted. "Or paid enough."

He had that so right. And he had a point. Even if no one else valued her skills, she needed to be sure she didn't undervalue herself. She lifted her chin, her self-confidence rising a notch. "Thank you," she said. "That was really nice to hear. And something I'm going to have to remember when I go back to my regular job."

He shuddered. "Don't say those horrible words."

She laughed, then turned the conversation back to him. "So what shows did you do?" she asked.

He started listing them. Soon they were lost in the realm of high-school performance stories. They even wandered into some of his football nightmares. Before long, they were both laughing and the meal flew by. As did the desserts. And the after-dinner drinks. Even the cab ride back to the hotel was filled with fun.

It wasn't until they were stopping right outside her bedroom door that things grew serious again. It was because he was going to kiss her. She could see the intention in his eyes, and she couldn't help but marvel at it. She'd been completely dateless for months, and suddenly she had a very full plate of men with Ken and Brian/Blake.

Blake was starting to lean in when she held up her hand. "This is not going to happen. I'm so sorry, but—"

"It has to, Ali. It's not newsworthy unless there's some sizzle."

She leaned back against her door and shook her head. "It's not newsworthy at all. You can't possibly believe that someone will print this."

"Someone will. Bloggers need content all the time. Ali, just once. For the camera."

She folded her arms, but he was already pulling out his camera phone. "I'm not kissing you for a blog."

"Then do it to help my career. Or Ken's product. Or because every bit of publicity helps." He waggled his eyebrows at her. "Come on. They're going to print a picture of two gorgeous people kissing because everybody likes looking at that. Especially if there's a little bit of scandal attached to it. Come on. It's Guinevere and Lancelot making time away from King Arthur."

None of that had the least bit of effect on Ali. None of it except the part about helping sell Ken's product. She couldn't forget how anxious Ken had been yesterday. And that the sales were on par with Leaper, his flopped product. She'd already sworn she'd do everything she could to help. What was the harm in a little kiss between Guinevere and Lancelot? She'd just chalk it up to acting.

"Oh, all right."

"Excellent!" he said. Then he carefully propped up his phone on a nearby fire extinguisher. A moment later, she heard the telltale beep as the timer started ticking down. Then he stepped up to her, pressed his pelvis way too hard against her, and adjusted his face for the right angle. Then he touched her cheek with his hand.

"Blake—"

"Shhh. And for you, it's Brian."

Then he kissed her. He came in too fast and she tried to pull back. But she couldn't and as she tried to push him off, he invaded her mouth. Yuck! Fortunately, she heard the click of the phone camera. Not so fortunately, Blake/Brian wasn't stopping. Or at least he didn't until she shoved him hard.

Sadly, he was really muscular so he barely moved. "Oh, Ali, you are a queen," he murmured.

Then an awful thing happened. Ken came around the corner and stopped dead, his eyes taking in the tableau of Blake with his hand on her face and both their lips wet. He went chalk-pale.

Ali shoved Blake off her. He went easily this time, damn him. Then she took a step toward Ken. "This isn't what it looks like," she said. *Oh, no! Lame, lame, lame!* she screamed at herself.

Meanwhile Blake—he'd shifted very much into his Blake persona—grabbed his phone and aimed it at Ken. "Don't be ridiculous, Ali," he said. "It looks like you and I were making out in the hallway. And got caught." Then as Ken's face shifted into a tight mask of anger, Blake snapped a picture. "And King Arthur is definitely pissed. Perfect!"

Ali all but rolled her eyes. "It's a publicity stunt," she said to Ken. "Ask Paul. It was his idea."

"Not all of it," said Blake with a suggestive leer. "Some parts we thought up all on our own!"

"Stop it!" Ali cried.

Blake laughed as he gave her a jaunty wave. "This is so going to kill on the blogs!" Then he went down the hall to his own room. Which left her standing there in the hallway with Ken.

"I swear. It was for publicity."

"I don't want that kind of publicity."

She might have said more. She would have said a lot more if she could think of what she could say, if she knew how to redeem the situation and if Ken weren't looking as though he'd just been betrayed. Which he had. But she never got the chance. He just shook his head and walked to his room.

"Ken—"

"Good night, Ali." Then he disappeared into his room.

15

KEN WAS CURSING at his computer in the back corner of another comic-book shop, this one in Chicago. The show out on the main mall stage had finished an hour ago. Fortunately, they were in the rising-suspicion stage between Arthur and Lancelot. That meant daily stage fights between the two men as Lancelot's betrayal burned between them both. Obviously, they'd taken a departure from the original legend. According to history, Lancelot and Arthur never fought against each other until they got onto opposite sides of a battlefield. But this made for a better show, especially with Paul playing Mordred and egging on the animosity.

And frankly, Ken really enjoyed trying to beat the hell out of Blake. All he had to do was bring up the memory of Blake pressing Ali up against her hotel door and Ken's aggression level soared. Made for a good show, though both men now had numerous bruises. It also made for good sales, which also helped.

But that was an hour ago. Now he was back at the comic-book shop and dealing with his own personal crisis. He was on the verge of throwing his laptop against the wall when Paul stepped in.

"Sales will pick up," he said. "We're building momentum. You'll see."

Ken blinked, then shrugged, shoving down the panic he felt deep in his belly. "Thanks," he said. "But that's not what I was cursing about."

"The website's fixed, by the way."

Ken leaned back in his chair. "Yeah, I noticed. Thanks."

Paul released a heavy sigh. "Not a problem, since I was the one who broke it in the first place."

Paul had been uploading video from their last event and had managed somehow to crash their online purchasing. The solution had required an emergency call to their web designers and about a thousand dollars, but it was up and running now. And that was only one of about a hundred other such mistakes that Paul had been making in the past month alone.

"Yeah," Ken said slowly. "So what's going on?"

"It was just a stupid mistake. Could happen to anyone."

"Maybe. But there have been a lot of stupid mistakes lately."

Paul nodded but didn't speak. As his friend, Ken didn't want to push. But as his employer with a product to launch and a company to keep afloat, Ken needed some assurances that this type of slipup wasn't going to continue. "Paul—"

"I know I've been a disaster lately. God, I know!" He rubbed his chin and looked absolutely miserable. "But I'm going to figure it out."

Ken exhaled, his mind weighing his choices here. "I can't let this kind of thing continue, Paul. I just can't."

"I know. Just please…give me a little more time. I'm figuring it out."

"Just what exactly are you figuring out?"

Paul shook his head, refusing to answer that question. "One more chance, Ken. If I screw up again, you can fire me. Or better yet, I'll quit."

"I don't want to do that," he said. And he didn't. He and Paul had been together since college.

"I know. And you won't have to. I swear."

He waited. Ken waited. They both looked at each other with the silent communication of longtime friends. And in the end, Ken nodded. Then he turned to the computer and grimaced. He considered trying to figure this out on his own, but he was desperate here, looking for a perfect date evening with Ali. Problem was, he'd been so busy with the events that he hadn't had time to properly prepare for what he wanted to do. Of course, he also had no idea what the perfect date was, so that made it extra hard.

"That doesn't look like sales projections," Paul said from right over his shoulder. "So what's got you scowling if it's not the website or the business?"

Ken glared at the computer screen. He'd been searching restaurants in Chicago, which was like finding a particular ant in an anthill. There were a zillion and he had no idea which one would provide the perfect date. He needed help. And besides, he reassured himself, there was a way to get the information he needed without giving anything away to Paul.

"So," he said, "you're familiar with Chicago, right?"

Paul's eyebrows rose. "I grew up here, but it's a big city. What are you looking for?"

"The perfect date. With a girl I met online."

Paul waited a beat. Then another beat more. Ken could see first relief on his friend's face, then laughter. Ken put on a fierce scowl to forestall the guffaws, but that only tipped his friend over into deep belly laughs.

"Fine. Don't help," Ken groused.

"No, no. I'm sorry. I'm just glad that you're worried about something other than the product. I just never thought it would be a girl you met online."

Ken was about to ask Paul to explain that statement, but then decided he really didn't want to know. "Look, it's not a big deal. I just need to know where to take her."

Paul's humor dialed back to low chuckles. "I assume you're

not talking about the kind of perfect date that can be found on bathroom walls or in the right section of the yellow pages."

"God, no! Look, I promised this girl a perfect evening. Yeah, that was stupid, but now I've got to try and live up to it."

"She's a girl in Chicago? Who?"

So here was the tricky part. Fortunately, Ken had a lie ready. "I met her online a while ago. We've been…emailing. I thought we could get together tonight."

"What kind of online?"

Ken frowned. "What do you mean what kind? On-the-internet online."

"On a dating website?"

"No!"

"Don't get huffy. There are a lot of nice girls on those sites."

Ken looked at his friend, who was working hard to appear innocent. There was a story there, but he didn't have time to pursue it.

"No. It was an…um…a chat forum."

"Really?" There was a wealth of unspoken comment in that one word and all of it was pornographic.

"No, not that kind of forum. It was a comic-book forum. You know. For collectors."

"I thought you'd stopped collecting when you were sixteen."

Mostly true and hell, lying was a lot harder than it should be. "Forget that. Tell me where I should take her for the perfect date."

"Comic-book-collector girl. From the internet. Take her someplace fun and unexpected. Collectors love the unexpected. Not too fancy. You don't want to intimidate her by going too ritzy." Paul snapped his fingers. "Go to Ed Debevic's in the city."

"Ed who?"

"It's like a Chicago landmark. If the date goes wrong,

you can say you've always wanted to try it. That you'll take her somewhere else next time." Paul waggled his eyebrows. "That'll get you set up for date two if you want it."

He'd want it, but he couldn't say that out loud. Not without risking a little too much curiosity from Paul. "You're sure?"

"Positive. It's fun. It's flirty. It's something a comic-book collector would get off on. Go late, when the crowd is more adult. It's way more fun."

No problem there. They weren't going to finish at the mall until almost nine. "What's the address?"

"Here," Paul said, pulling out his phone. "I'll text it to you."

And so it was done. Ken exhaled a sigh of relief, which lasted about two seconds because right after that, Tina came rushing back with an emergency. It wasn't a big emergency— a kid had been snooping around where he wasn't supposed to be and had tripped over some of the wiring. No biggie, but in today's world, it behooved them to make nice with the snooper's parents while involving mall security. Make sure everyone was okay, then cover their legal butt.

Not a big deal, but one that involved all of Ken's attention. Which was why—three hours later—when he was dressed in his best suit, he escorted a dazzling-looking Ali into Ed Debevic's—which was the equivalent of a raunchy burger-and-soda shop.

Oops.

WELL, THIS WASN'T AT ALL what she'd been expecting. Ali looked around the restaurant, seeing the tile floor, the chrome-and-laminate tables, the soda-shop decor. The waitresses were dressed in fifties diner dresses with aprons, and the waiters had on suspenders covered in buttons. She saw a woman in big sunglasses shaped like hearts, a plethora of white paper hats and most surprising of all, two busboys standing on the counter just finishing the song "YMCA," complete with hand motions and hip thrusts.

All in all, it looked like a fun place to get a burger and fries. But it was not at all what she'd expected. Especially since she was wearing her best dress, heels and jewelry, not to mention her makeup, which she'd taken an eternity to apply. Ken looked similarly dressed up in a great gray suit. He also looked equally surprised by the decor.

"I'm going to kill Paul," she heard him mutter.

"You told Paul we were going out?" she asked, a little startled.

"No. I said I had a date with a girl I met in an online chat forum. He recommended this place. For a first date."

"Well, it does look fun," she hedged.

"Ali, I'm so sorry. We can go somewhere el—"

"Did you two get lost looking for the opera?" asked a grinning hostess.

"Um—" Ken began, but the woman had turned to the restaurant at large and started bellowing.

"Hey, everybody! These guys were looking for the Opera House and came here. What should we do?"

The busboy who'd been doing "YMCA" jumped off the counter. "Guess they want an aria."

"We really don't—" said Ken, but it was too late.

The boy began belting out something that had to be in mangled Italian. He was really very good. His voice was pure, and his expressions were perfect comic exaggerations. In truth, he was hysterical in a Jim Carrey kind of way. By the time he finished, Ali was clapping along with everyone else.

"So, lost boy and girl," said the hostess. "Do you want a table in Neverland?"

Ken looked at her, and Ali shrugged. "You can really never have enough onion rings."

"Oh, onion breath," piped in the hostess. "Only a good idea if you both eat." Then she elbowed Ken. "What do you say, big boy? You up for a heaping pile of Screaming O?"

Ali laughed at the double entendre. It wasn't a perfect joke, but the way the woman said *O* definitely suggested *orgasm*.

"Um, yeah. I'm good with Screaming Os." He looked at Ali. "You sure?"

"Can't turn down a good O, can I?"

The hostess grinned. "I never do!"

So it was decided. They were escorted to a booth and settled down on red vinyl seats with menus that were approximately the size of the Dead Sea Scrolls.

"That's a lot of page to say cheeseburger and fries," Ken commented.

Ali grinned. "Well, they have to add in the Screaming Os, too."

"Oh, yes. Shall we share one or go for two?"

"I prefer to share my Os."

Ken was still grinning when the waiter came to take their order. They had to get it in before the hostess started singing "Over the Rainbow." By the time she was done, Ali's eyes were misting with delight. The waitress had been really good!

"I don't know about perfect date," she said, "but we've hit memorable for sure!"

"I was not going for infamy."

"I hope you were going for fun because you've hit that mark."

Ken sobered. "I'll make it up to you, I swear. We'll go someplace classy next time."

Ali shook her head. "Don't apologize. This is fun. Anybody can go classy. It takes a special date to take me over the rainbow."

Ken smiled and seemed to relax. Ali did, too, and for a moment she flashed on her date with Blake. This one was much better.

They started talking generally about the launch. She asked about sales. He hedged while the muscles around his eyes tightened. She took that to mean that sales continued to be sluggish, and he didn't want to think about it. She bit her lip, honestly intending to let it go. But the idea of financial disaster meant different things to different people, and she really wanted to know what it meant to him.

"So, um, let's say the worst happens," she said, watching his face closely for signs that she was treading on unacceptable territory. "How bad is bad? Are you going to end up homeless and eating out of trash cans?"

Ken blinked, then laughed. "Me? No. But I worry about Paul. He's not as careful with his dimes as I am. Besides, Paul has a life. He goes out on dates, wines and dines potential clients—I think on his own dollar, though I tell him to charge the business—and he generally lives the life of a charismatic man in Houston."

"And you?"

Ken shrugged. "I'm the original nerd. My mother died when I was young, so I had years with just me and my dad. He was a mechanic, but should have been an engineer. We liked nothing better than to tear stuff apart in the garage and put it back together. We tore apart lawn mowers and wet/dry vacs to build robots. If it had a motor, we tore it apart and put it back together."

"Sounds like wholesome guy fun."

"It was." His face grew wistful. "I miss those days."

"Is your father gone?"

Ken shook his head. "Worse. He remarried a woman he's crazy about."

Ali laughed. "That's bad?"

"That's great for him. But the two of them do everything together. Antiquing—her passion. Camping—his new hobby. And they're in a his-and-hers bowling league."

"The horrors!"

Ken shrugged. "It's embarrassingly cute to watch."

She nodded, listening to the note of loneliness in his voice.

"But it left you out in the cold? How old were you when they got together?"

"Fifteen. And she had kids, too, one of them troubled. He's okay now, but for a while there he was constantly in trouble."

"So good-boy Ken was left out."

"It wasn't bad. I was a teenager. Old enough to have a life of my own. I just…"

"You just missed being one-on-one with your dad. I get it. The same thing happened when my mom remarried. I like all my brothers, and I'm really close with my cousin. But the times that were just with my mom were really good."

He nodded, but she could tell his mind wasn't on his childhood. A moment later, his words confirmed it. "At this point, I don't think I'm in danger of bankruptcy. Sales are picking up. Slowly, but they're there. It's a good product. People will buy it once word of mouth gets going."

"That's a relief."

He flashed a smile that lasted less than a second. "But there's always a nagging fear of a problem, especially in this economy. Fortunately, I've got things covered for everyone."

"Everyone?" she asked, startled that he had contingency plans for his employees.

"Yeah, if QG goes belly-up, the programmers are covered. With a good recommendation from me, they'll get a job. Same with Tina. She's a genius at organization. Paul has some savings. Not as much as would make me comfortable, but that's him."

"And you?"

"Oh, I'll probably help out my dad at the garage while I figure out what to do next. I've got choices. There are a few companies that would be interested in a man of my background." He took a deep breath. "In short, if disaster happens, it will be okay. It will suck, but it'll be okay."

She reached out and touched his hand. "So why the long

face? Why the constant knot of anxiety between your eyebrows?"

He frowned then wiggled his eyebrows. "I have a knot?"

She smiled. "You do."

"Well," he said, "I guess it's because I don't want it to suck. I want to be really, really successful."

That was logical, but she sensed there was more to it than that. "Come on, Ken." She made pretend hypnotism gestures. "Tell me all."

He laughed, probably because she was trying to be funny, not because she really was. But it didn't matter. It broke the tension and got him talking again.

"I'm a nerd boy. Not quite the computer-programmer geek, but close enough. I was only average at sports, good in school, but nothing special. What I can do—what I want to do—is run a successful business. For my employees who depend on me being not-stupid with the company. For my dad who runs his own business very successfully."

"The garage?"

He nodded. "And then there's the most stupid reason of all."

She leaned forward. "Oh, I'm dying to know. What is it?"

"What every nerd-boy wants: to be rich and successful and get all the hot chicks."

She snorted. "Have you looked at your tour bus lately? You're buried in hotties."

He nodded. "Yeah…"

"But being up to your eyeballs in gorgeous models—both male and female—is not the same thing as taking them to bed."

"Or impressing them. It's very important to us nerds to impress the girls."

She smiled. "You're impressive, Ken. Trust me on this one. You're very impressive." Then she sobered, thinking through his words. "You want a wife, don't you? A house and kids. A dog and the mom-mobile van. The whole American-dream package."

"Yeah, I do. What about you? What do you dream about at night?"

She didn't have to think long about her answer. Despite the variety in her sexual fantasies, the truth was they all boiled down to one thing. "I dream about a man who loves me. That's it in a nutshell. A good man."

"To marry and have kids with? Or to rock your world in bed?"

She grinned. "Can't I have both?"

"In my world? Absolutely." Then he tilted his head and frowned at her. "Question is, why haven't you done it already?"

She blinked, startled by his question. "What do you mean?"

They had to wait a moment as their food was served. It was great. Good cheeseburger, better onion rings. They both took a few moments to stuff their faces. But all too soon, Ken was back on topic and Ali was surprised by how difficult his questions were for her.

"You're smart, organized and beautiful. College boys aren't that dumb. You would have been hit on. A lot."

"Frat boys hit on anything with boobs."

"It wouldn't have been just frat boys. There had to be others."

She shrugged and tried to take refuge in her food. But his words had unsettled something inside her. Eventually, she started to answer, though the words were difficult to get out.

"I took the risk once. It was a bad one. He was a jerk, and it nearly destroyed me when he left."

"You didn't kick him to the curb?"

She shook her head. "No, I didn't. I didn't have the strength. And I kept thinking it would somehow magically work out." She sighed. "You don't understand what I was like as a kid. I was home alone all the time until I was ten. Sure there were babysitters and stuff, but mostly I just lived in books. Then suddenly my mother remarries and I've got siblings. Younger brothers who were into everything. When I wasn't babysitting, I retreated into my room and read some more."

"Sounds lonely."

She toyed with an onion ring. "I was surrounded by family. Too much family compared to what I was used to. It wasn't until college that I forced myself out of my room."

"College does that to a person. Gets them out of their comfort zone."

"That's when I ended up feeling lonely. Then I met The Jerk who hadn't started out as an ass. A semester later I had to leave college because the money ran out, and well…"

"A bad situation became worse?"

She nodded. "It took me a while to get over The Jerk, then I was working full-time and I just don't meet that many guys."

He dropped his chin on his palm and looked at her. His expression was serious, but it was his eyes that really caught her. He was looking—at her—with all of his considerable attention and focus. It made her feel important. It also made her squirm.

"What are you thinking?" she asked.

"That there's something you're not telling me."

"There really isn't."

"It's okay. You don't have to tell me."

She shook her head. "No, I'm serious. I'm not hiding anything. There really just isn't that much to me. I read, I work, I…don't meet guys who ask me out on dates."

"I asked you out."

"A minor miracle, in my world."

"Blake asked you out."

Her food caught in her throat. "It was for a publicity stunt. He said Paul wanted us to do it."

Ken nodded, his expression excruciatingly neutral. "I know. But how did the date go?"

"It was fine except for posing for a zillion candid photos." Then she touched his hand and told him the truth. "The evening was fine, but it wasn't an evening with you."

His eyes widened, and he looked at her with those big puppy-dog eyes. Then he blinked, and the image was gone. No more puppy dog. Instead, it was a man there and his eyes were dark with hunger. The shift was so abrupt, she was momentarily taken aback by it. At least her mind was. Her body was way ahead of her, already growing liquid as she looked at him.

He slowly set down his fork. "I know I'm your boss—"

"Don't care."

"And I had wanted to keep this relationship quiet."

She nodded. That was just prudent.

"But if you want, I'd like to step things up a bit."

She swallowed, her heart speeding up until she felt it pounding in her throat. "Step it up?"

His smile came slowly, but when it hit its peak, he was more handsome than she'd ever seen. Gone was his usual geek-boy persona. The person before her now was all man. "Step it up, Ali. With me."

She looked into his eyes and saw his absolute certainty in what he was asking. He wanted a relationship with her. The kind that could end in marriage and that mom-mobile in the suburbs. She saw it right there in his eyes, and she couldn't believe how excited she was by the thought. "Yes," she suddenly forced out through her very dry throat.

"Yes?"

She swallowed and nodded.

He looked down at her plate, which had her half-eaten burger on it. "You still hungry?"

She shook her head.

"Dessert? Coffee? Want anything else here?"

Again she shook her head.

He grinned and waved to the waiter. "Check, please!"

16

KEN DIDN'T WANT TO BLOW THIS. He didn't want to screw up and say something stupid. On the other hand, he didn't want to be silent when he ought to be saying something. Which was a real problem for him because his brain was always telling him either to say something or not to say something, and the whole thing was rather unreliable when dealing with women.

So he went with his gut instead, even though it was tied in knots at the idea of confessing this particular sin.

They were outside the restaurant waiting for a cab. They were holding hands, which was the only reason he wasn't completely out of his mind with lust. She was keeping him steady and his brain relatively quiet. Mostly, he was enjoying the feel of her hand in his while his boner was gleefully anticipating another night like the last one they'd spent together.

But first he had to confess. So he took a deep breath and turned to her.

"I, um, well…did you ever wonder why you've always had a room to yourself this trip? When the other girls have to share?"

She blinked, then slowly shook her head. "I thought it was because I was the lead woman or something like that. Or because the other girls were friends."

Ken shook his head. "The others didn't know one another

before the tour and, yeah, I used the excuse of you being the lead female."

Always quick to pick up on the nuances, Ali lifted her chin. "The excuse?"

He nodded. "Despite my big stand on being your boss, I was hoping something like this would happen. And since Paul and I are sharing…" He let his voice trail off as she understood that he'd been planning to bed her from the very beginning. "I just didn't want it to be with Blake."

"I'm so sorry about all of that. I only did it—"

"For the publicity, I know. I don't know what Paul was thinking."

She released a breath. "So you did talk to Paul."

Ken nodded, then he took a deep breath. Might as well confess it all. "The truth is I heard Tina and Samantha talking about it. They said it was a date. Then, I guess I kinda stalked you. I waited for you guys to return and watched from around the corner." He grimaced. "I know. Real mature."

"I know this sounds stupid, but I only did it for you. Because Blake swore it would help get publicity for the game."

He felt a slight weight roll off his shoulders.

"And for the record," she continued, "I hated kissing him. Hated it."

A huge weight dropped to the ground with a thump. Of course, his conscious mind had known that. After all, she'd just said she wanted to up their relationship. Ergo, she had picked him over Blake. But it was really good to hear her say it. Really, really good.

He released his breath in a long, happy sigh. "And now, also for the record, we don't have to do anything—"

She stretched up on her toes and kissed him. It was a full kiss, one where she teased his lips with her tongue. And then she opened up completely as he wrapped his arms around her and dived right in. God, he loved kissing her. She seemed to love everything he did. Little nips, hard thrusts, it didn't matter. She was always flushed and breathless when he stopped.

"So…" he said when they finally separated. "You're okay with going back to your hotel room?"

She smiled and he caught a flash of real mischief in her eyes. "I'm so okay with it, I'm annoyed with the cab for taking so long."

Good. They were on the same page. "I, uh, I brought condoms this time."

She bit her lip and looked adorably flushed. It didn't take long for him to guess why.

"You have some, too, don't you?"

She shrugged. "I've had them for a while now."

He turned her to face him more fully. "Tell me now—while I still have some blood in my brain—tell me what you like."

She frowned. "Like?"

"In bed. I want to know. I mean—"

"You want to rock my world?"

He nodded. "Exactly."

Her tongue went between her teeth and again, there was that shy sparkle of mischief. "We got to live out my fantasy last time. Don't you think it's your turn?"

"You are my fantasy," he answered honestly. And he was a little startled by the truth in those words.

"But you have to have something more than that. A wish, a fantasy, something. You were a teenage boy, weren't you?"

He did. It was just that he wasn't sure she'd go with his idea of fun.

"Come on," she said with a laugh. "Spill it."

"In front of a mirror. Me behind. I want to see every part of you as…well, you know."

She grinned. "Yeah. And…um, okay."

"Okay?"

"Okay."

Okay!

THEY MADE IT TO Ali's room in record time, but it wasn't fast enough to keep Ken from doubting himself. He wanted this to be perfect for her. He wanted to *be* perfect for her. Consciously, he knew it was an impossible dream, but that didn't stop him from feeling inadequate to the task.

They were just inside her hotel-room door when he turned her to stand face-to-face with him. But he couldn't look at her directly yet, so he closed his eyes and dropped his head onto her forehead.

"I know performance anxiety is not macho," he said.

She laughed. "I've never been considered macha anyway, so why start now?"

He blinked, taking a moment to realize she was confessing to her own insecurities. "No," he said. "I was telling you I'm nervous. The last time was so incredible…" He shook his head, still awed by that particular memory.

"That was fun, wasn't it?" she whispered and even if he couldn't see her mischievous smile, he heard it in her voice.

"I want this to be equally good for you."

She blew out a low whistle. "That's a pretty tall order."

He groaned. "I know."

Then she pushed up on her toes enough to give him a quick kiss. "So how about we make this about fulfilling your fantasy?"

"But—"

"Come on…" she said, taking hold of his hand and drawing him deeper into her bedroom. "Tell me it from the beginning."

He felt his face heat to burning. "Really? You want to hear it…in detail?"

She glanced over her shoulder at him. Lord, she was beautiful when her eyes sparkled like that. "How else can I act it out?"

He turned her around again, pulling her into his arms. She warmed him. She got him to stop thinking. She made everything seem fun and good.

So he kissed her. He touched her cheek, lifted her face just enough and then pressed his mouth to hers. She opened easily to him, and he felt as if she were giving him this great gift. His fantasy. But also something more. Her heart.

It was a silly, girlie thought. He did *not* think about hearts and love and things like that. Sure he wanted it, but mostly he lived in a world of accounting tables and product-performance charts.

But with her, he thought of things like that. And he wanted things like that. And he wanted...to slowly take off her clothing. Slowly. Sensuously. While he watched every inch of her—front and back—with the help of the mirror.

"Are you sure you're up for this?" he whispered. His hands were already busy, stroking her shoulders, sliding down her arms and then reaching up behind her back. He had the zipper of her dress in his fingers, but he didn't pull.

Meanwhile, she bit her lip as she slid her hand down his belly until she outlined his erection. "I think we're both up for it."

That was all the confirmation he needed. So while he could still think—and coordinate the use of his hands—he pulled down the zipper of her dress.

She wore a very silky-feeling dress with a V-neck in front and a flirty skirt. There was some sort of pattern on it, but he really didn't care what. What he noticed was the way it showed off her legs and emphasized her cleavage. And now, wonder of wonders, he was watching it slip off her shoulders and down.

The hotel half mirror was behind her and he stood facing her, so he got to see both sides as a white lacy bra appeared and matching shortslike panties cupped her very sexy ass.

He stepped backward to admire and ran smack into the edge of the bed. She laughed as he stumbled slightly, and then she shoved him quick and hard on the shoulders. Down he went onto the bed, sitting there while she stood tall and proud before him.

"Take off your jacket," she ordered.

He grinned as he complied. He liked this take-charge attitude of hers. Then, before he could fully shed his jacket, she got hold of his tie and dragged him forward for another full kiss. She ended it much too soon for him, and stepped back to look at him.

"You going to dance for me?" he asked.

She blinked, apparently startled. Then he watched the blush creep up her chest into her face. "Uh…" she began.

"Don't worry about it. Dancing's overrated. I really like—"

"To watch?"

"To touch. Hard to do if you're moving all around." Then he fitted words to action. He pulled her toward him by her hips, extending his fingers around her waist and curving them down toward her very lovely bottom. "You have the smoothest skin."

She smiled, but didn't speak. She was too busy letting her eyes drift shut as she released a soft "mmm." Then he felt her belly tremble beneath his fingertips, and his dick nearly leaped off the bed in response.

"Keep that up," he growled, "and I won't last long."

She opened her eyes slowly and damned if she didn't look like a queen awakening by slow inches. "Then you'd better get undressed."

He nodded, unable to respond. His fingers fumbled on his tie, but she helped him. And together they got him out of his shirt, as well. Then she pushed his hands away as she bent to undo his belt buckle. He didn't mind, especially as he got quite the view of her behind in the mirror. In fact, he scooted back on the bed just so she would have to lean over more.

She knew what he was doing, of course. And rather than be shocked, she looked up at him, winked and then wiggled her bottom.

Again, he nearly jerked off the bed. But this time she was ready for him. As his hips thrust of their own accord, she took hold and let him push through the circle of her hand and fingers.

"Oh, God, Ali. I don't want this to end too soon."

"Not a problem," she said, as she gave him a squeeze that had his toes curling into the carpet. He didn't remember kicking off his shoes, but at some point he had. Ten seconds later, he thought *to hell with it* and just stripped out of everything.

He sat there naked on the bed while she gave him a tease of a smile. "That is a lovely sight," she said. "And before I forget…"

She slowly spun around on her toe and sashayed her way to her purse. Bending over from the waist, she kept her bottom high as she rooted around in her purse and finally produced a foil-wrapped condom.

"Want me to put it on you?" she asked without straightening.

"I want you to stay right like that," he answered. Then he stood up. Lord, it would be so easy to slip behind her. He wanted to, but he wanted it to last, too. And be good for her.

So while she was still bent over, he stepped near enough to fondle, but not close enough to be tempted where he didn't belong without a condom.

He took his time. He stroked her legs and slid his hands over her delicious ass. Her legs were strong, her bottom tight and high. And then he gently caressed his way up her back to pop her bra.

Then, while she remained frozen in place—except for her excited, breathy pants—he pulled off her bra and began to fondle her breasts.

"I love these," he said as he tweaked and pulled at her nipples. "I love the weight of them in my hands," he said as he cupped and lifted both breasts. "I love the sounds you make as I squeeze them." She was making them now. Soft gasps. Not a moan, not a vocalization at all. Just hitching gasps.

He felt the tension building in her. He wasn't sure how

he knew except that he had made a study of her body as he touched her. His thigh was pressing against hers and he could feel as she relaxed her legs enough to push back against him. She was growing really excited just from breast play, and he loved it.

She held up the condom. "Put it on," she gasped.

"Not yet. I'm not done yet."

She groaned, but in a good way. He stayed with what he was doing for a bit. Then he helped her straighten up even as he slid her panties all the way down. She was wearing strappy sandals that added about three inches to her height. That ought to be about enough, but he wasn't sure.

"Come over here," he said as he pulled her to the full-length mirror. He stood behind her, placing her so she faced the mirror as he stood behind. He could see both excitement and anxiety in her expression, and it took him a moment to realize why.

"Condom," she said, holding it out.

This time he agreed, and she watched as he ripped open the packet and rolled it on. It was cold and not at all what he wanted, but it warmed quickly enough. And it would lead to something much, much better.

Especially as she grinned at him. "Thank you," she whispered.

He frowned a moment. "For putting on a condom?"

She nodded. "Some guys don't like using them."

He looked at her face and guessed that her last boyfriend had been one of "some guys." "Well," he grumbled back, "some guys are assholes."

"Thank God you're not," she said as she reached up to kiss him. She pressed her mouth to his and he took full advantage of it, thrusting into her mouth and toying with her tongue until he was the one who had to break it off. Hell, she made him so hot he was going to explode!

Trying to cool himself off, he broke away and put his naked

backside against the wall. It was cold and really not that comfortable, but that was the point. Meanwhile, he turned her back to his front, facing the mirror.

And there, full-length in front of him, was her body in glorious detail. Full breasts, narrow waist, strong legs and at the juncture of her thighs, that coil of hair that seemed to beckon him.

He looked back up to her eyes in the mirror. He met her gaze and watched as she wet her lips. "What is your fantasy, Ken? What happens now?"

You tell me that you love me.

The words echoed through his thoughts enough to jolt him out of his lust. Holy moly, he hadn't been thinking love. Or at least he didn't want to be thinking love right now. It was too soon. This was a summer promotional tour, for God's sake. He knew that at the end of the summer, the whole tour would feel surreal. As though it had happened in a dream. It was ridiculous to start thinking words like *love* with a woman on a summer tour. Ridiculous, and yet his mind still echoed with the word.

Love.

She must have sensed his fear. She must have known his heart had sped up to near-lethal levels because she turned to look over her shoulder at his face. "Ken? Are you all right?"

He forced himself to nod, and then gently turned her back to the mirror. He could see that his reflection was pale. He could also feel that he was starting to recover as he forced that word out of his brain.

"Let me look at you," he said. And he did. He looked at her breasts as he cupped them again in his hands. He looked at her tight nipples, and he listened to her gasp. He looked at her curls as he slipped his fingers between her legs. And he felt her moisture as he began stroking her there.

By the time she let her head drop back against his shoulder and her legs eased wider, he had nearly forgotten *that* word. Instead, he felt her writhing against him. He heard her keening cries as the tension in her body built. So close, but he didn't want her to finish without him.

So he pulled his hand back and gently nudged her to support her weight. He urged her legs open and pressed her hands forward to frame the mirror. Looking over her shoulder, he had such a vision. Her breasts reflected in front of him. Her narrow waist and then a peek at her curls. Then he helped her adjust her hips as he pushed inside her.

"You feel so great," he groaned. Tight, wet, sweet.

"I was about to say the same thing," she said, her words short and breathy.

He was a little too tall for this and the angle was wrong for full movement, but that was the point.

"Ali—" he began, but then she gripped him with her internal muscles. Tight and hard, and it nearly made his head explode. "Oh, God!" he gasped.

She chuckled and he felt the rhythm of her laughter all the way through his organ and up his spine.

"Ali!" he gasped as she did it again.

She was moving too fast. He was going to come long before she did. And so he did the only thing he could manage. He kept his hips as still as possible so that he wouldn't unseat himself, and then he began to stroke her.

He started with her breasts, but in the end, he had to abandon them as he stroked her cleft. Up and down as she writhed on his pole. He didn't move. *Don't move!*

Her legs were tightening, her head was thrown back. What a sight she was! He stroked her. Faster and harder. And with a free hand, he pinched her nipple.

Again and...

She cried out, her entire body rolling as she came. He wanted to watch. He wanted to just feel what happened as she came apart, but it was too much. Her contractions kicked him over the edge.

He thrust deep, exploding.
And it felt like…
Love.

17

THE WAVE HIT—again—and Ali cried out. They were on her bed, and her head pressed back into her pillow, her pelvis ground hard into Ken's and her legs gripped him as the wave peaked and released, peaked and released.

Damn, they were good at this.

Fantasy sex had been great in front of the mirror. But they hadn't stopped there. They'd started talking as they cuddled close in her bed. And then postsex talk had progressed to caressing, then kissing. And in rather speedy progression, they'd gone on to another mind-blowing orgasm. Lord, she might even have screamed, and she was *not* a screamer. Well, not usually.

Ken collapsed, politely taking his weight onto his arms as he slid sideways. He groaned as he did it, tugging her close as he rolled to his side.

"Best queen ever," he said.

"Best boss ever," she returned.

He groaned. "Don't call me that. Not in bed."

"What if I want to play out my slutty secretary/horny boss fantasy?"

He stilled suddenly and cracked an eye. "Seriously? You have a—" He couldn't even say the words. Fortunately, he looked intrigued, not horrified.

She grinned. "I have a *lot* of fantasies."

"Marry me. We'll pick a different fantasy every night."

Ali didn't answer. The words *marry me* had effectively ended all power of thought or response. Especially since he had said it in jest. It wasn't that she had expected them to get married or anything. But his words blindsided her with their power. She could absolutely see marrying him. And so the idea that he could joke about it—that the idea was funny to him—well, that hurt. And the power of that hurt was what stunned her.

To his credit, he realized that he had screwed up. In truth, he looked as if the words shocked him almost as much as they had surprised her. But he was the one who'd put it out there. And so he was the one scrambling to recover.

"Uh…I mean…I—" He swallowed. "Oh, shit. I know better than to joke about that sort of stuff. I'm so sorry."

She forced a smile and a chuckle that didn't come off so well. "It's fine, Ken. Not a problem. I knew you were joking."

"Um, yeah. I was, but…" He rubbed a hand over his face. "But I brought it up. So let's talk about it."

Panic clutched her chest and she desperately wanted to run away. But they were wrapped together, their legs still intertwined, their faces just inches apart. She couldn't move away without making things ten times more awkward.

So she turned her face into her pillow and faked a big yawn. "It's really late, Ken."

"Don't run from me, Ali. Not now, after I've dropped a bombshell."

She peeked up at him. Nice that he could be so mature about the topic when she was acting like a three-year-old.

"Okay. We'll talk," she said as she forced herself to sit up. She pulled the sheets with her, covering her torso enough to be decent. He shifted to accommodate her, allowing her to pull the covers however she wanted, adjust them however she wanted, *delay* however she wanted. But in the end, she gave in. "So, Ken, what do you want to talk about?"

He gave her a grimace, but nodded. "Okay, here it is. I want to get married someday. I want kids. I want a successful company making a lot of money, and I want that with someone who can laugh with me."

She blinked, startled by his words. "Laugh?"

He nodded. "Yeah. Look, let's be honest, I'm not going to suddenly metamorphosize into a man with movie-star looks."

She smiled. "I think you look just fine. Besides, I'm not going to suddenly look like Michelle Pfeiffer either."

"Thank goodness. Blondes have never been my thing."

"Liar. All guys want blondes with big boobs."

"Yeah, all guys who are fourteen. But then we grow up and become more discriminating." He leaned forward and gave her a kiss. "Believe me when I say you look fine to me." He lengthened the word *fine* so that she felt like he was calling her both beautiful *and* sexy. How cool was that?

She would have deepened the kiss. She would have pulled him closer for another round of fun sex play. But he was being serious, so he pulled back.

"Okay, your turn."

"What?"

"Your hopes and goals and stuff. I told you mine."

"What do I want in a man?" She sighed as she tried to seriously answer the question. She ended up with one thing. "I just want someone who loves me no matter what."

"That's it?"

She shrugged. "Last boyfriend had conditions. He loved me if I cooked for him, cleaned the apartment and generally took total care of him and didn't challenge him too much."

"Loser. Him, not you."

She nodded. "Yeah, and when he dumped me, I was devastated."

He sobered. "I'm sorry, Ali. You deserve so much better."

"I agree. I am not that little girl anymore. I'm a woman who wants marriage and kids someday. With a guy who loves me."

He looked at her a moment, his head cocked to the side as if he were listening to something underneath her words. He probably was because a moment later, he'd accurately read her subtext.

"You mean you've gotten used to expecting so little from life."

She straightened. "Not true! And certainly not anymore." She huffed as she slumped backward. How did she explain this? "This summer has changed me. I'm stronger than I ever was before. I feel bolder, happier." She shot him a coy look. "Sexier."

"That's good."

"No, that's great. For the first time in my life I feel like I can go for what I want. If I can strut around in a corset in front of screaming fans, then I can also look my boss in the eye and demand a raise. I know the two don't exactly correlate—"

"Sure they do."

"But I can do it."

He touched her cheek with his index finger. It was a soft stroke with exquisite tenderness, and she couldn't help but close her eyes to feel every sensation as his finger slid to her lips. When he spoke, it was in a whisper.

"When I was younger and things got hard, I retreated into gaming."

"I read. Book after book after book. I read while I babysat my brothers. I read between classes and at lunch. I even read at my fast-food job when the drive-through lane got slow."

"So way back when, what were your dreams?"

She laughed. "You mean other than being a vampire huntress?"

"Yeah. Let's stick to the nonparanormal right now. Did you want to be a brilliant scientist with a Nobel Prize?"

"I hate science."

"First woman president?"

"Failure at politics. Too shy." Then she smiled in memory. "When I was little, I wanted to be a writer."

"There you go—"

"I tried it. Even had a poem published in a newsletter. But it was too hard and not what I wanted."

"Okay. Well, good. You tried something. It didn't work out, but you tried."

"And I was trying at college, but the money ran out. I ended up at the hospital and I've been there ever since. I'd like to finish school, but don't know in what."

"How about business? Marketing?"

She thought about it. A few years ago, her knee-jerk reaction would be that she wasn't smart enough to run a business or a marketing department. But after working under the head of the hospital PR department, she knew that she could do that job. And if she could run a PR department, what was stopping her from running a whole business?

"What are you thinking?" he pressed.

"I'm thinking that I should believe in myself more. That I should have believed a long time ago but that it took strutting around in a corset for me to see that I can do a lot more than I ever thought."

His eyebrows shot up. "Wow! I thought it would take way more time to get you there."

"I'm shy, not stupid," she said with a laugh. Then she sobered because he was still looking at her with a very serious, steady gaze.

"What would it take, Ali Flores, for you to reach for your dreams? For you to apply all those smarts and focus on something you really want? What would it take?"

The answer came to her quietly and very slowly. It was as if the word had to work its way through all her automatic denials until she heard it in her head. And even then, her heart quailed and her body tried to fight it.

"Ali? What are you thinking?"

That she needed *him*. By her side, pushing her to believe in herself every day for the rest of her life. But she couldn't say that. It would be too bold, especially after his "marry me" mistake. So she opted for something that he would accept. A partial truth, if not a full confession.

"I think I need to make a plan. I'm good at plans."

He nodded. "And?"

She shrugged. "And then I need to carry it out."

He smiled at her. "Have you ever done this before? Have you ever sat down and written out a plan for yourself?"

"Lots of times," she answered. "I've got a plan for how I'm going to pay off my car. How I'm going to get a coffee table. For how I'm going to manage which project at work."

"But nothing for your life. Why?"

"Because," she said, and this time she could see from his face that he wasn't going to accept a partial truth. So she told him it all. "Because then I'd have to do it. And I think I was just too tired to go for it. I've had a job since I was sixteen. I worked in college, too, plus babysitting for my mom because she needed the help. It's only in the last couple years that I've worked at one job and not filled in every waking moment with some other type of work."

"So are you rested? Are you ready to take control again?"

"I am," she said. A quiet excitement started to build inside her as she thought of all the possibilities before her. Suddenly the future was rich with possibilities instead of filled with frightening pitfalls. "After all, that's what this summer was about. Me stepping out of my comfort zone to do something new."

He stroked her face again. This time he used his full palm. "You could do so much, Ali. I can't wait to see where you go."

"Me, too," she whispered. She would make her plan. She would juggle the finances. She would see about a business degree or at least finishing college. And then, look out world! Ali was on her way!

With those thoughts spinning in her mind, she wrapped her arms around his chest. Together, they snuggled down into the sheets.

"You're good for me," she said.

"Well, it's about time someone was."

She smiled as he pressed a kiss to the top of her head. She closed her eyes, her head on his shoulder. And as she drifted off to sleep, she allowed herself to dream the big dream. Not college or even multi-zillionaire business. No, the big dream was being just like this, falling asleep on his shoulder, while they built their awesome future together.

Good thing she knew this was just a summer-tour fling. Otherwise, she might really be tempted to take everything that had just happened much too seriously. She was busy convincing herself of that when Ken's cell phone rang. Five minutes later, Ken was white as a sheet and Ali was driving them both to the hospital.

_18_

KEN RUSHED THROUGH the hospital emergency-room doors with Ali at his side. He quickly scanned the waiting area and found Paul sitting there, unnaturally still as he stared into the depths of a dark cup of coffee. Ken went to his friend's side immediately, but walking across the reception area took a little bit of time. About twenty steps, but it was enough for the pit in Ken's stomach to yawn wider and darker.

Paul wasn't moving. He wasn't making notes, checking his smartphone or doing any of the things that Paul did. He was just sitting motionless. And that meant things were bad. Really bad.

Without even thinking about it, Ken reached for Ali's hand. She was there at his side, her response immediate. And as they made it to Paul, she squeezed his hand for support.

"Hey," Ken said as he settled in the seat beside his best friend.

"Hey," came Paul's lackluster response. Then the man seemed to pull himself together. He took a deep breath and went into what Ken called his executive mode. He summarized the facts—just the facts—in a quick and brutal fashion. "Tina was…was doing something with the costumes. I don't even know what. Had to get them patched or something, but she took a cab. She was on the way back to the hotel when it happened. The cab got hit by another car. T-boned. Cabdriver was killed instantly. Other driver soon after."

"Oh, no," whispered Ali. This time it was Ken who squeezed her hand.

"Tina's alive, but she's beaten up pretty bad. She's headed for surgery."

"Surgery?" Ken asked.

Paul nodded. "Her legs are real bad. They've got to pin them and stuff. I...um...I wrote down all the details." He fumbled in his pocket and came out with a crumpled napkin. He held it out, and Ali took it from Paul's shaking hand.

Ali was the one who opened it up and showed it to him. The list was pretty extensive, but it all looked fixable. Assuming a shattered tibia and fibula were fixable.

"Is she in a lot of pain?" Ali asked.

Paul nodded and if possible, he went even more pale. "They doped her up pretty good, but she was screaming." He took a shuddering breath. "I was the contact person she gave to the paramedics. They called me on her cell phone and I could hear her screaming in the background. I could hear it."

Oh. Wow. Tina was not a screamer. Not a pain-screamer, that is. He didn't know about the rest. And his mind was just circling on stupidities because he couldn't process the rest. Tina. Car accident. Surgery.

"She'll be fine," Ken said to himself as much as to Paul.

Paul nodded. "She's a fighter."

"She's amazing," Ali said. "At everything. And that means she's strong. She'll pull through this." She held up the list. "Paul, none of this is life-threatening. Horrible. Going to keep her off stilettos for a while. But she'll pull through just fine."

Paul looked up, his heart in his eyes. "I know. I just keep thinking what if—"

"Don't go there!" Ali's voice was strong. Like superhero-strong. She had the ring of command and both Paul and Ken immediately responded to the tone. They straightened in their seats and looked at her. Meanwhile, she kept her eyes level and her voice calm. "She's alive and going to get better. I'm going to talk to the nurse over there and figure out what we can do. What's going on. You guys just sit here. I'll be right back." Then she glanced at Ken. "Do you want any coffee or anything?"

Ken flashed her a grateful smile. "No. I'm good, but thanks. And, um, thanks for…" He gestured toward the nurse and the crumpled napkin in Ali's hand.

"No problem," she answered. Then she put her hand on Paul's shoulder a moment before turning and heading toward the reception area.

"Hell," said Paul. Nothing more. Just hell.

Ken nodded. "Yeah."

ALI HAD NEVER SEEN Paul look so awful. In fact, she couldn't remember a time she'd seen him *not* moving, not smiling, not…anything. It was startling and made her wonder if there was more to Paul and Tina than anybody knew.

Her gaze traveled to Ken who was a rock of moral support. But he was also a guy, so that meant he sat there looking awkward and glancing at her. He was also surreptitiously making notes on a pad that appeared from somewhere. For all she knew, it was Paul's and Ken had just commandeered it.

Either way, she knew what he was doing. After all, he couldn't help Tina or Paul, except to sit there in case someone needed something. But he could make sure that all of Tina's hard work didn't go to waste. He was making lists of things that would have to be handled. Truthfully, she was, too. And between the two of them—plus a brilliant medical staff—she was sure everything would work out.

Ken looked up at her, and she smiled encouragingly at him. Tina was in surgery, the dawn was creeping over the city and soon the rest of the troupe was going to appear with their bags packed wondering where the two bosses were. She would have to figure out what they were going to do soon. The schedule was packed pretty tight. They couldn't afford to stay here.

She pulled out a water bottle from the vending machine and brought it over to Paul, forcibly putting it in his hands.

"Hydrate," she ordered.

He blinked, focused on her, then obeyed. After taking a few obligatory sips, he focused on his surroundings, his eyes narrowing as he looked out the window.

"It's morning."

Ken nodded. "I know."

"We're supposed to be leaving soon. We can't miss those dates. We need them. The sales—"

Ken squeezed his friend's arm. "I know, Paul. I know."

"But—"

"I can drive us," Ali interrupted. "I can drive the bus."

Both men cut their gazes to her. "You can? It's not the same as a car, you know. We had to take special classes and practice. A lot." That was Ken, his head tilted slightly, but his expression was hopeful. He, Paul and Tina were the three who had been driving the bus.

Ali grimaced. "Okay, *I* can't drive the bus, but I was checking on the internet. We can hire a bus driver. It shouldn't be too expensive."

"Great idea," said Ken. "Do it."

Paul grimaced. "You should go, too. You can do some of the driving."

Ken shook his head. "I'm not leaving."

"Don't be ridiculous—"

"Tina's my friend, too. I'm not letting her wake up alone in a strange hospital in a strange city."

Paul nodded slowly, his gaze slipping back toward the surgical wing. "She's got family. We need to call them."

Ali cleared her throat, feeling awkward, but knowing they needed someone to handle these things right then. "I've got her cell phone and her planner. The hospital got them from the police. All the information is there. I'm just waiting until a little later in the morning to start calling."

Paul frowned. "You got her planner?"

She nodded, but she didn't want to show it to him. There was blood on it. "Yeah. She kept everything in there."

"Not everything. Her laptop's in her hotel room. I think."

"Good. I'll check on that." Then Ali bit her lip. "If I could make a suggestion?" She looked at both Paul and Ken.

"Please," said Ken. "I'd love a suggestion."

"I know this might look opportunistic—"

"Ali, we know you're trying to help." That was Paul, his expression rueful. "It's not like I'm functioning on all cylinders right now. Whatever you can do is very welcome."

Meanwhile, Ken flashed a very brief smile at her. "How about I preempt the awkwardness here? Ali, how would you like a job? Just a temporary one until Tina can come back, but we need someone to take over the logistics here. I'll pay you what Tina makes—"

"We don't need to talk pay now."

"The hell we don't. You'll get what Tina gets."

She nodded, knowing that she was going to earn every penny. "Then I accept with gratitude. Now here's what we're going to do…" She pulled out her list. Ken pulled out his. And even Paul managed to find his iPad.

Five exhausting hours later, the bus was on the road with a new driver, she'd made her calls to Tina's family and helped them get flights, and she'd even figured out Tina's to-do list before the next event. Fortunately, Tina was almost as organized as Ali was. Unfortunately, taking her list plus Ken's and Paul's to-do lists was like trying to move three mountains all at once. But she didn't have much choice.

With that thought in mind, she abruptly stood up, balancing herself in the aisle since the bus was moving at a fast clip down the freeway. "Everybody, can I have your attention, please?"

Everyone quieted.

"Okay, so we've suffered a loss. A big one, but it's not fatal—to us or to Tina—thank God. But we're all going to have to pull together to make sure that the show goes on. So here's the deal. I've got about a zillion tasks that need to be done. I'm going to start reading them off. I suggest you volunteer to help because if you don't, I'm going to assign you something. And I can be very evil in assigning tasks. Understand?"

Every person nodded gravely.

She grinned. "Good. All right, task number one…"

KEN COLLAPSED INTO his hotel bed, his eyes gritty, his body aching from exhaustion. Tina was out of surgery, out of recovery and into a room of her own. Both Paul and Ken had been there when she woke up, but Paul was the one who had done all the talking. And his first words had stunned everyone.

He'd said he loved her. Paul loved Tina and wanted to marry her. That's why he'd been so distracted all tour, that's why he'd been screwing up left and right. Because his mind had been filled with Tina and the accident had given him a much-needed wake-up call. He loved her; he wanted to marry her.

Tina had said yes. Then she'd started crying—happy tears—between other equally loving words. So Ken had quietly left the room while his mind and his gut had churned. Paul and Tina were in love. And their happiness had him thinking of Ali. Was it possible for them, too? Or was the end of the tour going to end their relationship, as usually happened with these summer relationships?

Two hours later, Ken left the hospital. He'd stayed long enough to see that Tina was on the mend. The doctor said everything looked good. And since Paul was staying with her—currently sprawled in one of those awful hospital-room chairs—Ken had come back here to collapse on his bed.

All he wanted was to sleep, but he could not sink into oblivion. His bed was too empty and his mind too full. He'd already called Ali a dozen or more times for updates and the like. He knew he was interfering. Worse, he knew he was just wasting her time because she had enough things on her to-do list and not a one of them was chatting on the phone with him.

But he liked talking to her. He missed the sound of her voice and the feel of her body alongside his. And God, he wanted to curl into her side right now and smell her sweet scent. It wasn't a sexual need. He was too exhausted for that. He just wanted her by his side.

Ten minutes later, he was up and packing. Paul had everything under control here. Tina was going to be fine. Ken needed to be with the troupe. More specifically, he needed to be with Ali. So he called the airport, booked a flight and only winced once at the price.

He wouldn't arrive until midnight at the earliest, but he had to get there. He tried to convince himself that he would let her sleep. He tried to believe that he would get his own room and then he'd see her in the morning.

He failed. He knew that he was a weak man when it came to Ali, and he would find a way to get into her bedroom. Whatever time it was, he was going to slip into her bed if only to feel the heat of her again.

The thought terrified him. He really didn't want to need her so much. But he did, and right now, he was too tired to fight the draw. So he packed up and hailed a cab. And just before he boarded the flight, he texted her.

Catching a flight. Be there around 12:30.

He waited a long time before she answered, but when it came, he exhaled a great big sigh of relief.

My room is 824. Key will be at the front desk. If you want.

He grinned. He loved it when a woman read his mind. His text back to her was short and sweet.

I want you.

19

YES, YES!

Ali felt her eyes roll back as ecstasy pulsed through her body. She lived it, she relished it, she loved it…and then it faded. Ken collapsed sideways, his own orgasm leaving him spent and happy. She could tell because he was grinning. And even as he fell to the side completely boneless, his hands always sought hers. Her fingers, her palms, or whatever part of her was closest. He would touch her, absently rub his thumb across her skin, and he would grin.

They had been together every night for weeks now. Though they tried to keep their relationship low-key, everyone in the troupe knew. Fortunately, beyond a few teasing comments, no one had a particular problem with it. No one, that is, except for Blake who gave her long, puppy-dog-sad looks every now and then. She laughed them off, as did he, but inside she felt awkward and embarrassed. She was doing the boss. Every night. That was awkward.

And it was also increasingly sad. Because she felt the end of the summer coming like a big guillotine on their relationship. Sure they lived in the same city, but Houston wasn't exactly small. And besides, as everyone on staff had told her over and over, she should not expect this summer out of time to be anything but that: a summer fling. Everything changed once people got home. Best friends drifted apart. Romances ended—always. Some bitterly, some slowly, but they always ended.

The romantic in her wanted to believe that she and Ken were different. But her practical side said two words: *fat chance*. Summer flings didn't last past the first autumn leaf.

So she guarded her heart. She filled her days with work—doing her job plus Tina's was keeping her excruciatingly busy—and at night she and Ken explored all sorts of fun stuff. But every moment of every day, she had to remind herself that it wasn't going to last beyond October first.

They were on the last big stop before the end of the tour. It was Labor Day weekend at DragonCon, a fantasy/science-fiction convention with eighty thousand people. The event took over five hotels in downtown Atlanta, and was something that would have overwhelmed her at the beginning of the summer. Not so now.

Now, thanks to a summer of practice and the way Ken's eyes lit up every time she strutted into the booth, she had the confidence to act like a queen. Now she knew that the people—kids and adults—who came to hang out around her just wanted her to listen to them. She said almost nothing at all about the product, but they still bought. They just needed a friend.

In short, she had to realize being a queen had absolutely nothing to do with her as a person. She was simply a listener. And in listening, she had met all sorts of fantastic people.

Now it was time for the main event. The whole summer had been building to the big showdown between Arthur and Lancelot. Who would defeat the other in battle? Who would win Queen Guinevere's heart? And, in a marked departure from the traditional Arthurian legend, Ali didn't hide in the background on this one. For DragonCon, she was coming out in her Warrior Queen outfit complete with leather boots, short sword and *attitude*.

Looking back at the summer, Ali couldn't believe the changes in herself. Her first event had had her nauseous with anxiety. Today, she was actually excited to go on stage and kick some butt. But there were more changes, too. She'd been looking for something different for the summer. What she found instead was herself—different shades, different flavors, but all of them strong. She discovered that Sexy Ali was fun, Marketing Ali was good, but *Managerial* Ali was where she totally rocked. And that didn't even begin to address In Love Ali, but she wasn't going to think about that. Not with the end of the summer perilously close.

She was waiting behind the stage when Paul joined her. After Tina's accident, he had spent five days by her side. But then he'd returned to the troupe, and except for daily texts and calls, he acted as if nothing had changed. Except, of course, Ali had heard from Ken that he and Tina were engaged. The two kept it quiet for their own reasons, but every time Ali looked at Paul, she saw the happiness that simmered right behind his eyes. The man was in love, and that made all the difference.

"Hey, Paul," she said when he came up beside her. "Everything okay?"

He nodded. "Everything's fine, but…you know how we've been building to today? The whole tour has been set to reveal who wins you today. Do you go with Lancelot or Arthur?"

She knew. And all the blogs, web surveys and player input had been for Lancelot. By an overwhelming margin. So that was the plan for today. She was going to strut into the middle of the battle, declare that no one could pick her man for her and then choose the warrior everyone wanted her to pick. Which, sadly, was Lancelot. Blake's blond good looks plus that blog about their "date" had really turned the tide of public opinion his way.

"Yeah, I know," she said. "I'll drag it out, but in the end, it's gotta be Lancelot."

Paul grimaced and looked acutely uncomfortable. "It doesn't have go that way, you know," he finally said. "Just answer with your heart."

Ali frowned, not understanding what he was saying. Answer with her heart? This was a promotional tour. The fans wanted Lancelot and Guinevere to finally have their day. "But—" she began, but he just grabbed her hand and drew her closer to him. It would be almost romantic if it weren't so weird. "Paul—"

He kissed her on the cheek. "I'm not even supposed to be talking to you. Just, you know, answer honestly. That's the best anyone can do."

Then before she could say more, he just gave her a thumbs-up and hurried away. She would have followed. She hated surprises and damn if she was going to let a conversation like that just hang there. But then the music started and he jumped up on stage. Mordred was opening today's event, laughing and gloating over the war in the kingdom.

Meanwhile, Ali stood in the wings replaying the conversation in her mind. None of it made sense.

She waited, listening with half an ear as the battle scene began. Clash of swords, roar of the crowd, all the usual stuff. She peeked through and saw that both Blake and Ken were going all-out. She didn't really care what Blake looked like, but she saw Ken, his royal robe billowing behind him as he fought, his sword sweeping through the air. Good God, he looked amazing. Muscles, sword, cape—how could anyone look at Blake when Ken was there?

She was just about to go on stage when suddenly, Ken put on a burst of speed. Usually Blake was the better sword fighter. After all, he was younger and when he wasn't messing with his hair, he was working out. But this time, Ken was the greater one by far. Blow after blow after blow he beat Lancelot back. It was like Ken/King Arthur was possessed, and Ali couldn't take her eyes off him. She was supposed to step on stage and stop the battle, but she was so entranced by his victory, she couldn't move.

Then Lancelot tripped and Ken pinned him with his knee. The crowd was going wild, but not in support for Arthur. They wanted Lancelot to win, and this defeat in battle didn't sit well with them. Broken from her trance, Ali rushed on stage.

Except for her crown, she was dressed all in leather. Corset and boots and very little else meant the crowd's attention was riveted on her. She slowed just enough to remember to put some swagger into her strut and she went center stage. Ken was still there, his knee pinning Blake to the floor. And as Ali came up, she couldn't resist touching the sleek bulge of his biceps. Over the past month, she'd touched every part of his body. She'd kissed and caressed and a whole more, but this moment was special. He was special, and she looked at him with her heart in her eyes.

If only this summer could go on forever. If only they could live in this fantasy Camelot forever. But they couldn't. And she had a job to do.

So she stepped back and said her lines. "What foolishness is this? What makes you think a sword can win me or my favors?"

The crowd roared. There were at least as many women in the audience as men, and that statement was a real pleaser to the female set.

The swords came down. Blake's didn't have far to go since he was already on the ground. Meanwhile, Ken straightened and bowed before his queen.

"Of course," he said in his most regal tone. "My lady, I would speak with you."

Then Blake, mindful of his position as hero, also leaped up and bowed before her. "I, too, my queen, would beg an audience."

Ali nodded, stepping backward enough to allow the men the room on stage. Blake went first, going through his scripted lines of adoration. He loved her, he wanted her, blah, blah, blah. Ali knew the words and barely listened, especially since he seemed to be speaking more to the crowd than to her, though the audience, of course, was eating it up because Blake was actually a very good actor.

Then it was Ken's turn. "My Guinevere," he said, his voice pitched for everyone but his eyes on hers. "I have learned so much in my travels to this moment in time. I have laughed at the strangest times and found joy in places I never thought to look. I have discovered a value in silence and looked beneath the surface of your still pond and discovered such wonder."

He spoke the words with such passion, such power, even when he stumbled slightly over the word *pond*. And he kept speaking, though Ali could barely hear it over the roaring in her ears. He looked so earnest. If it weren't for the costumes and the crowd, she could imagine him trying to propose to her this way. And the sight hurt. It hurt because it wasn't real.

Meanwhile, he kept speaking, his words unrelentingly earnest. "Guinevere, you are everything to me. My day cannot begin except that I see you. Sleep will not come unless I cradle you close. No moment, no summer, no life, would be complete unless you are part of it."

He stopped speaking, and she just looked at him. Her eyes were watering, her belly was tight and her mouth was hideously dry. She had no idea what she was supposed to do now. How did this relate to the game? What was he doing? She didn't know, and the whole thing was too painful on every level. Her only urge was to run, but she couldn't. She was supposed to stay on stage.

"And so, my queen…" Ken reached into a hidden pocket beneath his breeches and pulled out a diamond ring. It had to be cubic zirconia because it was really large. And it sparkled under the stage lights. "Will you do me the greatest honor a man can have and become my wife? Um…again?"

She stared at the ring and then up at Ken. She couldn't tell.

Was this a proposal, as in a *real* proposal? It couldn't be. And yet it felt real. She looked out at the crowd, seeing the misty-eyed looks of some of the women. They were eating this up.

So did that mean this was a publicity stunt? A last ramp-up of the struggle between Arthur and Lancelot for her affection? She didn't know and her head was swimming with the possibilities.

She took a shuddering breath, struggling for some understanding. In the end, she fell back on the script. When all else failed, this was about selling a computer game. So she looked out at the crowd, pitching her voice to carry.

"Ladies, gentlemen, what should I do? Who is most worthy of my gifts and my love?"

The response was deafening, and the opinion was split. So she did what they'd been doing all summer. She looked out at the crowd and she asked them to vote. How did they vote? With their dollars. They played the game on the side of either Lancelot or Arthur, and then the game told them who had won her heart based on their score.

The crowd didn't like that. They wanted a winner and a loser. But Ali couldn't decide. Not until she knew if that had been a real proposal or a game one. And that's when Paul stepped in. He was Mordred, so he came on sneering and laughing, pushing the crowd to demand she choose.

So she did. She picked Lancelot because that's what the online players had demanded. With tears in her eyes, she rushed to Blake. She said the words she'd memorized and Lancelot was declared the winner. And as soon as she could possibly manage, she got off the stage and ran to her room.

KEN STARED AT THE SPOT where Ali was supposed to be. He stared at it, his knee throbbing and his heart in his belly.

She'd said no. He'd worked for a week on his lines, he'd bought the largest diamond he could afford, and he'd endured an agony of nerves as he prepared to bare his soul in front of a few thousand people.

He'd done all of that, and she'd said no. She'd asked the crowd what she should do and then let them force her to pick Blake. Then she'd run off stage.

The crowd was beginning to titter. What the hell had he been thinking to propose to a woman in so public a way? He'd been thinking about his female friends. He'd been thinking about his half sister who used to go on and on about how she wanted a proposal with a zillion witnesses. One that would be replayed on YouTube. That would be talked about with envy by all her friends. That's what he'd been thinking, and here he was, on his knee, while behind him a thousand strangers laughed at him.

He felt his face burn with embarrassment. And not just his face but his whole body—which was neatly exposed for everyone to see. Oh, God.

Thankfully, this was the last major stop on the tour. As the loser, King Arthur was supposed to disappear. It had always been part of the plan that he would leave after DragonCon. It was one of the reasons he proposed today because if Ali said yes, he would remain with her for the last couple of dates.

But she hadn't, and he couldn't face her. He just…couldn't.

So he put on a shirt, gave the sword to Paul because it wouldn't go through security and hopped a cab for the airport.

20

IT TOOK TWO HOURS before Ali realized her mistake. She'd left the main stage and headed straight to her room where she'd stripped out of all her "queen" clothes, showered off all the makeup and sweat and then put on jeans and a T-shirt. Finally, she felt exactly like herself!

Except, of course, she'd been dieting, so the jeans hung baggily. She'd also spent the summer getting used to a corset, so her T-shirt felt like a tent. Sure she could breathe easily, but her back felt unsupported.

It didn't matter. For this moment in time, she had ditched corsets and queens, geeks and freaks, and everything in between. And she had certainly, positively, had it with actors and Arthur!

Of course the Arthur in question would likely be coming in the door any second now. The show was definitely over. There would be cleanup and sales stuff to handle, but she had no doubt he would be headed her way soon. Part of her welcomed it. She wanted to have it out with him. Really express exactly what she felt in the privacy of their hotel room. And there was a measure of how much she'd grown over the summer because, frankly, this was exactly the type of conversation she would normally have run screaming from.

Was that a real proposal or not? Did he want to marry her?

Or was that a last-ditch publicity stunt to ramp up sales for "Team Arthur"?

And then, of course, was the really awful question: Did *she* want to marry *him?* Well, of course she did. She was in love with him, after all. But once again, this was a summer of fantasy and everyone had been telling her to not put faith in a summer romance.

Oh, hell. What did she want? To wait, obviously. Until the summer was over and she had some perspective. To see if he was going to dump her as soon as the next tour came along. Or a week after returning to Houston.

She heard footsteps coming down the hallway and held her breath in panic. Was that Ken? Apparently not, because whoever it was kept on going right past the room. Well, clearly she couldn't stay here. So with sudden resolve, she grabbed her purse and rushed out of the room. But where could she go?

The art room. She liked art, right? And she'd wanted to see the incredible display of beauty and whimsy that was part of fantasy art. She headed there as fast as the elevators, walkways and escalators could get her there.

And that's where Samantha found her an hour later. Ali was pretending to be enthralled by paintings of kittens with wings. It wasn't so much the little kittens that intrigued her. They were cute and all, like furry cherubs. But she'd been caught by an image of a fierce adult cat—a lioness—with her wings cut backward as she leaped to attack a hapless gazelle. It was fierce and bold and she was caught by the beauty of a creature so lethal.

"Thinking of killing Ken?" Samantha asked.

Ali started, turning to smile at Sam. "What? Oh, no. Well, maybe."

"Look, I'm not going to belabor this. If you want to talk, I'm here. But there's something I think you need to know."

Ali nodded, bracing herself inside. She could tell by the

set of Sam's face that she wasn't going to like whatever was coming next. "Okay. Hit me."

"I won't go into the stupidity of proposing to a woman like you while in costume in front of thousands of screaming fans. Or how dumb it is to completely spring something like that on anyone."

"So it was a real proposal?" Ali asked, feeling her gut roil.

"He thought he was being romantic. Which just goes to show how stupid these guys can be sometimes."

"Romantic?" Ali asked.

"Like the guys on TV. And YouTube and everywhere else."

"So, not a publicity stunt?"

"Nope."

Ali just stared at her. The words simply didn't compute. Sure they'd talked about marriage. Eventually. Someday. But she'd refused to think beyond the end of the summer. But apparently Ken had. Ken had been thinking very much beyond their last tour stop next week.

And while she stood there with her mouth hanging open, Samantha released a sigh. "Come on. Let's get something to eat. There's a cheap Chinese place around the block. I'm dying for some crab rangoon."

Ali nodded dully. Her mind had just stuttered to a stop. Ken had proposed to her. And she hadn't even known it was a real proposal.

They made it to the restaurant quickly enough. One glance inside told Ali that they would fit right in with the other customers. There was a table of Klingons, another of trolls and three with a mixed bag of zombies, fairies and kilted warriors. At least the robot had taken off most of his costume so that he could eat, which meant that someone else besides her wore a T-shirt, though his had a picture of a depressed Stormtrooper holding his head in his hands and the caption: REGRETS: Those were the droids you were looking for.

She and Sam didn't speak at all as they got their food from

the buffet and dug in. It was the end of the tour so all diets were at an end. Except for Blake, apparently, whose agent had hinted about something big but wouldn't say what.

Finally, after four crab rangoons and a pile of sweet-and-sour chicken, Ali felt strong enough to face the truth.

"Tell me again slowly," she said. "What do you mean that was a real...you know." She couldn't even say the word out loud.

Sam didn't even hesitate. "It was a real diamond, a real proposal. Ken was asking you—for real—to marry him."

Ali shook her head. "He couldn't have. He wouldn't. Haven't you guys spent the last month telling me this affair wasn't serious. That it—"

"Yeah," Sam said as she dropped her fork and leaned back in her chair. "See, we kept thinking he was one of us. You know, an actor. Summer gigs like this, lots of us have affairs. And we learn early not to put our hearts into summer tours."

Ali nodded. That's what every single one of the troupe had said to her either overtly or subtly for the past four weeks.

"The thing is," Sam said as she leaned forward, "we forgot that Ken's not one of us. At his core, he's a geek. He collects comic books, he has a couple of action figures on his desk, and he's got a regular online Dungeons & Dragons group from when he was a kid. He got one of his designers to put the game up online so they could all play from different parts of the country."

Ali knew that. At least those details. But she couldn't understand how Sam got from geek to proposal.

"You don't get it, do you?" Sam asked.

"No."

"In his mind, you've been engaged, married and have a couple kids by now. Ken isn't like Blake or Paul or any of the other guys you're thinking of. He hasn't dated girl after girl since the moment he hit puberty. In fact, I doubt you've seen any pictures of Ken in high school, have you?"

Ali thought back. "No, I haven't. But we've been on tour. It's not like he brought them along on the bus."

"He doesn't bring them anywhere. He didn't start working out until he was in his twenties. And even then, it's not like he can compare with Blake or even Paul. He just hasn't got the physique."

"So? I don't care about that. I never have."

"But don't you see? I don't know that he ever really dated in high school. He was a geek, through and through. So no matter that he owns his own company now, he's still got the geek I'll-never-get-a-woman mindset."

Ali took a deep breath, slowly processing everything Sam was saying. How could she have so misread the man she'd been sleeping with all summer? "You're saying that when we started dating, he was thinking marriage from—"

"The first moment you slept together. Probably the first time you kissed."

Ali looked down at her plate. "He's never spoken about love. Neither have I."

"He did in his proposal."

Ali thought back. "Um, no. Actually, he didn't."

Samantha frowned. "God, he is an idiot."

Ali might have agreed, except she'd just received a proposal of marriage and hadn't even realized it. In the grand scheme of things, that put her as the bigger idiot. With sudden resolve, she pushed back from the table. "I've got to go talk to him."

"You can't. He's gone."

Ali froze before she could take a step away from the table. "What do you mean, he's gone?"

"Paul told me. Ken left for the airport right after the show. Didn't pack a bag or anything. Just hopped a cab and was gone. Paul didn't even try to talk him out of it."

"What?" Ali gasped. Sure she understood—or was beginning to realize—the depth of how humiliated the man was.

After all, he'd just been refused in front of a zillion people. "But to just leave without talking to me…"

Samantha shrugged. "Yeah, I chewed Paul out for letting him go."

Ali shook her head. "When Ken is determined, there's nothing that Paul could say to change his mind."

"Yeah, that's exactly what Paul said."

"Which means he was very determined." And very hurt. Hurt, embarrassed and…heartbroken? The idea was so difficult to process. It had been real. All of it was real.

"Why wouldn't he stay and talk to me?" Even as she asked the question, she knew the answer. It was the same reason she'd fled the stage as soon as she could. It was the same instinct she had to run and hide the second things got too painful. The only difference was that she couldn't go back to Houston. If she'd had the means, she probably would have. Straight back to a pint of chocolate-fudge ice cream and a weepy movie sob-fest with Elisa.

"Besides," said Sam, "wasn't he planning on leaving tomorrow anyway? Wasn't that the schedule?"

Ali nodded as she collapsed back into her seat. "Yeah, that was the schedule." She'd seen it. She'd obsessed about it. She'd even tried to ignore the guillotine-like snick she felt every time she looked at the date. But she hadn't expected that their last night together would be…well, not.

She dropped her head into her hands. "What the hell am I supposed to do now?"

Sam touched her hand then ordered them both chocolate-chip ice cream. And after the bowls came and they both dug in, she finally answered.

"Personally, I'd bury myself in ice cream, then go back to work as if nothing happened."

Ali nodded, thinking that wasn't a bad plan.

"But," Sam continued, "you're not an actor any more than

Ken is. This summer has been about you changing things up, right?"

Ali nodded. "Yeah. You know, coming out of my shell, finding my outer beauty, and…hell, I don't know. It was mostly about just doing something different."

"Okay, so do you feel like a changed woman now?"

Ali shrugged. "I thought so. But some things will never change. I'll never relish the spotlight like you and Blake do."

"That's okay. There are enough of us out there. We don't need more competition."

Ali smiled. "No one can compete with you when you step on the stage."

"Well, maybe, but we were talking about you. So do you feel stronger, bolder, more I-am-woman, hear-me-roar?"

"Definitely."

"And what does Strong Ali think you should do?"

Ali dug out another bite of ice cream and stuffed it into her mouth. "I'll never get over how you actors can just split yourself into multiple personalities."

"Stop avoiding," Sam returned after she'd swallowed her own big bite. "What does the new strong you think you should do?"

"Have it out with Ken. If he really was thinking mar-riage—"

"Did you see the size of that rock?"

Ali flinched. Yeah, that had been a huge rock. "Okay, if he's thinking of marriage, then we've got to have a talk. We've got to talk about a *lot* of things."

Sam nodded, but her expression was pensive. "I suppose you could go that way. Talk. And more talk."

"And what would you suggest?"

"Me? I'd show up in a trench coat and nothing else. Then do him on his desk."

Ali laughed. "You would not!"

"Of course I would. And then when he was naked and vulnerable, that's when I'd force him to talk."

"Guys aren't usually so coherent at that point in time."

"Exactly! Because when I say talk, I usually mean, I talk and they listen."

Ali wasn't sure guys could handle listening at that point either, but she wasn't about to argue the image. Or that the men would have incentive to pay attention. But even after a summer of sexual exploration, she wasn't about to do that. It was too easy an out for her. In her mind, fantasy sex was fun, but it wasn't real life. And a marriage was built in real life, not bump and grind on a desk. Though there was definite appeal in the idea. Definite appeal.

Sam slowed eating long enough to look at Ali with narrowed eyes. "You're going to do the responsible thing, aren't you?"

Ali grimaced. "I don't know about responsible. I'm going to finish out the tour—"

"Because you're not one to skip out on your commitments."

"And I think I'll email him that I had no idea that it had been a real proposal."

"That'll be a hard thing for him to read."

Not a picnic to write either. But he had to know that she'd been confused. "I'll…uh…I'll tell him that when the tour is over, we should get together and talk."

"Oh, kiss of death."

Ali shook her head. "I'm not trying to be mean. But if he wants a white picket fence and children with me, then we've got to be able to talk like normal people."

Samantha rolled her eyes. "Geeks are *not* normal people."

"They're not space aliens either. We've got to meet halfway at least."

Samantha gave a fatalistic shrug. "Beats me. I'm an actress. I'm more comfortable around space aliens. At least these kinds." She gestured over to a group of guys dressed as aliens who were just now sitting down at a nearby table. And every single one of them was looking at her. "I bet I could get them to pay for our meal if I talked nice to them."

Ali laughed. "I bet you could. But this meal's on me. Which leaves you free to do whatever you want with the aliens."

"You could join me. Get a little geek compare and contrast."

Ali grinned but shook her head. "Sorry, no. I've got more than I can handle with just the one."

And with that she paid the bill and left. She had an email confession to write and absolutely no idea what to say.

21

KEN STARED AT a very nicely and calmly written email and tried not to choke. Only he could manage to propose to a woman and have her not even realize that he was asking her to marry him. God, he was such an idiot.

He read the email again. It was his hundredth time, and he still had no idea how he should respond. Ali's tone was calm, almost professional. There was no sign of emotion or desperate passion anywhere. It was simply an apology and a desire to speak again when the tour was over.

Translation: kiss off, loser.

He read it again trying as best as he could to not *feel* as he read. To look at it as if he were someone completely neutral reading the email. It took him three tries, and in the end he gave up.

The email was too neutral. For a woman who had done the things they'd done in bed, every word here was cool and dispassionate. But maybe it wasn't quite a kiss-off. Then again…

Hell, his mind was going in circles. And truthfully, it didn't matter what she'd written or how. There was a clear invitation to talk and Ken was too much of a masochist not to agree. Plus, he was too much in love with her *not* to grasp at straws. So if dinner and awkward conversation was the straw at hand, he would grab on to it and hold tight.

He typed back a quick email saying he would love to see her. Then he suggested the most expensive restaurant he knew—the kind of place he'd meant to take her on their first date—and added a day and time. Five minutes later, she accepted his offer in two quick sentences:

That sounds lovely. I'll meet you there.

ALI STEPPED INTO THE ELEVATOR that would take her up to the restaurant and hit the button, doing her best not to totter on her heels. She'd spent the summer strutting about in three-inch boots and the like, but now in a normal dress and heels, she felt completely off balance. Or maybe it was *who* she was about to see that had her off-kilter. Either way there was no turning back now.

The elevator dinged, the doors opened and Ali had to restrain a gasp of surprise. Talk about expensive! This was probably the ritziest restaurant she'd ever been to. Oh, hell. She'd planned to pay for her own dinner, if she and Ken politely went their own ways. But looking around, she doubted she could afford what even a salad at this place cost. Especially since she'd decided to quit her job and go to school full-time to finish her college degree. It would only take a year and if she filled in with a part-time job somewhere, she could manage it. But not if she blew her rent on a dinner at this restaurant.

"Good evening, miss," greeted the maître d'. He looked just like a man in his position should look, black tux and all. She flashed on her first date with Ken in Chicago. She doubted this man would burst into a rendition of "YMCA."

She repressed a hysterical giggle at the memory and stepped up to the podium. "H-hello," she finally managed. "I'm—"

"Are you perhaps Miss Flores? Here to dine with Mr. Johnson?"

Ali blinked. Of course a host at a place like this would know her name. They made a point of doing stuff like that. "Um, yes. That's—er, yes, I'm Alicia Flores."

"Then I believe—" he reached over to a nearby table and picked up a long florist's box, opening it with a flourish "—these are for you."

Ali gasped. They were roses. A dozen long-stemmed red roses. She looked, but there wasn't a card. Obviously they were from Ken, but...well, she just didn't know what to think.

"They're beautiful," she murmured.

"Shall I put them in water for you?"

"Oh...of course. Thank you."

He bowed and handed off the box to a waiting busboy. Ali was watching the box disappear when the maître d' turned back to her. "Mr. Johnson called to say that he has been unavoidably detained. This wretched traffic, you know."

"Wretched," Ali echoed because the man seemed to expect it. She hadn't really encountered any terrible pileups or anything, but Ken was likely coming from a different direction.

"Mr. Johnson hopes that you will order whatever appetizer pleases you, and as an added apology, we would like to offer you a complimentary glass of wine."

"Oh. Um, okay." What did one say when a restaurant apologized for one's date being late? "Thank you."

"Our pleasure, Miss Flores. If you would follow me?"

She did, trying not to fall flat on her face. The place was elegant, subdued and had what felt like half a dozen waiters and busboys prepared to meet her every need. There were a few fellow diners, all dressed in suits or sleek dresses. The amount of jewelry that sparkled in the candlelight was practically blinding. Her booth sported a pristine white tablecloth, classic table settings and her roses already artfully arranged.

And once again, she had to restrain an inappropriate giggle. Somehow she'd left the real world and stepped onto the set of a mobster movie or a spy thriller. She half expected

James Bond to appear at the bar and order a martini—shaken, not stirred.

She pulled it together and managed to slide into the booth. Her light sundress was chilly in the air-conditioning, especially since the day happened to be overcast and cool for late September. She shivered.

"I see you're a bit chilled. May I suggest a glass of wine and a lovely loaner shawl that should complement your dress perfectly."

She nodded numbly. What type of restaurant had loaner shawls? Apparently this one. "Thank you," she pushed out through her tight throat. "Red wine, please. Whatever you recommend and, um, the shawl would be welcome."

He bowed. "An excellent selection. And may I recommend the foie gras, as well? It is today's special appetizer, prepared with mustard seeds and green onion in duck jus."

Ali had no idea what all that was, but she hadn't the wherewithal to disagree. So she smiled and nodded, all the while wondering where Ken was. Was it possible? she wondered. Could he intend to stand her up? To get even in a small way for the humiliation she had dealt him?

She knew she was being ridiculous. She'd seen no indication that he was that petty a person. And really, he'd given her a dozen roses. That wasn't the action of an angry man. But Ali was really nervous, and her imagination kept coming up with all sorts of ways that this date could go horribly wrong. And one scenario was that this date was never intended to be a real date at all.

The foie gras arrived at the same moment as her loaner shawl, which was a simple thing of black embroidered with tiny seed pearls. It looked like something a rich grandmother would wear, but it was warm and so she wrapped it around her shoulders. Then she guzzled some wine and took a taste of the appetizer. Turned out foie gras was a yellowish-pink paste that tasted like liver, but wasn't all that bad. She might even have enjoyed it if her stomach weren't cramping with anxiety.

She'd finished her wine and was contemplating a second when Ken finally arrived. She was hyperaware of the muted ding of the elevator and had actually slid around in the booth so she could see it opening and closing without ratcheting her head around every time. So she got a good look—even in this light—at his haggard expression and his sideways-leaning tie.

The maître d' greeted him and smoothly stepped between herself and Ken, clearly blocking the view. When the two finally started moving toward the table, Ken's hair was no longer mussed, his tie was centered and smoothed and even his expression looked calm—or frozen with panic—it was hard to tell which.

It didn't matter. She'd seen him come off the elevator looking stressed, and that reassured her as nothing else could. This hadn't been an elaborate setup to a humiliation. He probably had been hung up in traffic. And, frankly, he was rather adorable-looking when his hair went every which way. Reminded her of the way he looked after some of their more adventurous nighttime sex-capades.

But he was smooth and put together when he made it to the table, even if his first words were an apology.

"I'm so sorry, Ali. I tried to get here as fast as I could, but I couldn't. I just…" He sighed and held up his hands. "I really tried."

"It's okay," she said, smiling in relief. "You're here now. Sit down and try some…uh…"

"Foie gras," supplied the maître d'. "Was it not to your liking?" he asked.

Ali tried to find the words that wouldn't insult the food but still wouldn't have her confessing that she'd been too nervous to eat. But before she could say anything, the man whisked the food away.

"Never mind. Goose liver isn't my favorite either. While

the gentleman gets settled, I will get you something less... French." He spoke the words as if *French* was synonymous with what-were-they-thinking?

Ali felt her lips curve at that, and one glance at Ken's face had her suppressing a laugh. He obviously didn't know what to think of such an attitude either.

"I don't even know what foie gras is," he confessed in an undertone.

"Liver, I believe. With mustard."

"Seriously? That sounds really, really...unappetizing."

"It actually didn't taste that bad. I just..."

"Not your style?"

"Not that hungry."

He stilled for a moment, his expression tightening into disappointment. "Oh. I'm sorry. You're not...hungry?"

"No, no!" she scrambled to say. "Actually, I am hungry. I just... I mean..." She shrugged and decided to go for broke. "I'm a little nervous."

He nodded. "Well, then you're doing a lot better than me. I'm *very* nervous."

"Good." She exhaled, her shoulders easing down with the motion. Then she caught sight of his face and scrambled to explain. "Not good that you're nervous. Good that we're both nervous and that means you're not here to punish me."

He blinked, obviously startled. "Punish? Why would you think that?"

She looked down at the crumpled linen napkin in her lap. "I did refuse your proposal of marriage."

"You didn't *know* it was a proposal of marriage." He said it as though it was his fault that she was so clueless.

She opened her mouth to say something—anything to ease the tension—but nothing came out. Thankfully, the waiter appeared asking Ken if he wanted a drink. Then there was the business of looking at the menu—Ali noticed that hers didn't even include the prices—and ordering something she hoped was modest. She picked a simple chicken dish. He ordered a steak and then they were alone again with nothing to say. Fortunately, Ali had thought of something while he'd been looking at his menu.

"The roses are beautiful, Ken. Thank you."

He smiled at her, not the roses. "*You* look beautiful. And I'm glad they got here. I'm sorry I couldn't present them to you myself."

"The maître d' did it just as you would, I'm sure. With flair and panache."

"I'm not sure I could find panache with a GPS, but thank you." Then he sobered. "Let me tell you why I was late. It wasn't on purpose, I swear."

"I never thought it was," she lied. And she noticed thankfully that he looked as if he believed her.

"I was in a meeting with some Hollywood studio guys."

She blinked. "Seriously?"

He nodded. "Yeah, that's exactly what I said when Paul told me they wanted to meet. Turns out one of the studio execs was at the theme park with his kid at the same time we were. They came into the booth because it was hot—"

"Everybody came in because it was hot."

Ken flashed a grin. "I know. That's why we book it whenever we can. Anyway, they came in, talked to us and played the game. Then they bought the game and junior played it with all the other studio-executive kids. Turns out, Winning Guinevere is a hit with the children of studio executives."

Ali grinned. "Of course it is. It's a great game."

"And apparently, they think it will be a great movie."

She blinked, her stomach squeezing tight for an entirely different reason than anxiety. Right then, it was joy. Pure joy. "It will make an incredible movie!"

"I'm not so sure. Games don't always translate well to film."

"But the story base is already there. It doesn't have to be gamelike. It just has to be a good quest story. Which it is!"

Ken smiled. "Well, it sounds like you and Paul agree. As do these guys. They flew out for the day just to talk contract details. They're right now in our conference room eating pizza while Blake's agent tries to squeeze them for extra seconds of title time on his name."

She frowned for a number of reasons. She started with the least important one only because it managed to somehow crowd its way to the front. "They want Blake in the movie?"

"It's low budget. They like him and his work so far, so they're willing to give him a shot assuming he agrees to being paid almost nothing."

She thought about Brian/Blake and knew that money would be the smallest of problems. "He'll want to do it. He wants movie stardom like he wants free hair product."

Ken snorted. "Yeah. Everyone knows that, though he's trying to play it cool."

"I'm so glad for him."

Ken paused, a frown starting to creep between his eyebrows. "They're talking about shooting next summer. He's talking about moving to California. That's okay with you, isn't it?"

She blinked. "Of course it is. Why wouldn't it be?"

Ken flushed and looked down at his fingers drawing circles in the condensation on his water glass. "Oh, well, I just heard that you and Blake got closer—you know, at the end of the tour. Have you two been—"

"Seeing each other?"

He looked up, his cheeks red. "Yeah. Have you?"

"Sure. We had nachos the other day. He needed help with ideas for a present to give his sister." She reached out and touched Ken's cold fingers. "We're just friends, Ken. That's all we ever were."

"Oh. Okay. Good."

Lord, she was handling this badly. But she couldn't find a way to get to the topic they both really cared about: their future relationship. And while she squirmed trying to find a way to get there, something else fitted into her brain.

"Wait a minute. You've got Hollywood types in for the day to negotiate a movie deal with you."

He nodded.

"So what the hell are you doing here with me? Isn't that kind of important?"

He shrugged. "Truthfully, it's awesome, but the business was doing fine even before the offer."

Ali nodded. She'd been watching the game blogs. It turned out that Ken's proposal had indeed hit YouTube, along with the leaked information that it had been a *real* proposal. Not surprisingly, that had sparked a flurry of Team Arthur gamers—all girls. Apparently girls could really get behind a product if properly motivated. Winning Guinevere was a huge success.

And now it was going to go Hollywood! "That's amazing. You're going to have a movie!"

He grinned. "Looks like."

"Assuming you guys agree to terms."

"We have."

"And you schmooze them right."

"Paul's on that right now."

"But *you* should be on that, shouldn't you? Not here with—"

Ken held up his hand, effectively stopping her words. And then he reached out and took her hands in his. "Nothing is more important than being here with you, right now, right here."

"But—"

"No buts, Ali." He swallowed and tightened his grip on her fingers. "Look, I know I screwed up. I know I shouldn't have proposed like that. But it was an honest proposal. I really want to marry you, Ali."

She blinked, startled to discover that her eyes were watering. "Why, Ken? Why do you want to marry me?"

He frowned as if her words made no sense to him. But he answered anyway. "Because I love you. Why else would I propose?"

Why else indeed? God, one look at his face told her that it was so simple for him. He loved her, ergo he proposed. That after everything, *she* was the one who had overthought it. *She* was the one who was jumping from what-if to maybe-this or maybe-that. God, she was such an idiot!

Meanwhile, he misunderstood her silence and tumbled into a babble of words. "I know I screwed up. You're not a geek chick or anything like my sister, who wants her proposal to be nationally televised. I don't know why I thought that. You're a normal girl—a great girl—and what you want—"

"Is a man who loves me. That's all. Just a man who loves me like I love him."

He nodded, his head bobbing up and down. "Right. So I figured we'd date for a while now. In the normal world. No tour."

"Me, too—"

"And then, after a few months—or longer if you need it— we can talk about marriage again. I still have the ring. I can propose to you however you want, whenever you want. I want you to be comfortable—"

"Ken—me, too."

"Good. Because marriage is a serious thing. And I don't want—"

She pushed her hand to his lips. "Ken!"

He shut his mouth and looked at her.

"I said, 'me, too.' As in yes, Ken, I love you, too."

He blinked. Then his eyes suddenly widened. "Me, too? I mean, you, too? I mean——"

"I've been thinking about you nonstop since you left. I know I haven't emailed much."

"You're not one to put stuff in writing like that. You like to internalize things. I get that. I do that, too. Which is why I didn't email much either."

And they hadn't. Just short, clear conversations of about two sentences max.

"But I loved every minute of the summer together. You told me—on stage—exactly what you love about me. Let me tell you what I love about you. You're grounded, Ken, even in a world of fairies, gnomes and barbarian warriors."

"I'm not big on the gnomes. Just an FYI."

She laughed. "And that's another thing. You make me laugh, you take me to amazing restaurants and you haven't said a word about this shawl."

He frowned. "Uh…it's lovely," he began.

"No, it's not. It's a loaner because I was cold, and it looks like Barbara Bush left it here by accident."

He looked around. "Actually, that's a possibility."

"I know it is! But you knew that it was nothing like what I would normally wear."

He shrugged. "It didn't seem like your style at all."

"And you know that. You know that even when I don't really know all of that. Ken, you spent the entire summer challenging me to do more, to be more, to…well, everything more. I'm *more* because of you. That's what I love most about you. You demand more of yourself and of me. And you love me even if I don't measure up."

"Of course you measure up—"

"I won't. Not always."

"And I won't get the right restaurants or propose in the right way all the time either."

She grinned. "Ken, I love you. I was an idiot to refuse you in the first place."

"You were shocked and unprepared."

"And you were feeling awkward and thought hiding behind King Arthur would make it easier to propose."

He looked startled for a moment then shrugged. "Yeah, you're right." Then he frowned. "Will you wear the ring now? Please? I've been dreaming of putting it on your finger since I first got it."

She nodded, pulling back enough to hold up her hand.

He fumbled in his pockets and drew out the jeweler's box, popping it open with speed if not style. Then he pulled the ring out and held it up to the light.

"Ali Flores, will you do me the greatest honor and marry me?"

She bit her lip, feeling the love she had for him well up inside her. They were rushing things. She knew they were. Hell, they'd only had two dates. But inside she knew it was right. So she nodded. "Yes, Ken, I will."

He pushed it on her finger, then scrambled around the table enough to kiss her deep and full, just like she adored. And then he pulled back, glancing up as the maître d' clapped his hands.

"Champagne!" the man cried.

Ali laughed. Now this was a picture-perfect proposal! And then she looked at the ring, twisting it in the light as she inspected it closer. The setting was unusual. The diamond wasn't sitting in the usual prongs, but was settled on what looked like a crown.

"Ken—"

"You don't recognize it, do you?"

"No, what is it?"

"At the end of the game, when Guinevere finally gets her man, she gets a new crown." He pointed at her ring. "She gets one shaped just like that."

"Wow," she whispered.

"It's so you know that you're my queen. You always have been. From the very first moment that I saw you."

"Ken, I'm a flesh-and-blood woman. Don't put me on a pedestal."

He grinned. "Well, then I guess you'll just have to remind me of the more…um…carnal nature of your life."

She laughed. God, she did love his sense of humor. "Agreed," she said. "Though I did enjoy it when you acted as my supplicant."

"For tonight, I'd just like to be your fiancé. Your ecstatically happy fiancé."

"Me, too." Then she leaned over and whispered in his ear, "We'll play tavern wench tomorrow."

"Oh my God, I love you!"

Ali grinned. It was amazing how well the man read her mind.

* * * * *

One touch was all it took...

Marley's tank top had ridden up, and Caleb found himself touching bare skin. Bare, warm skin, so soft that he hissed in a breath.

"I..." Marley's voice drifted and her mouth fell open when she saw the desire in his eyes.

He could do nothing to hide his swift response. Her flesh felt like heaven, and her sweet scent was far too intoxicating. Before he could stop himself, he moved his hand over her hip in a fleeting caress. An unsteady breath slid out of her throat.

Insanity. This was freaking insanity, and he was helpless to stop it. He'd been watching Marley Kincaid for seven days, watching and yearning and fighting the arousal he knew he shouldn't be feeling.

But he couldn't fight it now. Not when she was this close.

Screw it. Kissing her was wrong on so many levels, but at this point, he didn't care. He wanted her so badly his bones ached.

So he took her...

WITNESS SEDUCTION

BY
ELLE KENNEDY

MILLS & BOON

First published in Great Britain 2013
by Mills & Boon, an imprint of Harlequin (UK) Limited,
Eton House, 18-24 Paradise Road, Richmond, Surrey TW9 1SR

© Leeanne Kenedy 2011

ISBN: 978 0 263 90629 5
ebook ISBN: 978 1 472 01192 3

14-0613

Harlequin (UK) policy is to use papers that are natural, renewable and recyclable products and made from wood grown in sustainable forests. The logging and manufacturing processes conform to the legal environmental regulations of the country of origin.

Printed and bound in Spain
by Blackprint CPI, Barcelona

Elle Kennedy grew up in the suburbs of Toronto, Ontario, and holds a BA in English from York University. From an early age, she knew she wanted to be a writer, and actively began pursuing that dream when she was only a teenager. When she's not writing, she's reading. And when she's not reading, she's making music with her drummer boyfriend, oil painting or indulging her love for board games.

Elle loves to hear from her readers. Visit her at her website www.ellekennedy.com to send her a note.

For Amanda

1

"OKAY, HOW ABOUT THIS—you're walking down the
street and suddenly you bump into a tall, dark and
handsome stranger who sweeps you off your feet, looks
deep into your eyes and says, 'I have never seen such
exquisite beauty. Have coffee with me, my mysterious
maiden.' Would you go out with him?"

Marley Kincaid burst into laughter, nearly spilling
her coffee all over the oak work island in the middle of
her kitchen. She set down the mug and grinned at her
best friend. "'My mysterious maiden'?" she echoed.
"Uh, yeah, I'm not sure I could go out with any man
who called me that."

Gwen Shaffer rolled her eyes. "Okay, pretend he
didn't say that. He's just a drop-dead gorgeous guy
who wants to buy you a cup of coffee. Would you go?"

"I don't know. Maybe." Marley sighed. "Why are
you so eager to get me dating again?"

Gwen had raised the subject the second she'd walked
into the house nearly an hour ago, and Marley was
growing tired of it. She didn't usually mind when Gwen
popped in on her day off to chat over coffee, but this

conversation was beginning to annoy her. Somehow it had gone from Gwen trying to convince her to go on a blind date to what-if scenarios that made no sense. She knew her friend meant well, but what was the point in talking about all the possible ways she might meet a man?

"Because you've barely left this house in months," Gwen replied. "I want to see you having fun again. All you do is paint and put up wallpaper and—"

"I'm renovating," Marley interrupted. "And I'm enjoying it."

"You're hiding from the world, and you know it." Gwen's tone softened. "Look, I understand, hon. That bastard is still on the run. If it were me, I'd be worried, too. I mean, what if he shows up here pleading for help or something?"

Marley's entire body tensed. She swallowed hard, turning her head so she was spared the familiar flicker of sympathy in her friend's dark-green eyes. She hated it when Gwen brought up Patrick. Hated being reminded of the disastrous relationship that had ended in a train wreck she hadn't seen coming.

Eight months ago, she'd been on top of the world. Working at a job she loved, buying her first home, falling in love.

Well, she still had the job and the house, but the man she loved? Turned out he hadn't been all that worthy of her undying affection.

She'd met Patrick at the hospital, where he'd been recovering from a nasty stab wound to his side. Mugged on his way home from work, or so she'd believed at the time. She'd been assigned to his room, and it hadn't taken long for Patrick's easygoing charm to lure her in.

They went on their first date the night he got discharged from the hospital and, three weeks later, he practically moved into her house. Four months after that, they were engaged.

It'd lasted five months. Five months of great sex and laughter and that wonderful feeling of falling in love with a handsome, attentive man. He'd wrapped her in a protective bubble and made her believe anything was possible. Patrick had been good at that, playing make-believe. So good that when the cops had come knocking on her door, she'd actually defended him.

She still remembered the disbelief on those police officers' faces when she'd finally realized the truth. That her fiancé was not a freelance web designer, but a drug distributor. Not to mention the prime suspect in the fatal shooting of a federal agent.

God, what a fool she'd been.

"He won't show up," she said darkly. "He's probably lying on a beach in Mexico, laughing at the law-enforcement officers who couldn't catch him."

Fortunately, Patrick hadn't tried contacting her since he'd fled three months before, and good riddance. She never wanted to see that man again, and for the past few months she'd gone to great lengths to permanently erase him from her life. Burned his clothes in the backyard, flushed his engagement ring down the toilet.

Too bad none of that had succeeded in actually exorcising him from her mind.

"I'm not too happy with the cops, either," Gwen said with a frown. "I still can't believe they thought you were involved."

Marley's lips tightened. "Detective Hernandez couldn't accept that I was so naive. How could I not know my fiancé was a criminal?"

"You weren't naive. Patrick was just a good liar."

"Yeah, he was." Marley picked up her mug, along with Gwen's empty one, and set them both in the sink. "At least the police are finally leaving me alone. I only hope it stays that way. Now, can we please stop talking about Patrick?"

Gwen's face brightened. "Okay. Can we talk about Nick's friend then?"

Marley suppressed a groan. "I told you, I'm not interested."

"I'm not suggesting you marry the guy. It's just a date. One measly little date. You said you were ready to date again."

"No, I said I might be." She blew a stray strand of hair off her forehead. "But a blind date isn't the way I want to go about it, okay? I'm not having dinner with a complete stranger. It's too forced, too…intimate."

"Then we'll make it a double date."

"No." Without looking at Gwen, she swallowed back the bitterness sticking to her throat and added, "I can't agree to go out with a stranger. I can't do it, Gwen. Not now, anyway."

"Fine, but the subject's not closed, you know. We'll talk about it later." Gwen hopped off the stool, her brown curls bouncing on her shoulders, and reached for the black leather purse she'd set on the counter. "I have to run. I'm meeting Nick for lunch."

Marley followed her friend out of the kitchen, her bare feet slapping against the weathered hardwood floor. They reached the front hall, sidestepping the stack of two-by-fours obstructing the way. Marley's younger brother, Sam, had promised to extend the coat closet by a couple feet, so last weekend he'd come over and hacked away at the wall. Then he'd gotten a phone call and taken off to handle a work emergency. He hadn't been back since, and Marley was now left with a gaping hole in the floor and all the supplies he'd brought into her hallway.

She didn't mind, though. Sam was busy working at their dad's construction company, and it made her happy he was doing well. Her brother had always been irresponsible and scatterbrained growing up. It was nice seeing him act like an adult, even if it did mean he'd left his sister in the lurch.

Gwen paused on the front porch. "Want to come to lunch with us?" she offered.

"Thanks, but I'll pass." Marley was so not in the mood to watch Gwen make googly eyes at her long-time boyfriend. The two of them still acted as if they were in the mushy newlywed stage when in fact they'd been together for years.

Her friend looked suspicious. "How are you planning to spend the rest of your day off?"

"Cleaning out the eaves," she said, fighting back a smile.

Gwen blew out a frustrated breath. "You're incorrigible."

Marley's smile reached the surface. "Yeah, but you love me anyway."

"Can't argue that. All right, I'll see you at the hospital tomorrow." Gwen leaned in to give her a quick side hug, then bounded down the porch steps toward the shiny black Jeep parked behind the red Mazda convertible Marley had owned since she was eighteen years old.

Marley waved at her friend, watched Gwen speed away, then walked back inside. Alone, she let out a heavy sigh. Talking about Patrick always brought this awful feeling to her stomach. A cross between sorrow and bitterness, with a hefty dose of anger thrown into the mix. Everyone in her life kept pushing her to forget about him—Gwen, their friends from the hospital, her dad, her brother.

None of them seemed to get it. They didn't understand how badly Patrick had hurt her. Not only that, but he'd taken a skewer to her judgment and punched so many holes in it she wasn't sure she could ever trust her instincts again.

What kind of woman fell in love with a murderer? How could she have been so blind to Patrick's deception? She knew she wasn't the first and wouldn't be the last woman to be duped by a man. Heck, she'd once watched an entire documentary about serial killers and how they skillfully deceived their loved ones.

But that didn't make this situation any better. She still felt like a fool. She'd completely fallen for Patrick's lies and she hated how easily he'd conned her. He'd even convinced her to open a joint savings account, saying they'd need one anyway when they were married. Good thing she hadn't gotten around to depositing anything into it, but it still irked—especially since she couldn't close the damn thing because the cops had frozen it.

And sure, maybe she was hiding from the world, just a little, but the renovations on her house helped keep her mind off her fugitive ex-fiancé. Besides, she really was enjoying the work.

Her place was nestled in a neighborhood of quaint Victorians and leafy elm trees at the end of the cul-de-sac. Two stories high, it was painted pale cream and in desperate need of new shutters. But she loved the old place. She planned on tackling the exterior after the inside was all spruced up.

Heading to the laundry room, she grabbed all the cleaning supplies she needed. She slipped her feet into a pair of white sneakers, then hauled her bucket of supplies out to the side of the house, where the wooden ladder she'd set up earlier leaned against the slate-green roof.

Fine, so maybe cleaning out eaves wasn't the most exciting thing to do on one's day off, but it needed to be done. And who knew, maybe one of Gwen's what-if scenarios would come true.

A tall, dark and handsome stranger approaches the house. "My mysterious maiden," he says. "Your beauty overwhelms me. Let me clean your rain gutters."

Marley smothered a laugh. Rolling her eyes, she snapped a pair of rubber gloves onto her hands and climbed the first rung of the ladder.

"*This* maiden needs no man to take care of her," she murmured to herself with a grin.

CALEB FORD LEANED BACK in the plush swivel chair and wondered when exactly he'd become a voyeur. His job had forced him to sit through many a stakeout but somehow this one seemed…wrong.

Arousing as hell…but damn it, *wrong*.

He'd been a DEA agent for ten years, had put dozens of criminals behind bars, gotten shot twice in his career—and yet this one little stakeout was killing him. It should've been easy, a wait-and-grab he could've done in his sleep. The location was perfect, the electronic equipment was sweet, and his target, despite the irregular hours she worked, didn't leave the house much.

Yep, in theory, this stakeout should've been a piece
of cake.

But none of his theories had taken into consideration
the powerful allure of Marley Kincaid.

Caleb shifted in the chair, hoping to ease the ache
in his groin. A sip of the cold soda sitting on the desk
in front of him helped cool his throat, but did nothing
to snuff out the fire in his lower body.

A quick glance at the screens displaying Marley's
front and back doors showed no movement. Not that he
had to be so vigilant; the motion detectors they'd set up
caused the monitors to release a loud buzz every time
anyone walked by them. There was plenty of movement at the side of the house, however.

Marley was up on a ladder, wearing faded cut-off
shorts, a red tank top and yellow rubber gloves, and
she was cleaning out the eaves using a long brush. Wet
leaves and mud went sailing down to the grass ten feet
below, remnants of last night's thunderstorm.

Damn, she was cute up there on the ladder, her blond
ponytail swishing back and forth as she worked. When
he'd taken the case, he'd seen pictures of Marley, sure,
but seeing her in person was a different story altogether. It had been a week since he'd hunkered down
next door to her, and already he'd memorized every
detail of her face—her golden-brown eyes set over
a pair of unbelievably high cheekbones, her cute up-
turned nose, her full sensual lips. God, those lips. She
had a mouth made for sin. Not to mention a body that
could cause a man to forget his own name.

For seven days now he'd wondered what she looked
like naked. But they only had clearance to install cameras outside the house. And she always closed her
drapes when she undressed, forcing his imagination

to run wild as he stared at her enticing silhouette removing various undergarments.

His cell phone began to ring, a much-needed distraction from the woman next door.

Sighing, he snatched the phone from its perch near the computer keyboard and pressed the talk button. "Ford," he said. His voice came out hoarse, and he had to clear his throat before speaking again.

"I'm at the Starbucks around the corner," came AJ Callaghan's southern drawl. "Want some coffee?"

Caleb tore his gaze away from the monitor. "Hell, yes," he told his partner.

"Huh. You sound cranky. Ms. Kincaid doing yoga again?"

"Nope, cleaning the rain gutters."

"Darn. I won't hurry then. But call me if she starts up with the yoga." AJ's tone revealed the man was no doubt sporting a huge grin. "You know," AJ added, "I can't see Grier staying away from her for much longer. We already know he was infatuated with Nurse Hottie, and seriously, with that bod, who could blame the guy?"

Oh, Caleb couldn't blame Patrick Grier for craving Marley's extremely delectable body, either. Thanks to all the cameras Caleb and AJ had set up around the perimeter of Marley's house providing visuals of the kitchen, living room and bedroom, Caleb had firsthand experience with Kincaid's assets. And he was doing a little bit of craving himself.

Fortunately, all it took was one swift glance at the picture taped to the side of his computer monitor, and the need for vengeance replaced his desire.

As Caleb hung up the phone, he stared at Patrick Grier's grainy features. What pissed him off the most was how normal Grier looked. Brown hair, brown eyes, handsome in a preppy sort of way. That was drug-dealing murderers for you—they rarely ever looked like the scum they were.

If it were any other scumbag dealer, Caleb might have handed the case over to a junior agent and focused on the bigger fish swimming around in the drug pond. But this particular scumbag had murdered Caleb's best friend, and he wasn't going to rest until Patrick Grier was behind bars.

He looked back at the monitor and grinned when he noticed Marley leaning to the side, one slender arm stretched out as she attempted to tackle a clump of leaves that refused to dislodge. The grin faded, how-ever, when something caught his eye. One of the rungs on the ladder looked…wrong. He leaned closer, squint-ing at the screen.

"Damn it," he muttered under his breath.

Sure enough, the rung he'd noticed was sagging on one side. He couldn't see much more than that, but he suspected it was cracked. The thing would probably break the second she stepped on it.

Fortunately Marley's feet were on the rung below the broken one, but the way she was reaching her arms out, it wouldn't be long before she needed some more height to connect with her target.

Crap. What should he do in this situation? Sit around and wait for her to fall?

Caleb gritted his teeth. He couldn't go over there and warn her. Making contact with the person you were watching defeated the entire point of a stakeout. And he wouldn't risk the possibility of losing Grier. In his gut, he knew the other man was bound to show up here. When they'd raided the office Grier had been using for his web design company, they'd found more than a dozen pictures of Marley taped on the walls. Grier was obsessed with her, and Caleb knew he'd come for her.

He felt it deep in his gut, a certainty his supervisor, unfortunately, didn't quite agree with. But at least Agent Stevens had green-lighted this stakeout. How long he'd let it go on, Caleb wasn't sure, but for now, he could sit tight and see if his hunch played out. The local cops were already watching Marley at the hospital, but Caleb knew Grier wouldn't make a move there. Too many witnesses around. Here, though… Marley lived alone, didn't have many visitors and her house sat at the end of a cul-de-sac with a large park right behind it. This was the perfect place for Grier to make an appearance.

On the screen, Marley was looking up at the roof in dismay. An ominous feeling crept along Caleb's spine. He watched as she lifted one foot. His chest tightened with sickly anticipation.

"Don't do it," he mumbled at her, though of course she couldn't hear him. "Look down first."

But she didn't, and it was like seeing the chain of events that led up to a disaster, in slow motion, unable to do a damn thing about it.

She climbed up onto the next rung of the ladder, and he could practically hear the wood splintering beneath her feet. He couldn't see her face, but he could imagine the look of terror filling her pretty features as the rung gave way. She lost her footing, and the ladder swiftly toppled onto the grass down below.

Caleb shot to his feet, adrenaline pumping through his veins. A faint flicker of admiration lit his chest as he saw her arms whip up like an acrobat's, grabbing at the white-painted eave.

Relief flooded through him. She hadn't fallen. Instead, she dangled ten feet off the ground like a really crappy cat burglar attempting to scale a building. Caleb couldn't help but grin at the thought, but his mouth hardened when Marley twisted her neck, glancing down at the grass as if contemplating whether she could land the jump.

Sure you can, sweetheart, except you'll probably break your ankle. Or your neck.

Letting out a sigh, Caleb took one last look at the screen, then tore out of the room.

He ran out the front door of the house the agency had rented from a pair of retired teachers who were traveling for the summer. The afternoon sun nearly blinded him, making him realize he hadn't been outside in a week. It felt weird after being cooped up indoors for so long.

He crossed the perfectly kept lawn toward the side of the house. Only a couple of yards separated the two homes, and when he approached, Marley still hung from the eaves, cursing to herself under her breath.

He cleared his throat. "Need some help?"

She yelped in surprise and nearly lost her grip. Her legs swung wildly, making his heartbeat quicken. "Don't let go," he ordered.

"Who are you?" Her voice sounded tinny as it floated down from above.

"Your next-door neighbor," he replied. "And possibly the guy who saves your life."

She peered down at him, her light-brown eyes narrowed with suspicion. "I know my next-door neighbors, mister, and you aren't them."

"The Strathorns are in Europe. I'm renting their house for the summer," he called back, annoyance tightening his lips. "Now, do you think we can discuss this *after* we get you down from there?"

There was a long pause. Then she was scrutinizing the ground again. "I think I can make the jump," she said. "I once saw a documentary on stunt doubles."

He suppressed a laugh. "That's terrific. But no, you cannot make the jump." He swallowed. "I'll catch you."

She let out a squeaky protest. "What? No way. What if you miss? Or what if I crush you—"

"With the hundred pounds you're packing?" he interrupted in amusement. "You won't crush me, and I won't miss."

Caleb stepped closer, assessing the height and angle from which she was hanging. If he raised his arms, he could almost touch her sneakers. "I'll catch you," he said with confidence. "I need you to take a deep breath, and let go. Okay?"

"No, thanks."

He closed his eyes briefly, fighting back irritation. "What do you mean, no thanks?" He scowled up at her. "Are you always so difficult?"

"No, I'm scared," she retorted. "I'm only twenty-seven. I don't want to die today."

This time he couldn't stop a laugh from rumbling out of his throat. "You won't die. Trust me. Deep breath, then let go. On the count of three, okay?"

She hesitated for what seemed like an eternity. "Okay."

He rubbed his hands together, widening his stance. "One," he called. "Two—"

"Wait—on three, or one, two, three, let go?"

Caleb sighed. "On three."

"Fine."

He started again. "One…two…*three*."

A second later, her body came flying down and he suddenly found himself with an armful of warm, soft woman. One hand had instinctively reached out to cup her bottom, and his palm now cradled a firm, perfectly round backside, as Marley Kincaid's arms wound tightly around his neck.

She was breathing heavily, her body trembling a little. "You all right?" he asked. His voice sounded rough even to his own ears.

She nodded, tilting her head to look up at him. Her brown eyes widened slightly, her lips parting in surprise as she examined his face. She checked him out for so long he felt a pang of discomfort. "You should really let someone else clean those gutters for you," he grumbled.

Marley just stared at him, and then, to his extreme confusion, she started to laugh.

2

"SERIOUSLY," HER SEXY SAVIOR said in a deep voice. "If you don't tell me you're okay in the next two seconds, I'm calling an ambulance."

"I'm okay," she sputtered.

God, this was priceless. Her laughter came out in soft waves, while adrenaline still pumped through her blood. She suddenly wondered if Gwen had somehow planned this, though that seemed totally unlikely. But come on, what were the chances? Her friend had been babbling about tall, dark, handsome strangers sweeping Marley off her feet, and all of a sudden, a tall, dark, handsome stranger shows up and sweeps her off her feet. Literally.

"Can I let you go now?" he asked, a tad brusquely.

Her laughter finally trailed off. She nodded, and he set her down. Her legs were still quite shaky after her brush with possible death, but her brain seemed to have forgotten about her roof gymnastics—it was too busy analyzing the beautiful man standing in front of her.

He had that chiseled kind of face you expected to see on a movie screen, lines and angles put together to create a rugged landscape, vivid eyes the color of the Pacific Ocean. A pair of faded jeans clung to his long legs and taut behind, while a navy-blue T-shirt emphasized a broad chest and delicious set of rippled abs.

No doubt about it, this was one ridiculously gorgeous man.

Her heart did a few somersaults. "Thanks for catching me," she said.

"No problem." He took a step backward, looking like he couldn't wait to get out of here. "Be more careful next time, all right?" Another step. "I'll see you around."

"Wait, who did you say you were again?"

"I'm Caleb Ford." His blue eyes flickering with weariness, he extended his hand. "I'm renting the house next door to yours." As if to confirm it, he gestured to the redbrick side wall of the Strathorn house.

Since he was sticking his hand out at her, she had no choice but to shake it. The moment they touched, warmth suffused her palm, followed by a spark of awareness. Gosh, this guy was attractive. The messy black hair, the serious blue eyes, the drool-worthy bod. And his hand felt good on hers. Too good.

She quickly snatched it away, leery of the awareness sliding around in her body. Fine, so this guy was incredibly handsome, but he was also a total stranger. And the Strathorns hadn't told her they were renting their place out for the summer. She knew they were in Europe—they'd asked her to pick up their mail. So why hadn't they mentioned someone named Caleb Ford would be staying in their house?

"How do you know the Strathorns?"

Her voice held a note of suspicion, which she didn't attempt to hide. Since her experience with Patrick, she was far more careful about handing out her trust to strangers.

"Through a mutual friend. I heard they were going to Europe for a few months, so my friend arranged for me to rent this place while they're gone."

"Oh, that's convenient." She casually pushed a strand of blond hair off her forehead. Her ponytail had pretty much come apart after her near fall, and unruly blond waves kept getting in her eyes. "Isn't Stan and Debbie's house terrific? They have a lot of antiques in there."

Caleb arched one dark brow. "*Stu* and Debbie, you mean."

"Right, Stu, I don't know why I said Stan." She felt a little flustered, especially when a knowing glint filled his eyes. He knew exactly what she'd tried to do, but hey, at least he'd passed the test. So why was he still all fidgety?

"When did you say you moved in?" she asked, watching him carefully.

"I didn't. But it's been a week."

A week? And she hadn't seen him even once? She tried to rein in her misgivings. Okay, so maybe he didn't leave the house a lot. He could be one of those hermit types who liked being alone indoors.

"And you're here for the summer?" she said, trying to sound casual.

"Yep."

"On vacation?" she pressed.

"Work-related, actually."

For Pete's sake, getting answers from this man was like pulling teeth. She paused for a second, trying to concoct a way to draw some more details out of him, when a flash of red caught her eye. She glanced down, surprised to see an angry-looking scrape on her upper arm. She must have cut herself when she'd grabbed for the ledge, or maybe on her way down into Caleb's arms.

"Shoot, I should get this cleaned up," she said.

"Do you need any help?"

His voice was so full of reluctance she almost felt insulted. Jeez, was the thought of spending even a few more minutes with her that unappealing?

She frowned. "I'm a nurse, I can take care of it. But thanks."

Caleb slung his hands in the pockets of his jeans, shifting awkwardly. "You better go in and get that taken care of. Are you sure you didn't hurt yourself anywhere else?"

She examined her arms and legs, then flexed her back, wincing when a jolt of pain sliced up her left shoulder. "I think I pulled a muscle," she answered, "but it's nothing some yoga can't fix this evening."

Caleb coughed abruptly.

"Are *you* okay?" she asked, wrinkling her brow.

"Yeah, I'm, uh, fine." He began to inch away again. Lord, the way this guy acted, it was as if she was carrying the Ebola virus or something. "I really do have to go. Take care of yourself, uh…?"

"Marley," she supplied.

"Marley," he echoed. He lifted his hand, giving a stilted wave and a brisk nod, and then hurried off with long, smooth strides.

She watched as he walked away, shaking her head to herself. He disappeared around the side of the house and a few moments later, she heard the Strathorns' front door shut.

Okay. Well, that was kind of weird. He was probably

telling the truth, and really was renting the house next door, but maybe she ought to call the number Debbie had left for her just to make sure Caleb Ford was who he said he was. He'd been acting a little odd for her liking.

Yeah, she definitely should call, she decided as she bent down to take care of the ladder. She pushed it to the wall, leaning it length-wise against the house, then glanced down at her arm, which was beginning to ooze blood.

With a sigh, she headed into the house, making a mental note to contact Debbie Strathorn as soon as possible. Caleb Ford might be drop-dead gorgeous, but he was still a stranger.

And these days, Marley's guard went on high alert when it came to sexy men who made her heart skip a beat.

A girl couldn't be too cautious, after all.

"So…what was *that* about?"

Caleb nearly tripped over his own feet at the sound of AJ's voice. He'd expected to find the master bedroom empty, but AJ was casually sitting at the desk, sipping from a tall Starbucks cup.

With his military-style buzz cut, tattooed arms and black leather jacket, Adam James Callaghan looked like the type of guy Caleb would be slapping handcuffs on and dragging to jail.

But AJ was a damn good agent, a bit of a legend around the Drug Enforcement Agency. He'd spent three years undercover with a Colombian drug cartel, which was how he'd gotten all the tattoos. Had to prove himself, show he was one of them, AJ had told Caleb. He'd also managed to gather enough evidence to take down the entire organization. But now he was stateside, assigned as Caleb's new partner.

Caleb walked over to the desk and peered at the monitors, instantly spotting Marley in the kitchen. She was pulling a first-aid kit out of the cupboard under the sink.

"What was what about?" he asked, absently reaching for one of the steaming cups sitting in the cardboard tray on the desk.

AJ shot him a look loaded with disbelief. "You know exactly what I'm talking about. I come back from a coffee run to find—"

"You came in from the back, right?" Caleb cut in.

"Yes, I came in from the back. Same way I've been coming in for the past week. And yes, I parked the car two streets over. And no, nobody saw me when I cut through the park on my way here." AJ frowned. "Now quit interrogating me and tell me what the hell you were thinking, making contact with Kincaid."

Caleb walked over to the king-size bed and sank down onto the edge. "She fell off a ladder."

AJ swiveled his chair around to face him. "She fell off a ladder," he repeated.

"Yes, but she managed to hang on to the roof. She would have fallen off that, too, if I hadn't gone out to help her." The defensive note in his voice made him want to cringe, but he knew AJ's thoughts on the subject of Marley Kincaid. And none of them were too positive.

AJ put down his coffee cup in obvious annoyance. "Just in case you've forgotten, we're on a stakeout, man. The whole point of a stakeout is remaining out of sight, inconspicuous."

"I know that," Caleb ground out. "But what did you want me to do, watch her tumble to her death?"

"What I want you to do is focus on the bastard that killed one of our own." AJ frowned. "I've seen the way you look at her, Caleb, and I don't particularly like it, all right? She might very well be helping Grier and you know it."

"Yes, and she might not be helping him," Caleb countered, meeting his partner's hard gaze with one of his own.

"Then explain the hundred grand that was wired into her bank account after the DEA got the tip that Grier was heading to San Diego."

"It was a joint account, you know that. Grier could've made the deposit as easily as Kincaid."

"And she has no knowledge of what's going on in her own bank accounts? If a hundred thousand dollars mysteriously wound up in my account, I'd be talking to the bank, or calling the cops. Unless I know my slime-bag ex put it in there, and I'm planning on helping him get out of the country."

Caleb's jaw tightened at the thought of Grier taking off and disappearing. Oh, no, not happening. Caleb would catch the son of a bitch long before that happened. The DEA finally had hard evidence on the guy, after years of being unable to bring charges against the supposed web designer. Three months ago, an informant inside the Ruiz cartel—the Brazilian outfit they'd been trying to bust for years—had provided information about a shipment Grier was scheduled to distribute for the Ruizes.

Only, the raid they'd organized hadn't gone as planned, and Grier had yet again escaped arrest.

"If she's helping Grier, we'll find out," Caleb replied.

"All I'm saying is that we shouldn't jump to conclusions. Maybe she's involved, maybe she's not. But don't paint her with Grier's brush until we have some proof."

Even as he said the words, he knew AJ wouldn't heed them. His partner believed in Marley's guilt. Caleb, on the other hand…he was ninety percent sure Marley wasn't involved in any of this. He didn't quite believe Marley was in cahoots with Grier now, or that she'd been aware of his actions then. Grier was smooth, and according to his file, he'd fooled women before. Killed them, too, or at least he'd been suspected of it.

Still, ninety percent meant there was still that ten percent of doubt floating around in his head. He didn't want to believe Marley was somehow funneling money into her ex's hands, but it wasn't something he could rule out, either. At least their presence next door ensured they'd see Grier if he showed up.

"And if she's not involved," Caleb added, "she could be in danger. You know what happened to Grier's previous girlfriend."

"Yeah, she found out he was a criminal and tried to help the cops."

"Her dead body wound up in a Dumpster in Nevada, for Chrissake."

AJ sighed. "And I'm sorry that happened to her, but at least she was trying to take down Grier. Kincaid, on the other hand… I don't know, man, the hundred grand in that bank account makes me mighty reluctant to trust her."

"Well, you don't have to trust her. You just need to watch her." Unwittingly, Caleb snuck another peek at the monitor, where Marley had finished bandaging her cut. She was now in the second-floor bedroom, fixing her ponytail.

He wished he could find out exactly what was going on in her head. He needed to know more than what these brief glimpses provided. First and foremost, had she truly been oblivious to her fiancé's criminal activities?

Yet there were other questions he'd also love to get the answers to. Like what had she seen in Grier in the first place? Why was she doing all these renovations on her house by herself? What did she look like naked?

Caleb stifled a groan. It always seemed to come back to that, didn't it? Marley Kincaid's incredibly appealing body. It was the tease of watching, but not really *seeing*. Catching glimpses of her breasts in silhouette, but never knowing exactly what color her nipples were, never knowing how those firm mounds would feel in his palms or rubbing against his chest, pressed up to his mouth....

Jeez, AJ was right. This attraction really was getting out of hand.

"Grier will show up soon," Caleb declared. "Whether Marley is helping him doesn't matter. My gut tells me he's going to come for her."

AJ didn't look convinced. "You know I usually have the utmost respect for an agent's gut, but how are you so sure? I've read his file, Caleb, and he doesn't form attachments. He uses people, then walks away."

"She's different." Caleb's voice grew quiet. "He never moved in with anyone before, never proposed marriage, never opened a damned joint savings account. I'm telling you, AJ, he'll come for her."

"He'd better," AJ said with a trace of bitterness. "That bastard needs to pay for what he did to Russ."

The sound of Russ's name brought a deep ache to Caleb's chest. He hadn't had many friends growing up—being carted from foster home to foster home put a cramp in a guy's social life—but Russell Delacroix had been the exception. Caleb had met Russ at a group home when he was sixteen, and the two of them developed a friendship that had thrived for years. Russ had been the one who convinced him to join the DEA, and they'd been partners for eight years.

As long as he lived, Caleb knew he'd never forget the sight of Russ's body crumpling to the cold ground of that warehouse three months ago. Even now, the memory of Russ's blood staining the dirty floor sent a wave of rage through Caleb's gut.

Russ had been family, a brother. And losing him to a drug dealer had been a crushing blow.

Caleb tried to swallow the ball of fury lodged in his throat. "He'll pay," he said hoarsely. "He *will* show up here, I know it, and when he does, we'll be waiting."

AJ leaned back in the chair, giving a satisfied nod. "Nice to hear you have your priorities straight."

Caleb bristled. "What's that supposed to mean?"

"It means that you've been lusting after your cute nurse for a week now, and I'm glad you're still able to remember why we're here." AJ's voice took on an admiring note. Glancing at the screen, he let out a soft whistle. "Though I've gotta admit, she's fun to watch."

Caleb followed AJ's gaze, then stifled a groan. Marley had just come out of the walk-in closet in her bedroom, wearing black Spandex pants that hugged her shapely legs, while a tight yellow tank top stretched across her full, perky breasts.

Caleb's fingers curled into fists. A jolt of desire shot straight to his cock and turned it to granite. He knew Marley's routine to a T now, and when she put on the Spandex…that meant only one thing was about to happen.

Sexy yoga time.

He tore his eyes off the screen. "Have you made any progress figuring out where the money came from?"

AJ shook his head. "Still can't trace it."

Releasing a heavy breath, Caleb got to his feet and approached the desk. "Then we keep waiting."

"So, what, we sit around for another week, waiting for something to happen? How long is Stevens going to let this stakeout go on?"

"I don't know. But as long as we're here, all we *can* do is wait."

"For what?" AJ sounded frustrated. "There's been no activity in the account since the wire transfer, no appearances by Grier, no phone calls, nada. What do you suggest we do?"

"We keep watching," Caleb said, shrugging.

You mean torturing yourself.

He allowed himself another peek at the screen, swallowing when he noticed the sensual workout had begun. She always started out with sexy stretches that showcased her legs and emphasized her sleek calf muscles, followed by a series of little pelvic tilts that never failed to hold his undivided attention. *Oh, and look at that, now she had her hands and feet on the mat, ass thrust up into the air.*

Caleb smothered a groan. How much more of this could he take? He was only a man, after all. A thirty-one-year-old single man who'd always had a healthy appetite when it came to sex.

And the woman on the screen, with her lithe body and floor gymnastics, just screamed sex. The proximity of their houses, separated by mere yards, only made the situation worse. It was only ten steps from his porch to hers. Ten steps, and he could be at her door…in her bed…

"Maybe making contact wasn't such a bad idea," AJ said suddenly.

Caleb's head jerked up. "What are you talking about? You just chewed me out for that."

"Yeah, but I'm looking at it from another angle. You already laid some of the groundwork today," AJ said, a thoughtful look entering his harsh features. "You saved her life, chatted her up. Sure, she thinks you're a total weirdo, but—"

"What do you mean, she thinks I'm a weirdo?"

His partner shrugged. "You were like a panicked little rabbit out there. Seriously, you kept inching away, like you were going to bolt any second. I saw the look on her face, man. She's suspicious of you. And she thinks you're weird." AJ offered a big grin. "Fortunately, you're going to fix that by going over there tomorrow."

Caleb faltered. He didn't reply for a moment, running the idea through his mind. "No," he finally said.

"Why not? All you've gotta do is befriend her, get her to open up and figure out what she knows about Grier."

AJ made it sound like the easiest task on the planet, which, for AJ, it probably was. Despite his scary biker looks, AJ was never hurting for female company. Not Caleb, though. His problem wasn't finding female company; it was making sure nobody ever got too close. He liked his women the way he liked his cars—fast, bold and temporary. No strings, no hassles and definitely no relationships. He'd learned the hard way the price you paid when you formed attachments to people.

And he didn't want to get close to Marley Kincaid. His attraction to her had already proven too big a hassle—why make it worse?

"I won't sleep with her to find out what she knows about Grier," he grumbled.

"Who said anything about sleeping with her? Uh, one-track mind?" AJ snorted. "All I said was become friends with her. She cut her arm, right? Go over there tomorrow to make sure she's okay."

Caleb studied the monitor with a frown. The bedroom was now empty, but light spilled from underneath the closed bathroom door. Another part of the routine, a long shower after sexy yoga.

Indecision rippled inside him. Should he do this? It had been kind of amusing, talking to her outside. She had a great sense of humor, and she also happened to be the most beautiful woman Caleb had ever seen. Plus he was wildly attracted to her. An attraction that could equal trouble.

But AJ had a point. Caleb's supervisor, Ken Stevens, was a good man, but he wasn't known for his patience. If this stakeout didn't produce any results, if Grier didn't show up soon, Stevens would pull them out. Making contact with Marley and finding out if she knew anything might help move the case along. Hell, it might be the only way to keep the case alive.

"I guess I can do that," he said slowly. "Just to see if she knows something."

Right, because her fresh-faced beauty and killer body have nothing to do with it.

"You're a professional," AJ said, as if he knew where Caleb's thoughts had drifted. "Keep it casual, dig around and hopefully she leads us to Grier."

"And if she doesn't?"

AJ let out a frustrated sigh that revealed precisely how he felt about his next words. "Then we go back to waiting."

EMERGING FROM THE SHADOWS, Patrick Grier deftly hopped the fence leading into the backyard of the house across the street from Marley's. Darkness bathed the yard, which only helped his cause as he crept toward the back door. He'd purposely waited for the sun to set, killing time on a pier a few miles from here. He couldn't risk anyone seeing him in this neighborhood. A contact of his had warned him the cops were still watching Marley. Otherwise he would've broken into her house months ago. But he had to play it safe. Getting caught wouldn't help him or Marley one damn bit.

The door swung open easily when he turned the knob, and he stepped into the dark house. The temptation to run across the street to see Marley was so strong his legs started to itch. He swiftly fought the urge. He didn't have a death wish, after all.

Breaking into this house had been risky enough, but fortunately he knew the old bat who lived here. He'd spoken to Lydia White several times when he'd lived across the street, and during their talks he'd learned she lived alone and had zero family. No friends, either, though that wasn't a surprise considering her foul personality.

But even bitches had to eat.

Tucking the deli bag under his arm, Patrick headed upstairs without turning on any lights. The spare bedroom at the end of the hall had a perfect view of Marley's place, and when he peeked out the window, he noticed her bedroom light was on. Was she lying in bed, thinking of him?

Turning away from the window, he strode to the narrow closet and flung the door open. A pair of wide brown eyes greeted him, along with the muffled screams of Lydia White as she wiggled around on the closet floor like a scared puppy.

Patrick scrunched up his nose when the faint odor of urine drifted into his nostrils. "You couldn't hold it for a day?" he spat out.

The old lady whimpered, terror filling her wrinkled face.

Gritting his teeth, Patrick bent down and hauled her up so that she was sitting. He yanked off the duct tape stuck to her mouth. "Open your mouth, I brought you some grub. And remember what I said about screaming." As a reminder, he half turned to show her the black 9mm sticking out of his waistband.

Another whimper.

Ripping the wax paper covering the ham sandwich he'd picked up, he lifted one half to the lady's mouth and practically forced it down her wrinkled old throat. She objected at first, but then began to chew, unable to resist the first form of nourishment she'd had since he'd left the house early this morning.

He stifled a curse as he fed the old bat, wishing he could just kill her and be done with it. But he wasn't a cold-blooded murderer. No, he only killed when his own survival was threatened. Besides, he needed old Lydia around to answer the phone when some rare person called—while Patrick held a gun to her head, of course.

So far, Lydia had followed instructions like a pro. And using her house as his base of operations was ideal. For the moment.

"Here," he barked, uncapping a bottle of water and bringing it to Lydia's mouth.

The elderly woman drank fervently, but the glimmer of fear never once left her eyes.

"Don't look at me like that," he snapped. "I told you, I won't be here long. I'm just making some arrangements and then I'll be gone."

And so would Marley. No way was he leaving her behind. She was the love of his life, after all. So unbelievably different from the fast and loose women in his past. He'd known it the second she'd walked into his hospital room in her green scrubs, with that gentle smile on her face.

His smile dissolved into a frown as he thought about all the shit that had gone down three months ago. He still experienced an onslaught of rage every time he remembered what had happened in the warehouse. Damn cops. The shipment they'd intercepted had cost him millions of dollars. Not to mention that they'd officially made it impossible for him ever to live in the States again.

Tomorrow morning, he planned on driving to Tijuana to meet with a guy who was arranging the necessary papers, and he was still working on a way to contact Marley. Once he did, he could get hold of the money he'd hidden in her house. He'd stashed two hundred grand under her bathroom floor three days after he moved in; it was part of his routine—always have an exit strategy in case you need one.

And then there was the hundred grand in his and Marley's joint account. Earlier this week a European contact who owed him money had transferred the dough in there, since the feds had frozen all of Patrick's personal accounts and he didn't have the resources yet to open anything new. He wasn't sure why they'd left the joint account open—his instincts told him it was a trap—but if he could, he planned on transferring the amount to a bank in the Caymans when he secured the necessary ID papers.

Once he got the cash from Marley's house, though, he was outta here.

And Marley was going with him.

Sure she is, came the cynical voice in his head. *Women always love men who betray them.*

"She *does* love me," Patrick insisted, wishing he could punch that bothersome voice. "And she'll forgive me for lying to her. Marley doesn't stay angry at people, it's not her way."

He noticed the old lady staring up at him with eyes as big as saucers. Had he spoken out loud?

"She does, you know," he said to Lydia. "Love me, I mean."

The certainty surrounding his heart was as strong as steel, causing the worry in his gut to dissolve. Of course Marley would forgive him. She was still his. All he had to do was find a way to get to her. And once he had the cash, he was going to whisk Marley away to a place where nobody could ever tear them apart again.

3

"OKAY, SO HERE'S WHAT you're going to do," Gwen said, tightening the drawstring on her bright pink scrubs.

Marley flopped onto the narrow bench in the nurse's locker room and bent down to untie her shoelaces. "What are you talking about?"

"Your neighbor."

"You're still hung up on this?" Marley frowned. "I told you, he's kind of strange."

"But you said he was cute." Gwen grinned. "And he caught you when you did a swan dive off the roof."

"Fine, he gets two points for that. And then minus three points for being aloof. I swear, he couldn't wait to get away from me."

"But you spoke to Debbie, right?"

Marley nodded. "Before I left for work. She said she and Stu did rent the house, to a writer from New York, and, yes, his name is Caleb Ford."

"Well, there you go, he was telling the truth."

"Yeah, but... Something about him was really off."

"So he's shy. Which is why you need to make a move," Gwen answered as she tied her curly hair in a loose twist at the top of her head. "Tonight you're going to walk next door and ask for a cup of sugar."

Marley laughed. "No way. That's so lame."

"Wait, I'm not done. So you ask for the sugar, and then you bat your eyelashes and say, 'Actually, maybe I can give *you* some sugar instead.' One thing will lead to another and presto! You get laid and forget all about Patrick."

Marley shot her friend a firm look. "I'm not going to seduce my neighbor."

"Then at least promise to keep an open mind," Gwen pleaded. "There's no harm in saying hi to the guy next time you see him. Just don't be afraid of some flirting, or heck, even a casual conversation. Oh, and could you *please* come out with me and Nick on Tuesday? We're going to the salsa bar. It'll be a good time."

"I'll let you know." Marley took a step toward the locker room door. "I gotta go. My feet are killing me and I'm craving a long, hot bubble bath."

Gwen sighed. "I hate the night shift," she complained as she followed Marley out the door. "You're so lucky you're going home."

"Yeah, to sleep," she replied with a sigh. "I'm coming back for the graveyard shift, while you get to spend the night with your boyfriend."

"Good point."

They said goodbye in the hallway, and Marley headed for the elevator, her flip-flops snapping against the white linoleum floor.

When she exited the hospital, the early-evening air was warm, and she breathed it in, enjoying the fresh scent of salt and palm trees. She loved San Diego—the heat, the laid-back atmosphere, the ocean. She hadn't been to the beach in ages, she realized as she crossed the parking lot to her car. The renovations in her house were tedious and left little time for trips to the beach.

But maybe Gwen was right. Maybe it was time to quit using her house as an excuse not to go out and have fun. God knew she needed some fun after the past year.

Before she could start the car, her cell phone burst out in the Pussycat Dolls ringtone Gwen had downloaded as a joke. Her brother's number flashed on the screen, causing Marley to stifle a groan. Sam still hadn't come back to finish the closet he'd half gutted, and she had a feeling she was in for another excuse.

Sighing, she lifted the phone to her ear. "Hey, Sammy. What's up?"

"I wanted to touch base with you about the closet."

"Finally. So when are you coming to finish it?"

"That's what I wanted to talk about. It'll probably have to be at the end of the week."

"Why not earlier?"

"No time. We've got a massive renovation to finish this week, kiddo."

Marley rolled her eyes. "Don't call me kiddo. I'm three years older than you, Sammy."

"On paper, maybe. But in maturity, I win."

"In your dreams."

"See how immature you are? Only ten-year-olds say 'in your dreams.'" He suddenly sounded contrite. "I'll try to make it earlier, since you're being so difficult."

"What's difficult is having to jump over a huge hole in the floor every time I walk down my hall," she countered.

"I'll fix it soon, I promise. Anyway, I've gotta go. We'll talk this week, 'kay?"

"Hot date?" she teased.

"Yep."

Marley grinned to herself. "Should I bother asking for her name or will she be but a mere speed bump in the road that is your love life?"

"Very poetic. And the answer is we'll see," Sam said mysteriously. "I'll talk to you later, kiddo."

They hung up, and Marley was still smiling as she started the car and left the hospital staff lot. Sam always managed to brighten her day. They hadn't been very close growing up. He'd been the epitome of a pesky little brother, what with his unfunny pranks and that God-awful, year-long "why?" phase. Oh, and she most definitely hadn't appreciated the time he'd squeezed purple hair dye into her shampoo bottle. *Permanent* hair dye. But after their mother died, they'd banded together to console their dad, and a bond had formed. Now, Marley couldn't imagine not having Sammy in her life.

Turning onto the main street, she headed in the direction of home. As she pulled into her driveway, she noticed a shiny black Range Rover parked next door and her heart gave an involuntary jump. She thought of Caleb Ford's piercing blue eyes and lean, muscular body, then pushed the memory of her neighbor from her mind. She parked and climbed the rickety porch steps, her feet aching the entire time. Forget yoga tonight—she was heading straight to the bathtub and staying in there for hours.

Kicking off her flip-flops, she closed the door, hopped over the stack of two-by-fours on the floor and made a beeline for the narrow staircase. The moment she reached the top step, the doorbell chimed, startling the hell out of her.

Sighing, she headed back downstairs, determined

to get rid of whoever had rung the bell. No one she knew would show up unannounced, so it was probably someone selling newspaper subscriptions or something equally annoying, and she wasn't in the mood to deal with that right now. She paused in front of the door and peered into the peephole.

A shaky breath flew out of her mouth when she found Caleb Ford's blue eyes peering back at her.

Shoot. She was so not prepared for a visit from the hottie next door. She had convertible hair, wasn't wearing a spot of makeup and she hadn't even bothered putting on a bra when she'd changed out of her nursing scrubs.

But she couldn't *not* answer the door. He knew she was home. He'd probably seen her pull up just now.

The doorbell rang a second time.

Maybe she shouldn't answer it all. She didn't know this guy—just because he was renting the house next door, that didn't make them buddies. She didn't owe him anything.

Actually, you do. He helped you escape death.

A sharp knock rapped against the door, making her jump. Wow, this guy was overeager, wasn't he?

Taking a deep breath, she finally reached for the knob and opened the door. And then there he was, standing on her porch and looking even sexier than she remembered.

He hooked his thumbs through the belt loops of his faded blue jeans. The stance just screamed *cool,* emphasized by the way the sun was setting directly behind him. Dark oranges and reds lit up the sky, and in turn cast a ruddy glow over him. He looked like a cowboy in the Wild West, standing in the sunset.

Vivid imagination, Marley.

"Did I catch you at a bad time?" Caleb asked in a deep sexy voice that made her shiver despite the balmy breeze drifting into the hall.

She shook the cobwebs from her mind and tried to remember what she'd been doing before being assaulted by his sex appeal. "I was about to take a bath," she admitted.

Something flickered in his eyes. Heat?

"Oh." He cleared his throat. "Sorry I interrupted you. I came by to see about your arm."

"My arm?" Then she remembered, and glanced down at the bandage covering the cut. "It's fine, just a scrape."

"Oh," he said again, shifting awkwardly. "I guess I'll go then. I just wanted to see how you were doing."

Promise to keep an open mind. Be open to some flirting, or heck, even a casual conversation.

Gwen's words buzzed in her head. She hesitated. Okay, maybe she could manage some light-hearted small talk, a flirty remark or two. It wouldn't kill her. He was obviously trying to be nice, coming over to check on her.

Besides, did she really want to send away the first man who'd made her feel anything close to desire in months?

"The bath can wait a little while longer," she found herself saying. "Do you want to come in for a quick cup of coffee?"

He nodded. "Sure, if it's no trouble."

"None at all." She opened the door wider. As he stepped into her narrow front hall, she felt overpowered by the sheer maleness of him. He was at least six-two, his big firm body dominating the small space. Before she could stop herself, she imagined that big firm body dominating *her,* and her breasts immediately ached, her nipples poking out against the front of her tank top. She wasn't surprised when Caleb's eyes dropped to her chest, lingering only for a second.

And with that one brief look, a rush of heat filled her body. She was rooted in place, watching his face as he watched her, and for a moment she experienced a sense of familiarity. As if they knew each other. There was something unbelievably intimate about his gaze.

She cleared her throat. "Uh, the kitchen's this way."

Caleb followed her down the hall, keeping a respectful distance behind her. As they entered her kitchen, she experienced a twinge of embarrassment at the chaos in the large airy space. Last weekend she'd scraped off most of the awful flower-patterned wallpaper the previous owners had described as *charming* in the real estate listing, and the walls were now bare. Paint cans sat near the splintered oak counter, which she needed to replace, and since she planned on painting the pantry, too, all the food from there rested in boxes against the wall. The room was a disaster.

"Sorry for the mess," she apologized. "I'm doing some renovating."

He raised a brow. "On your own?"

"Yep," she replied, gesturing for him to sit at the table tucked in the corner of the room. "I'm about to start the kitchen, which leaves me with, oh, every other room in the house."

Caleb's mouth lifted in a crooked smile. Marley's breath caught in her throat. Wow. This man definitely needed to do that more often.

He sank into one of the tall-backed chairs and crossed his ankles. "You're a do-it-yourself type then."

"Of course. It's not fun hiring someone to do the job

for you." She shrugged. "Way more satisfying knowing that I did the work."

She flicked on the coffeemaker and opened the cupboard above the sink, pulling out two mugs. "So what brought a New Yorker all the way across the country?"

There was a long pause, and then he chuckled. "Checking up on me, huh?"

She turned around and met his knowing look. "What?"

"I never told you I was from New York."

Heat scorched her cheeks. Shoot. Totally busted. How could she slip up like that?

"I called Debbie in Paris," she admitted. "I just wanted to make sure you were on the up and up. They didn't mention a renter before they left."

"It was a last-minute thing," he said, not offering further explanation.

The coffee machine clicked, and she poured the hot liquid into the mugs, glancing over at him. "Let me guess, you take yours black."

His lips twitched. "How'd you know?"

"Just a feeling." She dumped two spoonfuls of sugar into her cup, then walked over to the table and handed him his. Rather than sitting, she leaned against the counter again, blowing on her coffee to cool it.

"You're just going to hover over me like that?" Caleb asked.

"I hate sitting down," she confessed. "Probably because of my job. I'm on my feet all day, and I've gotten used to it. I go a little stir crazy when I'm in a chair."

"So…" He held his cup in one hand, looking a bit uncomfortable. "Do you usually make sure everyone you meet is on the up and up?"

The blush returned to her cheeks. "Not really. I

just…well, I like the Strathorns and I wanted to make sure…" Her voice trailed, and she made a wry face. "Sorry, I guess I've been having some trust issues lately."

He appeared to mull over her remark, then raised his mug to his lips. She watched his throat work as he swallowed, her stomach doing a funny little flip. Caleb Ford oozed masculinity, even when he drank. She couldn't help wondering if he'd be like that in bed, controlled, powerful.

As if he'd read her mind, he locked his eyes with hers. Little sparks danced along Marley's skin. There were sparks in the air, too. Hard to ignore them, zinging back and forth between her and Caleb, heating her skin. Breaking the eye contact, she distracted herself by taking another sip of coffee.

"Yeah, I know all about those. Trust issues," he clarified with a shrug. "To be honest, trust isn't something I'm good at."

She was suddenly curious. "Giving it, or getting it?"

"A little of both, probably."

Before she could press for details, he glanced around the room, taking in the paint supplies scattered on the tiled floor. "So you're starting with the painting first?" When she nodded, he said, "What else are you planning to do?"

Considering the grief Gwen had given her about these renovations yesterday, it was nice talking to someone who actually seemed interested. Before she could stop herself, she launched into a recitation of everything she planned to fix up. She was vaguely aware that she'd gone into babbling mode, but hey, at least it helped her ignore the rampant flames of sexual attraction threatening to burn down her kitchen.

CALEB WAS HAVING a very tough time keeping his eyes off Marley. Leaning against the counter in her faded jeans and curve-hugging tank top, with her golden hair up in a messy ponytail and her bare feet, she made a seriously alluring picture.

Her mere proximity made his body burn. Despite the odor of paint fumes lingering in the air, he could also make out a more subtle fragrance. Strawberries. The feminine aroma drove him wild. So did her legs, encased in that stretchy denim, and damn but she had cute feet—small and dainty with bright-pink toenails.

He imagined those legs wrapped around him, her heels digging into his buttocks, and fought back a moan.

It had been a mistake coming here. He was pretty good at talking women into going to bed with him, but just talking to them? He sucked at it.

He sipped his coffee, using the pause in the conversation to figure out his next move. Okay, so he'd made contact, but sitting around in Marley's kitchen wouldn't land him any answers. He needed to get her talking about Grier. But though he'd been watching her for more than a week now, to her he was a stranger. And women didn't open up to complete strangers.

He glanced at the sliding door on the other side of the kitchen, pretending to admire her backyard while he planned what to say. The sight of the oak tree in Marley's fenced-in yard brought a flicker of guilt, as he realized AJ had set up one of their cameras in the tree's enormous branches. As if someone wanted to hammer the point home, the branches rustled, sending a few leaves fluttering down to the grass.

Caleb shifted his eyes back to Marley. He opened his mouth to speak only to be interrupted by the ring of his cell phone. "Excuse me," he said as he fished his cell out of his pocket. He glanced at the caller ID, saw AJ's number and stifled a curse. "Do you mind if I take this?"

"Go ahead."

He flipped open the phone and said, "Hey, Vic, what's up?"

"I thought you were going to make contact later tonight," AJ hissed.

"I was, but I decided to work on the chapters earlier," Caleb said smoothly.

AJ let out an expletive. "I need you to get her out of the kitchen."

"Are you still in New York?" From the corner of his eye, he saw Marley discreetly move to the sink to rinse out her mug.

"I'm in the freaking tree out back. Looking at your ugly face as we speak," came the heated whisper.

It took all of Caleb's willpower not to look through the sliding door again. Evidently the rustling he'd seen in the tree hadn't come from a mischievous squirrel. The image of AJ's huge leather-clad body up in those branches nearly brought a laugh to the surface, but he quickly clamped it down.

"What are you doing in Florida?" he asked with great interest. AJ had left the house next door an hour ago to grab some groceries. Now he was in Marley's backyard?

"I was coming back and saw the camera dangling from one of the branches. Must have gotten dislodged. She always goes upstairs and does the yoga/shower thing after work so I figured I had time to fix the camera before she saw it, but then you just *had* to show up and bring her into the kitchen. And now I'm in the tree. The end."

"Bird sanctuary, huh? Can't say that's my cup of tea."

AJ swore again. "Just get her out of the kitchen so I can hightail it back next door."

"Sure thing, Vic. I'll email you the chapters by the end of the week so you'll have them when you get back from your vacation."

Caleb hung up the phone and rose to his feet, just as Marley rounded the counter again. To his dismay, she headed right for the patio door and peered out.

He came up behind her. "What are you looking at?" he asked as casually as he could muster.

"I heard you say something about birds," she answered with a sideways glance. "It reminded me that I haven't put seed in my bird feeder for a few days."

She extended a dainty hand, pointing at the bright red bird feeder hanging from the largest branch on the elm. "I made it myself," she added. "The sparrows love it."

Panic rose up Caleb's spine, mostly because he could now see one of AJ's black biker boots camouflaged in the leaves. "I should go," he burst out.

She wrinkled her brow. "Oh. Okay."

"That phone call," he said in an attempt to explain his abrupt exclamation. "I'm a writer, and my agent reminded me I need to revise a few chapters. So, uh, yeah, I should go do that."

Moving away from the patio door, Marley nodded. "I'll walk you—" She tripped over one of the paint cans on the floor, letting out an unladylike curse as she stumbled forward.

Snapping to action, Caleb reached out to steady her.

And regretted it the second his palms made contact with her hips. Her tank top had ridden up, and he was touching skin. Bare, warm skin, so soft that he hissed in a breath.

"I..." Marley's voice drifted and her mouth fell open when she caught sight of the obvious desire in his eyes.

He could do nothing to hide the swift response. Her flesh felt like heaven under his hands, and that sweet scent wafting into his nose was far too intoxicating.

He coughed ever so slightly. "You all right?"

She nodded wordlessly, then glanced down at his hands, which were still on her waist. God help him, but he couldn't seem to let her go.

And she wasn't complaining. Rather, she shifted so they were face to face. Her liquid brown eyes searched his. "I'm...a klutz," she murmured without breaking the eye contact.

Caleb swallowed, his mouth in desperate need of moisture, his lips in desperate need of *her.* Before he could stop himself, he moved his hand over her hip in a fleeting caress. An unsteady breath slid out of her throat.

Insanity. This was freaking insanity, and he was helpless to stop it. He'd been watching Marley Kincaid for seven days, watching and yearning and fighting the arousal he knew he shouldn't be feeling.

But he couldn't fight it now. Not when she was this close.

As his pulse drummed in his ears, he finally gave up. Screw it. Kissing her was wrong on so many levels, but at this point he didn't care. He wanted her so badly his bones ached.

So he took her.

4

MARLEY LET OUT a little gasp as he captured her mouth with his, but the second their lips met, she melted in his arms. He thrust his fingers into her hair, angling her head for better access, while he slid his other hand to her waist and drew her body to his.

She made a gentle, keening sound against his mouth, and then lifted her arms to his shoulders, pulling him closer. Her lips parted, her tongue darted out to toy with his and Caleb nearly keeled over from the jolt of desire that shot through him.

She tasted incredible. Like coffee, cinnamon and heaven and he couldn't get enough of her. He deepened the kiss, drowning in her scent. Damn it, he hadn't known it would be so uncontrollable.

A muffled thud sounded from outside. Marley must have heard it, too, because her eyelids fluttered open at the same time as his.

And then she was out of his arms.

His arms felt empty without her warm supple body in them, his mouth going dry when seconds before it had been moist from the tip of Marley's tongue teasing his lips. Even as his body tried to recover from that unbelievable kiss, his brain went back to business, directing his line of vision to the now-empty yard. Relief coursed through him. AJ had managed The Great Escape.

"I'm sorry," he said hoarsely. "I didn't mean to do that."

"I..." She tucked an errant blond strand behind her ear. "It's fine. Just unexpected."

Understatement of the year. What had he been thinking, kissing her? He'd wanted to distract her, and instead, he'd opened Pandora's damn box, because now that he'd tasted Marley, he wanted nothing more than to do it again.

Information. You just need information from her.

Drawing in a breath, Caleb willed his desire away. "I should go," he said.

Something flickered in her eyes. Finally, she just nodded, and they stepped out of the kitchen. He saw her wringing her hands together as she walked. "So you're a writer, huh?"

He almost laughed. It seemed ridiculous making small talk now, after the explosive kiss they'd just shared. "Yeah, I'm, uh, working on my first novel."

"That's cool."

When they reached the front hall, he glanced down at the two-by-fours on the floor, then the gutted closet. "You sure this isn't a safety hazard?" he asked in a dry voice.

She sighed. "My brother keeps promising to finish it, but he never seems to get around to it."

Caleb ran a hand through his hair, pausing near the front door. "I did some construction a few years back."

The admission came out of nowhere, but at least it

wasn't a lie, like his writer cover story. He *had* done a lot of construction before he joined the DEA.

"I could help you with some of the renovations." Gruffly, he added, "If you'd like."

Marley seemed to hesitate. "No, I couldn't let you do that. You're here to work on a novel."

"It's really no trouble." Damn, why was he insisting?

Information.

Right, it had nothing to do with her stunning face and endless supply of curves. He needed to find out what she knew about Grier. If she even knew anything. AJ thought she did, but Caleb wasn't certain, not after he'd spent some time with her. Everything about Marley seemed so genuine, so refreshing. How did she do it, continue to smile and laugh and live her life after what Patrick Grier had done to her? Unless AJ was right, and she was still in contact with Grier, sticking by him, moving money around to help him escape....

Caleb forcibly shoved all the negative thoughts from his brain and focused on Marley. She considered his offer for so long that he grew certain she would say no, thank you. But then she gave a tiny smile and nodded. "Well, my brother's finishing the closet this week, but I could use some help with the painting," she confessed.

"Should I come by tomorrow?" Anticipation rose in his chest. He quickly banished it, trying to remind himself that he wasn't seeing her for pleasure, but business.

"Sure. Let's see...I'm stuck with a graveyard shift tonight. I start at two—" she made a face "—and I'll be home around eleven tomorrow morning. I'll probably pass out for a while when I get back, so how about four?"

"Sounds good."

Laughing, Marley opened the front door for him. "I'm not sure it'll sound as good when I put you to work painting my kitchen."

He gave her a faint smile. "I look forward to it."

Stepping out onto the porch, he thanked her for the coffee. After the door closed behind him, he released a ragged breath. Lord, that kiss. It was a miracle he'd been able to finish the rest of the conversation.

He could still taste her on his lips, and his current state of discomfort made walking next door difficult. He'd never been harder in his life, and if Marley were any other woman, it wouldn't have stopped with one kiss. He felt it in the way she kissed him back and saw it in the disappointment clouding her eyes when they broke apart. If they were different people, he could've buried himself inside her and eased the ache in his groin. But he couldn't. He couldn't sleep with her.

Getting close to her in order to learn the truth was a necessary evil, but sleeping with her would pretty much purchase him a one-way ticket to hell. Because if she was innocent, he would have slept with a woman while lying about who he was. A woman who'd already been used by one liar. And if she was guilty, he'd have to live with the knowledge that he'd had sex with the woman helping Russ's murderer.

He let himself in through the front door and went upstairs, where he found AJ in the master bedroom, manning the monitors.

The second Caleb entered the room, AJ let out a hoot, followed by a round of applause. "I'm thoroughly impressed," his partner drawled. "You move fast, man."

Caleb smothered a groan. He'd been hoping AJ hadn't seen the kiss, but from the lewd way the man wiggled his eyebrows, he'd obviously caught the show.

"I was trying to distract her," Caleb muttered.

"With your tongue? You could have just asked for a tour of the house."

Caleb ignored the remark and said, "Aside from climbing trees, did you do anything productive today? Any headway on where the wire transfer came from?"

"Still nothing." AJ leaned back in the chair. "But I'm close, and I can tell you, the money wasn't wired from the States. I traced it to Europe. Not sure which country, though."

Europe, huh? It made sense, if the money that had appeared in the account was being used to fund Grier's way out of the country.

"What if Grier tries to move the money?" he asked, a frown puckering his brow.

"He can't," AJ answered, looking smug. "We set it up so that money can come in—that way we can track it—but Grier and Kincaid can't move the money out. I hope they try, though. I'd love to be a fly on the wall when they realize the hundred Gs is stuck there."

They. The word hung in Caleb's mind like a black rain cloud. AJ still hadn't ruled Marley out as a suspect, and it was beginning to bother him. After these last couple of encounters with Marley, he was less suspicious of her than ever. Caleb's instincts continued to tell him Marley wasn't helping Grier, but he knew he couldn't rule it out entirely. Still, it grated a little, hearing AJ lump her into Grier's villainous category.

"What about you?" AJ asked. "Aside from playing tonsil hockey with the nurse, what'd you find out?"

"Nothing," Caleb said with a sigh.

Not entirely true, of course. He'd found out plenty of things. Like how sweet she tasted. How pliant and welcoming her lips were. How hot her skin felt beneath his fingers.

"You mean your overwhelming charisma didn't win her over?"

Caleb bristled. "I offered to help her paint tomorrow, so maybe we'll get lucky and she'll open up then."

AJ's black eyes narrowed. "And what about you?"

"What do you mean?"

"Will *you* be getting lucky?"

The sudden bite to AJ's tone was unexpected. Caleb met his partner's wary gaze head-on. "Come on, AJ, I told you I'm not going to sleep with her."

"You sure? Because that make-out session looked pretty damn hot. Actually, it looked like you were going to beat your chest a couple of times, throw her over your shoulder and drag her upstairs so you could screw her brains out."

Caleb's lips tightened. "I was playing a part. I have no intention of taking her to bed."

"Uh-huh…"

"For the love of—"

"How long has it been since you got laid?"

Caleb's eyes flashed. "That has nothing to do with anything."

"No? I think it has a lot to do with this. Look, I get it. She's an attractive woman. But don't—"

"Don't what?" Caleb cut in. "Forget why I'm here?"

"I'm just asking you to be careful. Grier needs to be behind bars for what he did to Russ. And I can't have a cute blonde distracting you from catching him if he shows up."

"She won't. Trust me, I want Grier as much as you

do." Caleb swallowed. "Russ was the best friend I ever had, damn it. And tomorrow I plan on getting the truth out of Marley. If she knows anything, I'll find out, okay?"

AJ looked unconvinced. "And if she suddenly rips all her clothes off and begs you to do nasty things to her?"

Caleb swallowed harder, forcing himself not to imagine the ridiculously tempting scenario AJ had just described. "Then I say no," he maintained. "I'm serious, man. I'm not going to sleep with her."

"And if she unrolls the yoga mat and starts doing naked pelvic thrusts…"

He gritted his teeth. "I'm *not* going to sleep with her."

But oh, how he wanted to.

Not gonna happen, man.

No, he wouldn't let it happen. The weeklong attraction he'd felt for Marley might have culminated in an explosive kiss, but he was determined not to let it go further.

He just hoped he had the strength.

Scratch that—he *prayed* he had the strength.

MARLEY WAS WIDE AWAKE and dressed for manual labor when the doorbell rang the next afternoon. She'd taken a power nap when she got home from the hospital, and her alert state was actually a bit of a surprise. There had been a massive car accident on Interstate 5 and half the nurses from the respiratory unit where Marley usually worked had been reassigned to the E.R. for a couple of days to tend to the onslaught of victims. Marley was one of them, and she'd been running around like a chicken with its head cut off for the past nine hours.

Yet here she was, bright-eyed and ready to paint her kitchen. Figure that one out.

Okay, well, maybe it wasn't that hard to comprehend, considering who she would be painting the kitchen with.

She opened the door and there he was, wearing a pair of faded blue jeans and a black T-shirt. The shirt clung to his muscular chest, a sight that made Marley's heart race like a Formula One car. Darn it, why did he have to be so attractive?

And why had she let him kiss her? They'd only just met, for Pete's sake. Only a couple days ago she'd been telling Gwen she wanted to take things slow when it came to her love life, that getting intimate with a stranger scared her. And what had she done? Gotten intimate with a stranger.

"Hey," Caleb greeted her. His deep voice had a sexy rasp that brought a rush of heat to Marley's belly. "Ready to paint?"

She gestured for him to come in. "Ready, yes. Excited about it, no."

His lips quirked and she instantly focused on his sensual mouth. Her legs trembled as she thought about the kiss they'd shared. The memory of Caleb's warm mouth and skillful tongue ignited a charge of heat through her body, hot little flames that licked at her skin.

"Tough day at work?" he asked as he followed her inside.

"Very tough," she admitted. "I was assigned to the E.R. because there was a huge accident this morning. A tour bus taking twenty people to a casino collided with an eighteen-wheeler."

"I saw it on the news. Was it as bad as it looked?" Caleb asked.

"Worse. Seven dead, twelve injured." She led him into the kitchen, where she'd already set up all the paint trays and rollers they'd need.

"How do you do it?" His voice was low and laced with awe. "How can you look at so much death and carnage day in and day out?"

"I like helping people," she said simply.

He didn't respond, and when she looked over, she noticed him watching her with some expression she couldn't quite decipher. Admiration? Or was it curiosity?

She cleared her throat and picked up the large paint can labeled Morning Sunshine. "Um, so, you can start on that wall," she said, pointing to the wall opposite the back door. She moved her hand toward the adjacent wall, adding, "I still need to get rid of the rest of the wallpaper on this one, and then we can prime it."

"Yes, ma'am." A glint of humor filled his eyes, but his face remained as stoic as usual.

She wondered why he smiled so rarely. Difficult childhood, or was he just serious by nature? She didn't mind, though. She'd faked enough smiles these past few months that it was refreshing not having to put on a happy face to avoid being on the receiving end of the sympathetic smiles she'd grown used to.

It was even more refreshing not having to make awkward small talk, which she discovered ten minutes later as they worked in comfortable silence. Caleb didn't say much, except for the occasional work-related remark, as he rolled bright-yellow paint on her kitchen wall.

She found herself sneaking sidelong glances in his

direction, admiring his perfect profile, the strength of his jaw, the confident way he moved. Her pulse sped up each time he lifted his arms, which made his powerful muscles bunch and flex. His body was incredible, hard and lean without an ounce of fat. And she loved how focused he was on his task, his head bent in concentration. As he painted, a rogue lock of dark hair fell onto his forehead. She wanted to walk over and brush it away, but kept her hands on the scraper she was using. Just because every nerve ending in her body crackled with the need to touch him didn't mean she'd give in to temptation.

She forced herself to keep working, succeeding in removing nearly all the wallpaper before her parched throat finally got the best of her. "How about a break?" she suggested.

Caleb glanced over with a slight grin. "We've only been at this for an hour. I thought you were tougher than that, Kincaid."

A tiny alarm went off in her head. Had she told him her last name? She couldn't remember, but she didn't think so. Or maybe…the mailbox, she deduced with relief. He must have seen her last name on the mailbox.

"I'm also thirsty," she retorted.

"And you had a long night," he added in concession. "So I'm willing to overlook your laziness."

Rolling her eyes, she headed for the fridge. "Iced tea okay?"

"Yep."

She poured two tall glasses, then grabbed a few ice cubes from the freezer. Caleb was sitting at the table when she came back, rolling his shoulders in a way that made his pecs flex against his shirt. Her dry mouth went even dryer.

She sat down, sipping her drink and hoping the cold liquid would ease the fire inside her. Silence hung in the kitchen again, only this time it made her feel awkward. God, it was strange having a man here. Three months ago, it had been Patrick in Caleb's chair, reading the paper and eating the scrambled eggs she used to make him.

Her chest squeezed with anger. Though she tried masking the shot of pain that streaked through her, Caleb evidently sensed it.

"Are you okay?" he asked.

Marley put down her cup. "I'm fine." Her stomach burned, and she tried to control the volatile reaction thoughts of Patrick evoked inside her. "I was just thinking about something…someone… Don't worry about it."

"Anyone important?"

She couldn't help a harsh laugh. "You could say that."

A knowing glimmer filled his blue eyes. "An ex?"

She nodded.

"How long ago did you break up?"

He sounded curious, but not pushy, and something about his tone compelled her to answer. "It's been a few months now." She sighed. "And let's just say it didn't end well."

"I'm sorry."

That was it. *I'm sorry.* Marley suddenly felt like hugging him. Everyone she knew, when they'd heard about Patrick, had grilled her about the breakup. Even her dad, God bless him, wanted to know everything—as if hearing every last detail could somehow help him protect her after the fact. But Caleb didn't dig, he didn't pry or demand, and for that reason, she found herself revealing things she would never usually tell a stranger.

"He wasn't the person I thought he was." She wrapped her fingers around the cold glass, needing to hold on to something. "He lied to me about everything, starting with who he really was."

Caleb's face remained expressionless, but she saw a muscle twitch in his jaw. "He sounds like a pretty awful guy."

"Big time." Her hand trembled. "I still want to kick myself for ever falling in love with him."

To her surprise, the sympathy she expected to see wasn't there. Instead, he just shrugged and, in a rough voice, said, "You can't always help who you fall for. Or at least that's what I've heard."

Marley studied his face. "Heard, not felt, huh?" She took a chance and decided to venture into dangerous territory. "So you've never been in love?"

CALEB WASN'T PREPARED FOR the question, but he knew he'd opened this can of worms by asking her about Grier. And the answers she'd given perplexed him. His gut still told him she wasn't helping Grier, that she hadn't known a thing about Grier's crimes. So why wasn't she angrier? Hell hath no fury like a woman scorned, right?

When she'd spoken of Grier just now, Caleb had only seen pain and bitterness in her eyes. Not the fury *he'd* be feeling if someone close had deceived him. Marley, though…she simply looked sad.

"Caleb?"

Her melodic voice drew him from his thoughts. He tried to remember what she'd asked him, but the sight of her was far too distracting. Her lips, pink and lush, looked so utterly kissable, and her hair was coming out of its ponytail again, loose blond waves falling forward in the most appealing way.

He curled his hand around his iced-tea glass. He had to quit getting distracted by her curvy body and beautiful face. What had she asked again? Oh, yeah, love...

"No," he said grudgingly. "I can't say I've ever been in love."

Curiosity and surprise pooled in her big brown eyes. "How old are you?"

"Thirty-one."

"And you've really never been in love?"

He focused on his drink, raising it to his lips and taking a long sip, delaying his response. Why did she look so bewildered? Lots of people had never been in love, right?

"It just hasn't happened to me," he said. "And you know what? Half the time I think that's a good thing. Seems like love ends in disaster more often than not."

"It does," she agreed.

"But you haven't given up?"

She leaned back in her chair, the action causing her breasts to jut enticingly against the material of her yellow tank top. Caleb forced himself to look only at her face. Anything lower than that was guaranteed to blow his concentration to smithereens.

"No, I haven't given up," she said in a soft voice. "Sure, I might have some trust issues now, thanks to my ex, but I'm working through those. You know, trying to understand why I didn't see the signs, why I let him manipulate me so completely. But I still think love can be a good thing, if you find the right person."

Caleb absorbed everything she'd just said. Love. It

was such a foreign concept to him, since growing up he hadn't had any of it. He'd never known his father, and his mother had decided drugs were more important than her five-year-old son. In a sense, his first relationship with a woman ended up with him finding his mom's overdosed body on the living-room carpet.

Could love be a good thing? To him, the answer was a big fat no. What was the point in opening yourself up to another person when they would only kick you aside sooner or later?

He scraped back his chair, discomfort gathering in his gut. This was too…intimate. He was getting too close to sharing a very private part of himself with this woman, and he couldn't do that. It made him uneasy.

"We should get back to work," he said.

Marley nodded. "I'm almost done with the wallpaper," she replied, getting up to drag a small stepladder toward the wall. She climbed up on it, looking over at him and adding, "I just need to finish this part near the ceiling and then we can—" A yelp flew out of her mouth as she lost her balance.

Caleb reacted instantly, reaching the spot just in time for her to topple right into his arms. A flash of heat tore through his body as he found himself yet again cupping her firm bottom. His groin stirred and hardened. Her sweet scent assaulted him, mingling with the paint fumes in the air and making him lightheaded with desire.

"What is it with you and ladders?" he asked roughly.

She stared up at him, amusement dancing in her eyes. "I never claimed to be graceful, okay?"

He choked back a laugh. "Good, because you're not."

They stared at each other for a moment and

something in the air shifted. She had one arm around his shoulder, the other pressed against his chest and her touch seared through the material of his shirt and heated his flesh. The room grew thick with tension, heavy with attraction. He wanted to taste her again. To drag his hands over that exquisite body, kiss her, touch her, until she cried out with pleasure.

Suddenly he couldn't move, couldn't breathe. He knew he should let her down, but his arms refused to cooperate. They just held her tighter, pulled her closer.

"Um, so…" Her voice came out husky. She stopped talking, the tip of her tongue darting out to moisten her lips.

"Don't do that," he burst out.

She froze. "Do what?"

"Lick your lips like that." Despite himself, he reached out to rub the bare flesh of her arm.

Marley's breath hitched. "Why not?"

He ran his hand up and down her hot skin. "Because it's already hard enough."

"What's hard enough?" she whispered.

"Trying not to kiss you again."

Those big brown eyes glimmered with heat. His cock swelled as her gaze moved to his mouth. For God's sake, didn't she realize he only wanted to kiss her more when she looked at him like that?

"You know what I think?" she said, her soft voice sliding over him like a sensual caress.

"What?"

She rubbed her palm against his chest in a feather-light stroke, then twined both arms around his neck and murmured, "I think you should just go for it."

With her head slanted up toward him and her lush

lips pursed, Caleb knew there was no way he could resist her. He wanted this. No, he *needed* this.

He slowly lowered his head. Their lips were inches apart, so close. Not close enough. An unsteady breath left his mouth. He shouldn't do this. His lips moved closer, nearly touching hers. He really, really shouldn't do—

A loud chime rang through the kitchen, startling them both. Their heads moved apart, and Caleb nearly lost his grip on the sexy woman in his arms.

"An email just came in," she murmured in explanation.

The annoying chime sounded again, and Caleb traced it to the open laptop sitting on the counter.

"Ignore it," she said, sounding a little breathless. "It's probably just my brother. He's supposed to send me pictures of tiles."

But the moment had passed, and the interruption had been much needed. Saved by email. Caleb's entire body shrieked in protest as he gently set Marley on her feet. His pulse was still racing, his cock stiffer than a two-by-four, but he knew his body would forgive him. He wasn't sure he'd be able to forgive himself if things went any further.

He was lying to her about who he was, for God's sake. Getting involved with Marley would be a terrible mistake. Not to mention unbelievably callous.

"You should check it," he said, taking a step backward.

The disappointment flashing across her face tore at him. *You don't want me,* he wanted to tell her. *You don't know me.* But he kept his mouth shut, and after a moment, she walked over to the counter.

He used the distance between them to collect his

composure, to steady himself and will away his massive erection. Marley was bent over the laptop, clicking away. She waited for a page to load, clicked again and then all the color rapidly drained from her face.

"Everything okay?" he called warily.

She didn't answer. Just remained glued to the screen, her face growing impossibly paler.

"Oh, my God," she whispered.

Caleb took brisk strides toward the counter, but Marley was shielding the computer screen from his view. "What's going on?" he demanded.

Slowly, she lifted her head and looked at him. The terror and confusion he saw in her gaze raised every warning flag he had.

"It's him." She shuddered. "Why won't he leave me alone? Why can't he just—" Her breath was quick and shallow. "Oh, God. I have to call the police."

5

"MARLEY, YOU NEED TO CALM DOWN and tell me what's going on," Caleb said in a firm tone.

But she was already marching over to the phone, mumbling unintelligible things. As she dialed, Caleb leaned forward to examine the page on the laptop, the message that had just shaken Marley's entire world. He hissed in a breath as he read the words on the screen.

I miss you, sweet pea. Stay strong. I'll see you soon.

Caleb's body hardened with icy fury. Grier. That son of a bitch had contacted Marley, just as Caleb had known he would.

"Detective Hernandez," he heard Marley stammer from behind him. "Yes…please…tell him it's urgent."

Caleb read Grier's message again. Short, but sweet. Each word was branded into his brain, the last four bringing a wave of satisfaction and a jolt of adrenaline. Grier was coming for her. Caleb had known Grier wouldn't be able to stay away. Yet along with the gratification of knowing that his hunch had been right, a knot of fear twined around his insides as he realized precisely how much danger Marley was in.

Grier's saccharine words rang of love, not hate, but when you were dealing with sociopaths there wasn't always a clear line between the two. Grier could turn on Marley any second. Hell, he could decide to strangle her to death if he didn't like the way she prepared his coffee. The knowledge of what had happened to the last woman Grier was involved with wasn't lost on Caleb. They'd never been able to conclusively tie him to her murder, but the circumstantial evidence was overwhelming. With nothing concrete to charge him with, the case had gone cold. Still, everyone involved felt Grier was their man.

Shit. He needed to call his supervisor and arrange for more agents to watch Marley, maybe get the local cops to patrol the neighborhood. Even Hernandez would have to agree this email spelled danger.

Hernandez. Damn. Marley was speaking to him at this very moment, her voice shaky as she told him about the message.

He had to get out of here. And fast. The local police detective knew about the stakeout, but not that Caleb had made contact. Which meant that his cover could be blown the moment the detective walked into the house and saw Caleb there.

"The detective in charge of the case is on his way over."

Marley's voice pulled him from his panicked thoughts. He turned to face her, glad to see some color returning to her face.

She gave him a rueful look. "I guess I have some explaining to do, huh?"

Caleb faltered. Explaining? Why would she need to—because he wasn't supposed to know about any of this... She wasn't aware that he knew about Grier, that he'd been hunting the guy for three months. That his best friend and partner had been killed because of her ex.

"Yeah," he said, finding his voice. "That might be helpful." He gestured to the laptop. "I'm sorry, I read the email. You were so upset, and I wanted to see—"

"It's fine," she interrupted. "Come on, let's sit."

He followed her back to the table, but even after they were seated, Marley didn't continue. She suddenly seemed lost, turmoil and anger roiling in her brown eyes.

"Who was the message from?" he asked.

"My ex," she said flatly. "Who made it pretty clear he's coming after me."

"I'm afraid I don't quite understand."

She inhaled slowly. "Remember I told you he wasn't who he said he was? Well, what I found out that he was a drug dealer."

Without preamble, she told him everything. She skimmed over the romance, but spoke in detail about the day she'd found out from the police who Patrick was, the investigation that followed, the shame and horror she'd felt when she learned the truth.

Each word made his temples throb. The disbelief dripping from her voice was unmistakable. So was the disgust in her eyes. AJ was wrong. There was now no doubt in Caleb's mind that Marley had been completely ignorant of her fiancé's criminal dealings.

Nobody could act that well. Nobody could fake the horror conveyed in each word she spoke.

"And now he emails me?" she finished, looking at him with wide eyes. "God, Caleb, what if he shows up here?"

Then I'll catch him.

He bit back the words, instead leaning forward in the chair and resting his elbows on the table. "I'm sure the police will do everything they can to protect you, Marley. They won't just let a murderer waltz into your home."

"Hernandez might," she said bitterly. "That man hates me. He thinks I knew about Patrick all along and that I'm somehow helping him now."

"Why the heck would he think that?"

"I don't know." She shook her head in anger. "He has it in for me, and I've never done a single thing to the man. And now he's coming over, and he'll probably grill me again and accuse me of sending the email myself."

Caleb stifled a sigh. Yeah, with Hernandez, some grilling would definitely be involved. He didn't understand what Hernandez had against Marley, but he made a mental note to ask AJ to get his hands on the detective's file. Caleb couldn't afford to lose Grier because of some stupid vendetta.

"Maybe he'll be more receptive this time," Caleb said, trying to sound positive. "He must be getting anxious, trying to find your ex, and this could be a big break in the case."

Marley didn't look convinced. "Will you stay while he questions me? I know this doesn't really involve you, but…" She exhaled. "I'd feel better if I had someone on my side for this."

How on earth was he supposed to say no to that?

Reluctance welled up in his chest. He couldn't stick around. Hernandez might slip up when he saw him, do something dim-witted like call Caleb "Agent Ford." If Marley found out who he really was, she would be furious. Most likely she'd throw him out and refuse to have any further contact with him. Then again, she was an intelligent woman; she might see the benefit of having a cop close by.

But he couldn't take the chance that fury might cloud her judgment. AJ had persuaded him to befriend Marley so he could gain information, but now that Grier had contacted her, Caleb had an even more important reason to stay by her side. He'd never be able to forgive himself if Grier hurt Marley—if he killed her, the way he'd killed Russ.

Caleb's blood pressure spiked. Marley was still waiting for his answer, and for the life of him, he couldn't leave her right now. "Let's sit in the living room," he said with a small sigh.

They walked into the spacious room, which contained a comfortable brown couch, a huge bookshelf crammed with novels, and a large window overlooking the front yard. As Marley sank down onto the couch, Caleb went to the window, fixing his gaze on the driveway.

How was he going to get out of this? Detective Hernandez would arrive any freaking second. Caleb needed to intercept the man before he entered the house.

Behind him, Marley sat with her back ramrod

straight. Caleb wanted nothing more than to draw her into his arms and offer words of comfort, but he couldn't. Not until he figured out how to get Hernandez alone before the man questioned Marley.

Tension coiled into a tight knot in his gut as he spotted an unmarked black sedan pulling into the driveway. He started for the front door. Marley followed him, but he placed a hand on her arm before she could reach for the doorknob.

"I want to go out there and talk to him first," he said.

She blinked. "Why?"

"To make a few things clear to him before he comes in here and starts treating you like a suspect," he improvised.

"Caleb, don't—"

Before she could object further, he darted out the door and descended the porch just as Hernandez stepped onto Marley's driveway. The detective was short and stocky, with a head of black hair streaked with gray, and dark eyes that widened at the sight of Caleb. "Agent Ford?" Hernandez said.

Caleb closed the distance between them, glad the detective hadn't spoken any louder. "Hey, Miguel."

Hernandez's thick black mustache curled as he drew his lips together in a frown. "What the hell are you doing in there with her? I thought Stevens had you next door."

"He does, but I had to make contact."

Hernandez looked suspicious. "Why?"

"It was necessary. Look, I'm undercover, Miguel. Kincaid thinks I'm her writer neighbor, and I need her to keep thinking that."

The detective's frown deepened. "The department still views her as a suspect, Ford."

"The department might need to change that opinion then," he retorted. "I don't believe Kincaid had any knowledge of her fiancé's previous or current crimes. But I do believe Grier will contact her again, especially after the message he sent twenty minutes ago."

"The email she *claims* he sent," Hernandez said.

"It's real, Miguel. And before we go in there, I need your word that you'll maintain my cover. We don't know each other."

Hernandez paused for a moment, looking both intrigued and wary. "We don't know each other," he finally agreed.

The two men crossed Marley's lawn and climbed the porch. Marley was waiting at the door. The moment she saw Hernandez, her delicate mouth tightened in a thin line. "Detective Hernandez," she said coolly, casting Caleb a suspicious look.

"Ms. Kincaid." Hernandez's nod of greeting was polite, but it was still obvious how he felt about Marley. He didn't trust her.

"Let's go into the kitchen," Caleb suggested.

Unable to stop himself, he placed a possessive hand on the small of Marley's back, ignored the slight raise of Hernandez's fuzzy black eyebrows and headed for the kitchen.

MARLEY HAD TROUBLE CONTAINING her distaste as she watched Hernandez read the email. He'd slipped on a pair of latex gloves before handling the laptop, as if he expected Patrick's fingerprints to be on it or something. Right, because she'd secretly met up with Patrick, let him use her computer so he could send her an email and then come home and called the police. Why did this man distrust her so much? She'd never been in trouble with the law, didn't even have any outstanding parking tickets and yet here he was, treating her like a common criminal.

"Has anyone had access to this laptop other than the two of you?" Hernandez asked.

"No," Marley replied. "I'm the only one who uses it."

He stared at the screen again. "Do you recognize the email address the message came from?"

"No. Patrick's address was the one on his domain name, for his web design company."

"He most likely used one of those free email accounts," Caleb spoke up, leaning against the counter. "He probably went to an internet café to do it."

"Maybe," the detective said, "but that's for us to figure out. Why don't you focus on—what is it you do, Mr. Ford? Writer?"

She noticed a muscle twitch in Caleb's jaw. "Yes," he muttered.

"Then focus on writing and let us do our job."

The detective's voice was so cold most people probably would've cowered and shut up, but not Caleb. To Marley's amazement, he crossed his arms over his spectacular chest and said, "I'm sure you have a bunch of tech guys at the station who can locate the IP address of the computer the message was sent on. But what about Marley? I assume you'll assign some officers to protect her."

The detective spared a pithy look in Marley's direction. "I'm afraid we don't have the budget for that."

Barely contained anger seethed in Caleb's blue eyes.

"Come on, Detective, you read the note. He's obviously planning to make a move soon. I was under the impression you've been searching for this guy for some time."

"We have been." Hernandez let out a resigned breath. To Marley's surprise, he caved in to Caleb's request. "I'll arrange some patrols around the neighborhood and talk to the captain about posting an officer outside the house."

Marley glanced from Caleb to Hernandez. There was a strange ripple of tension between them, and neither man seemed to like the other very much. She understood, at least from Caleb's perspective. She hadn't liked Hernandez from the moment they'd met. What she did like, however, was how Caleb didn't even flinch as he met the other man's gaze head-on.

A tiny thrill shot through her. She needed to stop being so closed off and suspicious. It actually felt nice, having someone in her corner.

"I'm going to have to confiscate the computer," Hernandez said, his words sounding stilted. He picked up the laptop and tucked it under his arm. "The boys at the station will try to figure out where the email came from."

"Thank you," Marley said.

Hernandez slowly studied her face. "Is this the first contact Grier has made?"

She nodded.

"Are you sure about that?"

Marley's spine stiffened. She opened her mouth to reply, but Caleb spoke before she could. "Why do you insist on treating her like a suspect?" he asked in an even voice.

"I'm doing my job, Mr. Ford. I'm expected to examine every angle."

"Well, you're wasting your time on this one. Marley didn't do anything wrong. She was used and lied to, and you might actually get a break in the case if you focused your attention on more important *angles*."

Hernandez looked absolutely livid. The tension in the kitchen skyrocketed, mingling with the rage radiating from both men. Marley sighed and quickly attempted to diffuse their volatile emotions.

"This is the first time Patrick has contacted me," she said loudly. "And yes, I'm sure. As I told you three months ago, Patrick went to a design convention and never came back. Two days later, you showed up at my door and told me who he really is. And a half hour ago, he emailed me. That's all I can tell you, Detective."

"Okay, then. We'll get on this email development right away." Scowling at Caleb, Hernandez took a step toward the doorway. "And if he tries to make contact again, call us immediately."

Nodding, Marley led the detective out of her kitchen and walked him to the front door. Caleb trailed behind them, his shoulders stiff. She offered Hernandez a polite thank-you for his help, then leaned against the door frame and watched as he strode to his car with her laptop under his arm.

The engine of the black sedan roared to life, and then Hernandez drove off. Marley turned to face Caleb. "I appreciate your sticking up for me like that, but I don't know if it was a good idea for you to interfere with Hernandez."

She still couldn't believe he'd done it. He didn't even know her, yet he'd reprimanded the detective, the conviction in his voice so strong when he'd insisted she couldn't be helping Patrick.

"He'll get over it," Caleb said, shrugging.

"You're a good man, Caleb. Not many people would defend someone they've only known a few days. For all you know, I really could be helping Patrick."

"You wouldn't do that," he said, sounding gruff.

Despite her reservations emotion filled her chest, making Marley's throat tighten. His faith in her came as an odd relief. She normally didn't care what people thought. As long as her family and close friends knew what kind of person she was, it didn't matter what jerks like Hernandez believed. But knowing that Caleb trusted her brought an unexpected rush of pleasure.

She realized she was starting to like him a lot. Not just because he'd caught her when she'd fallen off the roof or because he'd offered to help her renovate. There was something about his quiet strength and rare laughter that made her heart jump. She was shocked at how quickly her feelings were growing.

"I have to go," he said, then cleared his throat. "I'm next door if you need me. If anything happens, if your ex causes any trouble, don't hesitate to come and get me, okay? Day or night, Marley."

All she could do was nod, amazed by the sincerity in his deep voice. He really meant it. He would actually be willing to protect her, a woman he'd just met. Maybe there *were* some good and decent men left in this world.

As his hand reached for the doorknob, she burst out, "Wait."

Caleb turned. "Yeah?"

Without another word, she eliminated the distance

between them, cupped his strong jaw with both hands, and kissed him.

Like placing a hand on a hot stove, her body got an immediate reaction from the feel of his firm lips against hers. Heat torpedoed into her, and she deepened the kiss, needing to taste him. He hesitated when she ran her tongue along the seam of his lips, seeking entry, but then he let her in.

She flicked her tongue over his, eliciting a ragged groan from deep in his throat. He was restraining himself, and she didn't like it. So she pressed her body closer to his and wrapped her arms around him. Feeling bold, she let her hands skim down his body to touch his taut ass. Gave it a little squeeze, too.

Caleb chuckled against her mouth. "Did you just squeeze my butt?"

"Mmm-hmm." She brushed her lips over his. "Are you complaining?" Without letting him reply, she kissed him again. Caleb was so darn reserved all the time. She wanted to see some of his control crumble, wanted to feel him let go.

She got her wish seconds later, when he suddenly released a husky growl and returned the kiss with fervor. And then he was touching her, his warm hands stroking her hips, caressing her belly, reaching around to cup her bottom. He squeezed her the way she'd just done to him, then moved his hands back to her waist and began to drag his palms over her stomach, slowly traveling up to her breasts.

Her nipples pebbled, her core burning with passion. Marley shivered, whimpered, then gasped when he grazed the underside of each breast. God, she wanted

him to touch her. To fondle her and kiss her and slide
into her—

He abruptly broke off the kiss, his hands dropping
from her chest. "I should go." Each word was a hoarse
gasp.

Marley was still a little stunned, amazed by her own
boldness, but even more surprised by the sparks crackling between them like fireworks. She wanted him so
badly every inch of her body ached and tingled. What
was happening to her?

"Will you have dinner with me tomorrow night?"
she asked impulsively. "My treat."

He ran one hand through his scruffy hair, drawing her attention to the fleck of yellow paint caught in
his dark tresses. "No painting involved," she added,
grinning.

Hesitation flickered across his face. "I don't know,
I have a lot of work to do."

"Please?" She swallowed. "I could use the company."

She knew he was thinking about the email her psychotic ex-fiancé had just sent her—she was thinking about it, too. When he finally nodded, pleasure
bloomed inside her.

"Okay," he agreed. "What time?"

"I'll be home from the hospital around five, so how's
seven?"

"Seven," he confirmed.

She opened the door for him, smiling. "I'll see you
tomorrow then."

Caleb gave a slight nod, bade her goodbye and
stepped onto the porch. She watched him walk off,
then closed her front door and went back inside.

Her heart did a little jumping jack, and not even the memory of Patrick's disgustingly loving email could bring down her mood. The police would find Patrick. She had to believe in that, otherwise she'd be cowering in fear, hiding in her bedroom closet or something. No matter how apprehensive the thought of Patrick coming back here made her, she wasn't going to cower. She was stronger than that.

And right now, all she wanted to do was bask in the surprising and delicious feelings Caleb inspired in her and look forward to sharing dinner with a man who wasn't a psychotic criminal.

"SON OF A BITCH," PATRICK muttered under his breath, his eyes glued to the dark-haired man who'd just walked out of Marley's house.

Anger bubbled in Patrick's gut as he noticed the other man's cocky stride. The guy walked like a cop.

Probably because he was one.

Patrick's entire body had turned into a block of ice when he'd seen that unmarked cruiser slide into Marley's driveway, but the shock hadn't been as great as the one he'd experienced when a very familiar DEA agent strolled outside to exchange a few words with the detective.

He clenched his fists. He'd known the cops were watching Marley, but the DEA had someone right next door? Shit. That would make getting to her a hell of a lot more difficult.

Did she know her neighbor was a cop? Patrick froze as he pondered that question. No, the agent must be pulling the wool over her eyes. Marley would never work with the cops. She was on *his* side.

Then why did she give the fat detective her laptop?

"They were tracking her email," he mumbled after a moment. He'd thought about that when he was at the internet café sending her the message, but he'd figured it was a risk he could afford to take. The cops would trace the email to the computer at the café, but it wasn't like Patrick would be hanging around there, sipping lattes.

Marley had no choice. She'd had to give them her computer. What worried him more was the disconcerting presence of the agent next door. Patrick remembered him from the raid. The bastard had pointed a gun at him, ordered him to surrender. And now here he was, waiting for another chance to make his arrest.

"They won't catch me," Patrick said smugly, turning his attention to the woman on the bed.

He'd moved Lydia out of the closet to give her a little bit of air—he wasn't a monster, after all—but she was still bound and gagged. Still looking at him with those terrified eyes.

"Relax," he said with a sigh. "I'm not going to hurt you. I already told you that."

She whimpered, bringing a wave of irritation to his gut. Striding over to the bed, he sat down on the edge and stared directly at her. "I'm not a bad guy, all right? So quit looking at me like that. What's so wrong with wanting to make a little money?"

The old lady couldn't answer because of the gag stretched across her mouth, but the look in her eyes was annoyingly familiar. His parents used to sport that same expression, when he told them about all the big plans he had for himself. They didn't understand, though. His parents were too bland, too ordinary. They were perfectly happy living in their crappy little Iowa town, teaching math to snot-faced schoolchildren, and letting their lives pass them by.

Well, Patrick wasn't like them. All he'd ever wished for as a child was to get out of Nowhereville, Iowa, and *be* somebody. He wanted to live life. He wanted millions of dollars in the bank and yachts and trips around the world.

But above all that, he wanted Marley.

She was beautiful and kind and good. And a bad boy like him needed a good girl like her for balance.

Except now he had that asshole cop to contend with. It would be no easy feat, getting the money he'd stashed under the tile in Marley's bathroom, but he knew he'd find a way.

He always did, after all.

6

CALEB SPENT MOST of the morning going over his files on Patrick Grier, focusing on the list of known associates and persons of interest, and trying to figure out who Grier might turn to for help other than his ex-fiancée. By the early afternoon he gave up. The DEA and local law enforcement had already scoured that list for months, and so far it hadn't produced any leads. There was some hope with a former contact of Grier's in Mexico, but the man wasn't talking and no amount of pressure seemed to help.

Getting up from his chair, Caleb rubbed his eyes, then glanced at the bed, noticing that all the sheets lay in a tangled mess on the floor. He'd been awake most of the night, tossing, turning, cursing and trying not to think about Marley. Of course, he'd failed miserably, and in the end he'd been up for hours, tossing, turning, cursing and *totally* thinking about Marley.

He'd contemplated going to the guest room next door and dragging AJ out of bed, maybe getting a game of poker going, but he'd resisted the urge. AJ wouldn't understand the feelings Caleb was developing for Marley.

Disturbing feelings. His emotions, normally tightly reined in, now flowed like water from a leaky faucet, and he was helpless to turn them off.

He liked Marley.

No, he *really* liked her. And he wanted her so badly he couldn't think straight anymore. Just the thought of her made every part of his body ache. His head. His groin. His heart.

"Forget about that," he mumbled to himself, raking his fingers through his hair as he leaned back. "Focus on the job."

Unfortunately, his body wouldn't let him forget. He had an erection of colossal proportions straining against the front of his gray sweatpants, and in his groin an ache so deep his bones hurt.

His cell phone started ringing before he could slink off to the bathroom and resort to self-gratification. Noticing the caller ID, he suppressed a sigh and picked up the phone.

"Hello, sir," he said.

A vile curse battered his eardrums. "What's going on over there, Ford?" his supervisor demanded.

"What do you mean?"

Ken Stevens wasn't put off by his casual tone. "Miguel Hernandez just gave me a call, wanting to know why one of my agents is cozying up to Marley Kincaid."

Thanks a lot, Hernandez.

"I'm not cozying up to her," he replied. "I had no choice but to make contact with her." Quickly, he explained the ladder incident, finishing with, "AJ thought since I'd already interacted with her, I should keep it up to see if she knows anything about Grier."

"And does she?"

"No."

Stevens made a frustrated noise. "Next time, speak to me before you decide to go against protocol." Stevens paused. "What's this email Hernandez mentioned?"

Caleb told him what the message contained, even though Stevens probably had a copy of it sitting in front of him on his desk. "I told you he wouldn't be able to stay away from her," he said. "He's going to make a move soon, sir. I feel it in my gut."

"Then stay put and keep your eyes open."

Despite his sometimes hotheaded nature, Stevens had always possessed a great deal of faith in Caleb and his abilities, which Caleb appreciated at the moment. He knew his boss wasn't happy that he'd befriended Marley, but both men understood that there were bigger things to worry about at the moment.

"I'll catch him, sir," Caleb said "He's been lucky all these years, keeping his cover solid, avoiding charges, but his luck is up. I think he's obsessed with Kincaid, and he will come for her."

Stevens sighed. "He'd better."

"No breaks on your end?"

"Lukas is still monitoring the bank account Grier opened with Kincaid, but there haven't been any more deposits and no withdrawal attempts. I've got six agents on the airports, two watching San Diego General and a few more talking to Grier's associates. We're running out of manpower."

Stevens's voice hardened. "Don't get too close to her, Ford. Keep the contact casual—we can't risk having this case thrown out of court if you get involved with a witness. And keep me posted."

As usual, his supervisor hung up without uttering

a goodbye. Stevens didn't have time for pleasantries, never had.

Caleb set the phone on the desk and glanced down at his ratty sweatpants, then lifted his hand to his chin and rubbed the thick stubble he hadn't bothered to shave this morning. He should, though. He couldn't have dinner with Marley looking like a disheveled lumberjack.

He rubbed his forehead, wondering what the hell he'd gotten himself into. His job at the agency was all he had, all he cared about, and here he was, risking it for a woman with big brown eyes and a gorgeous smile.

Why couldn't he stay away from her? He had no reason to maintain contact—he was already convinced she had no information about Grier. He should be walking away from her, not running straight toward her.

He could always cancel their dinner date. Tell her he was sick or that he had to go out of town. But then he imagined the disappointment in her voice when he backed out, and knew he couldn't do it. He didn't want to disappoint Marley. He wished he knew where these protective instincts had sprung from and why he so desperately wanted to make her happy.

Don't get too close to her.

He almost laughed. What would Stevens do if he knew Caleb was going over there tonight for dinner?

Probably can his ass.

MARLEY DID ONE LAST SWEEP of the living room, making sure she'd dropped the clutter level from *this chick is a slob* to *organized mess*. She'd opted to serve Caleb dinner in the living room, since the kitchen reeked of paint. The Chinese food she'd ordered would be arriving any minute, and she'd already rid the coffee table of the paperback novels that usually resided there.

Now she stood in the doorway, wearing a pair of comfy black pants and her favorite stretchy green T-shirt. Butterflies danced around in her stomach.

"What am I doing?" she mumbled to herself, sinking down on the couch cushions.

She'd told Gwen she wasn't ready to get involved with anyone new, yet she seemed to be going out of her way to do just that. She pictured Caleb's face, wondering what it was about him that captivated her. Patrick had won her over with his easygoing smiles and almost youthful enthusiasm. He had a lust for life, charm that just poured out of him.

But Caleb...he was more intense. A little awkward around her, too, which she found kind of adorable. And whenever she thought about his hot kisses and lazy caresses, her body tightened with awareness.

Her head jerked up at the sound of the doorbell, immediately followed by the sound of her pulse drumming in her ears like the beat of a club song. She drew in a breath, willed her heartbeat to slow, then went to the door.

When she opened it, she found Caleb on the porch, wearing jeans and a long-sleeved navy-blue shirt, and holding two large paper bags with steam rolling out of the top. "I intercepted your delivery man at the door," he said.

Marley glanced past his impossibly broad shoulders, and saw the retreating headlights of a beat-up white Honda with Mr. Chow's logo on the side.

"I'll grab some cash and reimburse you," she said.

He shook his head. "No way."

"I said it would be my treat."

"I chose to ignore you." His deep voice brooked no argument as he entered her house.

"How very last century of you," she said sweetly.

He smiled—God, she loved it when he did that. "I'll take that as a compliment."

She led him into the living room, where they began laying out steaming hot cartons of food. Marley had already brought out plates and utensils, as well as a bottle of red wine and two glasses. She and Caleb got settled on the carpet, and she dug in immediately, too hungry to worry about the fact that she was stuffing her face when they'd barely said hello. She hadn't eaten a thing all day, thanks to another hectic shift at the hospital without a break and then because of the nervous flutters in her stomach at the prospect of seeing Caleb again.

She felt so drawn to the man, even though she still didn't know much about him, save for the fact that he was devastatingly handsome and kissed like a dream. Maybe tonight he'd finally open up to her a little.

"This is delicious," she moaned, popping another bite of sesame chicken into her mouth.

Caleb bit into an egg roll. "I haven't had Chinese food since I left New York. Back there, I live on this stuff."

"Is that where you call home?"

"I usually go where the job takes me," he answered.

She furrowed her brows. "You mean, for research?"

"No, I only started writing recently." He took another bite of the egg roll, then focused on the task of spooning chicken fried rice onto his plate. "I was doing construction before that, and the company I worked for did jobs all over the country."

"So you took time off to write?"

He nodded.

Marley picked up her wineglass, studying Caleb as she took a sip. He seemed completely uninterested in talking about himself. Patrick, on the other hand, had been all about his own ego, constantly regaling her with stories where he played the starring role. None of them true, of course.

Which did she prefer? A man who talked up a storm and only told lies? Or one who refused to talk at all? Still, she wasn't a quitter, and she was determined to pry some details out of Caleb.

"Does your family live on the East Coast?" she asked.

His face became shuttered. "I don't have any family. My mother died when I was five, and I never knew my dad."

She leaned closer, studied his face. "No aunts, uncles, grandparents?"

"Nope." His tone was casual, but she saw a flicker of pain in the depths of his eyes. He took a sip of wine, then said, "I was in foster care my whole childhood."

"Caleb, I—" Marley's words caught in her throat. "That must have been hard. What about close friends?"

Caleb's features creased with pain. "One. But he died a few months ago."

Her heart squeezed, just as it did in the hospital whenever she encountered a particularly sad case. "I'm sorry," she said quietly.

A lull fell over the room. Marley tried to focus on the food in front of her, but it was hard to ignore the flicker of sorrow on Caleb's face. She wondered how his friend had died, but didn't broach the subject. And he didn't share the details, making it obvious it wasn't a conversational path he wanted to venture down.

But his grief...she couldn't turn away from it. Couldn't ignore it, either. It was her fatal flaw. She saw someone in pain and felt compelled to help them. Setting down her fork, she slid closer to him, surprising them both when she lifted her hand to his face and traced the strong line of his jaw with her fingers.

"I'm sorry," she murmured again. "I know what it's like to lose someone close to you. When my mom died, it nearly tore my heart out."

Caleb covered her hand with his, but didn't move it away, just kept it pressed to his cheek. Slowly he turned his head to meet her gaze, and what she saw there stole the breath right out of her lungs. Heat. Lots and lots of heat, mixed in with that cloud of grief. His eyes dropped to her mouth.

He wanted to kiss her. His intentions were so clear they might as well be scrawled across a billboard in downtown San Diego. Yet he didn't make a single move. His cheek was hot beneath her palm, his hand just as warm as it covered her knuckles.

"Are you okay?" Her voice wavered.

A muscle in his jaw twitched. "No," he said roughly. "I never seem to be okay when you're around."

She didn't know what to make of the cryptic comment, and he didn't give her time to try and decipher it. He lowered his head and pressed his lips to hers.

Marley's entire body trembled. He tasted like soy sauce and wine and something distinctly male. And he kissed as if he actually gave a damn about kissing. Other men went through the motions, shoved their tongues into your mouth and made the appropriate groaning sounds, all the while wondering how they could move on to the more entertaining part of the evening.

Caleb, on the other hand, took his time. His lips and tongue toyed with her. He licked and nipped, as though he was sampling a mouthwatering dessert, a flavor he wanted to explore. Marley stroked his cheek, her hand tingling at the feel of his shadowy stubble chafing against her palm. Feeling bold, she slid her tongue into his mouth then retreated to sweep it across his bottom lip. She took the surprisingly soft flesh between her teeth and bit down gently, eliciting a low moan from deep in his throat.

He broke the kiss, tilting her head with one big hand so he could press his mouth to her neck. "You're a very dangerous woman," he rasped against her feverish skin.

She laughed. "Me? I'm the furthest thing from dangerous."

He left a trail of wet, open-mouthed kisses along her neck, his tongue traveling back to her lips, parting them and delving into her mouth again. This time, when he deepened the kiss, he brought his hands into play. They drifted down to her breasts, cupping the aching mounds through the fabric of her T-shirt, his thumbs flicking the nipples poking against her bra. Little sparks ignited in her belly, blazing a path up to her breasts, making them swell and tingle.

"No," he disagreed, pulling back so that his warm breath fanned across her lips. "You are dangerous."

With reluctance practically oozing from his pores, he dropped his hands from her chest and slid away from her, his broad back connecting with the edge of the sofa. "Which is why I need to focus on this delicious meal before I do something stupid." To punctuate the remark, he picked up his fork and speared it into the nearest carton, bringing out a tangle of spicy noodles.

"How about we skip dinner and go straight to dessert instead?"

The brazen suggestion flew out of her mouth before she could stop it. Once she'd said it, though, she knew she didn't want to take it back. Her breasts were heavy, achy. The tender spot between her legs quivered with need. Looking at Caleb, in the blue shirt that clung to his washboard abs, the dark hair falling on his forehead, the lust swimming in his eyes, she knew he was the only one who could soothe the ache.

The fork fell out of his hands and clattered onto his plate. He swallowed hard. "That's probably not a good idea."

"Why not?" She gave a wry smile. "Isn't sex always a good idea, according to guys?"

He coughed at the word *sex*. "Most believe that," he admitted. "But we've only just met, Marley."

He was right. She'd known him less than a week. But already she felt a connection to him. When he looked at her, she felt light-headed and vulnerable and so totally aroused. What would be so wrong about falling into bed with this man? She was old enough to know that sex didn't equal love and marriage. Sometimes it could just be about two people who were wildly attracted to each other, taking pleasure in what the other had to offer.

"Do you always date for at least six months before you sleep with someone?"

"No," he said. "But you're different."

"How so?"

"I don't know." His features furrowed with a hint of despair. "You just are."

She looked at him, and there it was again, that streak of white-hot chemistry, threatening to consume her whole. She wanted this. No, she *needed* it. Needed to feel wanted and appreciated. Needed to lose herself in this one passionate moment and forget about the stress and headaches of the last three months.

She rose to her feet. "Are you attracted to me?"

"You know I am." No hesitation on his part. She liked that. She also liked the way his eyes grew heavy-lidded, smoky with unconcealed desire.

"So let's do something about it."

Marley lowered her hands to the hem of her T-shirt. She brushed her fingers over the fabric, then lifted it just an inch, to reveal her midriff.

Caleb's breath hitched. "What are you doing?"

She raised her shirt another inch higher. "What do you think I'm doing?"

He gulped. "Marley…"

"For God's sake, Caleb, are you going to make me beg for it?"

Without waiting for an answer, she slid the shirt up her chest, over her head and threw it aside.

OH, LORD.

Caleb swallowed a few times, desperate to bring moisture to the arid desert his mouth had become. He couldn't tear his eyes off her. All that smooth, golden skin. The luscious, full breasts covered by a lacy white bra with a little pink bow. Christ, that bow. So proper and innocent and downright sexy. It drove him wild.

She drove him wild.

"Say something," she murmured.

He opened his mouth, but nothing came out. Every muscle in his body was taut, tight as a drum and wrought with tension that could only be eased by the thrust of his cock inside Marley Kincaid's sweet paradise. Oh, yeah, *paradise* was the word to describe her, all right. He could practically see her holding out the forbidden apple to him, her perfect skin and flat belly and out-of-this-world breasts taunting him to take a bite.

He stumbled to his feet and pressed his damp palms to his sides. Marley obviously took the action as a sign of assent because she moved closer, and closer, until they were mere inches apart. He knew he shouldn't be doing this. He was hunting her ex, for Pete's sake. So why couldn't he walk away?

His hand, of its own accord, touched her mouth, tracing the curve of her bottom lip. Her lips were red and swollen, the lips of a woman who'd just been thoroughly kissed.

Caleb smothered a wild curse. He'd been fantasizing about this woman for more than a week. He *craved* her.

But he couldn't have her. He gritted his teeth.

Her lips parted as she leaned into his touch. "Don't shut down on me," she said, as if reading his mind. "I know you want this, too."

He drew in a breath. Tried valiantly to resist the pure temptation she posed. Gathered up the courage to tell her he didn't want it, that it would be a mistake.

But then she touched him.

Just the feather-light brush of her fingers across his cheek and he was a goner. He kissed her, pouring all his frustration and pent-up lust into the kiss, pushing his tongue deep into her mouth until she was gasping with delight.

"Close the drapes," he choked out, pulling back.

She glanced at him in surprise. "What?"

"The drapes. They're wide open. Any of your neighbors could see us." One neighbor in particular. He wondered if AJ was watching. If he was shaking his head in disapproval.

"Shoot, you're right." She darted over to the window and shut the heavy drapes, officially closing out the world.

Closing out reality.

That's what he ought to be clinging to, reality, but it was too late now. The fantasy had taken over, and Caleb knew he could no longer walk away. He needed her too badly. Marley Kincaid had gotten under his skin from the second they'd met. He *had* to have her. He felt like an addict, and this insanely beautiful blonde was his fix. The only cure to the uncontrollable desire running rampant through his blood.

Marley sauntered back to him, her firm breasts swaying at each step. Lord, that bra scarcely covered her nipples. He could see the edge of her areolas. Dusky pink. Just as he'd imagined.

She stood inches away from him, her blond waves cascading down her bare shoulders. A moan lodged in the back of his throat. Before he could stop himself, he slid his fingers down her neck to caress her collarbone. Her skin was hot to the touch. Her sweet strawberry scent seized his senses and wrapped him in a hazy cloud of desire.

Marley stepped closer, pushed her barely covered breasts against him and whispered, "Your touch drives me crazy."

His pulse began to race. The fog in his brain deepened, making it impossible to form a coherent thought. His cock throbbed relentlessly, so stiff he could hardly move. He trailed his index finger up Marley's arm, stroking her shoulder, running his knuckles along the curve of her neck. She shivered.

"You have the softest skin I've ever felt," he murmured, then lowered his head to kiss the hollow at the base of her throat.

He looked up to see desire reflected in her deep-brown eyes, punctuated by her sharp intake of breath. "You're teasing me," she squeezed out.

He pressed his lips to her jaw, tongue darting out for a brief taste. "Do you want me to stop?" he asked in a rough voice.

"No."

Trying to ignore the heat flooding his groin, he moved his lips over hers. Softly, a mere hint of a kiss. She sighed into his mouth, rubbing her body against him like a contented little cat.

Capturing her bottom lip with his teeth, he swirled his tongue over it, then moved to lick her earlobe. He kissed the tender lobe, then her cheek, her jaw, her shoulder—everything but her lips, which were plump and moist and begging for attention.

She licked them, whispering, "Please," and finally he gave her what she wanted. What *he* wanted.

He claimed her mouth, and a rush of warmth assaulted him, pumping through his veins and making his pulse quicken. She tasted like heaven. As he possessed her lips, his hands cupped her mouthwatering breasts. He squeezed, then dipped his fingers under her lacy bra. Toyed with her nipples, pinched them, made them hard and stiff and watched as her eyelids closed and a moan of pleasure slid out of her throat.

"Please," she pleaded. "More."

Her hips moved restlessly, her pelvis sliding over the aching bulge in his pants. "More, Caleb, I need more."

He knew exactly what she meant. He needed more, too. So much more than he'd ever dreamed himself capable of wanting.

Swallowing, he reached between them and hooked his thumbs under the waistband of her pants. It was too late to stop this. Any of this. He was too far gone. And he knew that at this point, there was nothing he could do but hang on for the ride.

7

MARLEY'S ENTIRE BODY was on fire as Caleb peeled her pants off her legs and whipped them aside. That same fire smoldered in his blue eyes, the heat of it penetrating her bare skin. Something else flickered in his eyes, too. Wonder, maybe, and a hint of hesitation.

She reached out for him but he stepped back. "No," came his hoarse voice. "Just stand there for a second. Let me look at you."

Marley's arms dropped to her sides. Her cheeks warmed, but she didn't feel embarrassed. Caleb's gaze roamed every inch of her body, and each time he lingered, she grew hotter. Wetter. Nobody had ever looked at her like this before. As if she were the most beautiful thing in the world. And he was pretty damn beautiful at the moment, too. His eyelids were heavy, his handsome features creased with blatant sensuality. His breathing sounded labored. So was hers. In fact, if he didn't touch her soon, she feared she'd stop breathing altogether.

As if he'd read her mind, he moved closer and with

the softest of touches, grazed her collarbone with his thumb. "You're stunning," he murmured.

"You're exaggerating."

He shook his head, dead serious. "And you're underestimating yourself." He looked vaguely embarrassed. "I've fantasized about you since the day we met."

She swallowed. "Yeah?"

"Yeah." His fingers skimmed down her arm, then traveled toward her breasts, which tingled the second his strong hands came near.

He cupped her breasts and squeezed gently, eliciting a soft moan from her throat. Then he ran a finger under the edge of her bra and teased one rigid nipple. "Do you like this?" he asked quietly.

Pleasure coursed through her body, so strong she couldn't find her vocal cords. So she just nodded, her head lolling to the side as he continued teasing her.

Caleb reached for the front clasp of her bra and popped it open to expose her aching breasts. He sucked in his breath, the passion in his eyes darkening to midnight blue. "Tell me what you like, and what you don't." His voice was soft, his face slightly rueful. "I don't want to be too rough with you. I'm not always gentle."

He sounded genuine and awkward and she couldn't help but smile. God, who was this man? In her experience, men didn't usually take the time to find out what she liked. They just did what *they* liked.

She leaned her bare breasts into his waiting palms and said, "I like everything you do to me, Caleb."

A fleeting smile lifted the corner of his mouth, and then he lowered his head and pressed his lips to one throbbing breast, making her gasp. The heat of his mouth enclosed her nipple, his tongue darting out and swirling over the aching bud. And then he started to suck, so hard she nearly keeled over from the overwhelming wave of pleasure that crashed into her.

Caleb steadied her, rested one big hand on her hip while the other squeezed and fondled her chest. He shifted his head and tongued her other nipple. Sighed against her flesh as if he'd just discovered a treasure he hadn't believed existed. By the time the hand he'd placed on her hip slid to the juncture of her thighs, she was so wet and so hot and so ready she exploded almost immediately.

Marley cried out in a mixture of surprise and ecstasy as an orgasm that rivaled a category-5 hurricane slammed into her. Streaks of pleasure burned a trail through her body, growing more intense when Caleb rubbed his palm over her sex. She buried her face against his broad chest, shuddering violently, shamelessly writhing against his hand and taking every last iota of pleasure he could give her.

When she finally crashed back to earth, her pulse racing, her knees wobbling, she saw Caleb looking at her, his expression a combination of satisfaction and awe. Slowly, he slid her bikini panties down her legs, leaving her completely naked. And he was completely dressed.

"Gosh, you're such a tease. Are you going to take your clothes off sometime this century?" she grumbled, her core still throbbing from release.

Chuckling, Caleb reached for his collar, bunched the material between his fingers and yanked the shirt over his head. The sight of his bare chest sucked the remaining breath from her lungs. Smooth, tanned skin. Hard muscle and sleek sinew. A six-pack that made it extremely difficult not to drool...

"Better?" he taunted.

"Not yet." Her gaze followed the thin line of dark hair that arrowed down to the waistband of his jeans. "Take those off."

The corner of his mouth lifted. "If you insist."

Marley watched, mesmerized, as he tugged on the tab of his zipper. Her mouth went dry in anticipation. She couldn't wait to see him. All of him. Big and naked and—okay, so *big* was definitely the right word. Her thighs clenched at the sight of the long, thick erection revealed after he shucked his pants and boxers.

Caleb Ford was by far the sexiest man she had ever seen. His body was lean and solid, with muscular thighs, a trim waist and broad shoulders. She focused again on the impressive cock jutting toward her and before she could stop herself, she knelt down, bent forward and swiped her tongue along his tip.

Caleb jerked, a deep groan rumbling in his powerful chest. Emboldened, she took another taste, this time a long, slow lick along his shaft. He was velvety soft and rock-hard at the same time, and his salty, masculine taste made her sigh with pleasure.

"Who's the tease now?" he asked, one hand restlessly stroking her hair.

She looked up at him with a smile. "I'm not teasing. I'm exploring." Swirling her tongue over the pearly bead of moisture at his tip, she reached out and cupped his balls with one hand, squeezing gently.

This time his groan held a note of desperation. His grip on her hair tightened. He thrust his hips, his cock seeking her mouth. As little flames of excitement licked at her skin, she took him in her mouth and sucked.

"Yes," he hissed out. "That feels amazing."

His encouraging words sparked her confidence, inspiring her to take him in deeper. She purred against his hot shaft. She could feel him shaking, could feel the tension in his muscles, the raw passion building in his loins. His cock pulsed beneath her tongue. It thrilled her, knowing she was the one bringing him pleasure, the one stoking all that passion.

Caleb guided her head with his hand, groaning as she drew him in and out of her mouth, as she swirled her tongue over the tip of his cock at each upstroke.

She was just finding a rhythm, alternating between sharp pumps and long, lazy licks, when he made a strangled sound and withdrew. "I need to be in you, Marley."

He hauled her to her feet, nudging her so that she could sink down on the sofa. Then he faltered. "I didn't bring anything," he confessed.

"My purse," she squeezed out. "In the hall."

Nodding, he disappeared from the room, returning a moment later with her bag, which he handed to her instead of rifling through it himself. She found the plastic wrapper in the zippered pouch where she kept her mini first-aid kit. As a nurse, she was always prepared for everything.

Including, apparently, hot and impulsive living-room sex.

A hysterical laugh bubbled in the back of her throat as she hurriedly unwrapped the condom and handed it to Caleb.

He sheathed himself, looking at her with such longing and desire that she forgot how to breathe.

"Spread your legs wider for me," he whispered.

She obeyed him without question, as if spreading

her legs for this man was just another requirement for survival, like food, water, oxygen. Never breaking eye contact, Caleb stroked her tender folds with his thumb. He made a ragged sound in the back of his throat, his features taut with barely restrained lust.

Her thighs quivered. Parted even farther. Anticipation coiled inside her, but rather than sliding his thick erection where they both wanted it to be, he got to his knees first and pressed his mouth to her aching core.

When he captured her clit between his lips and suckled, she cried out, shocked to feel another spontaneous orgasm gathering in her belly. Ripples of pleasure danced along her skin, an unbearable fire of need building between her legs.

"I need you in me. Now." Her voice came out hoarse.

Before she could blink, his mouth left her, and his body covered hers. He positioned himself between her legs, then murmured, "Are you sure about this?"

She almost laughed. Her legs were wide open, his cock was prodding against her soaking-wet sex, and he was asking if she was sure? She wanted to say no, that she'd changed her mind, just to see what he'd do, but she had a feeling he would respect anything she said. Despite the fact that every muscle in his chest was straining with tension and his pulse throbbed in his neck, she knew he would stop if she asked, no matter how much pain he'd be in later.

Good thing she wasn't asking.

Gripping his strong chin with her hand, she pulled his mouth toward hers. "I'm more than sure," she said, and then she kissed him.

His tongue plunged into her mouth, and a second later, his erection followed suit and plunged inside her.

His thick cock filled her, stretching her in the most delicious way.

"You're so damn tight," he mumbled. "I'm afraid I'll hurt you."

Her heart did a little somersault. "I'll be fine."

She slid her hands down his back and found it covered by a sheen of sweat. The sinewy muscles there flexed beneath her fingers, tightening as he moved inside her with long, gentle strokes.

"You're holding back," she said, half teasing, half accusing.

His blue eyes flickered with uncertainty. "I'm too big for you. Are you sure you're okay?"

A laugh squeezed out of her throat. "Would you quit asking me if I'm sure about things? I'm dying here, Caleb."

His voice was husky as he said, "Me, too." Then he started to move. To *really* move. Marley let out a wild cry as he drove into her, his thrusts frantic. She curved her spine to take him in deeper, hooking her legs around his taut buttocks. The couch squeaked beneath them, cushions bouncing as Caleb pushed his cock in and out in a reckless pace that made her mind spin and her body throb.

Her breasts were crushed against him, nipples tingling as they brushed over the damp hairs on his chest. "You're amazing," he gasped, each word punctuated by the sharp thrusts of his hips.

She met his eyes, floored by the emotion she saw in them. He was looking at her as if she were the most beautiful creature on the planet, as if he couldn't possibly believe she was his for the taking.

Yanking his head down with her hands, she kissed him deeply, whimpering against his lips when he reached to where they joined and rubbed her clit with his thumb.

"Come with me, Marley."

He quickened his pace, filling her so deeply, so completely, it wasn't difficult to lose herself in another orgasm. As his fingers toyed with her clit, Marley arched her hips and toppled over the edge. Shards of light flashed before her, and her mind fragmented as a dizzying rush of pleasure flooded her body. Moaning, Caleb buried his face in the crook of her neck and shuddered as he gave himself over to a climax she suspected was as powerful as hers. His breath heated her neck, his cock twitching inside as he let go.

Their bodies were sticky with sweat, their breath coming out in ragged gasps. Marley wasn't sure which one of them started to laugh first, but they were both chuckling when Caleb finally lifted himself up on his elbows and brushed his lips over hers in a tender kiss.

"Wow," she said with another laugh. "That was... wow."

Amusement joined the remnants of release in his eyes. "Yeah," he laughed. "You're right."

Looking reluctant, he slid out of her, his gaze roaming over her naked body. She noticed a rosy blush dotting her breasts and moisture still pooled between her legs. She was amazed to realize she could go again. All he needed to do was shove that wicked cock back inside her and she'd be ready for him.

As if reading her thoughts, Caleb's shoulders squared in determination, and then he gripped her waist and hoisted her up to her feet. She squeaked in surprise. "What are you doing?"

"Carrying you upstairs." True to his words, he cupped her ass with one hand and lifted her into his powerful arms, holding her there as though she weighed no more than a feather. "Come on, we need a bed."

WHILE HIS HEART THUDDED against his ribs like a pair of fists, Caleb rolled off Marley's body and sucked in a gulpful of air. His cock twitched against his belly, throbbing from its third release of the night. He was still as hard as a slab of marble, and when he glanced at Marley, the haze of desire in her brown eyes told him she was nowhere near sated, either.

Hands down, he'd just had the best sex of his life. Three times. He couldn't think of any past encounter that even compared to what he'd experienced with Marley. The sheer thrill of sliding into her tight core. The body-numbing releases. He almost felt cheated. He'd always enjoyed sex, but this...this was sex to the max.

"Do you want to spend the night?" Marley murmured. "I don't have to get up early tomorrow." She moved closer and nestled her head in the crook of his neck.

Caleb ran his fingers through her sweat-dampened hair and stared up at the ceiling. The bedroom was dark—his doing, of course. He knew how transparent those damn curtains of hers were, and the last thing he wanted was AJ catching any glimpses of what he and Marley were doing.

The thought of AJ brought a rush of guilt so strong he nearly choked on it. Lord, what was he doing? The implications of what he'd done settled over him like a thick cloud of smog. He'd lied to her. He'd spied on her. Videotaped her.

Slept with her.

He'd always considered himself a man of honor, a man with principles, but he'd thrown honor right out the window when he'd succumbed to temptation.

He had to give her the truth. Shards of pain pierced his stomach at the thought. She trusted him, damn it. He saw that trust glimmering in her eyes like diamonds. How could he possibly tell her she'd been duped—*again?*

The confession burned in his chest, but he couldn't reveal the truth now. She'd kick him out, and then who would be there to protect her if Grier showed up?

"Caleb?" Her voice cut through his thoughts. "Are you staying?"

He swallowed. "Yeah, I'll stay."

"Good, because I'm way too tired to walk you out."

With a contented little sigh, she pulled the bedspread up and over the two of them. Then she slung one slender arm over his bare chest and gave another purr of pleasure.

"You realize you wore me out, right? I'm lucky I don't have to work tomorrow or I'd probably doze off in the middle of removing a catheter," she said with a sleepy laugh.

He continued stroking her hair, then stopped abruptly when he realized the gesture felt too damn right.

Okay, it was official. He was in deep, deep trouble here. Sleeping with Marley was one thing, but cuddling? Petting her? Whispering in the darkness? This was not good. In fact, all this non-sex stuff was far more dangerous than sex itself. It was relationship stuff. Commitment stuff. And he definitely didn't do either of those.

He had tried making connections over the years.

He'd latched on to his first few foster mothers, pathetically begging for their love, only to be carted off to another house within months. After that, he got smart. What was the point in opening yourself up to another person when they would only kick you aside sooner or later?

Smothering a sigh, he forced the memories from his head. "Did you always want to be a nurse?" he found himself asking.

She was silent for a moment. "No."

Her response aroused his curiosity. "What did you want to be then?"

He gave an inward groan after he'd spoken. What was wrong with him? Why was he so fascinated by her? He couldn't for the life of him remember ever asking the woman in his bed what she wanted to be when she grew up. He didn't care about things like that. Didn't care about anything but getting pleasure and giving it right back.

Until now. Now, he couldn't seem to stop himself from wanting to know everything about this woman.

"I was accepted to the fine arts program at UCLA," she confessed. "I've always loved art. Creating things."

"I can tell," he said, thinking about how passionately she'd thrown herself into making her house look beautiful. "So what happened?"

"My mom was admitted to the hospital." Marley's voice shook. "She was in so much pain. The cancer... it destroyed her inside and out, and I would sit by her side watching it, wishing I could do something to help her."

She fell silent again. Caleb waited for her to continue, all the while trying to ignore the strange somersaults his heart was doing.

"I enrolled in nursing school the day after she died," Marley finally said. "I couldn't help my mom, but that way I could at least help other people."

It suddenly became extremely hard to breathe. She had become a nurse because she hadn't been able to help her mother in her dying hours. God, what a woman. Shame gripped his gut in a tight vise. And here he was, lying to her.

"How did your mom die?" Marley asked, her tone gentle.

"Overdose." He'd been prepared to avoid the question, maybe even pretend to be asleep, so when that one word burst out of his mouth, he was overcome with shock. Why had he just told her that?

"And you were five?" she pressed, obviously remembering the meager details he'd provided.

"Yeah." It became difficult to draw a breath. "I was watching TV in our bedroom—we only had one bedroom in the apartment—and I went out to the living room to ask about dinner and…she was just lying there on the carpet." His chest went impossibly tight. "I remember shaking her, crying for her to wake up, but… she didn't wake up. She was already dead."

"Oh, Caleb," Marley whispered. "That's awful. I'm so sorry you had to go through that."

He tried to shrug it off. "I got over it."

There was a short silence, and then Marley released a small sigh. "I'm so sorry," she said again, turning her head to press a tender kiss to his chest.

What was the matter with him? Why had he told her about his mother? He hadn't even told Russ about that day, and Russ had been his best friend. His only friend.

He lay very still, trying to navigate the confusion

clouding his brain. This wasn't supposed to happen. He wasn't supposed to sleep with her. To share his past with her.

Growing up, he'd been guided by a sense of justice, going into drug enforcement because it was the only way he knew to find some sort of vengeance for his mother's death. He lived his life by a code of honor. There was a distinct line between right and wrong.

But Marley was blurring that line. His body ached at the feel of Marley snuggled up close to him. He listened to her breathing grow steady, felt her muscles loosen with slumber, and as he lay there beside her, he realized she was far more dangerous than he'd given her credit for.

8

MARLEY WOKE UP the next morning with a smile on her face and a naked man in her bed. Caleb was sound asleep beside her, lying on his stomach with one strong arm flung over her belly. Her smile widened. God, he was breathtaking. His stubble-covered cheek rested against the pillow, his dark hair messy and falling onto his proud forehead. And his face lost all of its hard edges in slumber. He looked peaceful, younger.

Trying not to wake him, she moved his arm and slid out of bed. Then she walked into the washroom, heading for the small shower stall. A jolt of pain hit her big toe.

"Shoot," she muttered, noticing that one of the tiles was loose. Good thing she was planning on retiling after she finished painting.

She opened the glass door of the shower stall, and as she turned the faucet and adjusted the temperature, she realized she was actually pretty sore. A slight ache between her legs, but one she was willing to overlook because last night had been totally worth it. She stepped into the shower and dunked her head under the hot spray, then turned to let the water slide down her body.

Her muscles sighed with relief as the water pounded against them. She was on her feet nearly every day of the week and did yoga regularly, but one night with the talented Caleb Ford had completely wiped her out. It had never been like that with anyone, not even Patrick.

The smile on her face faded as the memory of the last man she'd been with pushed its way into her head and the implication of what she'd done settled over her. Was she crazy? After what had happened with Patrick, she'd vowed to be more cautious, and yet she'd just slept with a man she'd known for less than a week.

She slowly lathered her skin with strawberry-scented body wash, forcing her mind to quit overanalyzing. It was just sex. Really great sex. Wasn't like she'd gotten engaged to the man.

Shutting off the faucet, she toweled off and left the bathroom, slipped into a pair of denim shorts and a red tank, and turned her attention to the man on the bed.

He was wide awake, and sporting a very familiar expression on his face.

The same shuttered stare he'd donned yesterday when he'd told her sleeping together wasn't a good idea.

"I'm going to make some breakfast," she announced. "Do you like pancakes?"

"I love them," he said quietly.

"Good. They'll be ready by the time you come down."

She headed downstairs, trying to forget about how stiff his shoulders had looked. Maybe he simply wasn't a morning person. Like her brother—Sam could be a total ass before he had his morning coffee.

When Caleb walked into the kitchen ten minutes

later, his hair damp from the shower and his blue eyes alert, she handed him a cup of freshly brewed coffee.

"Thanks." He took it gratefully, and sipped the hot liquid.

Marley moved back to the stove and flipped a pancake, wishing he wasn't being so distant. It was easy to pick up on the waves of tension rolling off him. Finally she turned to him and asked, "Everything okay?"

He didn't speak for a moment, just headed to the kitchen table and lowered his big body onto a chair. A line of indecision creased his forehead, and when he opened his mouth, she got the feeling she wouldn't like what he said.

"I'm fine. Just tired," he said with a shrug.

"Well, hopefully these will help." She turned off the burner, then walked over to the table and placed a plate loaded with pancakes in front of him.

Almost instantly, his expression perked up. She suppressed a grin. Men and their stomachs.

He inhaled the delicious aroma of blueberries and buttermilk, and groaned. "You neglected to mention you could cook like this."

"I only do breakfast," she clarified as she sat across the table. "For some reason it's all I can manage. Lunch and dinner? I'm lucky I haven't burned down the kitchen yet."

Caleb chuckled. "Thank God for that."

She picked up her knife and fork and cut her pancake in half, then fourths, then eighths. She noticed Caleb watching her in amusement as she finally brought a bite-size piece to her lips.

"You cut it up in advance?" he said with a laugh.

She finished chewing and shot him an indignant

look. "It's all ready to eat that way. No wasting time after each bite."

"You could always cut the next piece while you chew," he pointed out.

"Don't be a smart ass. Eat your breakfast."

She was pleased to see him devour the pancakes. For some reason, she liked making him happy. She got the feeling Caleb wasn't the kind of man who'd been served fluffy pancakes very often. There was an edge to him, something raw and vulnerable at times.

This morning, that edge seemed sharper than ever. He didn't say much as he drank his coffee. His dark eyebrows were furrowed, and he looked as if some inner dilemma was tearing him up.

"You okay?" Marley asked again, as she poured a hefty amount of syrup on her second pancake.

"Yeah. I'm fine." Setting down his cup, Caleb stood. He grabbed his dish and headed for the sink, keeping his back to her as he rinsed his plate under the faucet.

"You don't have to do that," Marley called. "I'll just shove everything into the dishwasher later."

"I can't not do the dishes after I eat," he replied without turning around. "It's a habit I picked up when I lived in one of my foster homes. My foster mom used to give me a quarter every time I cleaned up after myself."

"That was sweet of her," Marley remarked.

"Yeah, I guess it was. She was one of the nicer ones." She heard the smile in his voice. "She gave me this cracked yellow piggy bank to put the quarters into. I kept every quarter. I thought if I saved them all, I would have enough money to run away and be on my own." His shoulders tensed. "Not that it mattered. One of my foster brothers stole every last penny the night before he was transferred to another home."

Her heart melted in her chest, sympathy for that lost little boy tightening her stomach. "Caleb...I'm sorry."

She pushed away her plate and got up, walking over to him with purposeful strides. His back stiffened at her approach. She knew he probably felt uncomfortable for revealing what was obviously a painful memory. He'd looked and sounded the same way last night, when he'd told her about his mother's death.

"Sorry, didn't mean to depress you," he remarked.

She rested her hand on his arm and stroked the curve of his bicep. "It's okay to talk about things that hurt you," she said. "I do it all the time."

"I'm not great with talking about my feelings, or my past." His voice sounded thick as he admitted what she already knew.

Still, it might have been one of the most honest sentences he'd ever spoken to her, and she rose up on her tiptoes and kissed him, a slow, deep kiss filled with gratitude and warmth. He responded instantly, slipping his tongue between her parted lips and exploring her mouth with what felt almost like desperation.

Her heartbeat quickened. She wondered if every kiss she shared with Caleb would be like this. The racing pulse, the damp palms, the melting of her body into his. He placed his hand on the back of her head and drew her closer, teasing her with his mouth, his lips, his tongue. The air in the kitchen felt charged, like the streak of arousal crackling through her blood.

"Marley?"

She and Caleb broke apart like a pair of teenagers caught necking in a parked car. She swiveled her head and saw her brother in the doorway.

"What the hell is going on here?" Sam asked, his gaze shifting from her to Caleb. "Who is *he?*"

Marley found her voice. "*He* is Caleb. My, um, neighbor."

Her brother strode to the middle of the room and eyed Caleb like a guard dog that had just discovered a burglar in the house. Too bad Sam was more like a cocker spaniel than a rottweiler. In his sky-blue surf shorts and white T-shirt, with his blond hair windswept as usual, her brother posed the least menacing picture Marley could conjure up.

"Do you always make out with your neighbors?" Sam demanded.

"Just the cute ones," she replied.

Caleb snorted, then stuck out his hand. "I take it you're Marley's brother. It's nice to meet you."

Sam looked at Caleb's outstretched hand warily, but the good manners their parents had instilled in them beat out his obvious desire to play the role of Angry Brother. He shook Caleb's hand and said, "I'm Sam." His eyes narrowed. "Why are you kissing my sister?"

Caleb looked so uncomfortable she took pity on him and said, "Because we're seeing each other."

Sam's dark-blond eyebrows shot to his forehead. He glanced over at Marley. "Since when?"

"This week," she admitted.

"And you didn't tell me?"

"I don't tell you everything." Before Sam could continue the cross-examination, she said, "What are you doing here, anyway? Finally going to finish the hall closet?"

"Tomorrow. Dad's barbecuing for lunch," Sam said with a sigh. "He wants you to come."

"He sent you all the way over here to invite me to lunch? You could have just called, you know."

Sam shrugged. "I had to take measurements of the closet. I'm picking up some supplies before I come over tomorrow." He shot her a pointed look. "I'm glad I came, otherwise I would have never known about your new *boyfriend*."

Marley's cheeks heated up. "When's the barbecue?"

"In a couple of hours, but Dad wants you to come earlier. He has something to show you."

Marley blanched. "Oh, God. Is it what I think it is?"

For the first time since he'd marched inside, Sam broke out a lopsided grin. "Sure is."

Caleb shot her a quizzical look. "Do I get to be in the loop?"

She laughed. "Nope. Trust me, you have to see it to believe it." To Sam, she said, "Can you call Dad and tell him to expect a guest?"

The suspicion on her brother's face returned. "Sure, I guess." Shoulders stiff, he turned for the door. "I'll just take those measurements and meet you over at the house."

After Sam left the kitchen, Marley gave Caleb an apologetic glance. "Sorry, I didn't even think to ask you if you wanted to come along. I can tell them you can't make it."

He hesitated for a long time, but then to her surprise, asked, "Would you like me to go?"

She pondered the question. Would she? It might be awkward for him. Since Patrick's arrest and escape, the men in Marley's life had become super-protective. Sam, despite the fact that he was younger, now acted as if his only goal in life was to monitor and ensure her well-being, and their father wasn't much better. Each time she saw him, her dad quizzed her about every aspect of her life.

She wasn't sure how he would react when he met Caleb. Neither he nor Sam had liked Patrick, which only made her feel like a bigger fool. What had they seen that she hadn't?

But Caleb was different. He wasn't as smooth and polished as Patrick. Definitely not as talkative, either. And who knew, maybe her family would see something in him that she wasn't picking up on. She still didn't fully trust her instincts. It might not be a bad thing to gauge her family's reaction to Caleb.

"I'd like it if you came," she finally said.

He nodded. "All right then."

She leaned up and planted a kiss against his cheek. "Thank you."

THIRTY MINUTES AFTER they arrived at Marley's childhood home, Caleb was regretting his decision to join her. He should have stayed back at the Strathorn house. But he hadn't wanted to leave her side, especially with the chance that Grier was keeping tabs on her. Away from the safety of her home, Marley made an easy target, and Caleb refused to let her out of his sight.

But he knew he was totally out of his element here. He was a trained government agent. He'd arrested, interrogated and physically struggled with the slime of the world. Yet he was intimidated by a twenty-four-year-old guy in surf shorts and a salt-and-pepper-haired father in the process of showing off a castle he'd built.

Out of Popsicle sticks.

"It's…interesting," Caleb remarked as he stared, stupefied, at the structure.

The castle was about two feet wide and three feet

tall, made up of hundreds—no, had to be in the thousands—of little wooden sticks. Some were intact, creating walls and turrets. Others had been cut to accommodate little windows and doors. Oh, and a drawbridge. Who could overlook the drawbridge?

Next to him, Marley seemed to be fighting a grin. "Dad's very passionate about his hobby."

Sam Sr. lovingly picked up his creation from the crate it had been sitting on and set it on one of the long work tables in the garage. His brown eyes, the same shade as his daughter's, were animated. "My best one yet, don't you think, honey?"

"Definitely," she agreed.

Marley's dad linked his arm through hers and led her out of the garage. Caleb trailed after them as they stepped onto the driveway. He kept a watchful eye on their surroundings, determined to stay on guard during this visit.

His gaze focused on the intertwined arms of Marley and her father, and he was unable to stop the envy that rolled around in his chest. He could tell just by looking at them that they were close. And the way Sam Sr.'s eyes filled with warmth each time he looked at his daughter was almost painful to watch. Caleb had never had anything even close to that growing up. He'd known families like this existed, but he hadn't seen it up close before.

They walked around the side of the sprawling, Spanish-style bungalow and stepped into the spacious backyard. The grass was perfectly mowed, colorful flowers popped up around the perimeter, and the array of birdhouses and feeders hanging from the trees made Caleb smile. Evidently one of her father's hobbies had rubbed off on Marley.

Sam was manning the barbecue, flipping burgers with a spatula. He glanced up at their approach and grinned at his sister. "It's your turn to set the table, kiddo."

Marley let go of her dad's arm and took a step toward the patio door. "I'll help you," Caleb offered.

"No, sit down, relax," she called over her shoulder.

As Marley darted into the house, Caleb awkwardly crossed the stone patio and sank into one of the chairs by the large table. Marley's dad joined him. The older man settled into his chair, then fixed a frown in Caleb's direction. "So. Marley mentioned you're a writer?"

"Yes, sir." He swallowed, wondering why the lie that had come so easily a week ago now stuck in his throat.

"My wife was a writer," the older man revealed.

"Really? What did she write?"

"Articles, mainly. She freelanced for some of the top home and garden magazines in the country." Marley's father swept his arm in the direction of the garden. "This garden was her showpiece."

"There was even a feature about it in *Good House-keeping*," Marley chimed in, coming outside in time to hear her father's remark. She set four plates on the table, along with drinking glasses, utensils and a tray of condiments, then flopped down in the chair next to Caleb's.

"The garden is really pretty," Caleb remarked. "Who maintains it?"

"I do," Sam Sr. answered with a proud smile. "Before Jessie passed, I promised her I would do right by her babies." He winked. "The kids *and* the flowers."

"Well, you're doing a good job," Caleb said, and meant it.

"Food's ready," Sam boomed from across the patio. A moment later, he strode across the pink and gray stones and dropped a platter of burgers on the table.

Despite the fact that he'd eaten breakfast only two hours earlier, Caleb's mouth watered at the aroma of ground beef and melted cheese. Marley's brother joined them at the table, and the four of them didn't say much as they fixed their burgers and settled back to eat.

Caleb's eyes met Marley's. He found himself fighting a grin when he noticed a splotch of ketchup at the corner of her mouth.

Her brother noticed, too, and guffawed. "We eat food here, not wear it."

Shooting her brother a dirty look, Marley reached for a napkin and wiped demurely at her mouth. "Can it, Sammy."

"Would you like me to get you a bib?" he returned with a smirk.

Caleb choked down a laugh. At the same time, he wanted to hightail it out of here. This was too damn surreal. The bickering siblings. The father looking on in gentle amusement. The homemade burger patties and bright-pink petunias and napkins with little dancing goats on them.

This wasn't his life. This wasn't *anyone's* life, was it? Lord, it was bad enough that he'd slept with Marley under false pretenses, but hanging out with her family? A wave of discomfort crested in his stomach, especially when Marley offered a snarky comment to her brother, and Sam Sr. grinned at Caleb. Crap. Marley's dad was warming up to him. Heck, so was her brother. After an initial bout of curt sentences and suspicious looks, the two men were now beginning to drop their guard.

As lunch progressed, Sam Sr. spoke to Caleb about the east coast, where he'd apparently lived for a few years following college. And the younger Sam spoke at length about their construction business. From the sound of it, the business wasn't booming, but it paid the mortgage, and both Kincaid men obviously enjoyed the work.

They perked up when Caleb mentioned he'd worked construction in the past, and he found himself enjoying talking to them about it. His fake writing career was a topic he avoided, but since construction was something he'd actually done before the DEA, he felt comfortable discussing it, and Marley's family seemed to warm up to him even more.

By the time the food was gone and the table was cleared, Caleb's chest felt as if it were being squeezed in a vise. These people were...*nice.* They cared about each other. They *respected* each other. It was so unlike most of the families he'd been around growing up. The abusive foster fathers, the alcoholic mothers, the dilapidated houses, soiled sheets and empty refrigerators.

"You okay?" Marley murmured, flashing a tentative smile in his direction.

Next to her, Sam Sr. and his son were still talking about the renovation job they were currently working on.

Caleb lowered his voice. "I'm fine. I just spaced out for a second." Fortunately, his cell began to vibrate in his pocket before she could press him. "Excuse me for a second," he said, barely able to hide his relief as he pulled out the phone.

He left the table and walked a few feet away,

standing near the barbecue as he checked his phone. Nobody was calling, but a series of text messages were coming through, all from AJ.

Tech guys at SDPD tracked the email to an IP addy downtown. Beachside Internet Café. Grier used free email account, registered with fake name.

The next message beeped in.

Staff couldn't ID Grier from pic. Barista remembers guy in baseball cap, sunglasses, looked shady, but she didn't see his face.

A final text popped up.

Give me a couple of hours before you bring her home. Wiring got screwed up. Two monitors are down. Gotta fix them.

He put away the cell, experiencing only a fleeting spark of disappointment. He'd known Grier's message would be a dead end. The man was too smart to send an email from his personal account, or to register for a new one under his real name.

Caleb glanced at Marley. She was amused by something her brother had said, her blond hair bouncing over her slender shoulders as her body vibrated with laughter. She looked unbelievably beautiful in her old denim shorts and thin red tank top. Her face was shining, her plump lips curved with delight as another burst of laughter rolled out of her chest.

He suddenly pictured how she'd look when she

found out the truth about who he was. The shine in her eyes would fade to a dull matte. Those lips would tighten with fury. Her joy would fizzle like a candle in the rain.

Caleb bent his head and pretended to text something on his phone, his blood pressure rising. He'd screwed up, given in to temptation and now he had to live with the knowledge that he'd deceived a woman he was really starting to care about.

Marley would never forgive him for lying to her.

He was also pretty certain that he'd never be able to forgive himself.

GODDAMN ADULTEROUS *BITCH*.

Patrick could barely contain the streaks of fury shooting through his body like hot bolts of lightning. He'd been standing by the window for the past hour, still stunned by what he'd seen. The cop, strolling out of Marley's house at ten o'clock in the morning. And then the two of them getting into the cop's shiny Range Rover an hour later, going off to who knew where.

Patrick had watched Mr. DEA arrive on Marley's porch the evening before, and all night he'd paced the bedroom, his anger building, growing, until his gut was knotted with wrath.

That whore.

She'd slept with the cop. At the start of the evening, Patrick had tried making excuses for her. She was just being nice. A friendly neighbor. But he was all out of excuses.

Marley had slept with another man.

His Marley had let another man touch her.

Patrick drew his arm back and sent it smashing into the wall.

A frightened gasp sounded from the bed, where Lydia White lay in fear.

He ignored her, didn't even feel the pain in his hand. Nor did he pay much attention to the neat hole he'd just punched in Lydia's drywall. The acidic taste of betrayal burned in his mouth, making him want to unleash another upper cut at something else. Mainly the jerk who'd just had sex with his girlfriend.

Releasing a strangled shout, Patrick edged toward the canopy bed and sank down on the ugly flowered bedspread. His heart thudded, each sharp beat vibrating with rage and desperation.

"How could she do this to me?" he demanded, staring at Lydia. "Everything I've done the past few months was for her. Do you think I like hiding out in this shit hole, staring at your wrinkled old face? I could have left the country months ago!"

But he hadn't. He'd been getting cash together, calling his contacts in South America to help him disappear, arranging for new identities for him and Marley.

And instead of being patient, instead of trusting that he would take care of her, she'd gone out and slept with the first guy to come knocking at her door. Ungrateful little bitch.

Patrick dropped his head in his hands. Rubbed his aching temples.

"I can't let her get away with this," he mumbled.

Lydia let out a muffled yelp, beginning to struggle against the duct tape binding her hands and legs.

"Shut up," he snapped. "Just. Shut. Up."

How could Marley betray him? How *could* she?

Patrick slowly uncurled his fists and took a long,

calming breath. Fine, so she'd screwed around on him. Big deal. He'd get over it.

But first...

First he had to make Marley pay for what she'd done to him.

9

"THIS WAS A GOOD IDEA," Marley said, shooting Caleb a smile that made the drive to Coronado worth the traffic they'd encountered on the way.

Caleb watched as she dug her bare toes into the soft warm sand of Coronado Beach. After leaving the Kincaid house, he'd suggested coming to the beach in order to give AJ enough time to take care of the security cameras. His partner had said a couple of hours, but Caleb didn't want to risk bringing Marley back too early. He'd raised the beach idea on impulse, but now that they were here, he was glad they'd come. The tranquil turquoise water lapping against the shore a few yards away soothed him, making him feel more relaxed than he had in months.

Still, he remained vigilant, just in case Grier had followed them.

"I can't imagine growing up here," he admitted, looking out at the water. "It's so different from the east coast."

"Yeah, I don't think I'd like it over there," Marley said. "I would miss the Pacific Ocean too much."

"The Atlantic isn't bad," he protested. "Just a little cold."

She snorted. "A *little* cold? Tell that to the passengers of the *Titanic*."

She slid a hair elastic off her wrist and tied her hair up in a messy twist. Wavy strands framed her face and Caleb reached out to tuck some behind her ears. She smiled, then took his hand, interlacing her fingers with his.

"Thanks for coming to my dad's today," she told him as they moved closer to the water.

They'd taken off their shoes and left them on the sand, and the warm water splashed over Caleb's toes. The late-afternoon breeze felt like a soft caress on his face, the scent of sand and salt bringing a wave of serenity over him. Yet, even as his muscles loosened and his face tipped up to soak in the sun, in the back of his mind he couldn't stop thinking about how Marley would react when he told her who he really was.

On the drive out here, he'd considered not telling her at all. Just packing up and taking off, letting another agent handle the stakeout and the hunt for Grier. He knew Marley would be hurt, sure, but better a minor broken heart than another major dose of betrayal. But now, as he watched her smiling at a squawking seagull that swooped by, as the warmth of her fingers seeped into his palm, he knew he couldn't leave without telling her the truth. After all the lies Grier had told her, she deserved honesty.

"My dad likes you," she said. "Sam does, too, but he probably won't admit it."

"He's just being protective. I'm sure they were both pretty shocked and pissed off when they found out about Patrick."

Marley dropped her eyes. "Yeah, they were. But I don't think anyone was as shocked as I was."

Caleb tightened his grip on her hand. "You shouldn't blame yourself. It sounds like your ex was a pretty smooth liar."

"Let's not talk about him anymore," Marley said suddenly. "It's such a beautiful day. I don't want to spoil it."

"What do you want to talk about then?"

"I don't know. Anything. Tell me something. What do you do in New York when you're not working?"

Caleb scrubbed his free hand through his hair. "Honestly? Not much, really."

It was true. Now that he thought about it, he rarely took time off. It was one assignment after the next, and when he did have some down time, he usually spent it consulting with other agents about *their* cases. He and Russ had played poker every now and then, gone out to a bar a few times, but his partner had been a workaholic, too.

"You don't go out? Ball games? Movies?" Marley prompted.

"Nope. I just work."

She sighed. "There's more to life than work, you know."

"Not for me."

"Do you ever get attached to people, or are you only attached to your job?"

A wave of discomfort swelled inside him. He'd heard this before, from women he'd had casual flings with, women looking to turn it into something more. Somehow, though, hearing the criticism come from Marley bugged him. So what if the only real relationship he had was with his job? Was it really that unusual?

"My job is all I need," he said with a shrug.

Marley shot him a knowing glance. "That's what I thought, too, ever since Patrick took off. I told myself I didn't need anything or anybody else."

"And now you need that?"

"Need, no. But I want it." A smile stretched across her face. "It's because of you, you know."

His mouth ran dry. "Yeah?"

"I'm having fun again, Caleb, thanks to you. You reminded me that there are still some good guys left in the world."

Self-reproach crushed his chest. "Marley," he started, his voice thick. "I wanted to tell you—"

She cut him off with a kiss. He tried to pull back, but the feel of her lips on his drained all common sense from his brain. As Marley looped her arms around his neck, he curled his fingers over her slender hips and bent down to deepen the kiss. Their tongues danced. His pulse sped up.

"How do you always manage to do that to me?" she said breathlessly.

"Do what?"

"Turn me on so hard, so fast." She laughed. "You have a gift."

Caleb took her hand and guided it to the bulge in his jeans. "I think you're the one with the gift," he sighed.

He nearly came apart as she gently rubbed his erection. With a strangled groan, he moved her hand and said, "We're not alone."

Marley looked around, her eyes widening when she spotted another couple walking hand-in-hand on the beach, as well as three teenagers horsing around in the water a hundred yards away.

She laughed again. "Okay, I guess you can add

making me forget my surroundings to the list of things you're good at." Her brown eyes sparkled. "Wanna get out of here?"

Hesitation crept up his spine. He knew exactly what they would do if they left the beach and went back to her place, and talking wouldn't be on the agenda. If they stayed here, out in public, he could fight the temptation to tear her clothes off and muster up enough courage to tell her the truth.

But then Marley kissed him again, and the wave of lust that hit him was so powerful he could barely remember his own name, let alone anything else.

She took his hand and led him toward the narrow staircase leading up to the parking lot where they'd left his car. He followed her blindly, unable to combat the potent force of desire pulling him. When they reached the car, Marley hopped in, her enthusiasm bringing a smile to his lips.

He shut the driver's door and moved to start the engine, but Marley intercepted his hand. Before he could blink, she climbed onto his lap.

Heat coiled in his belly at the feel of her firm thighs straddling him. "What are you doing?" he choked out.

"What do you think?"

His cock thickened as she unbuttoned her shorts and began to wiggle out of them. All the wiggling succeeded in making him even harder. Fire seared through his blood, his mind turning to mush. All he could do was lean back and let her take control. Tossing her shorts onto the passenger seat, she stroked him over the denim then unzipped his jeans.

A streak of raw lust shot through him. He'd never done it in front of audience, but the notion of getting caught was an odd turn-on. There were no other cars in the lot, but someone could pull in at any moment.

Marley must have considered it, too, because as she slowly drew him out of his pants, she glanced out the window and said, "We'll be quick. I...I just can't wait."

He knew the feeling. He'd never wanted anyone as badly as he wanted Marley, and yet there was more than just desire pulsing through his veins. Emotions he hadn't allowed himself to feel in years bubbled up to the surface. Tenderness and sorrow and something hot and painful he couldn't quite label.

His head lolled to the side as she stroked his stiff shaft, bringing him to a level of pleasure he'd never known before. Gulping, he met her gaze, and everything he felt was reflected right back at him.

"You're amazing," he said in a quiet voice.

Surprise and joy filled her face. Then she laughed. "You don't have to woo me with sweet words. I'm the one doing the seducing here, remember?"

"I'm not wooing." His voice cracked, much to his dismay. "I mean it, sweetheart, you're amazing. You're the strongest woman I've ever met." Caleb cupped her breasts through the fabric of her top, fondling them gently, then moved one hand down to her stomach. "And the sexiest."

A pretty flush rose on her cheeks. "Now you're talking crazy."

He slid his hand under her tank top. Circled her belly button with his index finger, then stroked his way between her legs. "No," he disagreed. "It's true. You're sexy, Marley, so unbelievably sexy."

She gasped when he pushed aside the crotch of her panties and began to prod and tease her damp folds. She was more than ready for him, but he toyed with her for a few more seconds, drawing a series of soft, anxious purrs from her throat. Finally, when he couldn't stand it any longer, he withdrew his finger, covered himself with the condom she produced from her purse, and thrust his cock inside her. They released simultaneous groans, pressing their foreheads against each other for a moment. And then Marley started to move.

She rode him furiously, while he dug his fingers into her waist and moved his hips to meet each frantic motion. Something primal unraveled inside him, a wild and inexplicable need to claim her, to push deep into her and show her it was where he belonged.

Where he *wanted* to belong.

"You're so beautiful," he muttered, watching the pleasure seep into her face.

She moaned again. Sagged into his chest and pressed her lips to his neck as she moved over him. Caleb wrapped his arms around her, drawing her closer. The feel of her full breasts crushed against his chest made his heart rate soar. He could feel her heart, too, thudding against his pecs. What was happening to him? This was more than sex…this was… Lord, he didn't even know what it was. He just knew that he never wanted it to end.

He growled when her teeth captured his earlobe, and gave a deep upward thrust that had his knees knocking against the steering wheel. It was a reminder of their surroundings, and he urged her to move faster, to send them both over the edge.

"Come for me, Marley." The words squeezed out between gasps. "Now, sweetheart."

Their joint release was fast, but oh, so sweet. An intense rush of pleasure spiraled through him, scorching his nerve endings, as Marley convulsed in his arms.

She whimpered as waves of orgasm rocked through her, and he held her tight, riding it out with her.

"Like I said," she murmured, her breath hot against his neck. "You turn me on hard and fast." She paused. "You called me sweetheart."

"I did?" When she nodded, he swallowed a lump of unease. "Oh. I'm sorry, I didn't mean to make you uncomf—"

"I liked it," she cut in. "It's the first term of endearment you've given me. It was...nice."

Nice? More like scary as hell. He'd called her sweetheart without even noticing it. He'd made love to her in a car, in public, where anyone could have walked up and ambushed them. Including Grier.

Oh, Christ, and he'd just mentally referred to what had happened between them as making love.

He was in deep, deep trouble.

Caleb stared at Marley as she gingerly climbed out of his lap and slipped back into her shorts. She looked happy and aroused and so outrageously beautiful his heart ached.

He couldn't tell her the truth. Not now.

He'd do it tomorrow.

Just one more night with her, that's all he wanted. One more night to hold her and kiss her and lose himself in the sweetness that poured out of her.

He'd tell her the truth tomorrow.

FOR THE SECOND MORNING in a row, Marley woke up with a smile on her face. Next to her, Caleb was sprawled on his stomach again, and a rush of pleasure flooded her as she admired his long, lean body. He was fully naked, and she couldn't take her eyes off his strong, back and firm ass.

Was it possible to want someone this much? They'd had sex numerous times yesterday, including a hot session at four in the morning, when Caleb had roused her from slumber with his tongue between her legs. Yet each time she looked at him, she craved him again.

A twinge of discomfort pulsed in her belly as she realized there was more than craving going on here. She was developing feelings for Caleb.

She hadn't wanted to analyze her actions of the past week, but it was getting hard not to. Having sex with him in a car, in broad daylight, was one thing, but bringing him home to meet her father? Strolling down the beach with him?

Those things had nothing to do with sex, and everything to do with...with what? A relationship?

She gulped. Well, why *shouldn't* she want a relationship with him? He was an amazing lover, a great listener. He was smart, he made her laugh with that subtle, dry humor of his. Heck, he could even cook, which he'd proved last night when he'd fixed dinner for the two of them.

Then again, Patrick had been all of those things, too.

She scowled. Damn Patrick. That man had broken something inside of her. He'd stolen her capacity for trust. Trust not only for others, but for herself.

Marley pushed aside the distressing thought, got out of bed and headed for the bathroom. When she came out, she rolled a pair of socks onto her feet and tied her hair up, while Caleb continued to sleep. He didn't look so peaceful this time, though. A crease marred his forehead, as if he were agonizing over something, even in slumber.

She contemplated giving him a wake-up call that

would surely vanquish his inner demons, but decided against it. They'd been up late; she ought to give him time to recover before ravishing his body again.

Grinning to herself, she walked downstairs and opened the front door to check the mail. Her postman, Ernie, made his deliveries impossibly early, and sure enough, stacks of envelopes cluttered her mailbox, probably sitting there since seven o'clock on the dot. A few doors down, she noticed her neighbor Kim rooting through her own mailbox. Marley knew the other woman had recently lost her husband, and she offered a gentle smile when the tall brunette spotted her. They waved at each other, then walked into their respective houses.

Marley took the stack of envelopes into the kitchen, flipping through them while she turned on the coffee-maker. She normally paid her bills online, but with Hernandez confiscating her laptop, she'd have to use telephone banking.

After pouring herself a cup of coffee, she sat at the kitchen table and began to go through the mail. Bill, junk, credit card promotion, bill, bank statement—her hand hesitated on the last envelope. She furrowed her brow in confusion. She'd opted for online statements for her checking account, and the statement for her savings account had arrived last week. Why was the bank sending her another statement?

Frowning, she dug her nail under the flap and sliced open the envelope. She pulled out the sheet of paper inside and went utterly still when she noticed Patrick's name underneath her own at the top of the statement.

She quickly scanned the information, then gasped.

Why on earth was there a hundred thousand dollars in an account that was supposed to be frozen?

10

STARING AT THE BANK STATEMENT, Marley rubbed her forehead for a moment, just in case the hours of sex she'd engaged in last night had exhausted her more than she'd thought. But when she looked down at the paper again, the transaction record remained the same.

Marley could barely breathe. Why had money been deposited? The cops had led her to believe the account would be frozen. Was it just a bank error, or was the tremor of fear skittering up her spine justified? Oh, God. Was Patrick moving drug money through the account?

She pushed her chair back with a loud scrape against the tiles. Still clutching the statement, she picked up the cordless phone from the kitchen counter and punched in the number of the bank with unsteady fingers.

At the automatic prompt, she keyed in the account number and her PIN, and waited, reminding herself to exhale. An operator came on the line surprisingly quickly, sparing her the awful tinny music every company and institution seemed to use for its hold function.

"This is Jennifer, how can I help you?" came a bubbly voice.

"Hi, Jennifer." Marley took a breath. "I'm just glancing over my recent bank statement and I noticed some inconsistencies."

"I can definitely look into that. I need to ask you a few security questions first."

Marley stifled a grumble as she went through the security process, offering her birth date, address and verifying the account information.

"So what seems to be the problem?" Jennifer asked after the CIA interrogation ended.

Marley's jaw tightened. "I'm seeing a deposit here, but I was under the impression the account was frozen."

"Hmm. Let me check your file. Can you hold?" Without waiting for a reply, Jennifer sent Marley into the land of elevator music.

She released the groan she'd been suppressing, wanting to kick something. What was going on? She'd dealt with banking errors before—usually a potential fraud issue where they canceled her ATM card, or an interest reversal—but a one-hundred-thousand dollar deposit in an account that was supposed to be inactive? This was one monster of an error.

Jennifer popped back on the line. "Ms. Kincaid?"

"I'm here."

"All right, so I noticed on your file that you opened the account with a…Mr. Patrick Neil Grier, is that correct?"

Marley gritted her teeth. "Yes."

"Well, the account is still active."

"I can see that." She sighed. "I'm just wondering why. What about the recent activity I'm seeing on this statement? Can you tell me where the deposit came from?"

"Sure thing. I need to ask you a few more security questions first."

Oh, for the love of God.

Jennifer rattled off another series of questions, just short of asking Marley for the name of the boy she'd lost her virginity to. And then chirped, "Let's take a look-see, shall we?"

Marley was beginning to seriously despise Jennifer.

"All right, I'm seeing a one-hundred-thousand-dollar wire transfer from a European cash office. Other than that, it's anonymous."

A rush of fury flooded her belly, causing her to tighten her fingers around the phone. Patrick was responsible for this. She knew it. He just couldn't stop messing around with her life, could he? He'd lied to her, disappeared on her and now he was throwing suspicion right back on her by moving money into an account that had her name on it. Hernandez would only see this as another sign of her guilt.

She wished Patrick were here, standing right in front of her, so she could strangle him with her bare hands.

"Is there anything else I can do for you today, Ms. Kincaid?" Jennifer chirped.

"No, you've done quite enough," Marley muttered. "Thanks."

She disconnected the call and resisted the urge to whip the phone across the kitchen. Okay. She had to calm down. And she had to call the police again. They'd obviously misled her by saying the account was inactive, and were probably sitting around at the station, taking bets on whether she would call it in when she discovered the deposit.

Hernandez would no doubt bet against her.

Good thing she wasn't going to give him that satisfaction.

"YOU SLEPT WITH HER. You damn idiot."

AJ's harsh voice was not one Caleb wanted greeting him so early in the morning, but at least Marley wasn't in the room to hear the angry words hissing out of the phone. He slid up in bed and leaned against the headboard, wiping the sleep from his eyes. The bathroom door was open, the light off, so he knew Marley must be downstairs, probably making breakfast.

Caleb opted for the avoidance route. "You're okay there by yourself, right? Getting enough sleep?"

His partner sounded incredulous. "Yes, Agent Ford, I'm sleeping just fine. I'm getting in twenty-minute catnaps, and watching the monitors, one of which started shrieking last night when a stray dog walked past the porch motion sensor. I'm also eating my veggies and saying my prayers and all that fun stuff." AJ let out a loud curse. "Now how about we talk about you again. You know, about the fact that you *slept* with her."

Caleb drew in a breath. "I got caught up in…in the moment."

"Caught up in the moment?" Disbelief dripped from AJ's voice. "Look, I know you're having a ton of fun spending time with Nurse Hottie, but don't you ever forget why we're here, Caleb. This stakeout is about catching Grier, it's about Russ, not your goddamn libido."

Caleb closed his eyes. "I know."

There was a long silence on the other end.

"What?" Caleb asked. "Say whatever you're thinking."

"You don't want to hear it."

"Say it, AJ."

"Fine." His partner released a heavy breath. "I don't think you got caught up in the moment, man. I think you got caught up in *her*."

"What's that supposed to mean?"

"It means you've fallen in love with her, you moron."

The phone shook in his hand. Love? That was ridiculous.

Panic clutched at his chest like icy-cold fingers. No, he couldn't have fallen for her. So what if he liked being with her and making her laugh and seeing her bright smile when he woke up in the morning? So what if she made his body burn and amazed him with her constant optimism? So what?

It didn't mean he loved her, did it?

"You still there?"

AJ's tone was oddly gentle. It made Caleb's jaw tense. "Yeah, I'm here."

"You don't have a response to what I just said?"

He swallowed. "I have to tell her the truth, AJ."

"You can't do that."

"Why not?" he asked, running the fingers of one hand through his hair in frustration.

"Because if she *is* helping Grier, you'll tip her off, and then she'll tip him off."

"She's not helping Grier," he said through clenched teeth. "I know her, AJ. Like you said, I've been spending time with her, and I know in my gut she's not capable of that."

"Your gut isn't going to bring Russ back," AJ said.

"Nothing will bring Russ back." Caleb's chest squeezed with pain. "Russ is gone, and Grier is the one responsible for that. Not Marley."

AJ uttered another low expletive, but Caleb cut him off before he could object. "I can't lie to her anymore. I can't do it." A lump of grief lodged in his throat. "She trusts me. She *likes* me. And I feel like a total ass every time I look at her. I can't do this to her anymore."

Resignation lined AJ's tone. "And you still insist you're not in love with her, huh?" He paused. "Do what you want, Ford, I'm not going to stop you. But think real hard before ruining your cover. You don't want this blowing up in your face."

AJ hung up, and Caleb was left staring down at the phone. He wouldn't take his partner's advice, though. He *had* thought long and hard about it, and he knew in his heart that he couldn't lie about who he was any longer. He had to come clean, not just for Marley's sake, but for his own.

Getting out of bed, he slipped into his jeans and then searched for his T-shirt. He found it balled up on the floor and, with a sigh, pulled the wrinkled material over his head. After he used the bathroom and brushed his teeth, he headed downstairs. He found Marley sitting in the kitchen, staring at the half-painted wall. She still wore her pajamas, which consisted of tiny boxer shorts and a loose tank top, and she looked cute and fresh-faced as she sat there.

"No pancakes?" he teased.

At his question, her head popped up. She seemed confused for a moment, then she gave a dull shake of her head.

An alarm buzzed in his gut. With purposeful strides, he rounded the table, sank into the chair directly beside hers and cupped her delicate chin with his hands. "What happened?"

Without a word, she picked up a folded piece of

paper from the tabletop and handed it to him, looking tormented.

The bank logo immediately caught his eye. He scanned the details, realizing he was looking at the statement for the joint account she'd opened with Grier.

He pretended it was news to him. "What's this?"

"This," she said in a stiff voice, "is the account I opened with Patrick, which the cops told me was frozen." She snatched the paper from his hand and held it up as if it were laced with anthrax. "The account is still active, and he's putting money in it! Drug money, most likely. God, why can't the police just catch him already?"

Caleb rested his forehead in the palm of his hand.

"Why won't he stop haunting me?" Tears coated her dark lashes and her breath came in short gasps. "I'm so stupid. How did I fall for all his lies? I thought he was a good person."

A weight settled in Caleb's rib cage, causing his heart to constrict painfully. "He lied to you."

"Yeah, and I believed him. I was so wrong about him," she said, twisting her hands together. Then she swiped at her wet eyes. "I'm sorry. I didn't mean to dump all this on you."

He swallowed. "Don't apologize. You didn't do anything wrong."

"Hernandez isn't going to agree." She stared at him in dismay. "He's going to think I helped Patrick put the money in the account."

"You're going to call Hernandez?"

She looked surprised. "I have to. Obviously they lied and didn't freeze the account like they said they would. Or maybe it was the bank's mistake. Either way, I have to tell them. I'm going to do it in person, so hopefully

Hernandez will see I really didn't have anything to do with this."

"And if he doesn't believe you?"

"Then he doesn't believe me," she repeated in a flat voice. "I still have to let them know."

They already know.

Caleb drew a gulpful of air into his burning lungs. This was it. The time to tell her the truth. He opened his mouth, ready to do it, to bite the bullet and tell her he was a federal agent, but suddenly she placed her hand on his arm and said, "Will you come with me to the police station?"

He faltered. "You want me there?"

"I know it's a lot to ask, but I don't want to face him alone. Will you come?"

In a hoarse voice, he said, "Of course I will. But first I need to tell you—"

She cut him off with a desperate "Thank you" as she stumbled to her feet. "Let me just take a quick shower and then we can go."

Frustration rose inside of him. "Marley, wait—"

"You should go next door and change while I'm upstairs," she interrupted, a faint smile on her lips as she studied his wrinkled shirt.

"I will, but first—"

"I'll meet you out front in fifteen minutes." And then she bounded out of the kitchen.

Caleb stared at the empty doorway, listening to the sound of her footsteps thudding up the stairs. Damn it, why hadn't she let him finish? He needed to tell her everything before they went to the police station—if she even desired his company after the truth came out.

With a sigh, he stood up, realizing the truth would yet again have to wait. Until Marley came out of the shower, anyway. The sigh became a discouraged groan, which he tamped down as he headed toward the front entrance.

Might as well go next door and change his damn shirt. At least then he wouldn't look like a slob while he faced her wrath.

MARLEY HAD JUST PEELED OFF her pajamas when a disconcerting flash of clarity sliced through her. What had she been thinking, asking Caleb to accompany her to the police station? She'd only been thinking about herself, she realized as she sagged against the bathroom wall.

She suddenly felt like kicking herself. God, talk about overdependent. As much as she'd appreciate having Caleb's support while she faced Hernandez, she knew she couldn't ask that of him. He'd already been present for the last confrontation with the detective, and they hadn't even known each other that well then. She didn't want to keep dragging him into this mess. It wasn't fair to Caleb. Patrick had been *her* mistake. And she was the only one who could fix it.

Anyway, she didn't want him to view her as some damsel in distress that he constantly needed to rescue. They'd just started seeing each other, for Pete's sake.

Drawing in a long breath, she left the bathroom and quickly got dressed. She would go next door and tell Caleb she needed to do this alone. He didn't deserve to spend his morning in a police station.

She hurried downstairs, slipped into her sneakers and flew out the front door, approaching the Strathorn house with determined strides.

On the porch, she opened the front door without bothering to ring the doorbell. She already knew Caleb was home, and considering he'd been staying at her house for the past two days, she hardly thought he'd mind if she let herself in.

"Caleb?" she called as she walked into the house.

His voice drifted down from upstairs. "I'll be down in a second."

He sounded strained, panicked even, but it wasn't his tone that made her freeze. When he'd spoken, she'd heard a clatter, as if he'd dropped something—but the expletive that had followed wasn't uttered by Caleb. The voice had been deeper, raspier.

An alarm bell went off in her head. As her palms grew damp, she approached the staircase and peered up. The second-floor hallway seemed to be empty. Did he have someone up there?

With wariness wrapping around her spine like strands of ivy, she climbed the stairs, reaching the second-floor landing just as Caleb popped out of the bedroom at the very end of the hall.

"Hey," he said, looking frazzled. "I was just getting dressed and—"

"Who's in there?" she cut in, narrowing her eyes.

He hesitated, only for a second, but it was hesitation just the same. "What? There's nobody here. I was—"

Marley brushed past him, unable to let go of the misgiving pulsing in her bloodstream. "I heard someone, Caleb."

She headed for the doorway he'd just exited, knowing she was probably being ridiculous but completely helpless to stop the sudden onslaught of suspicion. This was a total invasion of privacy. Maybe she hadn't heard another voice at all. Maybe she was—

She froze as she entered the bedroom.

Her hands dropped to her sides, her entire body

growing colder than a glacial ice cap. All the oxygen rushed from her lungs, leaving her breathless.

The room was empty, but that wasn't what shocked her to the core. Oh no, it was the computer monitors sitting on the long desk pushed up under the window. At least half a dozen of them. A couple had switched into screen-saver mode, but the rest… She stumbled forward. Oh, God. The rest displayed very clear images of her house.

Her front porch. Her backyard. Her kitchen. Her bedroom window.

Oh, God.

Bile rose in her throat. Caleb had been watching her.

But why? Why the hell would he— She stiffened again when her gaze landed on the photograph taped to one of the monitors.

Her pulse shrieked in her ears as she moved closer. As she looked at the photo and saw Patrick Grier's face peering back at her.

She stared at the picture for a very long time, fighting back wave after wave of nausea.

A noise came from behind, causing her to spin around and face Caleb.

Their gazes collided, and she stood there, watching all the color seep out of his face. Watching as a thick cloud of guilt settled over his blue eyes.

"Marley," he choked out.

Her fingers curled into two tight fists. "You son of a bitch."

11

MARLEY SWAYED AS ice slithered through her veins. Rage was the only thing that kept her feet rooted to the floor while her heart slapped against her ribcage, urging her to run.

Never breaking eye contact with Caleb, she forced her vocal cords to work. "Who are you?"

"I…" His Adam's apple bobbed as he swallowed. "I've been monitoring your house in case Patrick shows up."

"Patrick," she echoed.

"Yes. We suspected he might come to San Diego, so—"

"We?" she interrupted, anger continuing to claw its way up her spine. "Who's *we?*"

"The DEA… I'm a federal agent."

"A federal agent," she said, feeling her stomach roil.

"Yes."

Marley wished she could crawl into a hole and disappear. Her heart felt as though it was full of little razor blades. Each time it beat, a shudder of pain shot through her body. And each time she took a breath, her lungs burned.

How could he do this to her? She'd trusted him, and all the while he'd been lying to her.

Caleb squared his shoulders, sucking in a breath and releasing it.

"How long have you been here, watching me?" she demanded.

He held his ground as he looked straight into her eyes. "Two weeks."

Marley staggered backward. She couldn't believe this was happening. Two weeks! He'd been spying on her for the past two weeks, one of which he'd spent conning his way into her life. Into her *bed*.

She'd slept with him. She'd taken him to meet her family. She'd laughed with him and kissed him, and the whole time he was pretending to be someone else. Resentment coursed through her, trailed by humiliation. At the moment, she wasn't sure whom she was angrier with—him, for deceiving her, or herself, for falling for it again.

"Marley, I'm sorry," he said. "I'm sorry I didn't tell you the truth earlier, but…"

She scowled. "But what?"

"I wasn't supposed to make contact with you in the first place," he confessed. "I only did because I saw you hanging from the eaves, and I didn't want to let you fall."

"Why didn't you tell me then?"

"I couldn't." He looked at the ground. "There was always the chance that you were still involved with Grier, that you'd tip him off."

A breath flew out of her mouth. "Involved with… You thought I was a suspect?"

He shook his head. "Maybe a little, at first. But not now. I know you're not involved with any of Patrick's dealings, Marley."

She glared at him. "How nice for me! The man who slept with me under false pretenses didn't think I was a criminal. I feel so much better." She clenched her fingers. "So, do you have sex with all your potential suspects, or am I the only one?"

He winced. "I have never gotten involved with a witness before," he said, emphasizing the word *witness*.

She shot him a cold look. "Lucky me."

"I was desperate. My best friend was killed in that raid, and the person who murdered him is out there somewhere, going unpunished. I didn't mean to get involved with you...it just happened...and I've been torn up in knots about lying to you."

"I'm sorry about your friend, but there were other ways you could have handled this." Her voice wobbled. "Telling me the truth would have been a good start."

"I wanted to, really." His claim meant little in light of his actions.

"What exactly have you been doing, Caleb?"

He hesitated. "Watching."

"Are you recording everything?"

"Yes."

"Recording everything," she whispered, remembering all the special moments they'd shared. Moments she'd thought were private. "God, I can't believe this."

CALEB STOOD PARALYZED as he watched Marley's feelings for him die.

Her shoulders were stiff as she turned and made a move for the bedroom door. "You're a bastard, Caleb."

"Marley, wait."

He tried to grab hold of her arm, but she shrugged him off as if she'd been stung by a scorpion. "Don't you dare touch me. You've been lying to me since the moment we met. I was always just a case for you. So don't you ever touch me again, do you hear me, *Agent* Ford?"

"Damn it, Marley, you're more than a case."

She stared through him. "Right."

"It's true." His heart twisted in his chest. "Something happened once we got involved. I started to care about you."

"You don't care about me," she said coldly. "You're just trying to butter me up with sweet words so I'll forget about all the lies."

"I'm not lying about this. And believe me, I'm not sure I even like it. My job has always been the most important thing in my life. I never wanted anything more than that. But then I met you, and now…now I realize what I've been missing all these years."

Marley moved toward the door again.

"A job isn't going to keep me warm at night, or make me laugh the way you do," Caleb continued in a soft voice. "A job isn't going to make me pancakes or seduce me in a car. Being with you has shown me that it's okay to open up to another person."

"Looks like you're going to have to be satisfied with the job." Marley stumbled to the door, tears coating her thick eyelashes.

"Marley, please," he burst out.

She turned around and paused in the doorway, slowly meeting his eyes. "I will never forgive you for this," she murmured.

Then she marched out of the room.

"Well." AJ's dry voice sounded from the bathroom

he'd ducked into when they'd spotted Marley's brisk walk next door on the monitors. "That was unpleasant."

Ignoring his partner, Caleb stared at the doorway for a second, then tore out of it. He heard the front door slam as he hurried down the stairs, but he kept going. He couldn't let it end like this. Every word he'd uttered up in the bedroom had been true. He *did* care about her. He'd told her things about himself that he'd never told another soul. His life in foster care, his mother's overdose, how hard it was to talk about his feelings. He couldn't lose her now, not when he'd finally found someone he actually wanted in his life.

He caught up to her on the front lawn at the same time a blue pickup truck came to a stop in her driveway. He bit back a groan when he saw Marley's brother slide out of the driver's side, pulling a tool belt from the passenger seat.

"Marley!" Caleb called after her.

She quickly ascended the porch steps. Sam must have noticed the anger radiating off his sister's body, because he darted toward them, reaching the porch just as Caleb did.

"What's going on here?" Sam asked, looking wary.

"Nothing," Marley answered. She avoided Caleb's face and glanced at her brother. "Come in, let's work on that closet."

"Marley, please," Caleb said. "Just let me explain."

"You've done all the explaining you need to."

"We can't leave things like this."

"Oh, yes, we can."

Sam's eyes moved back and forth between the two of them. He opened his mouth to speak again, but Marley raised her hand and gestured for him to come inside. "Agent Ford was just leaving."

Sam wrinkled his forehead, then walked up the steps and followed his sister into the house. "Agent Ford?" Caleb heard Sam say, and then the door shut behind them.

Caleb stood there feeling frustrated. He wanted to knock on the door, or hell, kick it open and try to make Marley understand, but he knew she wasn't in the frame of mind to listen right now. He'd blown it. She would never forgive him for this, and at the moment, he didn't particularly blame her.

His shoulders slumped. Slowly, he walked back next door and headed upstairs. When he entered the bedroom, AJ was at the desk, looking a little shell-shocked.

It killed him to do it, but Caleb turned to the monitors. He saw Marley lead her brother into the kitchen, where they sat down at the table. Sam leaned forward. Marley's eyes flashed as she filled her brother in on what had just happened. Sam's face hardened, and he tried to get up, but Marley forced him to sit back down.

He's not worth it, he could almost hear her say.

He hoped that one day he'd be able to convince her otherwise.

He tore his gaze from the screen, noticing that AJ was tentatively holding out a green folder to him. "What's that?" Caleb muttered.

"Hernandez's file. Lukas from headquarters faxed it over." AJ paused. "Read it. It might take your mind off…you know."

Caleb took the folder, but rather than reading it, he set it on the desk and walked over to the bed. He dropped onto the mattress, feeling beaten and battered.

Ravaged. The way he'd felt the night of the warehouse raid, as he held his dying best friend in his arms.

But this time, there was nobody to direct all that grief and anger at. Grier had killed Russ, but Caleb was the one responsible for bringing the anguish into Marley's eyes.

"Caleb...look, you were just doing your job," AJ said.

Caleb stared at his friend. "No, I wasn't. My job didn't require me to befriend her. Or to sleep with her."

"She'll forgive you."

"No, she won't."

Why would she? He'd screwed up big-time. Taken Marley's trust and whipped it out the window, along with his own code of honor.

"HE'S A COP?" GWEN EXCLAIMED later that evening, ten minutes before their shift was scheduled to begin.

Marley sat down on the bench with a weak nod.

Gwen shook her head, her eyes wide. "A *cop?*"

"Yes," Marley said gloomily.

"And he only got close to you to find Patrick?"

"Yep, but apparently he developed feelings for me along the way." Right. He'd been spying on her for weeks, yet he expected her to believe that he gave a damn?

She suddenly wished she'd called in sick. She'd spent the entire day stewing over Caleb's lies. Berating herself for being such an idiot and yet again placing her trust in the wrong man. Sam had wanted to stick around, even tried distracting her by saying they should work on the hall closet together, but she'd ended up sending him away. She couldn't bear seeing the pity on her brother's face.

Caleb's betrayal continued to haunt her. It pulsed through her veins and buzzed in her mind and pretty much made it impossible to focus on anything else. She'd come into work only because she needed a diversion from her thoughts.

"I can't believe this," Gwen said.

Marley's lips tightened. "Neither can I. I thought he actually cared about me."

Gwen tied the drawstring of her scrubs and stepped toward Marley, gently touching her arm. "Maybe he does, Mar. It might have been a case for him at first, but that could have changed."

"That's what he claims, but why should I believe him? He's lied to me about everything, Gwen."

Gwen looked thoughtful.

"Maybe you should talk to him again, try to make some sense of all this."

"Sense of it? He *lied* to me."

"He lied about what he did for a living," Gwen clarified. "That doesn't mean he lied about how he feels for you."

Marley fell silent. She thought about the times they'd had sex, the emotion overflowing in his blue eyes as he'd held her tightly, as he'd told her she was beautiful. She hadn't picked up on anything insincere in those actions, in those words, but how could she trust her own judgment after being duped. Twice.

"I don't know." She rubbed her forehead in frustration. "I keep thinking about all the time we spent together. It felt real, Gwen."

"Maybe it was."

"The way things were so real with Patrick?" she retorted.

"Patrick was a soulless jerk who dealt drugs and

killed people. Caleb is a cop. A drug-enforcement cop, to boot." Gwen sounded conflicted, a deep crease in her forehead. "He cleans up the streets, tries to make them safe—does that make him a bad man?"

"He *lied,*" Marley said through clenched teeth. She took a breath. "Whatever, it was just a fling and it's over. I'll just have to deal with it, the way I dealt with everything that happened with Patrick."

Her friend sat down next to her and took her hand. Squeezing her fingers, Gwen searched Marley's face, a perceptive glimmer in her eyes. "What are you really angry about, hon? Because if it really was just a fling, you wouldn't care this much. You'd just chalk it up as another stupid mistake, the way it was with, what's his name, the guy you went out with before Patrick."

"Brad," she murmured.

"Right, Brad. He was a total ass, remember? He stood you up on your birthday."

Marley sighed. "I really pick winners, don't I?"

"You're missing the point," Gwen said with a sigh of her own. "I'm just saying, some men are jerks. Brad was, and you barely blinked after you dumped him."

"And Patrick? Are you saying I shouldn't have been furious about *him?*"

"No, I'm not saying that. Patrick is different. You were with him for five months. You lived together. Of course you should have been furious. But you've only known Caleb a week. It's normal to be angry, sure, but not devastated." Gwen hesitated. "Unless you care about him more than you're willing to admit."

Marley smothered another sigh. "I...liked being with him," she finally admitted. "He's such a hard man to get to know, hardly ever talks about his feelings, but I thought he was starting to open up to me."

She swallowed. "And when we had sex, I felt really... connected to him."

"Then you need to talk to him again," Gwen advised. "You need to find out if he felt that connection, too."

"I don't know. I just don't know."

She thought about Caleb's confession, the regret flickering in his eyes, and for a moment she experienced a pang of doubt. But then the memory of all those computer monitors pushed its way into the forefront of her brain, and the doubt transformed into anger again. She imagined Caleb sitting at that computer desk, watching her, talking about her, wondering if she was helping Patrick leave the country.

How could she ever trust him again?

Her mind was spinning, but considering she was about to start her shift, she couldn't afford to be distracted.

Taking a breath, she stood up and said, "I can't talk about this anymore. I need to worry about my patients right now."

"Just promise you'll think about what I said," Gwen said.

"Sure," Marley said, then kicked off her sandals. Determined to change for work, tend to her patients and forget all about Caleb and Patrick and every other headache pulsing through her mind, she walked to her locker and opened the door.

"Oh, my God," she choked out.

"What?" Gwen rushed to her side, sucking in a gasp when she saw what Marley was looking at.

On the inside of the metal door, scrawled in the red lipstick she kept on the top shelf, was the word *Whore*.

And underneath it, attached with a piece of silver duct tape, was a photograph of Marley.

A photograph she recognized as the one Patrick used to keep in his wallet.

A photograph that now featured a big black X directly over her face.

12

Two hours later, Marley sat on her living-room couch, stiff as a board, unable to erase the memory of Patrick's vile message. She and Gwen had called the police immediately, and officers had turned the nurses' locker room into a crime scene, dusting Marley's locker for fingerprints and questioning everyone who'd been working on the floor that day. So far, none of the hospital staff had admitted to seeing Patrick.

She fought a wave of nausea as she pictured what had happened. He'd waltzed into her place of work, strolled into the locker room. Opened her locker. Touched her things. She wanted to throw up just thinking about it. Was he fearless, or just crazy?

Crazy, obviously. And apparently enraged. She shivered and wondered what on earth she'd done to earn Patrick's rage. The disgusting message was so different from the sweet email he'd sent only days ago. Something had changed during that time, something had infuriated Patrick so much that he'd decided to paint a target on her.

Fortunately, the police had decided to take this

matter seriously. Her house was swarming with law-enforcement officers. Hernandez was in the armchair next to the couch, a notepad in his hand so he could take her statement. Three other officers from the SDPD hovered behind him, while three DEA agents, including Caleb and his partner, stood near the door. Caleb's partner had introduced himself as AJ Callaghan, and Marley had been angry just shaking his hand, especially when she learned he'd been next door with Caleb this entire time.

Caleb had reacted with a brief flash of guilt during the introduction with AJ, but now he leaned against the bookshelf, his face completely expressionless.

She couldn't bring herself to look at him for more than a few seconds. He wore a long-sleeved black shirt and snug black trousers. The butt of a gun poked out of the holster on his hip. The weapon was a reminder of his true identity.

He hadn't said a word to her since entering the house, but concern creased his handsome features.

How concerned had he been when he'd slept with her while pretending to be someone else?

She shoved aside the bitter thought and focused on Hernandez's latest question. "It's the picture from his wallet," she said for the second time. "I gave it to him a few days after he proposed. You can tell from the creases that it was folded a few times to fit somewhere small."

Hernandez jotted a note, then looked up at her with hard eyes. "And you say the locker was that way when you opened it?"

"Yes." She gritted her teeth, wondering how many times she'd have to answer the same questions. "My last shift was yesterday morning, and I didn't go back to the hospital until eight o'clock tonight. When I left yesterday, my locker looked normal."

Hernandez made a harsh sound under his breath. Annoyance pricked at her skin like tiny little needles. For the love of God. What would it take to convince this man she was innocent, that *she* was the victim?

She opened her mouth to ask him just that, only to be interrupted by Caleb's husky voice. "Detective Hernandez?" he called from behind. "May I speak to you for a moment?"

Looking irritated, Hernandez excused himself and made his way over to Caleb. As Marley watched, the two men went out into the hall, heads bent together, voices low. Whatever Caleb had to say, the detective didn't like it. She could tell from the way his thick black eyebrows bunched together. Then Hernandez looked at the ground and his shoulders slumped.

What was Caleb saying? Whatever it was must have worked, because when Hernandez returned, his normally frosty tone had thawed considerably.

"Ms. Kincaid, do you have any idea what this message means?"

"I'm pretty sure he thinks I'm a whore," she said dryly.

"Yes, but do you know why he might think that? Do you have a new boyfriend?"

She forced herself not to glance over at Caleb. "No."

"Are you casually seeing anyone?"

She hesitated. "I did have a date two nights ago."

Hernandez leaned forward. "Where did you go on the date, which restaurant? Perhaps Grier saw you with another man and—"

"We didn't go out," she cut in. "We stayed in and ordered take-out."

For a moment she was tempted to stand up, point directly at Caleb, and yell, "It was him! We slept together that night, too."

Instinctively, she knew to keep her mouth shut. It wouldn't look good for Caleb if she announced his involvement with her. But she wasn't simply covering for him. The truth made her look like a total idiot, and she was tired of Hernandez glaring at her with that belittling and antagonistic expression.

Right now, he just looked disappointed. "You stayed in," he repeated. "Okay, well, my gut tells me Grier knows about that date, Ms. Kincaid. Somehow, he heard about it, or maybe—"

"He's close by," Caleb stated.

The room fell quiet at his words. Hernandez turned to Caleb. "You think so?"

Confidence lined Caleb's face. "He has to be. We know from the email that he had planned to reunite with Marley soon, and he's smart. He wouldn't risk walking up to her door, not unless he knew for sure what the law-enforcement situation was."

"He'd need to scout the area first," Hernandez agreed.

"I think he's doing more than that. He's watching her. He knows she had another man over—" there was a slight crack in Caleb's voice "—and in order to see that, he had to be close."

A tremor ran along Marley's skin. The notion that Patrick was lurking outside somewhere, watching her, was too frightening to contemplate. God, would she ever be rid of that man? She wished she'd never gone into his hospital room all those months ago, never agreed to that first date, never opened her heart to him.

"Okay, he can't be next door, since AJ and I have

occupied that space," Caleb said in a brisk voice. He glanced at Marley. "How well do you know your other neighbors?"

Since he'd spoken to her directly, she had no choice but to meet his eyes. Damn. Why did he have to be so attractive? Her heart shouldn't skip a beat anymore when she looked at him.

"Don and Melinda live in the house on the other side of mine," she answered. "They have three kids, but they're all away at camp for the summer. Next to them is Kim, she's a widow." She racked her brain for more names and faces. "Across the street is Mrs. White, she lives alone, kind of grumpy all the time but she can be sweet. I'm not sure about anyone else."

"Do you know if any of the ones you mentioned are on vacation, like the Strathorns?" Caleb asked.

"I don't think so. I saw Don and his wife the other day, and I saw Kim yesterday when I checked the mail." She paused. "I haven't seen Mrs. White in a few days, come to think of it, but she hardly ever leaves the house."

Caleb and the other men sprang to action before she even finished talking. She tried to hide her admiration as she watched Caleb bark orders at everyone. "We canvass each house one by one, only the ones that have a direct visual on Marley's. Teams of two. Hernandez, you're with me. Officer Thompson," he said to the thin, uniformed blond man, "you stay with Ms. Kincaid. Radio us if there are any disturbances."

"Yes, sir."

Marley's chest tightened with alarm as Caleb and the others unholstered their weapons. What if they got hurt? What if Caleb got hurt? She wanted to urge him to be careful, but clamped her mouth shut. She refused to let herself feel anything for him. Besides, he was a trained government agent. He could handle himself.

Still, her heart thudded as she watched him disappear through the doorway, his strides long and determined.

Please don't let him get hurt.

CALEB CROUCHED BESIDE the tall hedges of Lydia White's two-story Victorian home, silently gesturing for Hernandez to take the back. AJ and the other agents, as well as two of Hernandez's men, were already approaching the other houses in the vicinity, moving stealthily in the shadows.

With adrenaline coursing through his blood, Caleb held his Glock in his right hand and the radio in his left. He crept to the front door while Hernandez circled the house. As he reached the porch, his radio crackled and AJ's voice came through. "Kim just let us in. Preparing to search the house."

The radio went silent. Caleb stood in front of Lydia White's door and rapped his knuckles on it. There was no doorbell, just a sign on the mailbox that said No Solicitors. He knocked again, but still no answer.

"Lydia White?" he shouted. "This is Agent Caleb Ford with the Drug Enforcement Agency."

Nothing.

The radio came to life again. "Kim's house is clear." A moment later, one of Hernandez's officers checked in. "Don and Melinda Levenstein's house is clear."

"Lydia White," he said again. "With your permission, I'd like to search your house. There is a possible fugitive on the premises."

He debated picking the lock when static hissed out

from the radio. "Back-door lock's been jimmied open," came Hernandez's grim voice. "I'm going in."

The adrenaline in his veins flowed harder. No time to pick a lock. Instead, he kicked Lydia White's door open with his heavy black boot and then he was in the front hall, shrouded by darkness. Holding his weapon, he moved through the shadows, clearing the living room and a small den, before rendezvousing with Hernandez in the hallway.

"Kitchen's clear," the detective murmured.

The two men headed for the staircase, Hernandez falling into step behind Caleb, letting him take the lead. You could say a lot of things about Hernandez, but Caleb felt good knowing the detective had his back. The two of them moved together as if they'd been a team for years, scouting the hallway, using hand signals to direct their movements. They found the bathroom and master bedroom empty, then crept down the carpeted hall toward the single door at the end of it.

Caleb's instincts began to hum, growing stronger when a muffled sound broke through the silence.

He signaled for Hernandez to pull back. They paused in front of the white door, exchanging a significant look. Someone was in there. Slowly, Caleb rested his hand on the door handle, glanced at the other man again, then pushed his way into the room, weapon drawn.

A strangled cry came from the bed.

Caleb's eyes adjusted to the darkness, a soft curse exiting his mouth as he stared at the elderly woman bound and gagged on the bed. Had to be Lydia White.

Caleb held up his hand to silence the crying woman, scanning the bedroom. There was a door, ajar, at one end of the room. Hernandez slipped toward it, then kicked it open and yelled, "San Diego Police Department!"

Nobody was in there. After examining the narrow closet, Hernandez stepped back and said, "Clear."

Disappointment tightened Caleb's chest. Damn it. Grier had been here, and for a while, judging by the empty food containers littering the carpet.

Caleb went to the woman's side, pulling off her duct-tape gag as gently as he could. "Lydia White?"

"Yes," the woman croaked. "Oh, thank heavens you're here! He was going to kill me!"

Caleb helped her into a sitting position. He pulled the knife from the holster on his ankle and quickly sliced open the tape binding her hands and feet together. Holding it by the corners, he set the pieces of tape on the table next to the bed for forensics to print and bag. He knew without a doubt whose prints they'd find on the tape, all over the room, in fact.

That son of a bitch had been here, scheming and watching Marley. Caleb's eyes drifted to the window, then narrowed at the hole in the wall beside it. His pupils contracted as Hernandez flicked on the light, but adjusted quickly, and he noticed flecks of blood on the plaster where the drywall had been broken. Grier's DNA would be on it.

"Mrs. White, can you identify the man who did this to you?" Caleb asked.

She nodded, a soft sob sliding from her mouth. "Yes, yes, I'll never be able to forget that face."

"I know you've been through quite an ordeal," he said, keeping his tone quiet. Behind him, he heard Hernandez barking into the radio, arranging for a forensics team and an ambulance. "We're going to take you to the hospital, to get you checked out, all right?"

The elderly woman's eyes filled with tears. "It was so terrible, officer," she said in the raspy voice usually heard from long-time smokers. "He was here for that dear girl across the street. He was so angry!"

"Don't worry, Ms. Kincaid is under police protection. You are, too, now," Caleb assured her. "Mrs. White," he continued, "the man who did this to you— did he say he would be coming back? Did he give any indication of where he might have gone?"

"No. No, nothing," Lydia stated.

Caleb turned to Hernandez, who carefully walked through the bedroom, making sure not to touch anything. "Miguel, can you stay with Mrs. White while I go across the street to Kincaid's?"

Hernandez nodded, taking Caleb's place at Lydia's bedside, offering surprising words of comfort as he reassured her the paramedics would be there soon to examine her.

But Caleb wasn't worried about Lydia White as he left the house. The elderly woman was dehydrated and in shock, but she would be fine. Marley, on the other hand…

His chest constricted as he realized how close Grier had been this entire time. He bit the inside of his lip so hard he could taste the blood in his mouth. Christ, he was scared for her. He'd seen the digital photo one of Hernandez's men had taken of Marley's locker at the hospital, the thick black X marking her face in that picture.

He couldn't let Grier hurt Marley.

Swallowing hard, he ignored the sharp metallic taste and walked faster. When he marched into Marley's living room, she was still on the couch, her hands clasped in her lap. Officer Thompson stood by the window, watching the scene outside.

"Is the old lady all right?" the young officer inquired.

"She'll be fine. Thompson, do me a favor and excuse us for a moment."

With a nod, the officer left the room. Caleb heard the front door open and shut, then Thompson's footsteps as he descended the porch steps to help out the others.

"You have to listen to me right now," he began, his throat tight as he looked into her gorgeous eyes. "I know you're angry with me, and I don't blame you for that, but please, Marley, just hear me out."

"Okay," she said softly.

"I need you to understand how much danger you're in." An eddy of fear swirled in his stomach but he ignored it, trying to remain calm as he laid it all out in front of her. "When I first moved in next door, I suspected Patrick would come back for you. Not to hurt you, but to convince you to leave town with him, or maybe just to say goodbye. I suspected he was obsessed with you, and when he sent that email, I knew it was a matter of time before love, or infatuation—whatever you want to call it—pushed him to see you."

Marley unclasped her hands and pressed them on her knees. "And now?"

"Now he wants to hurt you." He sank into the armchair Hernandez had occupied earlier. "He was across the street for who knows how long, and he must have seen us together. He also has to know I'm with the DEA, because he saw me there during the warehouse raid."

"So he thinks I'm working with the cops."

"Or at the very least, sleeping with one." He flinched when he saw her eyes darken. "What he did to your locker was an act of violence, and it's an indication of what he wants to do to you."

"I know." Her bottom lip quivered. "I know the danger, Caleb. I can feel it. Where are you going with this?"

"Someone needs to stay here in the house with you," he said. "And I'd really appreciate it if you wouldn't object. You need protection."

"Okay," she said without any argument.

"Though I'd prefer it if you'd agree to stay in a safe house," he added.

Bitterness flickered across her face. "I'm not leaving my house, Caleb. Patrick has already turned my entire life upside down. I won't let him chase me from my home."

He'd known she'd say something like that. "Then an agent will stay here. Grier is going to find out what happened tonight. We might get lucky and he'll waltz back to White's house, unaware that we found his hideout, but I'm not holding my breath. He was probably in the area, saw the police activity and took off."

"So search the neighborhood," Marley burst out, sounding frustrated.

"We are. Units are combing the area as we speak, though my gut tells me Grier will be long gone by now."

"But he'll be back."

"He'll be back," Caleb echoed. "He might consider it too risky to come to this house, but he'll find a way to get to you, Marley. I'm certain of that."

She released a shaky breath and turned her head away, but not before he saw tears forming in the corners of her eyes. He wanted so badly to pull her into his arms and comfort her, but he knew she wouldn't allow it.

"You probably shouldn't go into work for a while," he continued. "It'll be too hard to protect you there, and today Grier showed us that he can find a way into the hospital without getting caught."

Marley's jaw tightened. "So I'm just supposed to sit around and wait for him to kill me?"

"He won't kill you." Caleb's pulse sped up at the mere thought. "I won't let him."

She fell quiet for a few long moments, then cleared her throat. "It can't be you, Caleb."

"What can't be me?"

"The agent who stays here. I don't want it to be you. Or your partner for that matter."

Something shifted in his chest. There, his heart had officially cracked in two. He wanted nothing more than to stay here with her, to protect this beautiful, generous woman who had once trusted him so willingly—and so misguidedly. It killed him that she didn't want him around, though he understood perfectly why that was.

But God, he wished she would trust him now, to protect her, at least. He'd still be next door, but what if that wasn't close enough? What if he wasn't fast enough?

His palms began to sweat and he rubbed them on the front of his pants. "No," he finally said, his voice sounding hoarse even to his own ears. "I'm not going anywhere. I'm not leaving you, Marley."

THE SHRIEK OF SIRENS reverberated in the night, causing Patrick to sink farther into the bushes. He'd been hunkered down in the small park directly behind Marley's cul-de-sac for the past hour, ever since he'd heard that first siren wail in the distance. Seconds from hopping the fence at the edge of the park, he'd been forced to retreat, and now he hid, waiting for the opportunity to get the hell out of here. Evidently the cops had discovered his hiding place, which sent a rush of fury to his gut.

A flash of color caught his eye, and he peeked out to see a cop car cruising along the street in front of the park. Patrols. They were obviously casing the entire neighborhood.

"Damn it," he muttered, ducking into the bushes again.

What was he supposed to do now? He'd planned on going for the money tonight. The black backpack slung over his shoulder contained the syringes and sedatives he'd stolen from the hospital earlier this afternoon. He still couldn't believe he'd walked in undetected and managed to break into one of the medicine cabinets. Managed to leave Marley a nice little message, too.

Now his plans were shot to hell. It could've been so easy. Break into the house next door to Marley's and stick a needle in that cop bastard's throat before he knew what hit him. And then, with the cop in a drug-induced slumber, Patrick would get his money from Marley's bathroom while she worked the night shift. He'd considered going back to the hospital after that, waiting outside in the parking lot for her to come out. Even contemplated forgiving her for sleeping around on him. God knows, starting a new life would be a lot more fun if he had someone with him.

But now…now everything had changed.

He peered out again, breathing a sigh of relief when he noticed the cruiser had disappeared. He needed to make a run for it. If the patrols turned up nothing, the cops might start searching the area on foot soon, and he couldn't afford to stay in this damn park all night.

He crept out of the bushes and stayed in the shadows, using the oak trees for cover, his guard on high alert with each careful step. Rocks lined the edge of the playground. He bent to pick up a decent-size one, then kept moving. He neared the sidewalk, his gaze darting up and down the street, and finally he zeroed in on a beat-up old Toyota with rust coating the doors. There was no telltale flash of an alarm as he approached the decrepit vehicle. Perfect car to hotwire.

Fingers tightening over the rock, he glanced around the dark, deserted street, then smashed in the driver's-side window and held his breath. No alarm sounded.

He was in business.

Rapidly, he opened the door and slid into the car, his hand reaching under the dash and yanking out a bundle of wires. Two minutes later, the engine rumbled and Patrick sped away as if his life depended on it.

Because it kind of did.

He drove fast. His breath came out in sharp puffs, growing steadier the farther he got from Marley's neighborhood. He glanced in the rearview mirror every two seconds, but no police cruisers appeared behind him. No flashing lights. No sirens.

Relief pounded into him. Shit. That had been close. Too close.

When he decided he was far enough away—he'd driven for a good half hour—he pulled up at the curb in front of a small strip mall and let the car idle.

Then he slammed his hands against the steering wheel in fury.

Damn it. What the hell was he supposed to do? He needed that money.

Then you're just going to have to get her to bring it to you.

A slow smile stretched across his mouth. Yeah. Yeah, that could work. Marley would have to bring him the money. But how? How could he get her to—He straightened his shoulders, the smile widening.

And just like that, he knew exactly what he needed to do.

13

MARLEY LIFTED HER HEAD in surprise. Caleb stood in front of her, his broad shoulders squared, his defiant expression making it clear he would not back down.

"I know you're angry with me," he began. "And you should be. I lied to you, and I abused your trust. But the only thing I lied about was what I do for a living. Everything else was real, Marley."

"Forgive me if I have a little trouble believing that," she replied.

"It's true. I'm still the same person. I never lied about my background. I never hid my personality." His voice grew wry. "Don't you think, if I was playing a part, I'd choose to be someone more charming, more likable? I know I'm flawed, Marley. I'm rough around the edges, I'm too serious, too intense, too…broken."

Her heart squeezed in her chest. No, she would not allow herself to be swayed by his words, no matter how earnest they sounded.

"That could have been part of the act," she said, wincing at the feeble pitch in her tone. "Make yourself out to be…to be *broken* so I'd feel some silly urge to fix you. You knew I was a nurse, that my job means I like to help people. Maybe you wanted me to help you."

"Remember when you told me it's okay to talk about things that hurt you? Well, for me, it's never been okay. Do you think I liked telling you about the day I found my mother overdosed on the floor? That it was all part of some sick game? I've never told anyone about that before." Caleb made a frustrated sound in the back of his throat. "I didn't plan on opening up to you, Marley. It just happened."

"Yeah, it conveniently happened."

He flinched at her harsh retort, but the determination on his face never wavered. "I won't leave you. Grier will try to get to you, but I refuse to let him. Did Hernandez tell you what happened to the last woman who got involved with Grier?"

She nodded, unable to speak.

"Well, I won't let that happen to you. You can be angry with me all you like—you can hate me if you want—but I'm not leaving this house. If I left and something happened to you…" Agony clung to his husky voice. "I'd never forgive myself. No matter what you believe, I care about you, and I'm staying right here to protect you."

She tried to ignore the rush of warmth that heated her belly. There wasn't a single false note in his heartfelt words. Was Gwen right? Was it possible Caleb truly did care for her? Patrick had covered up the fact that he was a criminal, had lied about his very nature. But Caleb was a cop, a man who'd sworn an oath to protect others, and now he was determined to protect her. If anything, that made him honorable, but did it excuse the lie he'd told her?

She sucked in a slow breath. "Caleb—"

"I'm not going anywhere," he interrupted, jutting out his chin. "Even if I have to sit on the front porch all night, even if I have to stand on a ladder outside your bedroom window, I won't leave."

As if a higher power were eavesdropping on their discussion, a loud crack of thunder sounded from outside. Seconds later, rain poured from the sky, pounding against the house. Marley turned to the window in disbelief, watching as raindrops streaked down the glass.

"I swear, you planned this," she grumbled, shaking her head at him. "Now I'll spend the whole night picturing you getting soaked on the porch, or struck by lightning while standing on a ladder."

His lips twitched, but he didn't say a word.

"Fine," she said. "You can stay. But this doesn't mean I forgive you, Caleb."

"I know."

They stared at each other for one long moment, and a kaleidoscope of emotions spun around in her body. A part of her wanted to break the distance between them and find solace in his strong arms. She wanted to feel his firm lips pressed against hers, his dark stubble scraping her cheek. But then there was the other part of her—the angry part—that looked at him and remembered the cameras next door.

The sound of the front door opening interrupted her thoughts. Her pulse quickened, as a feeling of foreboding shot up her spine. She'd been on edge ever since the incident with her locker, and she found herself jumping at shadows, startling at the merest sound. She kept expecting Patrick to pop out of a closet or blaze into the house with a gun.

Her heartbeat slowed when Caleb's partner appeared

in the doorway, shaking out his clothing and sending water droplets onto her parquet floor.

"Hernandez left for the hospital to get Mrs. White's statement," AJ said. "The other officers from the SDPD are continuing the patrols, and our guys are setting up posts around the neighboring houses. Are we heading next door?"

Caleb shook his head. "I'm staying here."

His partner's eyes flickered with surprise. "All right."

"Keep your radio on, and your eyes on the monitors," Caleb said brusquely. "If Grier decides to come back tonight, we're going to see him."

With a nod, AJ bid an awkward goodbye and left the room. Caleb walked him out, and she heard the metallic scrape of the lock sliding into place. He returned a few seconds later and said, "You should go up to bed. It's past midnight."

Marley was quite aware of the fact that they were now completely alone. The same way they'd been alone last night, when they'd made love for hours in her bedroom. A traitorous flame of desire licked at her skin.

No. No way. She couldn't let herself be tempted by this man. No matter how gorgeous he looked in his all-black get-up, with his dark hair falling onto his proud forehead.

She stumbled to her feet. "Yeah, I should go upstairs."

To her dismay, he followed, trailing after her as she climbed the stairs to the second floor. "I guess you can sleep in the guest room," she offered, gesturing to the doorway across from hers.

He shook his head. "I'll stay outside your door."

Annoyance tickled her throat. "For the love of—"

"I'll be right here if you need me," Caleb cut in. "Now stop arguing and go to bed."

She rolled her eyes. Fine, if he wanted to be all macho about this, she would let him. So what if he chose to sit on an uncomfortable hardwood floor all night? That was his problem.

The first thing she did after she walked into her bedroom and shut the door was make a beeline for the window. She closed the drapes, her lips thinning as she pictured Caleb's scary partner next door, watching her on the monitor. She fought the urge to give him a big fat scowl. Instead, she took the higher road and turned away from the window, heading to the bathroom to get ready for bed.

Ten minutes later, she slipped under the covers and stared up at the ceiling. Outside, the rain continued to pound against the house, drumming out a staccato beat on the roof.

Sleep did not come. She was too keyed up and afraid, unable to erase the memory of what Patrick had done to her locker. That angry red word, designed to scare, to accuse. She pushed the image from her mind, only to have it replaced with one equally disturbing—Caleb sitting outside her door. He was actually prepared to spend the night there. In the morning, his back would be throbbing, his legs stiff from— God, she was such a bleeding heart.

Or maybe she was just looking for excuses to invite him into her room.

Marley sighed in the darkness. Why couldn't she just stay angry with him? She shouldn't want him around. After Patrick's betrayal, she'd banished her former fiancé from her heart and mind. Had had zero desire ever to see his sorry face again. So why wasn't it that way with Caleb?

She lay in bed for eighteen more minutes, watching the red numbers on her alarm clock roll over. Finally, she couldn't stand it anymore.

Groaning, she pushed away the comforter and got up, bare feet padding toward the door. She threw it open, and sure enough, Caleb sat on the floor, his head resting against the door of the guest room.

"Get in here already," she mumbled.

He shifted, one hand on the gun holstered at his hip, the other behind his head as a makeshift pillow. "I'm fine out here."

She set her jaw. "Seriously, come in. I can't sleep knowing you're spending the night on the floor."

"I—"

She held up her hand to silence him. "Stop arguing," she mimicked, "and come in."

Looking extremely reluctant, Caleb stood up and followed her into the bedroom. He eyed the bed, and she noticed his throat working as he swallowed. She knew exactly what he was thinking. She was thinking it, too, and her body grew hot as she remembered everything they'd done on this bed only last night.

A wave of longing hit her as she thought about Caleb's hands touching her skin, the seductive swirl of his tongue, the strength of his body as he drove into her, over and over.

"Now what?" he asked with a sigh, turning to her for his next orders.

She hesitated. "We'll share the bed. It's big enough for both of us."

"Marley…this isn't a good idea."

"I don't care. It's one o'clock in the morning, I'm

exhausted, and I can't sleep knowing you're sitting on the hard floor." She marched to the bed and got under the covers, then shot him a pointed look.

Caleb seemed ready to protest again, but finally he just nodded, a resigned light in his eyes. Slowly, he removed his gun and holster and carefully placed them on the top of her dresser. Then he glanced down at his clothing, as if trying to figure out what the heck to do.

Marley averted her eyes as he reached for his zipper. She heard the soft rustle of his clothing falling to the floor and then he was lowering his big body onto her bed. The mattress sagged from the weight of him. Her pulse sped up.

He didn't get under the covers, just lay on top of them, flat on his back with his arms pressed to his sides. She was on her back, too, suddenly feeling nervous and slightly upset with herself. Her fingers tingled with the need to touch him. From the corner of her eye, she saw his bare chest rising and falling with each breath he took. And his masculine scent wrapped around her, spicy and musky and totally intoxicating.

She curled her fingers into fists to keep from reaching over and touching him. Staying completely still, she closed her eyes and tried to sleep, but her mind refused to shut off. She suddenly remembered something, and rolled onto her side to look at him. "What did you say to Hernandez in the hall?" she asked.

"Nothing important."

"It seemed important," she said. "And when he came back to question me, he was actually being kind of… nice. So either hell froze over or you got him to change his mind about me."

Caleb went quiet for a moment. "I reminded him that you're not Amanda James."

She wrinkled her forehead. "Who?"

"AJ got me a copy of Hernandez's file, which included the last case he worked." Caleb paused. "I probably shouldn't be telling you this."

"Don't you think I deserve to know why he's treated me so badly?"

He paused for a second beat, finally letting out a breath. "Amanda James was the girlfriend of a guy Hernandez was trying to pin a series of bank robberies on. She insisted she had no idea what her boyfriend was doing, that she played no part in the robberies, and she was inconsolable when Hernandez brought her in for questioning. She was just a kid, barely nineteen, and Hernandez felt protective of her."

Marley propped herself up on her elbow. "What happened?"

"The boyfriend was arrested but the judge let him out on bail. The day he got out, he and the girl robbed a grocery store, trying to get money to skip town. They ended up killing three people, including a ten-year-old kid."

Marley sucked in a breath. "Oh, God, that's awful."

"Yeah, it was," he agreed. "It turned out James knew about the robberies all along, she'd even participated in some, and Hernandez looked like a total fool."

Despite herself, she felt a pang of sympathy. "And then Patrick and I came along, and the Bonnie and Clyde thing was happening all over again."

"He didn't want to make another mistake, but he took it to the other extreme. Too lenient on the first suspect, too harsh on the second."

"I still don't like him," she said. "I get now why he was so hard on me, but I'm not sure that's a good enough reason to totally railroad someone."

"I agree."

They fell silent, and she lay there watching the rise of his chest, the way he stared directly at the ceiling as if he couldn't bear to look at her.

"Was it honestly real?" she whispered.

That got his attention. Very slowly, he turned to face her, looking into her eyes. "It was real," he murmured. "I lied about my job, but I didn't lie about who I am."

"And who are you, Caleb?"

"I'm...I'm just a man. I make mistakes. I obsess over the job sometimes. I've never been in a serious relationship, probably because I'm used to being alone. I've always been alone."

Each word sent an ache to her heart, until it squeezed so tight in her chest she could barely draw a breath. His voice was heavy with emotion, his face showing vulnerability she knew he hated to reveal.

"But not with you," he said, so quietly she had to lean forward to hear him. "I don't feel alone when I'm with you."

She couldn't help herself—she moved closer to him. Their faces were mere inches apart. Alarm bells rang in her head, warning her to stop this insanity before she fell into the same damn trap as before.

"It was real," he said again, his breath warm against her face. "More real than anything else in my life, sweetheart. All these years I've gone through the motions, done my job and made conversation with my coworkers. I pretended to be normal, all the while knowing I wasn't quite whole."

She shivered as he lifted his hand to touch her cheek, tenderly caressing her skin. "I wasn't pretending with you," he finished. "I lied, but I didn't pretend."

God, what was she supposed to do, to say? This was

the most open he'd ever been with her. His gruffness and cool composure was stripped away, leaving him bare and raw and *honest*.

Was she an idiot for wanting so badly to believe in that honesty?

Sensing where her thoughts had gone, Caleb's voice became desperate. "I'm not lying to you, Marley. It might be better if I was, because then I wouldn't have to feel…whatever it is I feel for you. It scares me. *You* scare me."

Her breath hitched as he slid closer, so that their bodies were touching. She felt his heartbeat vibrating against her breasts, which grew heavy with need. His eyes dropped to her mouth, and her surroundings faded as Caleb kissed her.

She couldn't pull back, couldn't push him away. Goosebumps rose on her bare arms, which twined around him. Her fingers touched the soft hair at the nape of his neck.

"We shouldn't… I shouldn't…" Her words got lost in the kiss, swept away as he teased her lips with his tongue then slipped it into her mouth, where she met each greedy thrust, swirling and exploring until they were both breathless.

"Can't you feel it?" he rasped against her trembling lips. "It feels right, Marley."

She wanted to disagree, but the objection refused to leave her mouth. She didn't want him to be right. She didn't want *this* to be right. But she couldn't stop kissing him, couldn't stop the need that rose inside her like a tidal wave.

She reached between them and slid her hand under the elastic waistband of his boxers. She grasped his erection, stroking it as he let out a husky groan. She couldn't fight the crazy urge to touch him. He nuzzled her neck, his mouth latching onto the soft flesh there.

A slow-burning fire spread through her body, pulsing between her legs and making her breasts tingle. When Caleb groaned against her throat and moved his hips to meet her hurried strokes, the fire burned even hotter.

"I need you inside me," she whispered.

Both his hands suddenly cupped her chin. He searched her face, looking hopeful and anxious and unbelievably aroused. "Are you sure?"

She nodded, shifting onto her back and parting her thighs. God, this was insane. She should hate this man, not want him. Kick him out, not pull him close. But the fire inside her refused to cool. Every nerve ending she possessed crackled with urgent need.

Caleb leaned over her and yanked open the drawer on the nightstand, rummaging around for the condoms they'd stashed there. He had his boxers off and a condom on before she could blink, and then he peeled her tiny boxer shorts and tank top off her body. He tossed them aside, along with her panties, and covered her body with his. With a slow and delicious thrust, he was inside her, eliciting simultaneous groans from each of their throats.

Pleasure gathered in her belly, intensifying as Caleb began to move. There was nothing rushed about his thrusts. He slid in and out, out and in, an indolent rhythm that made her whimper.

His warm hands stroked her face, his lips peppering kisses on her jaw, her neck, her shoulder.

"This is real," he murmured. "It's real, sweetheart."

His pace remained lazy, and not even the restless

lift of her hips deterred him. He made long, slow love to her, and when she looked up at his gorgeous face, the emotion she saw took her breath away.

Real. Yes, this felt real. She wrapped her arms around him and dragged her fingernails up and down the hard muscles of his back. The gentle tempo he'd set wasn't enough anymore. She wanted more. Needed more. With a little moan, she urged him to go faster, arching her back to take him deeper. When he still didn't comply, she raked her nails down his back and resorted to begging. "Please, Caleb...*please.*"

Whatever restraint he'd been holding onto snapped like a bungee cord, and then he was driving into her like a man possessed. "Christ," he choked out. "You're... I..."

He gave up on talking and kept moving, plunging into her until she could no longer bear it, until all her muscles tensed and...oh, *yes.* All thoughts drained out of her head as her body fragmented in sweet release. Flashes of light blinded her, while bursts of ecstasy went off in her body. She felt Caleb let go and she held him as he shook from release.

When the waves of her orgasm finally ebbed, common sense returned, urging Marley to push him away. She'd experienced a momentary relapse, a foolish lack of self-control, but now was the time to come back to reality. Caleb had lied to her, he'd hurt her, and even though she'd trusted him with her body just now, could she really trust him with her heart?

Yet her arms refused to let go of him, her legs refused to unhook from their perch on his trim hips. And her heart...her heart implored her to hold him even tighter.

So she did.

CALEB HAD NEVER BEEN ONE to question good fortune. Even that one Christmas when his current foster mom presented him with a brand-new baseball glove, he'd forced himself not to ask, "Why?" In his experience, people didn't give gifts without expecting something in return, but Marley…she'd given him something so incredibly important last night. He wasn't about to ruin that by spitting out all the questions biting at his tongue.

Do you forgive me?

Can you ever trust me again?

He couldn't help but remember the day in Marley's kitchen, when she'd asked him if he'd ever been in love and had looked so astounded when he'd admitted he hadn't. He might have a different answer now, if the unfamiliar warmth flowing through his veins was what he thought it was. It was funny—the women he'd dated in the past had wanted so badly for him to love them, but how could he, when he wasn't even sure what love felt like?

Now, he thought he might have an idea. The lump of tenderness that lodged in his throat whenever he looked into Marley's eyes. The heat that unfurled in his body whenever he touched her. The protective rush that shot through him when he thought about the danger she was in.

Was that love?

Sitting up in bed, Caleb watched as Marley moved around the bedroom, folding clothes, shoving a pair of shoes into the closet. She'd barely said two words since they woke up, and he was beginning to grow uneasy. Any second now, he expected her to tell him last night was a mistake and throw him out.

But she didn't do that. Rather, she strode to the

bathroom, then hesitated in the doorway and glanced over her shoulder. "Want to take a shower?"

He was off the bed and moving toward her in a nano-second.

Taking off the T-shirt she'd slipped into before they'd gone to sleep, she stepped into the shower stall. Caleb shucked his boxers and followed her in, wrapping his arms around her from behind as she turned on the faucet. Hot water poured out of the showerhead and Marley tilted her head, letting the water soak her honey-blond hair. She took a step back, giving him a turn under the spray while she reached for a poufy-looking thing and squirted a generous amount of body wash onto it. The scent of strawberries filled the small space. It smelled like Marley, sweet and feminine and unbelievably sexy.

He couldn't take his eyes off her as she washed herself, white suds sliding down her body and gathering in the valley of her breasts. She was so freaking gorgeous, creamy white skin, gentle curves and full breasts tipped with tight pink nipples.

He opened his mouth to say something. Tell her she was beautiful. Ask her if she needed help. But what came out was, "What does this mean?"

Handing him the pouf, she moved under the spray and let the water wash away the suds. For a long time, she didn't answer, and he just stood there, feeling slightly awkward as he dragged the fluffy sponge across his body, branding that strawberry scent into his own skin.

When she finally spoke, her voice came out in a sigh. "I don't know what it means."

Do you want me to stay?

He didn't utter the words, fearful of how she might respond. Instead, he asked the question to himself.

Did he want to stay?

His entire adult life had revolved around his job. He worked out of the New York office, but his assignments took him all over the country. Staying with Marley would mean not being able to take certain assignments, or maybe even leaving the agency altogether. It would be too hard, living apart for long periods at a time.

It astounded him that he could even consider any of this. His work was all he'd ever cared about. Previously, the notion of not having his job had brought a knot of panic to his gut.

Now, that panic arose when he imagined leaving Marley. He wanted to stay here with her. To help her renovate her house and go to Sunday barbecues at her dad's place. To make love to her every night and wake up next to her every morning.

"We shouldn't talk about it right now." Marley's soft voice pulled him out of his disconcerting thoughts. "I don't have the energy for it. I just want Patrick to be caught."

Sliding open the steamed-up door, Marley got out of the shower, her body slick and rosy pink. Caleb quickly rinsed, then turned off the faucet. He was just getting out when Marley let out a squeak followed by an irritated curse.

"You okay?" he asked.

She hopped on one foot, holding the other one with a wet hand and rubbing her big toe. "Yeah, I'm fine. I just stubbed my toe on that loose tile again."

He looked at the floor. One of the tiles had popped out of place, thanks to Marley's foot.

"I definitely need to retile," she grumbled, moving

to the door and swiping a terry-cloth robe from the hook there.

Caleb continued to stare at the tile. Why had a tile in the middle of the floor come loose? Something wasn't right. "I think…" Getting out of the shower, he bent down to the floor, dripping water all over the place. "There's something here."

He lifted the tile, squinting into the space beneath. Instead of the plywood that should have been there, someone had sawed out a jagged square, revealing the cavity beneath the sub-floor. A dark little hiding place. Slowly, Caleb stuck his hand in, feeling around until his fingers made contact with plastic. He gripped what felt like an envelope, using only his thumb and forefinger to pull it out.

"What is that?" Marley asked.

Caleb studied the envelope, which was enclosed in a clear plastic bag. It felt bulky, and when he gingerly removed it from the bag and lifted the flap, his breath caught in his throat.

Marley stepped closer, peering down at the envelope in his hands. She gasped. "Is that…money?"

He stared at the thick stacks of bills, four of them individually wrapped with elastic bands. All hundreds, and each stack had to contain at least fifty grand.

Dropping the flap, Caleb tucked the envelope back in the bag and stood up. "Well, I think we know why Patrick's still in town," he remarked with a sigh.

14

Marley stood in front of the sliding door leading to her backyard and stared at the sparrows pecking at the seeds in her bird feeder. Male voices drifted in from the living room—Caleb was in there with Jamison and D'Amato, the two DEA agents who'd been posted outside during the night. They were discussing the money Caleb had discovered in the bathroom, and she preferred not to be there for that.

She still couldn't believe it. Patrick had stashed two hundred thousand dollars under her floor. She'd probably walked over that spot hundreds of times in the past few months, completely oblivious to what lay below. The thought that her bathroom floor had been housing Patrick's drug money for so long made her want to cry.

Caleb was certain Patrick would come back for the money. It was probably the only reason he hadn't fled the city earlier. He had to know by now that their bank account had been frozen. Caleb told her that the bank wouldn't authorize any transfers *out* of the account.

Patrick must be pretty desperate by now, she thought,

her stomach churning. She grew even more uneasy when her cell phone vibrated in her purse, which sat on the kitchen counter. It was probably Gwen, or maybe her brother or her dad, whose calls she'd been avoiding since last night. Her best friend and family had no idea what had happened yesterday—finding Lydia White tied up in her bedroom, discovering Patrick's drug money.

She hadn't called because she didn't want to scare them any further. Patrick's stunt at the hospital already had everyone on edge.

She fished the phone out of her bag, sighing when she saw her dad's number flashing on the screen. This was his third call in the past hour. If she continued to not pick up, he and Sam would probably drive over in a panic. That was one scene she wouldn't mind avoiding.

"Hey, Dad," she said as she pressed the talk button.

"Hey, sweet pea."

Shock slammed into her like a baseball bat, sucking the oxygen right out of her lungs.

"Don't say my name," Patrick added swiftly. "Are you alone?"

Her fingers shook against the phone. "Y-yes."

"Good. If anyone comes in, you're talking to your father."

She choked down the hard lump of terror obstructing her throat. "Why are you calling from this number?"

"Because I'm having a nice little visit with your father," Patrick answered in a pleasant voice. "Sammy's here, too, but I'm afraid I had to knock him out. He was being very difficult."

A chill rushed over her. "Don't you dare hurt either one of them."

"I'm not going to hurt anyone." He sounded annoyed. "Your father's sitting right here beside me, not a hair on his head disturbed."

"Let me talk to him," she blurted. Her heart hammered in her chest, so fast she feared it might stop beating altogether. "I want to talk to him."

"Fine, but be quick. You and I have some things to discuss."

There was a shuffling noise, and then, to her sheer relief, her father came on the line. "Sweetheart?"

"Daddy?" she whispered. "Oh, God, Dad, are you okay?"

"I'm all right," her father replied, but the slight quiver in his voice told her he was anything but all right.

"Has he hurt you?"

"No." *Not yet,* was what he seemed to be saying. Her dad grew urgent, his words coming out so fast she struggled to keep up. "Don't do a thing he asks, Marley. Your brother and I will be okay. Whatever he wants, don't give it to him. Do you hear me, sweetheart, don't—"

An angry curse whipped through the extension, and then Patrick returned. "Your father's trying to be a hero," he said with a chuckle. "But we both know you're not going to leave him at my mercy, right, *sweet pea?*"

"What do you want?"

"I need you to bring me something. There's some money stashed in your house. It's hidden under…"

Marley tuned him out, the sound of footsteps sending alarm spinning through her. She heard the front door shut, then more footsteps coming toward the kitchen. Caleb appeared in the doorway a second later, and she quickly held up her hand to silence him.

His blue eyes immediately hardened as he looked at the cell phone pressed up to her ear.

"—and bring it to your father's house," Patrick finished. "One hour, Marley."

An unsteady breath squeezed out of her lungs. "I c-can't. They're watching me."

"The cops?"

"Yeah. They're next door. And one is upstairs right now," she said, avoiding Caleb's eyes. "I can't leave without them knowing."

"You're a smart girl. I'm sure you'll find a way." Patrick's voice turned to ice. "You sure found a way to screw someone else while I was gone."

She swallowed. "I…"

"I don't want to hear your excuses," Patrick snapped. "Get the money and bring it to me, or you can say goodbye to your baby brother and your daddy."

"Please, don't hurt—"

"And you'd better be alone," he interrupted. "I'll be watching you pull up, and if I sense anything funny, your father and junior die."

He hung up, and Marley sagged against the counter. She gasped for air, salty tears welling up and coating her eyelashes. A pair of warm arms surrounded her, steadying her before she could keel over.

She whirled around and pressed her face against Caleb's strong chest, her tears soaking the front of his shirt. "He has my dad and brother," she wheezed between sobs. "He's going to kill them if I don't bring him the money."

Caleb's hands stroked her back, soothing her, bringing warmth to her suddenly freezing body. He tangled his fingers in her hair and angled her head so she was looking up at him. "It's okay," he murmured. "It'll be okay."

"How can you say that? He's going to kill them!"

"I won't let him," Caleb replied. He used his thumb to wipe away her tears. "I won't let him hurt them, Marley."

"What are we going to do? He wants me to bring the money in an hour, and I have to go alone. If I bring the cops, he said he'll kill them."

Whatever confidence she lacked at the moment, Caleb made up for in spades. He released her and picked up the radio he'd put on the counter, alerting AJ and the others to the situation. As she stood there, shaken up and afraid, he placed a call to Hernandez and then to a man he referred to as Stevens.

Fifteen minutes later, Caleb had efficiently assembled a team in her living room, except for Stevens, who listened in on speakerphone.

Marley could barely focus as the men discussed the situation in urgent tones. Patrick had her father and Sam. He'd taken so much from her already. Several pieces of her heart, her ability to trust, her confidence and now he wanted to take her family?

"We can use a decoy," she heard Hernandez suggest.

Marley's head whipped up.

"We've got an officer in vice who's about Marley's height and build," the detective continued. "We'll set her up with a wig and a wire, and send her in to—"

"No."

The men swiveled their heads in her direction, stunned into silence by the vehemence in that one word.

"Marley," Caleb began, "I know you're upset, but

we're doing everything we can to get your dad and brother back."

"You can't send in a decoy," she insisted. "He'll know."

Hernandez glanced at her in annoyance. "Officer Gray is trained to—"

"I don't give a damn what she's trained to do," she snapped. "I'm telling you, Patrick will know the second she gets out of the car that she isn't me. We were engaged, Detective. He'll *know*."

Silence descended over the room again.

"What exactly are you getting at?" Caleb asked, sounding extremely wary.

She drew in a steadying breath. "I should be the one to go."

"No way," Caleb jumped to his feet. "No way, Marley."

"Why not? I can take the money, give it to him in exchange for my dad and Sammy, and then you guys can catch him when he tries to leave."

"It's not that simple," Caleb said. "He's bound to have a weapon. He could shoot you and your family the second he gets the cash."

She lifted her chin. "So give me a bulletproof vest."

"And if he shoots you in the head?"

She swallowed hard. "I need to do this, Caleb. I won't let him hurt my family, and if you try to send in some fake version of me, he *will* hurt them."

She studied the faces of the men. Caleb's partner was looking at her with what appeared to be admiration, the two DEA agents looked as if they were mulling over what she'd said, the SDPD officers were stone-faced and Hernandez watched her with serious dark eyes.

"Do you think you can get him outside?" the detective asked.

Caleb spun around to glare at Hernandez. "What are you doing? She's not going in there, damn it!"

"It could work," Hernandez replied. "She gives him the money, and then convinces him she wants to run off with him. Kincaid Sr. and Jr. remain in the house, and Marley and Grier head outside where we'll have a team waiting."

"He'll spot us," AJ spoke up.

"Not if we stay out of sight until Marley gives the signal they're coming out," Hernandez countered. He looked over at her again. "Do you think you'll be able to do this?"

She hesitated. Convince Patrick she still loved him, that she wanted to flee the country with him? The very idea of seeing his face again made her feel sick.

But what about her dad? What about Sammy? Could she really let them be taken away from her simply because she felt ill at the thought of being near Patrick?

She exhaled. "I can do it."

"No," Caleb said again. He stepped toward her, his features hard. "I won't let you put your life in danger. We can handle this."

"No, you can't. Patrick won't open that door to anyone but me."

She stared into Caleb's blue eyes, floored by the agony she saw in them. He was scared. Scared for her.

"I'm scared, too," she murmured as if he'd vocalized his fear. "But you'll be right outside to protect me."

He nodded. "Always," he said softly.

Something inside her chest dislodged. It took her a moment to figure out what it was—the jagged little pieces of anger and bitterness that had clung to her heart after Caleb had told her the truth. The shards had disappeared, as an important realization dawned on her. This man would do anything to protect her. She mattered to him.

Acceptance settled over her like a warm blanket. Caleb wasn't a sick voyeur who'd decided to prey on her. He was a cop on a stakeout, a man trying to avenge his friend's death. Could she really hold that against him? He might have lied to her, but now he was doing everything in his power to keep her safe.

"I can do this, Caleb," she said, her voice barely a whisper. "Trust me to do this."

His shoulders tightened at the word *trust*. She knew what he was thinking. The question he'd been wanting to ask her since last night. *Can you trust me again?*

Now she was asking it of him.

And even though she could tell it went against everything he believed in, letting someone else venture into a dangerous situation instead of him, he nodded and said, "I trust you."

MARLEY'S ENTIRE BODY trembled as she shut off the engine of her convertible. The bungalow she'd grown up in, where her dad and brother still lived, looked so harmless and cozy, but there was nothing harmless about this situation, was there? Patrick was inside that house, holding her family hostage, all so he could get his greedy hands on some cash. To flee from the law, to get away with murder.

"I really hope you can hear this," she muttered.

She didn't look down at her chest, in case Patrick was watching her from the window, but the transmitter taped inside her bra dug into her skin, reminding her of the danger she was about to walk into.

Caleb's partner assured her that every word would be recorded and transmitted to the team's earpieces in real time. They would know what was going on every second she was in the house. If she said the panic word, agents would storm the house in less than a minute. If she convinced Patrick she wanted to leave town with him, she would say the go word and the arrest would be made after Caleb gave her the signal to wrench away from Patrick's side.

Taking a breath, she picked up her purse, which contained the two hundred thousand dollars. The agents had opted not to tag the money with dye, instead tucking a tiny GPS transmitter into one of the stacks, in case Patrick managed another great escape.

She slung her purse over her shoulder and got out of the car. Her legs shook as she stepped onto the gravel driveway. She took a few more seconds to breathe, to gather her composure, and then she walked up the path to the front door.

Her hand wavered as she knocked on the door. It opened instantly, and for the first time in three months, Marley laid eyes on the man she'd been engaged to marry.

He looked exactly the same. Brown hair cut in a neat, no-nonsense style, wiry body covered with a pair of khakis and a polo shirt. Only his brown eyes looked different. Wilder. Colder.

Patrick looked pleased as he peered past her shoulders and examined the deserted street. He also seemed completely unruffled by the fact that he was pointing a gun at her.

"You came alone. Good girl."

She yelped as he grabbed her arm and hauled her into the house, closing and locking the door behind them.

"Where's my dad and brother?" she demanded.

He ignored the question. "Did you bring the money?"

She nodded.

"Give it to me."

She reached into her purse, pulled out the envelope, and handed it to him. Keeping his gun trained on her, he stuck a hand into the bag and took out the envelope. Opening the flap, he flipped through the thick stacks of bills.

Marley held her breath, praying he wouldn't stumble across the transmitter. It was smaller than a watch battery, hard to find unless he diligently examined each bill, which he didn't.

She exhaled slowly. "It's all there."

"I can see that," he replied.

"Can I see my family now?"

"You don't get to ask me questions." He leaned closer and jammed the barrel of the gun into her side.

She stared up at him, shocked by the emptiness she saw in his eyes. How could this be the same man she'd fallen in love with? The last time she'd seen Patrick, he'd been playful and loving as he kissed her goodbye and left for a web-design convention that would last all weekend.

There had never been a convention, only an illegal gathering to distribute drugs.

He looked like a total stranger now. Those empty eyes. The effortless way he gripped the gun, as if holding someone at gunpoint was no biggie to him.

Marley blinked back tears. She pressed her lips together, forcing herself not to plead with him. She was anxious to make sure her dad and Sam were alive, but she didn't want to push him.

Patrick's hard gaze connected with hers, and the unrestrained anger on his face made her apprehensive. She suspected he might snap at any second, just go ahead and shoot her, but to her surprise, his features crumpled with anguish. "How could you cheat on me?" he asked.

This was it. Her chance to diffuse the situation.

"You slept with that cop," Patrick continued, bitterness drenching each word. "You couldn't wait three damn months?"

She tried to speak, but he cut her off, his expression suddenly wistful. "You know, I came back here for you, Marley."

She feigned surprise. "You did?"

"Yeah." A faraway note entered his voice. "I had it all planned. We'd head for South America, buy a little house on the beach, spend the rest of our lives lying on the sand, just the two of us."

Marley was tempted to point out how delusional that sounded—he was a fugitive, for Pete's sake—but she stayed quiet. She couldn't blow this. She'd promised Caleb she could handle this, and antagonizing Patrick was not the way to do it.

"That sounds wonderful," she said, smiling up at him.

"Then why couldn't you wait for me?" he spat out. "Instead of having faith that I'd come for you, you went out and screwed the first guy you saw."

She took a deep breath. "I did it for you."

Patrick's entire body stiffened. "What did you say?"

"I said I did it for you," she whispered.

Patrick didn't speak, but she could swear the pressure of his gun eased up. His dark eyes searched her face. For what seemed like hours. She grew uncomfortable, scared, panicked, under that intense scrutiny. When she couldn't stand it anymore, she said, "Why are you looking at me?"

"I'm trying to figure out if you're telling me the truth."

Her heart raced. "I am."

"How?" he asked. "How was that for me, you banging another guy?"

She edged closer to him, flinching when the gun dug into her side again. "I missed you so much," she confessed. "I was so worried, Patrick. I didn't know where you were, if you were okay… And then this cop showed up, pretending to be my neighbor. I knew right away what he was up to."

"You did?"

"Of course. I would never go to bed with another man unless I had a good reason. You know that."

He looked deep into her eyes, a hesitant smile lifting one corner of his mouth. "You got close to him to get information? To protect me?"

"I got close to him so he wouldn't get close to finding *you,*" she replied. "I had to be sure he wasn't making headway locating you."

Patrick hesitated, then released a sigh. "I would have done the same thing, babe."

"Really?" She gave him a pleading look. "Do you forgive me, Patrick? I was only trying to help."

He lowered the gun and slid closer to her, stroking her cheek with his cold fingers. "Of course I forgive you. I love you, Marley. I've been thinking of nothing but you the last three months."

"Why didn't you tell me the truth? You know I would have stood by you, no matter what you did for a living."

He lowered his eyes and shrugged. "I know. I'm sorry. I should have trusted you."

"Yes," she agreed in a petulant voice.

"Well, I trust you now." He gently tucked a strand of hair behind her ear. "And I promise I'll spend the rest of my life making this up to you."

He stuck the gun in the waistband of his jeans, every last iota of rage and resentment draining from his face, replaced with pure, delusional joy. Oh, God, he was insane. He seriously believed she was telling the truth. That she'd gotten close to Caleb to find out what the cops were doing.

So she could protect Patrick.

Choking back her disbelief, she said, "Can I really go with you?"

He gave her a warm smile, reminding her of the day she'd met him in the hospital, how charming he'd been. "I want you by my side, sweet pea, and I always will." He wavered for a moment. "What about your dad? And Sam? Can you leave them? I know how much your family means to you."

Then why are you holding them hostage? she wanted to scream.

Her nerves began to unravel like an old sweater, and she had to force herself to stay in character. "You mean more," she said simply.

His entire face lit up, and all of a sudden he was the man she'd been going to marry. Preppy, handsome, easygoing smile.

"We should go then," he said, urgency lining his tone. "How did you get away from the cops?"

She fed him the story she and Caleb had concocted. "I insisted I wanted to go into work. An agent followed me to the hospital, and then I switched clothes with Gwen and snuck out."

Patrick sounded surprised. "Gwen helped you?"

"Of course." Marley smiled. "She knows how much I still love you."

"God, sweet pea, I missed you so much," Patrick burst out, taking a step toward her.

His gaze dropped to her mouth and something in his expression shifted. To her dismay, she saw a spark of lust there. Horror gripped her insides as he dipped his head. He was going to kiss her.

There was no way she would be able to kiss him back. The very thought of placing her lips on his repulsed her.

Faking a smile, she pressed her index finger to his mouth and laughed. "Hold that thought. We need to go, remember?" She put on a concerned look. "But first I want to make sure Dad and Sam are okay, and say goodbye to them. Is that okay?"

The reverent expression on his face told he would give her the moon if she asked.

"Okay, you can say your goodbyes," he conceded. "Let's get this show on the road before I go crazy with impatience. I want to start our life together, Marley."

She looked him square in the eye and said, "Me, too."

15

CALEB CROUCHED BEHIND the tall hedges of the house three doors down from the Kincaid bungalow. Fear continued to slither up and down his spine like a hungry snake, cold and relentless. He'd been in this state since the moment he'd agreed to let Marley go and meet Patrick.

For the last ten minutes, he'd been listening to their conversation on his earpiece while AJ and Hernandez coordinated with the other agents and police officers on the scene. Four teams had been set up—all out of Patrick's line of sight—and they were all raring to go. Waiting for Marley to say the word.

"She's good," Hernandez admitted with great reluctance as he came up beside Caleb.

Marley had just convinced Grier she was willing to leave her family for him. To anyone else, her tone must sound strong and confident. Ringing with conviction.

But Caleb had spent enough time with her to recognize the nuances of her voice. He knew when she was fighting back laughter, when she was aroused, when she felt vulnerable.

And when she was scared out of her wits, the way she was right now.

"She's terrified," he corrected.

Hernandez's shoulders drooped. "I know." He sounded ashamed as he added, "And I know you despise me for the way I treated her."

Caleb sighed. "I already told you, I understand what drove you to it. The James case hit you hard, I get that."

The detective gave a sad nod. "Yeah, it did." He glanced at the four men standing nearby. They were armed and ready to take down the bastard whose clutches Marley had willingly put herself in. "But I'm not sure that excuses the way I acted."

Caleb didn't answer, too distracted by the relieved cry that rang in his ear. Patrick had just taken Marley to her father, who Caleb figured was tied up as he heard Marley ask about his wrists. Sam Sr. was apparently in perfect health, unlike his son. "Did you have to knock him unconscious?" Marley asked.

"He tried to attack me," came Patrick's muffled voice. "It's only a sedative, sweet pea. He'll come to in an hour or so."

As Caleb listened, Marley tried to convince Patrick to untie her father, but he wouldn't have it, insisting that her brother would take care of the bindings when he woke up. Now that Marley had seen to her family's safety, Patrick was all action, going on about the money and the new IDs he'd arranged for them.

Footsteps echoed in Caleb's ears. His muscles tensed. They were heading for the door.

"I'm so happy we're doing this," Marley said, sounding nearly giddy. "I've always wanted to go to South America." She giggled. "The most exciting place I've ever been to is Disneyland."

Disneyland—there it was, the go word.

Caleb and his team sprung into action.

"Let's move," Hernandez hissed.

The men emerged from their hiding place, moving in unison toward the Kincaid bungalow. They reached the front lawn just as Patrick and Marley stepped outside.

Grier's eyes flashed with red-hot fury at the sight of Caleb and the other men. He spun around as two cruisers, along with an unmarked SUV, flew into sight. One cruiser drove directly onto the front lawn, another came to a grinding halt in the driveway, while the third skidded over the curb. Car doors opened and slammed, men in tactical gear, carrying gleaming black weapons, swarmed the yard.

Caleb heard his own voice shout, "Hands in the air, Grier!"

Rather than obey, Grier's right hand snapped down to his waist and he whipped out a gun. Caleb's heart dropped to the pit of his stomach as Grier then took that gun and jammed it into Marley's temple.

"I'll shoot her!" Grier screamed, his face bright crimson.

"Put the gun down," Caleb ordered. He took another step forward.

"Don't move!" Patrick yelled.

Caleb stopped in his tracks and shot a sideways look at Agent Tony D'Amato, who was kneeling behind the open door of the police cruiser on the lawn. D'Amato lifted his rifle slightly, asking a silent question, which Caleb answered with a hard glare. D'Amato wanted to take out Grier. Caleb wanted the same thing. But there was no way in hell he was doing anything until Marley was out of the line of fire.

He forced himself not to look at her, but it was damn near impossible. Her heart-shaped face was ashen. She stood motionless, with Grier's weapon pressed to her temple.

"You're completely surrounded," Caleb told Grier. He lowered his voice. "Just let her go and give yourself up, Patrick. This doesn't have to end with another life on your hands."

"I killed that agent in self-defense! I'm not a murderer!"

"Of course not," Caleb soothed. He took another step. "But you will be, if you use that gun on Marley."

"Don't say her name," Grier hissed. "She doesn't belong to you. She belongs to me!"

Another step. "Then I'm sure you don't want to hurt her, Patrick. I know you care about her."

Grier's features twisted. "She's mine." He jabbed the gun into Marley's temple again. "But I will kill her if you sons of bitches don't get out of my way. Marley and I have a plane to catch."

Caleb moved closer, then stopped and caught Marley's eye. The panic on her face tore at his insides, but he pushed away the primal urge to launch himself at Patrick Grier and wrench Marley away from him. Instead, he sent her the signal they'd agreed on back at her house, two quick nods and the lift of his right shoulder.

She answered with an imperceptible nod and followed his orders to a T.

Pride mingled with the fear pumping through Caleb's blood as Marley made her move. With a little cry, she pretended to trip, then dove to the side, pressing her body flat to the ground.

While Patrick blinked with shock at losing his

hostage, Caleb charged forward. "Put the gun down!" he yelled.

Grier blinked again. He suddenly snapped out of whatever trance he'd gone into, his lips tightening. He stared at Caleb running toward him, then at Marley, who was a couple of yards to his left.

With lightning speed, he spun the gun at Marley.

Caleb didn't hesitate. He squeezed the trigger of his Glock, eliciting an outraged shriek of pain from Patrick as his arm took a hit. The other man stumbled, but not before his gun spat out a wild, desperate bullet in Marley's direction.

A bullet that Caleb dove in front of.

MARLEY LIFTED HERSELF onto her elbows in time to see Caleb's big, strong body thudding to the ground.

Chaos ensued. The hurried footsteps of the other agents rushing for Patrick. Patrick's shouts of indignation as he was thrown down, his arms yanked behind his back.

Still stunned, Marley watched as a pair of handcuffs were snapped around Patrick's wrists. And then the agents hauled him toward one of the cars, while he spat and struggled.

She winced when she heard him call her name.

"Marley!" he wailed. "You tricked me! You little bitch!"

He was still shouting at her as the cops shoved him into the cruiser.

"Are you okay?" a deep voice asked, and then a big hand helped her to her feet.

She flinched when she realized the hand belonged to Detective Miguel Hernandez. "I'm fine," she squeezed out.

"Ms. Kincaid," the detective started awkwardly. "I wanted to apologize for—"

She was already rushing away before he could finish the sentence. She didn't want or need Hernandez's apology, not when Caleb lay there on the grass after taking the bullet that was meant for her. What if the bullet had missed the vest?

"Caleb," she said urgently as she fell to her knees beside him.

He let out a groan and then, to her relief, sat up. Marley scanned his torso, wincing at the neat hole in the middle of his dark-blue button-down shirt.

"It got the vest, right?" She ran her fingers over him, checking for damage.

With a soft chuckle, he unbuttoned his shirt and spread it apart, revealing the black Kevlar vest molded to his broad chest. A small bullet was lodged in the material, an inch to the right of Caleb's heart.

"They always aim for the vest," he said gruffly.

"Unless they're aiming at your head," she said, mimicking his earlier words. "Seriously, are you okay?"

"I feel like I got the wind knocked out of me, but I'm okay. I'm more worried about you." Caleb stumbled to his feet, pulling her up with him. "Did he hurt you?"

She stared into his gorgeous blue eyes and the love and concern she saw shining there robbed her of breath. He was worried about *her*. He'd just taken a bullet while trying to save her, and he was thinking about her?

"He didn't hurt me," she assured him. "He was too busy planning our happy little life together. I did good, didn't I? I really had him going."

Caleb's eyes became cloudy. "You took a big risk, Marley. You could have gotten yourself killed."

"I knew you would protect me," she murmured. "I knew you would save me."

He opened his mouth to respond, but someone called his name. Agent D'Amato, a tall man with shaggy red hair, stalked toward them. "Agent Ford, we're taking the perp to lock-up. Stevens said you'd want to head up the interrogation."

Caleb didn't even glance at the other man. "You take care of it, D'Amato. I'm staying here."

"Yes, sir."

As the other agent walked toward the cruiser by the curb, Marley shot Caleb an inquiring look. "Shouldn't you go with them? You've been working this case for months. Don't you want to be there to see it come to a close?"

He shook his head. "I'm not leaving you. D'Amato and AJ can take care of Grier. I need to take care of you."

"I told you, I'm fine. I—" She halted. "But I do want to see Dad and Sam."

He reached out for her arm, stopping her. "Wait. I...I wanted to tell you something."

He bent forward a little, and she experienced a spark of concern, but when he met her eyes again, she realized the pain he was feeling had nothing to do with the fact that he'd been shot. "I thought he was going to kill you," Caleb whispered.

"But he didn't. I don't even have a scratch, Caleb. I promise you."

"I..." He released a breath with obvious effort. "I watched him hold that gun to your head, and I knew that...that if he pulled the trigger, I'd die right along with you."

Her heart did a little flip. "Caleb..."

"Please, I have to say this." He swallowed. "I know this isn't the time to ask for your forgiveness, or to figure out the future, but I need to say this."

Tears pricked at her eyelids. She tried to speak, but he pressed his fingers to her lips. "I love you," he said thickly.

All around them, things were still bustling. The cruisers were speeding away, sirens flashing. Several residents gathered on their front porches and lawns, whispering as they stared at the scene across the street. But Marley was oblivious to the activity. She couldn't look away from Caleb.

"I didn't think it could ever happen to me, I was always too shut off from people, but I fell in love with you." His voice cracked. "You made me see that there's more to life than just work. That I don't need to control my emotions all the time."

Marley was stunned. It was impossible to breathe, let alone speak.

At her lack of response, Caleb barreled on. "I'm sorry I lied to you. But I do love you, Marley, and I want to be with you."

She stood rooted in place, so overcome with joy she was unable to say a word.

Caleb's broad shoulders sagged. "Sorry, I guess this isn't the time to unload all this on you. I know you want to see your family." He let out a breath. "Okay, go do that. I guess I'll go to the station and we can talk later."

He started to walk away. His normally smooth strides were ungainly, as if walking in a straight line took too much effort.

She stood there, dumbfounded, then cleared her throat and shook her head, regaining her senses. "What the heck are you doing? Come back here," she called after him.

He froze, then looked over his shoulder, revealing his unbelievably gorgeous profile. Slowly, he turned to face her. A few yards separated them, but despite the distance, Marley could swear she heard his heart pounding.

"You're angry," he said with a sigh, bridging the distance between them.

She shot him a no-kidding look. "You were going to leave just like that?"

"You didn't say anything. I figured…you might need space or something."

The awkwardness of his voice made her laugh. God, he could be totally clueless sometimes. She thought of the way he'd launched himself in front of her when Patrick pulled the trigger. How he'd chosen to stay behind with her instead of going to the station to process the criminal he'd been hunting for months. He'd been so confident, so determined to protect her. And now he was standing here, back to his gruff, serious self, missing every last signal she sent in his direction.

"I didn't say anything because your words made me all emotional, you idiot."

The corner of his mouth lifted in a hopeful smile. "So you don't want me to go?"

"Of course I don't want you to go."

"Are you sure?" he asked, searching her face.

She nodded. Her throat went tight again, but she managed to say the most important thing. "I love you."

"You love me," he echoed in amazement.

"Yes." She drew in a breath and decided to do something crazy—trust him again. "I'm willing to work on the whole trust-and-forgiveness thing…if you're willing to stay."

Caleb touched her cheek so gently she felt like crying again, this time with joy. "I'm not going anywhere." He smiled ruefully. "Scratch that. I will need to go to Virginia to be debriefed about the case, but when I'm there, I'll request an immediate transfer to the west coast." He stroked her lips with his thumb. "And if they deny my request, I'll quit."

Her heart skipped a beat. "Are you serious?"

"You're more important to me than a job," he said.

Marley stood on her tiptoes and brushed her lips over his. Smiling, she pulled away. "I have one more condition for taking you back."

He grinned. "I knew this was too easy. Okay, lay it on me."

"You have to promise never to videotape me again."

A glimmer of guilt filled his eyes. He opened his mouth, but she raised her hand, adding, "At least *ask* me first, will you?"

The guilt faded into amusement. His smile consumed his entire face as he drew her into his arms and bent close to her ear. "There will never be another videotape of you again, sweetheart. Unless you want it." His voice grew husky as he murmured, "And if you do, let's make sure you're naked next time. I really like it when you're naked."

Laughing, Marley wrapped her arms around his neck and leaned in for one of Caleb's warm, toe-curling kisses. As their lips met, her heart sang with delight and forgiveness and trust.

And most importantly, love.

Epilogue

Eight months later

"SO WHAT DO YOU THINK?" Marley asked, holding up the two paint swatches so Caleb could give his opinion.

He frowned. "They're both green."

"Actually, this one is Serene Forest and this one is Leafy Splendor."

"They're _green_."

Marley sighed. Okay, it was official. When it came to paint advice, Caleb was terrible. From now on, she'd just ask her dad or brother for input.

"I'm picking Leafy Splendor," she said. "If you don't like it, tough."

Caleb looked beyond relieved. "You know, it amazes me that it took you this long to figure out I don't know anything about picking colors. Put a hammer or paintbrush in my hand and tell me what to do, and I'm fine, but colors? That's your job, sweetheart."

"I'm just trying to let you in on the decision-making process. That's what engaged couples do, you know." She held up her left hand and wiggled her ring finger.

The diamond engagement ring sparkled under the kitchen light.

Caleb's mouth curved in a crooked smile, not so rare these days. He always seemed to be smiling when they were together. "I still can't get enough of hearing that word. *Engaged*."

The wonder in his eyes made her smile, too. She knew exactly what he meant. She couldn't stop looking down at the ring, just to make sure she hadn't imagined its presence.

The past eight months with Caleb had been the best of her life. She still couldn't believe all the changes he'd made for her. Leaving the DEA, taking the detective job with the San Diego Police Department. Ironically, his partner was none other than Miguel Hernandez, but Marley had begun warming up to the man who'd formerly treated her like a criminal. Hernandez had apologized numerous times for his behavior, though she'd barely thought about any of that for months now.

She'd have to think about it again soon, however. Patrick's trial started next month, and she'd been called as a witness. With all the charges her ex faced, she doubted her testimony even mattered. Murder, trafficking, attempted kidnapping, attempted murder. The prosecutor had assured Marley that Patrick would be in jail for the rest of his life, a notion that pleased her immensely.

But she didn't dwell on Patrick much anymore. What she and Caleb had was better than anything she could have imagined. Love, trust, laughter… Even her brother admitted the two of them made a scarily perfect match. It didn't hurt that Caleb had helped Sam and Marley's dad finish a huge construction job the other month. Nothing to kick-start some male bonding like renovating a house.

Caleb grabbed the Leafy Splendor paint swatch from the counter and sighed. "So, Color World?"

She was about to nod, but then she met his eyes, and the familiar expression on his face made her laugh.

"Don't give me the sex look," she said, wagging her finger. "One of these days you're just going to have to suck it up and buy some paint with me."

"One of these days," he agreed. He let the paint swatch drop from his hand and moved his fingers to her mouth, stroking her lips as his blue eyes smoldered with heat. "But today? No, I think we can find something more interesting to do."

She tilted her head. "Prove it."

With a grin, Caleb removed every scrap of clothing from her body.

And proved to her that there were, indeed, *much* more important things than paint.

* * * * *

Have Your Say

You've just finished your book.
So what did you think?

We'd love to hear your thoughts on our 'Have your say' online panel
www.millsandboon.co.uk/haveyoursay

- 🌹 Easy to use
- 🌹 Short questionnaire
- 🌹 Chance to win Mills & Boon® goodies

The World of Mills & Boon®

There's a Mills & Boon® series that's perfect for you. We publish ten series and, with new titles every month, you never have to wait long for your favourite to come along.

Blaze.

Scorching hot, sexy reads
4 new stories every month

By Request

Relive the romance with the best of the best
9 new stories every month

Cherish™

Romance to melt the heart every time
12 new stories every month

Desire™

Passionate and dramatic love stories
8 new stories every month